PRAISE FOR THE NOVELS OF
#1 NEW YORK TIMES BESTSELLING AUTHOR
BARBARA FREETHY

"I love *The Callaways*! Heartwarming romance, intriguing suspense and sexy alpha heroes. What more could you want?"
-- *NYT Bestselling Author* **Bella Andre**

"I adore *The Callaways*, a family we'd all love to have. Each new book is a deft combination of emotion, suspense and family dynamics. A remarkable, compelling series!"
-- *USA Today Bestselling Author* **Barbara O'Neal**

"Once I start reading a Callaway novel, I can't put it down. Fast-paced action, a poignant love story and a tantalizing mystery in every book!"
-- *USA Today Bestselling Author* **Christie Ridgway**

"*BETWEEN NOW AND FOREVER* is a beautifully written story. Fans of Barbara's Angel's Bay series will be happy to know the search leads them to Angel's Bay where we get to check in with some old friends."
-- ***The Book Momster Blog***

"A very touching story that shows the power of love and how much it can heal."
--***All Night Books*** *for BETWEEN NOW AND FOREVER*

"In the tradition of LaVyrle Spencer, gifted author Barbara Freethy creates an irresistible tale of family secrets, riveting adventure and heart-touching romance."
-- *NYT Bestselling Author* **Susan Wiggs**
on Summer Secrets

Also By Barbara Freethy

The Callaway Family Series
On A Night Like This
So This Is Love
Falling For A Stranger
Between Now And Forever
All A Heart Needs
That Summer Night
When Shadows Fall
Somewhere Only We Know

The Wish Series
A Secret Wish
Just A Wish Away
When Wishes Collide

Standalone Novels
Almost Home
All She Ever Wanted
Ask Mariah
Daniel's Gift
Don't Say A Word
Golden Lies
Just The Way You Are
Love Will Find A Way
One True Love
Ryan's Return
Some Kind of Wonderful
Summer Secrets
The Sweetest Thing

The Sanders Brothers Series
Silent Run
Silent Fall

The Deception Series
Taken
Played

To my writing pals, Anne and Poppy, who share tea, chocolate and words of wisdom!

BETWEEN NOW AND FOREVER

The Callaways

BARBARA FREETHY

HYDE
STREET
—PRESS—

HYDE STREET PRESS
Published by Hyde Street Press
1819 Polk Street, Suite 113, San Francisco, California 94109

Printed in the United States of America

Cover design by Damonza.com
Interior book design by KLF Publishing

ISBN: 978-0-9906951-3-4

One

It felt like earthquake weather. Nicole Prescott slipped off her bright orange sweater and tied it loosely around the waist of her jeans. It was unseasonably warm for the last day of October, not a trace of breeze blowing off the bay, not a hint of fog sweeping across the tall red spires of the Golden Gate Bridge, just blue skies, and an eerie stillness, as if something momentous was about to happen.

It was just her imagination, she told herself, heightened by the ghosts and goblins running through the Halloween carnival at Washington Elementary School. The school sat at the top of one of San Francisco's many steep hills and overlooked the bay and marina.

The auditorium had been turned into a haunted house, and wooden booths dotted the playground, offering games ranging from darts to a water balloon toss and a cakewalk. Smells of popcorn, hot dogs with mustard and salty pretzels warmed the air while children in costumes roamed the playground. Everything seemed normal, and yet it wasn't—at least not in Nicole's quiet corner of the yard.

Glancing at her six-year-old son Brandon, Nicole bit back a sigh of frustration. She'd hoped that Brandon would find a way to join in the carnival fun. She'd dressed him up as Hercules, with a chest plate, a black cape and some muscled armbands. She'd even given him a sword to carry. Her son had ditched the sword upon arrival, and a few minutes ago had tossed the chest plate onto the ground. Instead of playing games with the other children, Brandon knelt by the line of rosebushes that ran along the fence at the furthest end of the school property and as far away from the carnival action as he could get.

Digging into the dirt, he pulled out pebble after pebble, his entire being focused on the stones as he arranged and rearranged them in patterns on the cement path. Every few minutes, he would swap one rock with another, his small fingers moving with a passion and a purpose Nicole could not begin to understand. She watched as Brandon picked up a stone, sweeping his finger across the surface, tracing the rough edge, as if he were memorizing the curves, the cracks, the weight. Then he set the stone down and picked up another one, seeking a pattern, a conclusion, that would bring some sort of closure to his obsession, but the end never came. Even when he seemed to find the perfect match, he was never completely satisfied with the result. Lately, there appeared to be a greater urgency to his movements, as if he thought he was running out of time.

Nicole yearned for some way to connect with her only child, but most days Brandon seemed unaware of her presence, his focus so pure, so single, and so solitary. His world was his own, and she had no place in it. When she tried to interfere or help, he would go into an angry, agitated frenzy, hitting his forehead with the palm of his hand over and over again until she backed away.

For three years she'd battled her son's diagnosis of autism, researching every new therapy, constantly changing his diet, taking him to doctor after doctor, but while she'd seen small changes in his behavior, nothing significant had occurred. Her son was trapped in his own head, and she couldn't find a way to get through to him. The pain of that broken connection was relentless.

While Brandon might not remember the first few years of his life, she had forgotten nothing, from the sweetness of his joyous smile when he woke up in the morning, to the feel of his soft arms around her neck when he'd hugged her, the sound of his laugh—half snort, half giggle—and the touch of his hand in hers. He'd been perfect for two years, eleven months, and six days, and then he'd changed. He'd become withdrawn, isolated, and unresponsive. It was as if the light in his brain had gone out.

Terrified, she'd fought desperately to find first a diagnosis and then a cure. But the enemy she fought was winning the war, invincible at every turn. She'd prayed for a miracle, but none had come. She'd put Brandon before everything and everyone else in her life, including her soon-to-be ex-husband, Ryan.

Another ache filled her heart, this one having nothing to do with her son and everything to do with the man she'd vowed to love for all time. She tried to shake Ryan out of her mind. There were only so many emotions she could handle at one time.

Brandon paused, his body stiffening as he stared down at the two stones in front of him. He glanced over at her, and Nicole's heart stopped in amazement. There was a rare spark in his blue eyes, a moment of triumph, satisfaction, and in that brief glance he connected with her in a way he hadn't done in a long time. He had looked to her to see his achievement.

Her eyes blurred with shocked tears. Maybe this was the momentous thing she'd been anticipating. But the moment vanished as quickly as it had come.

Brandon's gaze dropped away, and he sat back on his heels. After a moment, he picked up the rocks and put them in the pocket of his jeans. Then he scampered down the path, searching for more stones among the rose bushes. Even though he had found the perfect pair, he would have to do it again and again and again.

She wanted to take him by the hand and lead him over to one of the game booths, get him involved in the world around him, but she wouldn't be doing it for him; she'd be doing it for herself. Brandon had no interest in playing with the other children. And while she could interact with the mothers, the truth was—she rarely did. The moms were always polite to her, but they were often wary, as if they thought their kids could somehow catch autism from Brandon. They wanted distance, and most days she let them have it.

She glanced across the playground, seeing Theresa and Kathleen organizing the cakewalk. At one time they'd all been so close. They'd taken walks together, bought strollers, complained about sleepless nights. They'd looked to each other for advice about pacifiers, night terrors, and thumb sucking. Seeing them huddling together now, she could imagine their conversation. They were probably planning their evening. They'd gather at Kathleen's house before trick-or-treating, share wine and appetizers while the children ate pizza. The men would take the kids through the neighborhood while the women stayed behind to hand out candy. Kathleen's husband, Patrick, would take pictures.

Patrick, she thought with a sigh, another good friend gone. Since she and Ryan had separated, Patrick had chosen to stick with Ryan. It was no surprise. Patrick and Ryan had grown up together. She couldn't blame Patrick; she couldn't really blame anyone. A lot of the distance was her fault. She'd drifted away, and they'd let her go. That was the way of relationships. If no one fought for them, they ended. Or maybe that was just the way of her relationships. She had only so much fight in her; what she had left she saved for

Brandon.

Taking a seat on a nearby bench, she reached into her purse and pulled out the folder of essays she needed to grade. She'd cut back on her teaching in the past three years, but she still taught a class in Greek Mythology at San Francisco City College three mornings a week. The Gods had always fascinated her. They represented the best and the worst of humankind. While they rose to heroic proportions, they also battled deep and sometimes fatal flaws within themselves, representing the good and bad within each individual.

A passion for history and mythology was something she'd inherited from her biological father, David Kane, who was a professor of history at UC Berkeley. Her love of learning was the only thing David had given her before he divorced her mother, Lynda, when she was six years old. Everything else she'd gotten from her stepfather, Jack Callaway, a man who had given her love and treated her like his own daughter.

A soccer ball came rolling towards her. She put down her folder and grabbed it. Then she stood up as Derek, Kathleen's three-year-old son, came running over, followed by his mother.

"Sorry about that," Kathleen said, her cheeks red from chasing after Derek. She was a tall, slim woman with blonde hair and a lightly freckled complexion.

"No problem." Nicole tossed the ball back to Derek, who squealed with delight. "Your baby is getting big."

"That's for sure, and he's hard to keep up with. He has so much more energy and stubbornness than William did at this age," she finished, referring to her six-year-old, who was in the same class as Brandon.

Derek dropped the soccer ball and kicked it in Nicole's direction. It took her a second to realize that Derek was playing a game with her. It had been a long time since a child had played with her. It felt surprisingly good and ridiculously sad all at the same time. She kicked the ball back to him.

"Don't encourage him," Kathleen warned. "He'll never leave you alone."

She wanted to encourage Derek. She wanted to keep on playing. She just wished it was Brandon who was the child kicking the ball to her.

Kathleen snagged the ball. "Sorry to break this up, but I have to do my duty in the haunted house. Why don't you and Brandon come by tonight, Nicole?" Her gaze softened. "We miss you. Everyone would love to see you."

"I miss you all, too," Nicole admitted.

A guilty expression flashed in Kathleen's eyes. "I know I haven't been in touch since you and Ryan split up. It's not because I don't care. It's just—"

"It's fine," Nicole said, cutting her off. "You're busy. We're all busy."

"It is that time of the year."

Kathleen had barely finished speaking when the buzz of a small plane drew Nicole's head upward. It was a reflex she couldn't quite shake. The plane dipped its wings as if it were saying hello. Her heart skipped a beat. An old memory of Ryan flashed through her head. He'd been seventeen years old, cocky as hell, taking off at the small airport in Half Moon Bay with his flight instructor. Back then he'd thought he could conquer the world; she'd thought the same thing.

With a sigh she lowered her gaze from the sky. Kathleen gave her a speculative look. "Do you miss Ryan?"

More than she'd ever imagined.

"It's complicated." She looked past Kathleen to see Joni waving at them, and she was relieved at the interruption. "Joni is calling you."

Kathleen groaned. "I have to go. Sorry."

"No problem."

"We need to catch up, Nicole. Let's make it happen before too much more time passes."

Nicole nodded. "See you later."

As Kathleen and Derek returned to the carnival, Nicole thought about trying to take Brandon through the haunted house. Even as the thought crossed her mind, she immediately dismissed it. Brandon would hate it. He'd throw a screaming fit, and everyone would be uncomfortable.

Enough was enough. It was time to put an end to yet another moment of wishful thinking that this day would be different—normal. She had to accept the fact that this version of her life was normal.

She could put Brandon in a costume. She could bring him to a carnival, but she couldn't make him care about Halloween. She couldn't really make him care about anything. It wasn't his fault. It just wasn't in him.

She turned around to see what Brandon was doing, and it took a moment for her to register the fact that Brandon wasn't playing in the rosebushes where she'd last seen him. Her gaze moved down the fence. Brandon wasn't there. Had he gone over to the carnival while she was talking to Kathleen and Derek? She looked around the playground, trying to catch a glimpse of Brandon's tousled blonde hair, his black cape, but all she could see was a blur of costumes and children in the playground, and none of them were her son.

Her heart began to pound against her chest, her breath coming short and fast. She told herself to calm down. Everything was fine. This was Brandon's school. He knew his way around; he'd probably just gone to the bathroom.

The sound of a car speeding down the street brought her head around. She caught a glimpse of the tail end of a white SUV. Then her gaze fell on the black cape lying on the ground by the gate.

Had Brandon left the yard?

It seemed to take forever to get her feet to move. She was frozen in fear, a terrible certainty ripping through her soul. Brandon had gone through that gate. But why?

He didn't like change, new environments, or strangers. He wouldn't leave on his own.

Her feet finally took flight. She ran across the yard and picked up the cape. It was still warm from the heat of Brandon's body. She walked through the gate to the sidewalk, looking in either direction. There was no sign of her son. Where was he?

She ran back into the playground, calling Brandon's name. She searched every game booth, every corner, running into the halls of the school. A couple of the other moms came over to help her search. The principal made an announcement over the loudspeaker. Everyone started looking for Brandon.

Forty-five minutes later it became clear that Brandon wasn't in the school or the yard. She'd checked under every desk, looked in every closet. The lights had been turned on in the haunted house to make sure Brandon hadn't gotten lost in the cobwebbed maze.

And then the police arrived.

She answered their questions with what little knowledge she had and took them out to the spot where Brandon had been playing. Then she saw something she'd missed before— a small trail of rocks leading down the sidewalk. They must have fallen out of Brandon's pockets. The trail ended at the curb. She looked up and down the street again.

The two cops were talking to her, but she couldn't hear what they were saying. The fear was overwhelming.

The scream came from down deep in her soul, the raw agony of the torn connection between mother and child.

Her baby was gone!

The ground shook beneath her feet. It wasn't an earthquake—it was worse.

Two

---><>><<<-—

Midnight. The nightmare should have been over by now. Brandon should be tucked in his bed, not lost somewhere in the night.

Nicole walked out to the front porch with Max Harrison. Max was engaged to her younger sister Emma and was also a homicide detective for the SFPD. Upon hearing of Brandon's disappearance, he'd jumped in on the case and had assured her that everything would be done to locate Brandon as quickly as possible.

Unfortunately, eight hours had passed since Max had made that declaration, and *quickly* no longer seemed like a possibility.

They'd scoured the neighborhoods around the school and also her house. The police had put out an Amber alert for Brandon. His picture had been flashed across every television newscast and Internet news site. But so far no tips had come in.

A chill of fear ran through Nicole as she looked at the quiet street and thought about how late it was. The idea of her little boy alone in the night made her physically sick. She crossed her arms in front of her chest as Max put a reassuring hand on her shoulder.

"Hang in there," he said. "We're going to find Brandon,

Nicole."

His steady, determined gaze gave her some comfort. Max was a strong, confident man, the kind who got results, and she wanted very much to believe in his ability to find her son, but with every passing hour, her terror grew.

"What else should I do?" she asked.

"There's nothing more you can do tonight."

"I feel so helpless, Max. Every minute counts. How can I sit here and wait?"

"We're *making* every minute count. We've got everyone in the department looking for Brandon, and your father has alerted all the fire stations in the city. Brandon's photo has been on the news, and by morning Emma and the rest of your family will have thousands of flyers up all over the city. Someone is going to see Brandon and call us."

"If he's still in San Francisco," she said, voicing the thought that had been forming in the back of her mind the past few hours. "What if Brandon was taken out of the city?"

"It's a multi-state alert throughout California, Nevada, and Oregon," he told her.

"I wish we had a license plate. Something more to go on."

"Hopefully, we'll get that something soon. We'll re-interview some of the kids and parents tomorrow in case someone remembers something. I'm going back to the station now. I'll call you as soon as I have any news." He paused. "Any word from Ryan?"

"Emma reached him about fifteen minutes ago. He just got off his flight. He should be here soon." She had mixed feelings about Ryan being on his way home. She wanted his support, but she was too distraught to handle the awkward relationship that had developed between them since they'd separated several months earlier. It was still difficult to believe their great love story had fallen apart.

"I'll talk to him later then."

"He won't be able to add anything, Max. He hasn't seen Brandon in two weeks."

"We need to cover all the bases, Nicole."

"I understand."

As Max walked out to his car, her younger sister Emma stepped onto the porch. Emma was a slender blonde, whose blue eyes matched Nicole's, although there was usually more mischief and fire in Emma's gaze. Tonight there was only worry.

Nicole didn't want to see concern in her sister's eyes. Emma was a strong, kick-ass fire investigator, brilliant at taking small, random clues and figuring out how they went together. And she needed Emma to believe that everything was going to be all right, so she could believe it, too.

"You should come inside, Nicole. It's cold out here," Emma said.

"In a minute. I need to catch my breath."

"Is the family driving you crazy? Do you want me to start kicking them out?"

"Soon," she said. The Callaways had descended in full force on her small house, and while she appreciated the support, their increasing worry was only making her more nervous. "It's getting really late."

"They'll stay here all night if you need them."

"Well, Sara should be home in her own bed," Nicole replied. "She's eight months pregnant."

"Aiden made that suggestion a few minutes ago, but no one wants to leave you alone, including me." Emma gave her a compassionate look. "It's going to be all right, Nic."

"You don't know that, Em. I can't lose Brandon. Since Ryan left, it's been Brandon and me against the world. He's like my other half." Panic ran through her. "What am I going to do without him?"

"You won't be without him. You have to stop imagining the worst."

"I can't help it. Every hour that passes—"

"I know it's terrifying," Emma said, cutting her off. "But you have to keep the faith. And I know you will, because when it comes to Brandon, you don't give up. And neither does the rest of your stubborn-as-hell family. The Callaways don't accept failure."

Emma's tough talk was just the kick that Nicole needed. She straightened and threw back her shoulders. "You're right. Brandon is coming home. There is no other option."

"Exactly. Now, why don't you come inside?"

"I will in a minute. I want to speak to Ryan alone, and he should be here soon."

As Emma went into the house, Nicole glanced down the street, willing Brandon to appear. Minutes passed, and a shimmer of fog began to cover the streetlights, adding darker, deeper shadows to the night. The air grew cold, the street eerily quiet. The empty candy wrappers scattered on the lawn by impatient trick-or-treaters reminded her that Brandon had completely missed Halloween. Not that he would have cared to participate. In fact, he probably would have hidden in his room the whole time. He didn't like the sound of the doorbell. He didn't like noise or strangers. Maybe he'd hidden away in some dark yard to avoid all the chaos of the night.

She strained to see some sign of her little boy trudging home. She could imagine Brandon suddenly appearing through the trees, from behind a bush. She could picture herself running down the walkway, gathering her son in her arms, squeezing him so tightly he would scream in dismay. He hated to be touched, hugged. But she'd weather the screams if only she could hold him again. She ached with yearning, and tightening her arms around her waist, she held on to the only thing she had left—herself.

Her heart jumped as a car turned the corner, the headlights sweeping across the street. The taxi stopped in front of her house. A tall man in a navy blue pilot's uniform got out. He tossed money at the driver as he pulled his black suitcase out of the cab and hurried towards her with long, impatient strides. Ryan had been on a flight from Hong Kong when Brandon disappeared.

"Is he here? Is he back?" Ryan demanded, dropping his suitcase on the porch. "Did you find him?"

She heard the fear in his voice and shook her head, her throat too knotted with emotion to speak.

Ryan ran a hand through his thick, dark brown hair as he'd probably done a hundred times since he'd received her message. He paced around the porch, every jerky movement a reflection of his worry. "What the hell happened, Nicole?"

The anger in his voice took her by surprise. He was blaming her?

"He's six years old," Ryan continued. "How could you let him out of your sight? You always tell me over and over again not to take my eyes off the kid."

"You? You're asking me that? You?" Fury ripped through her body.

Ryan was the one who'd promised to love her for better or worse, but when worse had come, he'd bailed. He was the one who couldn't be counted on to watch Brandon, not her. She was the one who was there, who was always there.

Her hands clenched, and all the emotions of the day sent her fist flying towards his face. Her knuckles cracked against his cheekbone. She'd never hit anyone in her life, but it felt good—amazingly good. She drew her hand back for a second time, but this time he caught her by the arm.

"God dammit, Nicole! Stop it. I'm sorry. Okay? I'm just—scared."

The agony in his words, the fear in his eyes, took the

fight out of her. This wasn't Ryan's fault. It was hers. And that was the bitter truth.

He was right. She'd let her child out of her sight. She'd been distracted by a game of kickball with another child, with selfish, yearning thoughts for a normal life. And now Brandon was paying the price.

"I looked away for a second." She bit down on her bottom lip as she struggled to hold back the tears. "He was there, and then he wasn't."

Ryan let go of her arm, the brand of his heated grip still stinging. But it was a pain she could deal with, not like the one ripping her heart in two.

The skin around Ryan's right eye was swelling already. She felt a momentary twinge of guilt that she'd hurt him. "You should go inside and put some ice on your face."

"I don't care about my face."

"I'm sorry," she whispered. "I didn't mean to hurt you."

"Forget about it. Just tell me what you know. Do the police have any leads? Did Brandon run away? Did he wander off and get lost? That's the most likely scenario, right?"

"I thought it was, but every second that passes makes it seem less likely. If he was anywhere in the neighborhood, we would have found him by now. They even brought out a search dog to try to pick up his scent. But the dog came up with nothing."

Ryan swallowed hard, the pulse in his neck beating fast and furiously. "What are you saying? Do they think someone—someone took him?" he asked, stumbling over the question.

Her stomach twisted at the thought. "I don't know. A few seconds after I realized Brandon was gone, I saw the back end of a white SUV turning the far corner. And a second grader, Stephanie Bennett, said she saw Brandon get into a big white car, but she couldn't identify the make or remember a license plate number. She didn't even notice who was inside. She started crying when the police kept asking her questions. And then she said she wasn't sure, maybe it wasn't Brandon but someone else. There was more than one kid wearing a cape at the carnival."

"I don't understand how anyone could grab Brandon. Brandon will barely let me touch him," he added, pain in his voice. "I can't imagine how a stranger could get close to him. Why didn't he scream? Why didn't he struggle? I've seen him take a swing at the pediatrician he's known all his life. I've seen you wrestle him to the ground to get a toothbrush in his mouth. This isn't a kid who just goes along with things."

"It doesn't make sense to me, either." She gave a frustrated shake of her head, his words echoing her own thoughts. "I was right there, Ryan. I was watching him play. I moved away for a couple of minutes when Kathleen came over. I couldn't have been more than twenty feet away from him. When I turned back around, Brandon was gone. I don't know how anyone could have taken him away without him screaming."

"What do the cops say?"

"That maybe someone waved him over with an enticement—a puppy, a toy, a candy bar."

"Brandon can't be tempted like that."

"I told them that. Luckily, Max arrived and got everyone straightened out on Brandon's condition, and then they sprang into action. Everything that needed to be done was done, but Brandon still isn't home." She paused. "All I can think about is how terrified he must be. He can't tell anyone what he needs. And if someone took him, how will they know when he's hungry or cold? Will they give him a sweater or a blanket? Will they feed him? And what will they do when they find out he has problems? What if he doesn't do what they want him to do? What if he won't stay quiet, or won't stop screaming, or stop kicking his feet and his hands? Will they understand that he can't help it? That he's just scared? Or will they try to make him shut up?"

Ryan put up his hands on her shoulders, cutting off her hysterical ramble. "Don't, Nicole. Don't go there."

She looked into his eyes. "I can't stop myself. I'm terrified, Ryan."

His jaw tightened. "We'll get him back." He let go of her and walked across the porch, staring out at the street.

She wanted to believe everything would be all right, just the way she'd wanted to believe that Brandon would snap out of his autistic state, but she'd been wrong before.

Three

The early morning sun crept through the slits in the living room blinds. The hands on the grandfather clock in the corner were finally making their way towards seven o'clock after a seemingly endless night. Ryan turned on his side, his legs and body cramped on the short and uncomfortable couch in Nicole's living room.

It had once been his living room, too.

Five months ago he'd moved into a two-bedroom condo by the Embarcadero. Brandon had been to his home exactly three times, and the room he'd put together for his son had never been slept in. Brandon didn't like change, not even when that change came with his father.

After those couple of visits, which consisted of Brandon hiding under a desk in a corner of his living room and screaming at the top of his lungs for most of the afternoon, Ryan and Nicole had agreed that Ryan would see Brandon at her house. That hadn't worked much better. Eventually his visits had dwindled down to nothing. He felt guilty about that. He felt guilty about a lot of things. But it seemed apparent that Brandon didn't miss him. The child who had once slept on his chest, cried on his shoulder, held his hand and looked to him for courage, safety and love didn't even notice his existence.

Nicole didn't seem to miss him either. He couldn't blame her. He'd let her down. And the sad truth was that he'd always known deep down that that would happen. From the minute things had turned serious between them, he'd worried that he'd be a lousy husband, a terrible father, just like his own father had been. He'd fallen in love with her, but he'd felt destined to disappoint her.

He'd hoped it wouldn't happen. With Nicole and Brandon, he'd finally found the family he'd always been looking for, a family that didn't include an abusive, alcoholic father or a weak-willed mother who could barely take care of herself, much less anyone else. He'd counted himself lucky to marry into the Callaways. And Nicole and Brandon had been the center of his world. Now they were in their own world, and he was on the outside—where he deserved to be. He'd screwed up. And he couldn't fix it. He couldn't fix one damn thing. He turned over onto his back and stared at the ceiling.

Things had started out so good.

The first time he'd seen Nicole she'd been seventeen years old and in her favorite class—art. She'd had on a smock covered in streaks of paint, her gaze focused intently on the easel in front of her. She hadn't even noticed him, and that had surprised him. All the girls looked at him. He was an athlete. But Nicole didn't care much for sports. She liked art and history and was wildly interested in obscure subjects like Greek mythology and the Trojan War. Even though she was a pretty blonde, and one of the Callaways, she wasn't in the popular group. When he'd finally gotten her to look at him, she'd simply been annoyed, not impressed. She had dreams, ambitions, and she had no time for him.

And from that moment on he'd had no time for anyone else.

Her blonde hair and beautiful blue eyes had pulled him in. Her passion, her drive, her view of the world had changed him. She was the prettiest thing he'd ever seen, and she put a bright slash of color in his dark, ugly life.

They became inseparable, spending weekends at the beach, in the mountains, sometimes even in the library where Nicole would force him to read obscure texts about mythological gods. She'd made him look at life in a whole new way. She'd made him care at a point where he'd given up caring about anything. He'd been going down the road to nowhere until he met her and she'd yanked him back, making him want to pursue his dreams again. She was the one who'd talked him into asking his neighbor for flying lessons. She was the one who'd watched him take off that first day, who'd made him see that the world was a lot bigger than he'd ever realized. Nicole had made him want to be someone, not just for himself, but also for her.

He'd screwed it up, all of it.

Which was why he was on the couch and not in bed with the woman he'd once loved more than anyone.

Not that Nicole was in their bed. He'd heard her go into Brandon's room hours ago, and she hadn't come out. She was either sitting in her grandmother's rocking chair, or she was lying in Brandon's twin bed, her arms probably wrapped around Brandon's honey bear, a stuffed animal that had once been his favorite sleep buddy but had been discarded along with so many other things and people that had once been important to his son but no longer were.

He'd thought he'd come to terms with the fact that he was no longer a husband or a father, but now—back in the house that had been filled with so much promise, so much love, he was achingly aware of just how wrong things had gone.

Too restless to sleep, he sat up and stretched his arms over his head. Then he got up, walked into the kitchen and started the coffee maker. As he moved toward the refrigerator to get some milk, the picture on the door gave him pause.

It was a hand-sketched drawing. The artist had used colored pencils. But it was the familiarity of the scene that made his heart stop. He could hardly believe what he was seeing. The focus of the picture was the living room of his condo. Every piece of furniture—from the leather couch, to the big screen television, to the bookshelves under the window, was depicted in painstaking detail. He pulled the paper out from underneath the colored magnet to take a closer look.

He couldn't believe Nicole had spent time sketching his apartment. She'd only been inside a handful of times, yet everything was so carefully delineated. She hadn't left out a thing—not the clock on the wall, the magazines on the coffee table, the empty coffee mug, his tennis shoes sticking out from under the couch, the basketball in the corner.

What the hell? Why would she draw this? Did she miss him? Was he seeing a crack in her armor?

He looked up, startled to see the object of his thoughts walk into the room. Nicole's long blonde hair was tangled, her eyes bloodshot and weary. In her arms she held Brandon's teddy bear, just as he'd predicted.

"Coffee," she mumbled.

"Almost done."

She shuffled over to the table and sat down. She was wearing the same clothes she had on yesterday, a pair of blue jeans with a cream-colored camisole top under the bright orange sweater she'd worn every Halloween since the first day he'd met her. She stared down at the bear in her hands, her fingers rubbing over the nose that had long ago lost its fur. As a baby, Brandon had gone to sleep sucking his thumb and rubbing his other fingers over the bear's nose as he lulled himself to sleep.

"Do you think Brandon misses Honey Bear?" she asked.

"Brandon gave up on that bear a long time ago."

She slowly nodded. "Yeah, I guess he did."

"Nicole, when did you draw this? More importantly, why did you draw this?"

She gave him a confused look. "What are you talking about, Ryan?"

He hated the way she said his name now, as if it exhausted her to speak to him, to deal with his needs. She used to say his name with eagerness, passion and love. He turned the picture around so she could see it. "I'm talking about this. Why did you take the time to make such a detailed sketch of my living room?"

Her eyes widened. "You think I drew that?"

"Who else? It's perfect—the symmetry, the lines, the angles. You were always a talented artist."

"I didn't do it." She got up from the chair and took the paper from his hands. She turned it to face him. "Take a good look. Where do you think the person was who drew this? What's the perspective?"

"I don't know what you mean."

"Yes, you do. Try again."

"I guess the view is from the living room looking towards the dining area."

"Looking up," she said pointedly. "From the ground. Brandon drew this, Ryan. He did it the first time he came back from your condo. Do you remember where he spent the day?"

"Under the desk in the living room," he said in bemusement, trying to make sense of what she was saying. "He didn't have any paper under there."

"He drew it when he came home."

Ryan shook his head in disbelief. "How is that possible? It's like a snapshot."

"He has a photographic memory. Brandon sees

something once and he can draw it perfectly. It's a savant skill, one of the doctors said."

He met her eyes. "God, Nicole, what the hell goes on in his head?"

"I wish I knew," she said softly.

Ryan took the paper out of her hands. "Why do you have it up on the refrigerator?"

"Brandon put it there. I took it down once, and he put it back up. I think it might be his way of staying connected to you."

Now he was more confused. "Brandon hated every second that he was in my home. He hates every second that he's with me."

"That's not true," she said with a definitive shake of her head. "He doesn't hate you."

"Even when I'm here, he doesn't look at me, doesn't acknowledge I'm in the room."

"And you think he acknowledges me?" she challenged, a spark of anger in her eyes. "He doesn't. He treats me the same way."

"No, he's better with you."

"Because I've stuck with him, but he knows when you're around. He is paying attention, even if he doesn't show it."

"That's your fantasy, Nicole."

She bristled at that. "I'm not delusional, Ryan."

"I didn't say you were delusional, but you have to admit that you're very optimistic where Brandon is concerned."

"I'm hopeful. There's a difference. But you want proof? Come with me." She marched out of the kitchen.

He followed her into Brandon's room. His son's bedroom looked nothing like it had when Brandon was a baby. Back then, the walls had been covered by a beautiful mural that Nicole had painted. There had been piles of stuffed animals, shelves of books, crates of toys, and piles of stuff everywhere. Now the shelves were almost empty, the walls were painted a light blue and the bedding was the same color. Everything was very neat with the exception of a box of building blocks next to a half-built fort and a group of pebbles and rocks on Brandon's floor. His son was obsessed with rocks.

Nicole opened the top drawer of the desk and pulled out a stack of papers. She flipped through them until she found the one she wanted, and then she handed it to him. It was another drawing, this time a portrait of him. He was sitting on the back steps of their house, a red ball in his hand. He'd wanted to throw that ball to Brandon, but his son had been too busy digging for pebbles under the bushes. So he'd sat on the steps, bouncing the ball, and after an hour of complete quiet and total rejection, he'd gone inside.

As before, Brandon's drawing was perfection, down to every detail, including the look of disappointment in his father's eyes, the scowl on his lips. God! Was that the way his son saw him? Was that the way Nicole saw him? He felt sick to his stomach.

"Brandon sees you, Ryan, even if he doesn't appear to be looking at you," Nicole said.

"Why didn't you show me this before?" he demanded. "Brandon drew this weeks ago."

"When would I have shown you? You canceled your last two visits and the time before that you stayed about ten minutes."

"That's not the reason you didn't show me." He saw the truth in her eyes. "You didn't want me to know, did you?"

Guilt flashed across her face. "Fine. I didn't want you to know."

"Why?" he asked in bewilderment.

"Because Brandon has never drawn a picture of me." Her words came out in a heated rush. "He sees you for ten minutes and draws you down to the freckle by your left eye, but has he ever drawn me? No. Make of that whatever you want." She grabbed the picture out of his hand and stuffed it back into the drawer.

There was pain in every taut muscle in her body. He wanted to take her in his arms, protect her, comfort her, the way he'd promised to do a lifetime ago. But she wouldn't welcome his touch. She didn't want his comfort. She didn't want anything from him.

"You're with him all the time," he said quietly. "Brandon doesn't need to draw you. He *has* you."

She met his gaze, her eyes blurry with tears. "He should have you, too."

A phone rang, and they both jumped. They started for the door at the same time, colliding in the doorway. Nicole shoved past him, running down the hall to the kitchen. She grabbed her cell phone off the table. "Max? Did you find him? Did you find my son?"

His heart jumped into his throat as Nicole listened to whoever was on the other end of the phone.

"Yes, I understand," she said finally. "We'll be there as soon as we can."

"What happened?" The words bolted out of his mouth as she hung up the phone. "Did they find Brandon? Is he all right?"

"They haven't found him yet. Max wants us to come down to the station. They've put together a task force, and they have questions for us."

"What kind of questions?"

"I don't know. They say the family is always suspect. I don't care what they ask. I just want to get this over with. The sooner they clear us, the better. Then they can spend their time finding the person who took our son. I'm going to change clothes, then we'll go."

Four

⟶⟫⟪⟵

Nicole walked down the hall to her bedroom and shut the door behind her. She paused long enough to take a deep breath. The call from Max had been both welcome and also terrifying, because Brandon was still as lost as he'd been the day before.

With her stomach churning and her head pounding, she moved into the bathroom, stripped off her clothes and stepped into the shower. As the warm water ran over her head, neck and shoulders, she tried to force some calm into her system. She needed to be able to think, to make decisions, to give the police whatever information they needed to help them find Brandon. She just didn't know what else she could tell them.

She suspected that they really wanted to talk to Ryan. They'd asked her a lot of questions about her estranged husband the day before.

She really hated that word *estranged*. It shouldn't be a word that described their relationship, but what would work better?

They'd been separated for months, and divorce seemed to be inevitable. She tried not to think about it. It was easier to deny reality when Ryan wasn't around, but when he got close to her, when she looked into his beautiful brown eyes, she felt a deep aching pain in her heart. And it wasn't only pain she felt, it was also attraction, yearning for the love they'd once had for each other.

Ryan had been her whole life since she was seventeen. And she'd been his.

They'd been so caught up in each other that they'd gotten engaged when they were twenty and married at twenty-one. Their families thought they were too young. Her friends tried to tell her that she should date other people, make sure Ryan was really the one. But she didn't want to see anyone else.

So they'd had a simple wedding in her parents' backyard and a quick trip to Lake Tahoe for a honeymoon. Then they'd moved into a studio in San Francisco. The apartment was so small they could only fit a bed and a dresser, and meals were cooked in a toaster oven and a microwave. In reality, the place was a dump, but through the eyes of love, all Nicole had seen was Ryan. She didn't care that they were tripping over each other. She was in love, in lust, and crazy happy.

It had all been so perfect.

Until it wasn't.

Was it her fault? Was it his? Who even knew anymore?

She felt a little guilty that she hadn't shown Ryan Brandon's artwork. It might have helped Ryan connect to Brandon, but she'd hated the fact that she was the one Brandon saw every day, yet he chose to draw his father on the few occasions they were together.

She jumped out of the shower and dried off. She pulled her damp hair into a ponytail, then grabbed some clothes out of the bedroom closet and threw them on.

When she got to the front door, Ryan was waiting. They didn't talk on their way to the station, which was fine with her. She didn't want to think about anything except getting Brandon back.

➤➤◄◄

After arriving at the police station late Friday morning, Nicole was whisked away by her future brother-in-law, Max Harrison, while Ryan was taken into an interrogation room to face Inspector Michael DeCarlo of the Missing Persons Unit. DeCarlo was a forty-year-old cop with twenty years of experience. His weathered, cynical expression told Ryan he was not going to go easy on anyone, not even the father of the missing child.

"Has Brandon ever wandered away before?" Inspector DeCarlo asked.

Ryan considered the question, the automatic 'no' not quite rolling off his lips.

Four and a half years ago, on the morning of Brandon's second birthday, before his son's world had gone dark, Ryan had taken Brandon to the park so that Nicole could decorate the house for the party. It had been a beautiful sunny Friday in early June, the scent of summer in the air. He'd pushed Brandon on the swing, helped him down the slide and watched him dig in the sand with his shovel and bucket.

Brandon had been a normal two-year-old, happy, eager to join in the play, not at all disturbed by the noise or squeals around him. His son had been the way he was supposed to be. And Ryan hadn't appreciated that moment as much as he should have.

Then his friend, Patrick, had called. Ryan had walked a few feet away from the sandbox to talk to Patrick about the upcoming Giants game. The call hadn't lasted more than a couple of minutes—at least he didn't think it had. But when he turned around, Brandon wasn't where he'd left him.

The memory made his heart stop. He could still feel the adrenaline rush, the fear. He'd found Brandon a few minutes later, hiding in the tube part of the play structure. Brandon had given him a big smile, said "Daddy" and crawled over to him. He'd thrown his chubby little arms around his neck and held on to him as if he would never let him go.

Ryan had never told Nicole that their two-year-old son had been out of his sight for a good five minutes. He'd just thanked God that Brandon was all right and sent up a silent promise that he'd do better in the future.

He really hadn't done any better.

"Mr. Prescott?" the inspector prodded.

"No," he said, not wanting to confuse the current situation with some old memory. "Brandon isn't a kid that wanders away, especially not since he was diagnosed with autism. He doesn't like change, new places, or strangers. He gets upset, hysterical sometimes. I can't imagine how anyone could have lured him away without a struggle."

"That's what your wife said."

"Are we about done?" Ryan asked. Every minute that passed reminded him that Brandon was still missing, and he was doing nothing to find him.

"Not quite."

"Look." He waved a frustrated hand in the air. "You know I was on a flight from Hong Kong to San Francisco when Brandon vanished. We need to wrap this up so I can look for my son."

"Just because you were out of town doesn't mean you don't know anything about your son's disappearance."

"Why would I want to kidnap my son?"

"Having a child with disabilities can be very stressful," the inspector answered in an even, reasonable voice. "It obviously caused a break in your marriage. I understand you and your wife are separated. I'm sure there must have been moments when you wished you didn't have such a difficult child."

The inspector had been trying to get some sort of reaction out of him since he'd walked into the room, but it wasn't going to work. The truth was on his side. "I love my son," Ryan said. "And Brandon belongs with his mother, who adores him, who does everything she can to help him get better. I would never take him out of his home environment. I would never tear him away from Nicole."

"How did it feel to come in second to your own kid? Did it make you angry? Did it make you want to get back at your ex-wife for devoting herself to your son instead of to you?"

"No! What the hell kind of man do you think I am?" he asked, unable to keep the anger out of his voice.

"I have no idea, Mr. Prescott. That's why we're having this conversation. Why don't you tell me how you got that black eye?"

He hesitated, realizing his reply was not going to help their situation, but he had to tell the truth. "Nicole hit me last night. I implied that losing Brandon was her fault. She took offense. It was the heat of the moment. She was stressed out, and I deserved it."

"Was your marriage often violent?"

"It was *never* violent. Nicole was pushed beyond the limit. I don't blame her."

"You've never hit her?"

"No," he said tersely, the question reminding him of another time, another cop, another person with bruises—and that person had been his mother. But unlike his father, he had never hit a woman, nor had he even contemplated the idea. The thought of being like his father made him sick to his stomach. "You can ask Nicole if you don't believe me," he added, seeing the speculation in the inspector's eyes.

"We will."

"Fine. What else?"

"Your wife stated that you rarely see Brandon. What is your relationship with your son?"

"There is no relationship. Brandon doesn't have

relationships with anyone. He's more comfortable with Nicole, but even she can't reach him."

"Does it bother you that you can't connect with your child?"

"Of course it bothers me. He's my son." He looked DeCarlo straight in the eye. "I didn't kidnap Brandon. I don't know where he is, but I'll do anything to help you find him. So keep asking me whatever questions you want, and I'll keep answering, but the end will be the same. I am not involved in Brandon's disappearance. If he didn't wander away on his own, then someone has him." His stomach clenched at that unimaginable thought. "Someone you need to find. That's the bottom line."

"Would you be willing to take a polygraph test?"

"Absolutely. I have nothing to hide. The sooner you can move past me, the sooner you'll start looking for the person who actually did this."

"I'll set it up," the inspector said, getting to his feet. "Wait here."

As DeCarlo left the room, Ryan blew out a breath. He glanced down at his watch. An hour had gone by—a wasted hour. He wanted to be out searching for his son. He looked up as the door opened, relieved to see Nicole.

She quickly answered his unspoken question with a shake of her head. "No news."

He let out a sigh, then got to his feet and paced around the small room, feeling a wave of anger and anxiety sweep through him. "This is so messed up, Nicole."

"I know."

"I don't want to sit in this room while Brandon is out there somewhere, lost and afraid."

"I know," she repeated.

"The inspector wants me to take a lie detector test. He thinks I had something to do with this."

"No, that's crazy."

"He asked me if I ever wanted to get rid of Brandon, because his illness was too difficult," he said, as rage swept through him. He might not have been the best father. Hell, he might not have even been close to the best, but he had always loved his son. "And then he asked me if I hit you, if I hit Brandon," he added, waving a frustrated hand in the air.

"Oh, God," Nicole muttered, guilt flying through her blue eyes. "I didn't even consider that your black eye would focus attention on us instead of Brandon." She paused. "I'm sorry, Ryan. I shouldn't have hit you. I don't know what came over me."

"Fear and anger."

"At the situation more than you."

He was a little surprised by the apology in her gaze. There had been so much anger between them the last few months.

"The inspector was trying to rattle you," she continued. "He doesn't know you, but I do. And you would never ever hurt a child."

Her words put a knot of emotion in his throat. She reminded him of the old Nicole, the woman he'd fallen in love with, the one who'd trusted him, loved him—and made him believe that he would never be like his father.

She ran a hand through her hair, tucking the loose strands behind each ear. "If this is anyone's fault, it's mine," she added. "I was with Brandon at the playground, not you. When you asked me last night how I could let him out of my sight, I hit you because I really wanted to hit myself. Brandon was my responsibility, and I screwed up."

"I never should have said that. I know you watch him like a hawk."

"But I did look away. And just so you don't feel completely special, I've been asked to take a lie detector test, too. You're not the only suspect."

He shook his head in disbelief. "You'd die for Brandon."

"I don't care. I'll do whatever it takes to find our son."

It was the first time in a long time that she'd referred to Brandon as *their* child. "I lost Brandon once," he said, the words slipping out before he could stop them.

Surprise flashed through her eyes. "When?"

"The day of his second birthday party. When we were at the park, I answered my phone. I was on the call for a couple of minutes. I looked up, and Brandon was gone. I'll never forget that feeling of terror. I found him a couple minutes later. He was in that tube between the slides. He smiled when he saw me. And I thanked God that nothing bad had happened to him."

"You never told me that."

"I didn't want you to think less of me. I guess that was bound to happen sooner or later. I'm just afraid that…"

"That what?"

"That I used up our miracle that day. That we weren't supposed to lose Brandon again, because we already got him back once."

"Don't say that." She shook her head, her eyes glittering with determination. "We're getting another miracle. I'm not settling for anything less."

The door opened and Inspector DeCarlo returned to the room. "I received some new information," he said briskly. "A six-year-old child was kidnapped from a playground in Angel's Bay two days ago."

Ryan stared at the inspector in surprise. "How is that relevant? Angel's Bay is miles from here."

"We don't know yet."

"What's the child's name?" Nicole asked.

The inspector glanced down at the yellow pad in his hand. "Kyle Schilling." He looked up at them. "Ring any bells?"

"No," Ryan said.

"Do you think there's a connection?" Nicole asked.

"That's what we need to find out."

Five

⟶⟫⟫⟪⟪⟵

It had been sixty-four hours and eighteen minutes since Kyle had disappeared from a birthday party at the miniature golf course arcade in Angel's Bay on Wednesday night. The birthday child's mother and her sister were supposed to be watching the seven children invited to the party. She'd promised Jessica that six-year-old Kyle would be well supervised, but at some point in the party, Kyle had gone missing.

Jessica Schilling stared into the bathroom mirror, wishing she could stop reliving the horrific phone call and four terrible words—*your son is missing*.

She'd thought it would be minutes until they found him, then hours, but now they were going on three full days, and despite the dedicated and determined help of the Angel's Bay Police Department, Kyle had not come home.

A knock came at the door. "Jessica, are you all right in there? Are you almost ready?"

The voice belonged to her friend, Charlotte Adams. It took Jessica a minute to remember why she was even in the bathroom. She'd been operating on no sleep and too much coffee.

The television interview—that's why she was here. She was supposed to be getting ready to go in front of the cameras again and make a plea for Kyle's safe return. Her hair was oily and limp. She couldn't remember when she'd last taken a shower. Was it yesterday or the day before?

She took a band out of her drawer and pulled her long brown hair into a ponytail. Her skin was pale and blotchy from crying. The shadows under her dark brown eyes made her look like she'd been in a fight. She looked far older than her twenty-six years. In fact, she barely recognized herself.

Two years ago, at the age of twenty-four, she'd fallen hard for a much older man, a man with a four-year-old child, who had also stolen her heart. In three months, she'd gotten married and become a stepmother. For fourteen months, she'd been happy, finally finding the family she'd always wanted. Then Travis was killed in an accident, and she had to raise Kyle by herself.

She'd thought she'd been doing an okay job, although her mother-in-law had a lot of complaints, but Kyle had been happy to be with her. Now he was gone. She'd lost him. And she was starting to lose hope that she was going to get him back.

"Jessica?" There was worry in Charlotte's voice now.

"I'm coming," she said as she splashed some water on her face.

She was grateful for Charlotte's support. Charlotte had taken her under her wing after Travis's death, introducing her to her friends and helping her find her way in the community. She'd been so wrapped up in Travis and Kyle that she barely knew anyone in Angel's Bay.

Charlotte, on the other hand, knew everyone. She'd grown up in Angel's Bay and had even dated Travis's cousin Andrew back when they were in high school.

"Jessica?" A new voice rang through the door, this one belonging to one of Charlotte's good friends, Kara Lynch. Kara had also been born and raised in Angel's Bay, and her family ran the Angel's Heart Quilt Shop.

She dried her face and opened the door. "Sorry."

Charlotte and Kara were standing at the end of the bed. Charlotte was a slender blonde wearing a navy blue pencil skirt and a button-down blouse. She'd obviously come straight from work; she was an OB/GYN at the local hospital. Kara wore a light blue sweater over black leggings and boots. She was a curvy redhead, who'd added a few curves five months into her second pregnancy.

As Jessica's gaze moved to the photo in Kara's hands, her breath caught in her chest. It was a photo of Kyle wearing his soccer uniform—Kyle, with his blond hair, blue eyes, and happy smile. Her son was an outgoing, friendly kid, open and fearless in his innocence. He trusted far too easily, and someone had taken advantage of that trust.

"The press wanted another picture," Kara said tentatively. "Is this one okay to give out?"

She nodded her head, too filled with fear to speak.

"If you can't do this," Charlotte began, her gaze narrowing in concern. "One of us can be your spokesperson. Or Mrs. Schilling—"

"No," she said forcefully. She was not going to let her mother-in-law take over, even though Paula had been trying to do just that. Jessica was Kyle's mother, and she was the one who would speak for him. "I'll do it. I have to do it. I can't let anyone forget about Kyle."

"No one is forgetting," Kara said, compassion in her voice. "There are flyers up on every storefront, and this interview will put Kyle back on television."

"We're not giving up," Charlotte added. "Miracles happen all the time around here."

"Thanks for the pep talk."

"It's the truth," Charlotte said, kindness in her eyes.

She knew both Charlotte and Kara felt connected to

Kyle's disappearance because she'd been with them that night. They'd been at dinner for Charlotte's bachelorette party, a party that had come to an abrupt halt with that phone call.

They left her bedroom and walked down the stairs together. At the front door Charlotte and Kara hung back while Jessica continued down the steps. The media had set up a microphone on her lawn. A barrage of cameras and reporters faced her. It was so surreal. She'd been an ordinary person living an ordinary life—until last Wednesday night.

As she stepped closer to the microphone, she realized it was a smaller group today, and that made her more scared. She needed the media not to lose interest in Kyle.

"I'm here to plead for the safe return of my son, Kyle Schilling. He's a wonderful, caring, loving boy," she said, her voice cracking with emotion. "And he needs to come home. If you see him anywhere, please call the hotline. The police need your help." She drew in a deep breath. "I love my son, and I want him back."

As she finished, the reporters started asking her questions. One of the detectives who'd been working the case, Jason Marlow, came forward to provide some answers. As he stepped in front of the microphone, she made a hasty retreat into the house. Her mother-in-law, Paula Schilling, met her in the entryway.

Paula looked a lot like Travis, very tall, square jaw, dark brown hair, but where Travis had warm, friendly eyes, Paula's eyes were cold and hard. She hadn't liked Jessica from the minute Travis brought her home.

"That's how you dress to represent your son?" Paula asked sharply.

Jessica glanced down at her layered tank tops and skinny jeans that were ripped at one knee. She hadn't given her clothes any thought at all, but even if she had, she wouldn't have found anything too different in her closet, certainly not the kind of dress that Paula would approve of.

"I thought you did a good job," Charlotte cut in.

Paula rolled her eyes and brushed past Jessica as she left the house.

"Forget about her," Kara advised. "She's worried about Kyle."

"She blames me for his disappearance."

"You weren't even there," Kara said.

"Exactly. I wasn't there. I was at a party. I was being selfish. She's reminded me of that at least a dozen times," Jessica said.

Charlotte frowned. "You weren't being selfish; you were helping me celebrate my engagement. This wasn't your fault, Jessica. You can't let her get to you, and having a mother who is very much like Paula Schilling, I know that's easier said than done, but you have to try to blow off whatever she says."

"I can't even think about her right now," Jessica said with a sigh. "I just want to find Kyle."

As Charlotte finished speaking, the front door opened, and Charlotte's fiancé, Joe Silveira, walked into the entry. An attractive man with olive skin and dark, intense eyes, Joe was the chief of police in Angel's Bay.

He gave Charlotte and Kara a brief smile, then turned to her. "I have some information, Jessica. There was a kidnapping in San Francisco yesterday afternoon, a six-year-old boy by the name of Brandon Prescott."

Jessica stared at him in confusion. "What does that have to do with Kyle?"

"Maybe you can tell me." He handed her a photograph.

As she stared down at the picture, her heart stopped. "Who is this?"

"Brandon Prescott."

Her pulse began to race as she noted the blond hair and familiar blue eyes. This boy's name was Brandon?

Blood pounded through her veins, and her vision grew blurry. It was suddenly too much—the fear, the lack of sleep, and now more shock.

Her head began to spin, her breath coming short and fast. She heard Charlotte call her name just before everything went black.

Nicole sat down in the chair next to Inspector DeCarlo's desk. Ryan stood behind her. They both waited as the inspector finished his phone call.

As he hung up the phone, the inspector gave them a quick glance, his expression thoughtful. "Wait here a moment. I'm printing out a photograph." He got up from his chair and walked across the room to the printer.

Nicole gave Ryan a worried look. "I don't understand what's happening. Is someone going around kidnapping six-year-old boys? How could this child in Angel's Bay have anything to do with Brandon?"

"Kidnappers can go after the same type, blondes, kids, boys, girls." Ryan rubbed a hand across his tired eyes. "I just don't want to believe that someone took Brandon. I keep hoping that he wandered away and we'll find him hiding somewhere, like in the tube at the park."

"I keep hoping the same thing," she said, but deep down she knew that hope was fading. Someone or something was preventing Brandon from coming home.

A moment later the inspector returned. He sat down behind his desk and handed her a picture. It was a photo of a child along with vital statistics noting age, height, and weight.

She stared at the picture in bemusement. It was a picture of Brandon, but the name and the other details were wrong. "Kyle Schilling?" she murmured. She looked up at the inspector. "I don't understand."

"What the hell is this?" Ryan demanded, looking at the photo over her shoulder.

"It appears that Brandon has an identical twin," the inspector said. "Now, does someone want to tell me what's going on?"

"Brandon isn't a twin," Nicole replied, staring down at the photograph, her heart beating way too fast. The boy in the picture was Brandon, and yet he wasn't. This child gazed straight into the camera with a smile, with warm, interested eyes. Brandon hadn't smiled in more than two years. And he never looked directly at anyone.

But there were details about this little boy that made her heart turn over: the cowlick on the corner of his head, the tiny freckles that dotted his nose, the slightly crooked teeth. He looked exactly like Brandon—but this child wasn't her son.

"This isn't Brandon," she said, handing the photo back to Inspector DeCarlo.

"No, it's Kyle Shilling. But this boy's looks and his birthday are the same as Brandon's. Was your son adopted?"

"Yes," she said.

"Why didn't you tell me that before?" he questioned sharply.

She didn't like the suspicious look in his eyes. "I didn't think I needed to. We adopted Brandon when he was four days old. He's our son. I don't think of him as being adopted. We've been with him almost every second of his life."

"Almost," the inspector said, his gaze moving to Ryan. "What about you? Anything to add?"

"When we adopted Brandon, we weren't told he was a twin."

"What adoption agency did you use?" DeCarlo asked.

"We went through an attorney," Nicole answered. "Jim Edwards. He has an office downtown. He's very well-respected and specializes in private adoptions. He would have told us if there was another child, because we would have adopted him, too." She paused, wanting the inspector to understand her motivation.

"I've known since my teens that I wouldn't be able to have children of my own," she continued. "I have a medical condition that makes that impossible. So Ryan and I started exploring options right after we got married. But it still took years for us to get a baby. When Jim Reynolds told us that we were getting a son, we were over the moon. If there were twins, Mr. Reynolds would have asked us to take both, and we would have said yes."

DeCarlo jotted down some notes on a pad and then gave a nod. "All right. I'll check with your attorney. At the time of the adoption, were you given any information about the birth mother or father?"

"All we knew was that the mother was a teenager," Nicole said. "Otherwise, it was a totally blind adoption." It was the way she'd preferred it. She hadn't wanted Brandon to be confused by two sets of parents.

"What about when your son was diagnosed with autism? Weren't you concerned about the family medical history?"

"Of course I was concerned, but the doctors told me that there's no familial link where autism is concerned, at least as far as they know." She licked her lips, her gaze moving to the photograph of Kyle Schilling again. It hurt to see Kyle's smiling face, hurt in a way that only a mother of an autistic child could understand. Because this boy, this exact replica of her son, looked so happy, so normal. This was supposed to be her son. This was what Brandon should look like now.

Ryan's hand came down on her shoulder, and she welcomed his warmth. It had been a long time since she and Ryan had been in sync, but in this moment she felt like he was the only person who could possibly understand what she was feeling. She cleared her throat, turning her attention back to the inspector.

"It doesn't appear that Kyle is autistic," she said.

"No, he's not," DeCarlo confirmed.

"What do Kyle's parents know about the adoption?" Ryan interjected. "Were they aware that their son had a twin?"

"I haven't yet spoken to the Schillings, but the police department in Angel's Bay informed me that Mrs. Schilling is as surprised as you are that her son has an identical twin. They also used an attorney; not the same one you mentioned, but I suspect there's a connection somewhere."

"So what do we do now?" Nicole asked. It was mind-boggling to know Brandon was a twin, but that fact wasn't bringing him home."

"Continue investigating," the inspector said. "We'll start with the attorneys and go on from there."

"This other boy," Ryan began. "How long has he been missing?"

"This is the third day," DeCarlo answered, his expression grim.

Nicole's heart sank. Three days?

"But," the inspector said, obviously reading the disappointment in her expression. "The connection between the boys gives us a new lead to work."

"You think they're together?" Ryan asked.

"Yes, I do. And I'm very interested in finding the biological parents. I don't believe it's an accident that someone kidnapped two brothers who have been separated since birth."

"Why is this happening now?" Nicole asked. "Brandon is six years old. Why would anyone wait so long to try to get him back? And why not find us, talk to us, see if we wanted to connect? Kidnapping is such a drastic step. I don't even understand how they made it happen."

"They must have planned it in great detail," Ryan said slowly. "This kidnapping took some coordination. They had to get each child away from his parents in a very short amount of time. They had to have been following Brandon, waiting for an opportunity."

Nicole hated the idea that someone had been watching her and Brandon.

"I agree," the inspector said. "This wasn't a crime of opportunity, a grab of a random child. It wasn't a stranger who kidnapped your son."

"Yes, it was a stranger," Nicole said forcefully. "Brandon doesn't know his biological parents or his brother. He's going to be terrified and confused and wondering where we are, and why we're not coming to get him. You don't understand how hard it is for him to connect with anyone, to adjust to even the smallest change in routine. He hits his head against the wall when he gets agitated. And then he starts screaming in this super high pitch. I don't know what they're going to do to him when they realize he's not—normal." Her voice broke as she choked on a knot of fear. "You have to find him."

DeCarlo's gaze filled with compassion. "We're going to do everything we can, Mrs. Prescott. Brandon is our top priority. I do think that Brandon's chances of being found are greater now than they were before. And if the biological parents are involved, I doubt their intent is to harm the boys."

She really wanted to believe that. "But you don't know that for sure."

"No, I don't, but let's try to stay positive. Why don't you go home? We'll be in touch as soon as we know anything."

"What about the polygraph?" Ryan asked.

"That's on hold. If you remember anything or anyone that might have had something to do with the adoption proceedings, please let me know."

Nicole was suddenly reluctant to leave. Going home and

waiting were unappealing, but the inspector was picking up the phone, and Ryan tipped his head toward the door. She got to her feet and followed him down the hall and out the front door. She paused when they got to the sidewalk, the bright sun seeming so at odds with the darkness surrounding her life.

"I can't believe what's happened," she said. "Brandon has a twin? How could we not know that? And his twin..." She had to bite down on her bottom lip to stop the trembling.

"I know," Ryan said, meeting her gaze. "He's not autistic."

She shook her head. "It's all so strange. Do you think Mr. Reynolds knew there was another boy?"

"Only one way to find out. Let's go talk to him."

"What about the police?"

"They can talk to him, too. But I don't feel like waiting around for them to get to that."

"I don't, either." As they walked to the car, she was relieved to have something purposeful to do. And she had a lot of questions for Jim Reynolds.

Six

Jim Reynolds's law firm was on the thirty-second floor of a downtown skyscraper with a view of San Francisco and the Bay Bridge. It had been six years since Nicole had been in this office, but she vividly remembered the last time, the day that Jim had placed Brandon in her arms and said, "I'd like you to meet your son."

Emotion choked her throat, and she sniffed back a tear. This was no time to break down. There was too much to do.

She followed Ryan to the reception desk, happy to have him take the lead while she pulled herself together.

"We need to speak to Mr. Reynolds," Ryan said, his voice firm and demanding.

"Do you have an appointment?" the woman asked.

"No, but Mr. Reynolds handled our adoption six years ago, and the child we adopted is now missing. I'm Ryan Prescott. This is my wife, Nicole. We'd like a few minutes of his time."

"All right," the woman said, a wary look on her face. "Wait here."

She got up from her desk and disappeared down the hall.

Nicole walked over to the window and gazed out at the city below. The narrow, crowded streets were teeming with tourists and business people. In the distance she could see

Coit tower, Fisherman's Wharf and Pier 39. The view was beautiful, but from here, the city seemed huge and filled with a million people. Where on earth was her little boy?

She'd never *not* known where Brandon was. For every second of his life, she'd been in control. But now she had no idea where Brandon was or who he was with. The biological parents were nameless, faceless people that she'd stopped thinking about a long time ago. That had obviously been a mistake.

"I should have asked more questions," she said, turning to Ryan, "about Brandon's real parents. But I didn't want to know anything about them. I wanted to pretend that Brandon was ours."

"He is ours, and we are his real parents. We were there when he had colic every night as a baby. We took turns holding him when he had a fever. We were there when he learned how to walk and talk. We comforted him when he cried. We were by his side every moment of every day." Ryan's jaw tightened. "At least you were."

She saw the anger flash in his eyes, and habit made her want to reassure him. But she couldn't quite bring herself to let him off the hook.

In the first year after Brandon's diagnosis, Ryan had been very present. But as the years passed, his hope had faltered, and she couldn't handle his realistic viewpoint. They were suddenly at odds all the time. They couldn't hear each other. They couldn't connect the way they used to. Brandon's condition was always between them. Their strong bond frayed, and then it eventually snapped.

But they were together again now. It seemed the bitterest irony that Brandon's presence had split them apart and his absence had brought them back together.

As the tense silence between them lengthened, she cleared her throat and said, "Do you think the biological parents will tell Brandon that he's their son?"

Ryan stared back at her. "If the parents are the ones who took him, probably so. I don't think he'll believe them or even understand them."

"I wanted to tell him when he was older. And then after he got sick, it seemed like the last thing we needed to try to get into his brain."

"That was the right decision," Ryan said.

"I thought it was." She paused. "What if we did something wrong, Ryan? What if the right papers weren't signed? What if Mr. Reynolds cut some sort of corner?"

"Jim Reynolds is a reputable attorney. Look around this office. He's been in business for years. He's helped coordinate thousands of adoptions."

"I know, but I remember thinking back then that it was too good to be true. Didn't you?"

He frowned. "No. I didn't think that. We tried to adopt for five years, Nicole. I thought our turn had finally come up." He glanced at the empty reception desk. "What's taking so long?"

"Maybe he doesn't remember us. It's been six years."

As she finished speaking, the receptionist returned to her desk followed by Jim Reynolds. The attorney was in his early fifties and was a short, stocky man with a receding hairline. He waved them into a nearby conference room.

"Mr. and Mrs. Prescott," he said. "What can I do for you?"

"Our son is missing," Ryan replied. "And apparently, he's a twin, something you didn't disclose to us at the time of the adoption."

"His twin has also disappeared," Nicole put in. "The police think the biological parents could be connected."

Jim stared back at them for a long minute. Nicole couldn't read his expression. He seemed surprised, but he was also wary.

"We need to know everything you know about Brandon's biological parents," Ryan added.

"You've caught me off guard here," Jim said slowly. "As I recall, your adoption was closed. Is that correct?"

"Yes," Ryan said.

"I'm afraid I can't give you any information without the consent of the biological parents."

"Then get them on the phone," Ryan ordered.

Jim stared back at them. "Tell me what happened with your son."

"He disappeared from his school playground," Ryan replied. "And his identical twin was taken from a party a few days ago."

"His identical twin," Nicole repeated, watching the attorney's face for some clue as to whether or not he had known there were two boys. "Why didn't you tell us our son had a brother? We would have adopted both of them."

"I don't remember the circumstances of your case. I'm sorry. I've handled thousands of adoptions. Quite frankly, I didn't even remember your name until I saw you in reception. I will, however, check the file and see what information is available."

Nicole's heart sunk at his answer, but she was used to fighting for Brandon. She had no intention of letting the attorney blow them off. "Every second is critical. Our son has been missing since yesterday afternoon, and the other child has been gone for three days. We need you to open the file now."

"I understand your desperation, and I sympathize. I have children of my own, and I can only imagine what you're going through."

"You *can't* imagine," Ryan said forcefully. "No one can imagine the horror of losing a child. We'll wait while you look up our case."

The attorney frowned. "It was six years ago, right? I'm afraid those files were moved to storage several years ago."

"They're not computerized?" Ryan asked.

"No, but I will have a search conducted for the records."

Nicole didn't think that sounded like a fast process. "We've just come from the police department, Mr. Reynolds. They'll be contacting you soon."

"I understand. I'm happy to cooperate."

"You don't seem cooperative," Ryan said bluntly, his words echoing Nicole's thoughts.

Mr. Reynolds tipped his head. "I'm under legal constraints, Mr. Prescott. California has very strict laws when it comes to unsealing adoption records. There's little I can do without the consent of the biological parents. If I can help you, I certainly will. I promise to be in touch as soon as I know anything."

Jim opened the conference room door, making it clear their meeting was over.

Ryan strode forward, then paused in front of the lawyer. "Whoever kidnapped two six-year-olds from the only families they've ever known doesn't deserve the protection of the law. The children do; they're the only ones who are important here. Please help us."

"I will do everything I can," Jim promised.

They walked out to the elevator in silence. Ryan slammed his hand against the elevator button. "Asshole," he muttered under his breath.

She didn't disagree with his opinion of the lawyer. Jim Reynolds had seemed like their benevolent savior six years ago. Now he was a hard, ruthless man, who was obviously worried about protecting himself. He was not going to help them unless the court ordered him to open up his records. And how long would that take?

Suddenly overwhelmed, she put a hand on the nearby wall to steady herself.

Ryan's gaze shot to hers. "Are you all right?"

She shook her head. "No."

"What can I do?"

"Bring Brandon home," she said helplessly.

"I'm trying."

"I know you are," she said, meeting his gaze. "I'm glad you're here with me, Ryan."

His eyes darkened with emotion. "There's nowhere else I want to be. Let's go home."

⟶⟫⟪⟨⟵

When they returned home, Ryan found himself surrounded by Callaways, and his tension increased. In the past several months he hadn't had much contact with the family, and he didn't know what Nicole had told anyone about their separation, but he doubted her family was too high on him, especially her father, Jack Callaway.

The patriarch of the family, Jack was also second in charge at the San Francisco Fire Department. He was a man who was bigger than life, with a loud booming voice, sparkling blue eyes, and innate leadership qualities. Ryan had always admired Jack. Jack was the kind of father that Ryan had wanted to be, but he'd fallen short of that goal.

As they entered the living room, the group chatter came to an immediate halt. On the couch next to Jack were Nicole's mother, Lynda, and her grandmother, Eleanor. Nicole's sister, Shayla, was perched on the arm of the recliner next to her grandfather, Patrick. Nicole's brother, Drew, and his new love, Ria, were on the loveseat. Burke stood by the window, his arms folded in front of him, a serious look on his face, but that wasn't unusual. He was the most intense and focused of the Callaway brothers.

After a tense moment, Jack stood up and opened his arms to Nicole. She walked into his embrace.

Ryan felt very much like the odd man out.

"Ryan," Burke said, drawing his attention. "What have you found out?"

"A lot." He ran a hand through his hair as he glanced at Nicole. "Do you want to tell them?"

"Go ahead," she urged.

"All right. We learned today that Brandon has an identical twin brother," he said. "And that little boy, Kyle Schilling, was kidnapped on Wednesday night. The police obviously believe now that there's a connection, perhaps a link to the biological parents."

Jack shook his head in disbelief. "That's shocking. You had no idea your son was a twin?"

"None. Our lawyer didn't tell us—if he knew—and he wasn't willing to state whether he did know or he didn't. He said he would have to look up our case file, which doesn't appear to be on his computer system. Apparently, it's going to take some legal maneuvering to get to the identity of the biological parents, maybe even a court order."

"That's crazy," Drew said. "If the kids have been taken by the biological parents, can't someone be compelled to open the file?"

"The police are working on it," Nicole said. "But Ryan and I found our attorney to be pretty uncooperative. We don't know why. Hopefully, he didn't do something wrong at the time of the adoption."

"Is that a concern?" Burke asked.

Nicole met Ryan's gaze, then she shrugged, turning back to her brother. "We don't know. Everything is happening so fast; we're trying to keep up."

The doorbell rang, and Lynda jumped to her feet. "That's

going to be a team from the Center for Missing Children. They've offered their resources to help search for Brandon."

"Thanks for reaching out to them, Mom," Nicole said.

"They called you, honey. They have a lot of resources we can tap into. Even if the biological parents are involved, I think it's still worth talking to them."

"I agree," Nicole said, following her mother out of the room.

"You look tired, Ryan," Eleanor said, drawing his gaze to hers. "You should drink some chamomile tea. It always works for me when I can't sleep."

"He doesn't need tea, Ellie," her husband Patrick said.

"How do you know what he needs?" she snapped back. "You don't know everything, Patrick Callaway. I know a few things, too."

"We should go," Patrick said abruptly.

"What did I say?" Eleanor asked in confusion as Patrick held out his hand to her.

"It's time for dinner," Patrick said.

"We haven't eaten yet?"

"No," Patrick said gently, taking his wife's hand as he brought her to her feet.

It saddened Ryan to see Eleanor so confused. Nicole's grandmother had been one of his biggest supporters when he and Nicole had first gotten together. Eleanor had told him once that she completely understood what first and furious love felt like, because she'd felt that way about Patrick.

But while he and Nicole had been derailed by the problems of life, Patrick and Eleanor still clung together, even after fifty years of marriage and Eleanor in the throes of Alzheimer's disease.

"Grandpa always shuts Grandma down," Shayla commented. "Emma's right. It's like he doesn't want her to tell us something."

Ryan didn't know what Shayla was talking about, but he had his own puzzle to solve. "I'm going to take a walk around the neighborhood." He'd wanted to go down to Brandon's school and also look around the few blocks in between the house and the school. Dozens of people had already searched the surrounding area, but he hadn't had a chance to actually look for his son until now. And he needed to do that.

"I'll go with you," Drew said, getting to his feet.

"All right." If he had to have a Callaway with him, he'd take Drew. They'd always had a lot in common, starting with their love of aviation. Drew had flown helicopters for the Navy and was now working for the Coast Guard.

As they walked to the door, he saw Nicole and her mother in the dining room with three other people. He paused to say, "Drew and I are going to look around the neighborhood."

She nodded. "Okay. I'll be here."

He walked out to the porch and down the steps, Drew on his heels. They didn't say anything for a few minutes, and he was grateful for the silence. He felt like he'd been on a sprint since he'd gotten off the plane and raced home, his heart beating out of his chest, terror running through his veins. And today had been one shock after the next. He needed to get his head together.

"Where are we going?" Drew asked after a moment.

"To the school. It's three blocks away."

"You need to see where it happened."

"I do," he admitted. "I know the school has been checked many times, but I have to start somewhere."

As they walked, his gaze swept every yard of the residential neighborhood, which was a mix of houses and small apartment buildings. He knew the streets well. Nicole and he had always been walkers. They'd loved exploring the city on the weekends. Before they'd adopted Brandon, their walks had been longer and more vigorous. After Brandon, they'd stayed closer to home, visiting local parks and the beach on Sunday afternoons.

Brandon had loved to walk with them, before he'd gone into his head and gotten lost. After that, it was a struggle to get him to go anywhere. Sometimes Nicole would have to drive him the three blocks to school just because she knew it would take close to an hour to coax him to walk that far. Oftentimes, Brandon would sit down on the curb and refuse to budge. Then they'd have to try to pick him up, and he'd scream loud enough to bring out the neighbors. Ryan let out a sigh, thinking that even with all the problems, he wanted desperately to get his son back.

Drew shot him a sharp look. "You okay, Ryan?"

"I don't remember what *okay* feels like. Brandon is lost, and Nicole and I are headed for divorce. I don't know what the hell happened to my life." His gaze moved upward as a small plane flew overhead.

Drew followed his gaze. "I bet you'd rather be up there."

"Yes. I know what I'm doing up there. Down here—not so much."

"The sky has always been a great escape for me, too. But eventually we all have to land. Any chance you and Nicole can work through your differences?"

"Maybe if we spent more than five minutes talking about our marriage," Ryan replied. "But Nicole never has time to talk and even less time to listen. It's all about Brandon, and I understand why her focus is on him. But I can't be in this marriage alone. If I can't give Nicole what she needs, then maybe I should let her go, let her find someone who can."

"What about what you want?" Drew challenged. "Or *who* you want—is it still Nicole?"

Ryan thought for a moment. "Yes. It's always been her." He paused. "I thought things had gotten so bad that being apart wouldn't matter, but I've missed Nicole these past few months, and I've missed Brandon, too. Unfortunately, there's a big wall between us, and I don't know how to tear it down."

"Take out a small hammer and start chipping," Drew suggested.

"Your sister is tough," he said dryly. "I might need a big hammer."

Drew smiled. "Of course she's tough; she's a Callaway. But you knew how to get to her once. Do it again. Make her hear you. Make her see you. I don't think you should give up on her, not if you still love her."

"Maybe I'll try again after Brandon comes home." He shot Drew a thoughtful look. "So now that you have a girlfriend, you think you know everything about women and relationships?"

Drew grinned. "Not everything, but at least a little more than I knew before."

"So you and Ria are a couple now?" he asked, having heard bits and pieces of their love story. "How's that going?"

"Great."

"She has a kid or a sister…"

"Megan is Ria's niece, but Ria is her legal guardian now. Megan is seventeen years old and a senior in high school. She's a wonderful girl, very resilient. She lost both her parents and was terrorized by her mobster uncle, but she came through it all. And now she's a normal teenager. I've actually been teaching her how to drive."

"You?" Ryan said with a laugh. "Didn't you get like three speeding tickets in one year?"

"That was a long time ago."

"Yeah, when you were Megan's age."

"We don't need to share that information with Megan."

"Got it. So you're kind of playing a father role these days?"

"Megan is basically grown, but I like watching out for her."

"And Ria?"

"She's the woman I always dreamt about. I just didn't know who she was until I met her. And then that was it for me. I was hooked. I know she's the one. I'm going to propose next month on her birthday. No one else knows yet, so keep that under your hat."

"I will," he promised. He was a little envious of the happiness in Drew's voice, the love in his eyes when he spoke about Ria. He'd had that kind of amazing love, too, but somehow he'd let it slip through his fingers.

"So we're here," Drew said, pausing by the gate to the schoolyard.

"Yes." He turned his focus back to the present. "Nicole said Brandon was playing in the bushes over there. He likes to collect rocks and match them up."

"Yeah, I know," Drew said. "He's a little obsessed with that."

They walked into the yard and stopped next to the bushes. Ryan's gaze swept the grounds, and he silently measured the distance from the street to this part of the playground. It was only about thirty feet. Even with the Halloween carnival in full swing, it seemed unbelievable that anyone could have drawn Brandon away without Nicole realizing what was happening.

"How did they do it?" he muttered. "How did they get Brandon away from Nicole? Or from his rocks?"

Drew shrugged. "Brandon must have seen something that drew his interest."

Ryan stared back at Drew, his words striking a chord. "Oh, my God! Why didn't I think of that?"

"What?"

"Brandon's brother, his identical twin, was probably in

the car. If Brandon saw his mirror image, he might not have been afraid at all." Ryan's mind raced as a piece of the puzzle fell into place. "He might have run to the car."

"That makes sense," Drew said slowly. "If his brother was in the car. Of course, that doesn't explain how they got Brandon's brother."

"Kyle disappeared from a miniature golf course arcade. Maybe it was easier to get him away from a busy place. But with Brandon, there needed to be some special enticement."

"At least they're together. I know that's not much consolation."

"It's something," he agreed. "The brother is the key."

"The key to what?"

"I'm not sure yet."

"But there's a plan brewing in your mind."

"There is," Ryan said, feeling like he finally knew what he needed to do next.

Seven

⟶⟫⟪⟵

"You're going to Angel's Bay?" Emma asked, as Nicole threw some clothes into her overnight bag just before five o'clock Friday afternoon. "Are you sure that's the right move? Wouldn't it be better to stay close to home? Angel's Bay is at least a four-hour drive from here."

"I have absolutely no idea if it's the right move, but after spending the day waiting for the phone to ring, taking any kind of action is appealing. And I think Ryan's plan is a good one."

"That's the first time in a while that you've given Ryan credit for coming up with a good idea," Emma said pointedly.

"Well, I guess he was due," she retorted. "When he told me that he thought Brandon was enticed into the car by his brother, everything fell into place. I have been beating myself over the head trying to figure out how anyone could have snatched him out from under me, and I finally have an explanation."

"But what good will going to Angel's Bay do? The boys aren't there."

"We don't know where they are. But the other child's family is there, and maybe if we put our heads together, we can come up with a lead or something that neither one of us has thought of yet."

"I suppose that makes sense."

"Mom said she'd stay here in case Brandon comes home on his own, although that's extremely doubtful. And Sara said she could also hang out here if Mom needs to do something since she's on maternity leave. If Sara can't be here, then someone else will take over."

"I know the family will make sure the house is covered," Emma said. "And of course I'm happy to do whatever you need. I'm just worried about you, Nicole. It might be best to let the police investigate."

Nicole frowned. "You would never stand around and do nothing, Em. You took on a serial arsonist all by yourself."

"Because I'm a trained fire investigator. I knew what I was doing. You're not a detective. And we don't know what kind of people you're dealing with." She frowned. "Maybe I should come with you. I can get some days off work."

Nicole shook her head. "I appreciate the offer, but I need you here, Em. You and Max can stay on top of the investigation. Inspector DeCarlo seems like a good investigator, but I know that as time passes, Brandon's case will lose priority."

"Max and I won't let that happen."

"I know you won't."

"So what are you going to do when you get to Angel's Bay?"

"Probably knock on the Schillings' door."

"You could call."

"Ryan already called. He wasn't able to speak to Mrs. Schilling, but he talked to a neighbor who did give us a little more information. Apparently, Mrs. Schilling's husband died a year ago, so she's a single mother now."

"That's sad."

"Yes, and it's already been three long days for her. I

guess she finally passed out from exhaustion. Anyway, we'll figure out a plan on the drive. I know I want to ask her about her adoption process. Perhaps her attorney will be more forthcoming than ours." She took a breath. "And I want to talk to her about her son."

"Nic…"

She glanced at Emma and saw a question in her eyes. "He's not autistic. That's what you wanted to ask, isn't it?"

"Actually, Max already told me that the other child was fine. What I wanted to ask was how you're going to handle dealing with that fact?"

Nicole wanted to pretend like it didn't matter, but this was her sister, and they'd always been honest with each other. "It shook me up to see a picture of a child who looked exactly like Brandon but had all the life and light that Brandon is missing. It's like Brandon is a dim shadow of his brother. And I have to say it made me sad."

"I'm sorry."

"I know you are. I am too, but it is what it is. And I love Brandon unconditionally. I'll do anything I have to do to bring him home." She zipped her suitcase. "I think I'm ready."

"Good luck," Emma said, giving her a quick hug.

"Thanks. I could definitely use some good luck."

--->>><<<---

Ryan walked restlessly around the living room of Nicole's house. After convincing Nicole to go to Angel's Bay, he'd run back to his apartment, showered and grabbed some clothes. Now he was back and eager to get on his way, but Nicole was upstairs with Emma. He hoped Emma wouldn't try to talk Nicole out of making the trip. He'd already had Max caution him against getting in the way of the investigation.

He knew the cops wanted to handle things on their own, and he'd been assured that both police departments were working together, but he didn't give a damn about their partnership. He wanted—needed—to talk to Kyle's mother. The boys had been taken together, and it made sense to him that the two families should be together. Nicole hadn't taken much persuasion. Like him, she was itching to do something else besides wait.

For the first time in a while they were a team again. He'd missed being her partner, seeing her turn to him for advice or support, and being able to help. And while he hated the reason that had brought them together, he was determined not to let her down this time. Nor did he want to let Brandon down.

He'd told himself for a long time that Brandon didn't care about him, didn't notice him, didn't even realize they were father and son, but maybe that wasn't true. The pictures that Brandon had sketched of him had revealed at least a snapshot of what was in Brandon's head. Maybe Brandon knew a lot more than he let on. If that were true, then Brandon was counting on his parents to come and get him, and that's exactly what they were going to do.

He turned as the front door opened. It was his sister-in-law, Sara Davidson, now Sara Callaway. Sara had married her first love, Aiden, several months ago. In fact, they'd moved up the wedding date to accommodate Sara's unexpected pregnancy. Judging by the size of her belly, she was getting close to her due date.

"Hi, Ryan," she said with a compassionate, worried smile. "How are you doing?"

"Hanging in there. Can I help you with that?" he asked, noting the casserole dish in her hands. "You really don't need to be cooking for us."

"I didn't. Your neighbor stopped me on the way up the

walk. She didn't want to bother anyone by ringing the bell. And no, I've got it," she added as he reached for the dish. "Is Lynda here?"

"In the kitchen."

"And Nicole?"

"Hopefully almost done packing. We're going to meet the family of the other child. You heard about Brandon's twin?"

She nodded. "Yes. It's unbelievable. You must be incredibly curious about this other family."

"I'm more interested in the attorney they used for their adoption." He suddenly remembered that Sara was a lawyer, too. "The guy we used is not cooperating, Sara. He claims he can't do anything without the consent of the parents, probably the same people who kidnapped Brandon."

"Aiden told me that you used Jim Reynolds. I don't know him, but he has a good reputation. Opening sealed adoption records in California is a difficult process. You have to have the consent of all parties or get a judge to open the records. I'm sure that's not what you want to hear, but it is the truth."

"That's what Reynolds told me. Max said they're working on getting a court order. How long will that take?"

"Hopefully not long, but it will depend on how strong a case the police have for believing the records are crucial to finding the boys."

"They seem convinced someone wanted to reunite the kids, and who better than the biological parents?"

"Or it could be one parent and not the other. Were you given any information about either of them at the time of the adoption?"

"Only that the mother was a young teenager and the father was unknown."

"Which would make her still pretty young," Sara commented. "If she was sixteen when she gave birth, she'd only be about twenty-two now. Kind of young to pull off a double kidnapping all by herself."

Another piece of the puzzle fell into place. "You're right. I hadn't added that up. Nicole kept wondering why now, and suddenly it makes sense. The mother had to grow up first."

"Or the father may not have been party to the adoption and now wants his children," Sara suggested.

"Another good point. And he could be older than the birth mother."

"I hope the other family can give you more information. If there's anything I can do, let me know."

"Thanks."

As Sara went into the kitchen, Nicole and Emma came down the stairs together. Emma shot him a thoughtful look. Emma and Nicole were very close, and he had no doubt that Emma had heard about some of his less than stellar qualities. But right now he wasn't interested in her opinion of him, so he was happy when she didn't say anything.

"I'm ready," Nicole said.

He grabbed her overnight bag out of her hand.

"I can carry that," she protested.

"So can I." He disliked the fact that she couldn't accept even the smallest offer of help when it came from him.

"All right."

"Ryan," Emma said, drawing his attention to her.

"Yes?" he asked warily.

"Bring our boy home."

He gave her a nod. "I will," he promised. There was no other option.

It was six by the time they got on the road, and traffic leaving the city was predictably heavy for a Friday night. Ryan hated the slow pace. Patience had never been his strong suit. "We should have flown," he muttered.

"The closest airport to Angel's Bay is an hour away," Nicole said. "And we're going to need a car to get around down there."

Which was exactly why he hadn't insisted on flying. "I know." He flung her a quick look. "I just want to get there as fast as possible. At this rate, it will be ten before we arrive. We may not be able to speak to Mrs. Schilling tonight."

"Then we'll do it first thing in the morning, or maybe we won't have to talk to her. Maybe the police will find Brandon before then."

"That would be my hope."

She sighed. "Are we making the right move, Ryan? Should we be at home waiting for Brandon? What if he wasn't kidnapped? What if he was just hiding or lost? He could still find his way back to the house."

He heard the hope in her voice and wondered why he was always the one who had to kill her dreams. He'd done it so many times over the past few years. She'd come to him with some crazy idea for a cure, and he would have to be the one to point out the flaws or the unscientific evidence. And she always hated him for it.

"Ryan?" she said when he remained silent.

"I think we've made the right decision." He didn't want to address her other concerns. He'd used reason before, and it had never gotten him anywhere. Nicole was all about heart and emotion and rarely about logic. It used to be one of the things he loved about her. And his practicality was one of the things she used to love about him. But somewhere along the way, their strengths had turned into flaws.

Nicole turned her gaze out the window, and for the next half hour they didn't speak. The traffic eventually thinned as they got south of San Jose and the scenery became more rural. With more open space, he pressed down on the gas pedal, eager to make up some time. He already felt a little better now that there was some room to breathe.

As Nicole shifted in her seat, he glanced over at her. She wasn't looking at him, and seemed lost in thought as she played with the ring on her finger. It wasn't her wedding ring that she was twisting around her middle finger; she'd taken that off months ago. This ring was a silver band with some odd etchings on it. Nicole's biological father had given it to her on her birthday a few years back. He'd told her he'd bought it in Greece and that it would bring her good luck.

Ryan didn't think they'd had a speck of good luck since Nicole had put that ring on her finger. And he'd been a little surprised that Nicole had even wanted to wear it. Her relationship with her father, David Kane, had been awkward and distant for most of her childhood and adolescence. But when Nicole had gotten interested in history and in teaching, her father had suddenly reappeared in her life. Since he was a professor at UC Berkeley, apparently he felt he now had something in common with his daughter. But where the hell had he been for most of Nicole's life? He didn't know how she could let him off the hook.

"Have you spoken to David?" he asked.

Nicole started and turned to look at him. "What?"

"Your father—David. Have you talked to him about Brandon's disappearance?"

"No, he's in Greece. I sent him an email, but he's on an archaeological dig, and I don't know if he has access." Her gaze narrowed. "Why did you suddenly bring him up?"

He tipped his head toward the ring on her finger.

Her fingers stilled. "Oh. Bad habit." She took a breath. "I'm scared, Ryan."

He was shocked that she'd admit it. It was probably the most honest thing she'd said to him in years.

He wanted to reach out to her, to put his hand on her leg, to tell her it would be okay and have her believe him.

But Nicole was already looking away. She'd gotten really good at putting the brakes on her emotions. Unfortunately, putting her feelings on ice had turned their relationship very, very cold. And that coldness was so at odds with the passion that had sparked so hot and so fast when they first met. Sometimes, he wished they could go back to seventeen and remember what it felt like to be in love, to have hope, to see their whole lives in front of them, no obstacle too big, no mountain too high. Being together had made everything seem manageable.

He smiled to himself as the range of mountains in front of them reminded him of a very special hiking trip they'd taken the summer in between sophomore and junior years in college. They'd been twenty years old, and the hike was going to be their last big adventure before school started again.

Nicole had not been as in love with nature as he was, but she was in love with him. When he'd told her that he wanted to show her the amazing views from the Skyline Trail near Big Sur, she'd agreed to go with him.

As his hands tightened on the wheel, his mind drifted back to the past.

They were four miles into the hike with another quarter mile to go, the terrain growing steep as they headed toward the summit. As Nicole paused, he put his hand on the small of her back. She glanced over her shoulder.

"I don't think I'm going to make it," she declared, her breath coming fast.

"You'll make it. You're strong."

"I can barely breathe. The view is good from here. Isn't this high enough?"

"It's better at the top. Trust me, it will be worth it. You'll feel just like one of your Greek Gods looking down from Mount Olympus."

"Nice," she said dryly. "You think you know me so well."

"I do know you. And you're not a girl to back down from a challenge."

She sighed. "Okay, but after this you're going to owe me."

"Oh, yeah? What am I going to have to do?" he teased.

"Take me to the Modern Museum of Art and not complain for at least one hour."

He groaned. "Really? That's what you want?"

She smiled back at him. "Take it or leave it."

"Fine. I'll take it."

"Do you want to think about it for a few more minutes?"

"No, I'm good," he said with a grin. "Stop stalling."

"It's steep. I don't want to fall."

"If you do, I'll catch you. Trust me, Nicole."

She gazed into his eyes. "You know I do, Ryan."

His chest tightened, his heart overflowing with love for her. The fact that she could trust him was amazing. As a kid, he'd been told so many times that he was a worthless piece of shit by his father that sometimes it was hard to believe that not everyone thought that way.

Nicole turned back to the path in front of her and started to walk.

He followed close behind, just in case she slipped, but they made it to the top of the mountain without incident.

As they reached the summit, they stopped and looked out at the spectacular view. There was nothing but hills below and the wide blue Pacific Ocean in front of them.

"Oh, my God," Nicole whispered. "It's amazing."

"Told you." He dropped his backpack on the ground. Inside the bag was water and snacks, but their picnic could wait.

"Thanks for not letting me quit," she said.

"You're welcome." It was about time he'd returned that favor. She'd kept him going on more than a few occasions.

"I feel big and small—at the same time," she added. She pulled out the band from her ponytail and shook out her blonde hair, letting the long strands blow in the breeze.

She was so beautiful, her blue eyes sparkling, her cheeks pink from the sun and the hike, her smile so wide, so full of life and fun. He wanted to look at her face for a lifetime. He wanted her to be the last person he saw at night and the first person he saw in the morning. He couldn't imagine not having her in his life.

"You're staring," she said. "What are you thinking about?"

"How much I want you," he said quietly.

She caught her breath as she gazed into his eyes. "Really?"

"Yes. I want to make it official, Nicole."

"Ryan," she said warily. "I think the altitude is going to your head."

"It's not the altitude that's making my head spin; it's you. I want to marry you, Nicole."

The words came out in a rush. He hadn't considering proposing in this moment, but now that he had, it seemed perfect. It was just the two of them on top of the world. What could be better?

"Oh, Ryan," she said, a breathy note in her voice. "Are you sure?"

"Absolutely. I love you. I want to spend the rest of my life with you. Will you make me the happiest man on earth? Will you marry me, Nicole?"

Her pause made his blood thunder through his veins. He couldn't stand it if she said no.

"Yes," she said, a smile spreading across her face.

His heart stopped. "Seriously?"

"Yes," she repeated, as she slid her arms around his waist. "I will marry you, because I love you." She pressed her

mouth against his.

He put his arms around her and kissed her until they were both breathless.

"When?" she asked with a laugh.

"Whenever you want. But let's make it soon."

"Everyone will think we're crazy. We're so young. We're not done with school."

"I don't care about anyone else. We can finish school together. It's you and me, Nicole. It's us. Now and forever."

Her gaze grew more serious. "I like the sound of that."

"I wish I had a ring," he said, realizing his spontaneous proposal was a little lacking.

"We'll get one."

He leaned over and pulled a long blade of grass from the hillside. He tied the ends in a knot and slipped it over her third finger. It almost immediately fell apart.

"Damn. I thought that was going to be really romantic," he said.

Nicole laughed. "It was romantic."

"I'll get you a ring as soon as we get back."

"Oh, sure, with all the extra cash you have lying around," she teased.

Her words reminded him that he was a long way away from being able to buy her a ring. "Maybe we should wait until we can do it right—"

She put her finger against his lips. "No. I don't care about jewelry. I just want you, Ryan. But..."

He saw the sudden hesitation in her eyes.

"What about children?" she asked. "I told you before that I might not be able to have any of my own. And if that's important to you..."

"There are a lot of kids in the world, Nicole. We'll find one who needs us. I don't care about biology. In fact, this kid might be better off if it doesn't have my family genes. We'll

make it work. Together we can do anything."

"Together," she agreed as she threw her arms around his neck and kissed him again.

"Ryan."

Nicole's voice suddenly seemed so much louder, so much sharper. He blinked and straightened in his seat, realizing that the happiest day of his life was a long time ago.

"Are you okay?" she asked with a worried look. "You almost drifted off the side of the road."

"Sorry," he said, focusing his attention on the highway.

"Can we stop for a moment?" Nicole asked. "I could use a restroom and some coffee."

"Good idea." He changed lanes so he could get off at the next exit. He didn't need caffeine, but he did need to regroup. He found a Starbucks a few blocks off the highway and turned into the parking lot.

As he shut off the car, Nicole said, "What were you thinking about, Ryan? You got really quiet there for a while."

"I was wondering how we got to where we are. And I'm not just talking about Brandon," he added.

"I know," she said, her gaze filled with pain and what almost seemed like yearning.

His chest tightened, but before he could say anything more, she was out of the car and on her way into the café. Maybe it was better that way. This wasn't the time to have that conversation.

Although there never seemed to be a right time to talk to each other, which was probably why they'd ended up in separate houses living separate lives. But they were together now. Maybe they could find Brandon and their way back to each other.

Now who was the hopeless optimist?

Eight

As Nicole waited for her coffee, she glanced out the window of the café and saw Ryan leaning against the hood of his car. He had his hands in the pockets of his jeans and was staring off into space, the same odd expression on his face that he'd worn earlier in the day.

Her nerves tightened as she remembered what he'd said just before she got out of the car—wondering how they'd gotten to this place. She'd wondered that, too.

They'd once been insatiable for each other. Kissing for hours, spending days and weekends in bed together. And every time they made love, it was better than the time before, because they'd each wanted the other to feel as good as possible. There had been so much generosity back then, so much unselfishness.

Her skin tingled with memories.

Ryan had always loved to touch her. It was as if he were making up for the affection he didn't get as a child. When they watched TV, he'd put his arm around her shoulders or a hand on her thigh. When they slept together, she always woken up wrapped in his arms. And anytime they walked anywhere, his hand had been in hers.

She'd loved being so close to him, feeling like they were deeply connected in every possible way. And it wasn't just his touch that she craved, it was the laughter, the shared dreams, the feeling that they were building something important—a family, a home, a life together.

But when Brandon came along, their tight bonds had loosened a little. They were still madly in love, but now there was someone else to hold, to talk about, to worry over. Brandon became the center of their world, and she'd been happy with that. Ryan had been happy, too.

And then one day Brandon woke up lethargic and very, very quiet.

She'd thought he had the flu. She'd forced fluids on him and taken him to the doctor, who'd told her it was probably a virus.

But the virus had gone on for over a week. And then there was another doctor's visit, a consultation, increasingly worried looks, and new tests.

When the diagnosis came a few days later, she'd been both shocked and unsurprised, because she'd known that something was terribly wrong with her son. And now it had been confirmed.

For days she'd gone over everything she'd done, questioning whether she'd fed him something he was allergic to, whether she'd been too lax in keeping his brain stimulated. Had she read to him enough? Had she sung to him enough? Had she missed some important developmental step? And what about the vaccinations? Some people thought they were responsible; others said absolutely not. She didn't know who to believe.

She supposed that Ryan had asked himself the same questions. But now it occurred to her that that was when the first break in their union had occurred. Her focus had turned completely to Brandon, and when she wasn't thinking about her son, she was wondering about herself, what she could do differently to help her son.

Ryan—Ryan had just been somewhere in the background.

He'd been supportive the first two years. He'd gone to the doctor appointments with her. He'd listened to her rant and complain that they weren't getting enough answers. He'd held her when she slowed down enough to let him, which wasn't that often, because she'd been acutely aware of a ticking clock from the moment of Brandon's diagnosis. They only had a short window to get through to him, so she had to make every second count.

But the seconds turned into minutes, hours, days, months and years. And there was still no improvement. Nothing had changed—except her relationship with Ryan.

Deep down, she knew she was as much to blame for their separation as Ryan was; she just didn't know how to fix what had broken. Brandon was always between them, and he still was.

But as she stared at Ryan, a knot grew in her throat and an ache filled her heart. She had tried not to miss him. She had filled her days with Brandon and work and more doctor appointments so she wouldn't have to think about Ryan. And she'd managed to push him out of her head most days. But Ryan was easier to handle from a distance than up close. When they were apart, she could remind herself of everything he did that annoyed her. When they were together, she stopped seeing his flaws and started remembering all the good times they'd had together.

She let out a sigh as her gaze traveled down his beautiful, masculine body. He'd always been attractive, but he was better looking now that he'd grown into his looks. His hair was thick and wavy with gold highlights lightening the dark strands. His shoulders were broad, his body lean and fit. He'd always loved to run, bike, or hike, and there wasn't an ounce of fat on his body.

A familiar yearning ran through her, making her feel frustrated and restless and needy. She'd always been attracted to Ryan. She'd loved his body and she'd explored every inch of it with her hands and her mouth, as he'd explored hers. He'd been her first time, and her first love, and she'd never been with anyone else besides him. She'd never *wanted* to be with anyone else.

Her sisters had thought she was crazy to marry the first and only guy she'd slept with, but she'd known Ryan was the one. She'd been so certain that they would last forever.

Forever had turned out to be way too short.

She started as the clerk called her name. Her coffee was ready.

Thank goodness. She turned away from the window, grateful for the interruption. She needed to stop thinking about Ryan and everything they'd lost and concentrate on the present. She picked up her drink and made her way out to the parking lot.

As she neared the car, she saw Ryan talking on the phone. Her pulse sped up, wondering if there was news.

"Thanks," Ryan said, as he ended the call.

"Who was that?" she asked impatiently.

"Max. I called for an update. They're still working on a court order to get Mr. Reynolds's records. The Angel's Bay Police Department informed them that the Schillings' attorney passed away two years ago. Their lawyer ran a very small office, which closed after his death. They're trying to locate his records."

Her heart sank. Every time they turned around, they seemed to hit a wall. "Anything else?"

"Max assured me that Brandon's photo will continue to be shown on the local news broadcasts and in the newspapers. Your family is working with the Center for Missing Children, so everything that needs to be done is being done."

She really hoped so. She'd thought it was a good idea to go with Ryan to Angel's Bay, but now standing by a lonely highway in the middle of California, she was assailed with doubts.

"We're doing the right thing," Ryan said, reading her mind. "We need to join forces with Mrs. Schilling, compare notes. Find out what the Schillings knew at the time of adoption. Perhaps it's more than we knew. Together, hopefully, we can figure out who has our kids."

She stared back at him, a little surprised by his optimism. He'd become so cynical in recent years that she'd forgotten he could be any other way. "It's weird, but I feel like we've changed places," she murmured.

"What do you mean?" he asked, a wary note in his voice.

"You're the one leading the impossible charge, pushing aside the doubts, forging ahead with a plan you're sure is a good one, even if it might not be. Sound familiar?"

"A little." His gaze clung to hers. "Are you still with me, Nicole?"

It was such a charged and complicated question, but there was really only one answer.

"I'm with you."

He nodded approvingly. "Good. Next stop, Angel's Bay."

———➤➤◄◄◄———

It was after ten by the time they reached the outskirts of Angel's Bay, a small community on the central California coast. Nicole had called the Schilling residence from the car but had been told by Jessica's friend Charlotte that Jessica was finally sleeping, and she didn't want to wake her up.

Knowing that Mrs. Schilling had already gone through two more days of hell than they had, Nicole had asked Charlotte to tell Jessica they would stop by to see her in the morning.

"So, I guess we should find a hotel," Nicole told Ryan, feeling like their arrival was more than a little anticlimactic.

"I wish we could talk to her tonight," he grumbled. "How can she sleep when her kid is missing?"

"She's been dealing with this longer than we have. Her friend said she collapsed when she found out about Brandon's disappearance. I guess the shock sent her over the edge. So the morning will have to do. We need to find somewhere to stay tonight." She glanced down at her phone, surfing the Internet for hotel recommendations. "The Seagull Inn is about two miles away. It has good reviews and four stars."

"I don't care where we go."

"Then turn right at the next corner," she said, giving him directions to the boutique hotel, which was located on a bluff overlooking the Pacific Ocean.

As they got out of the car, a cold, blustery wind and a misty spray of salty seawater greeted them. Nicole shivered. It definitely felt like fall in Angel's Bay.

They grabbed their bags out of the car and walked into the warm, cozy lobby. A middle-aged man with gray hair and glasses greeted them with a smile.

"Hello, folks," he said. "Need a room?"

"We do." Nicole hesitated, glancing over at Ryan. "Should we get two?"

Before Ryan could answer, the innkeeper said, "Oh, I'm sorry, but we only have one room tonight. It has two beds, though. Will that work?"

"Fine with me," Ryan said shortly.

Sharing a room with her almost ex-husband didn't seem like a great idea, but Nicole was tired and didn't want to spend time driving around town looking for somewhere else to stay. "We'll take it."

"It's one of our best rooms. You'll have a great ocean

view. How long will you be staying?"

"We're not sure yet."

"Well, we don't have anyone coming into that room for another week, so if you want to stay a few days, you're welcome. Or if you want a second room tomorrow, we should have one opening up."

"Thanks," she said, as he ran her credit card and then handed her key cards.

They walked down the hall to the elevator. As Nicole pushed the button, she was shocked to see a flyer for Brandon. Actually, it was for Kyle, but once again the similarity between the two boys took her breath away.

She turned to Ryan. His jaw was tight, the pulse in his neck beating fast. She wanted to say something, but she had no words. Neither did he.

The elevator doors opened and they stepped inside. They got off at the third floor; their room was two doors down.

As they stepped inside, Nicole realized that the innkeeper hadn't been bragging; the room was beautiful with two full-sized beds covered with beautiful quilts, fresh flowers on the table and seascapes on the walls.

Ryan dumped his bag on the floor and then walked to the double doors leading out to the balcony. He opened them and stepped outside.

She followed him a moment later.

Large, white-capped waves crashed on the rocky beach below. It was a wild, rugged scene under an incredibly starry sky.

Looking up at those stars, Nicole sent up a silent prayer to the universe to watch out for her little boy.

"I think I'll take a walk," Ryan said.

"Really? It's late."

He shrugged. "I'm not sleepy." He hesitated. "Do you want to come?"

She'd been sitting in a car all day. And she wasn't in the mood to sleep, either. "All right."

She grabbed her coat as they headed back out of their room.

There was a lighted path that ran from the front of the inn, down the side, to a long stairway leading to the beach below. Once they hit the sand, the moon and stars provided just enough light to see where they were going.

They walked along the water line for almost a mile until an outcropping of rocks prevented them from going any further.

Nicole flopped down on the sand, breathless from the brisk walk.

"I like it out here," she said, as Ryan sat down next to her.

"You always loved the beach."

"You're right. The sea makes me feel happy and optimistic. I need those emotions now more than ever."

"Then I'm glad we came."

Silence followed his words, but she wasn't in a hurry to break it. It was soothing to listen to the relentless pounding of the ocean on the beach. She tried to slow her pulse down to match those beats, and after a few minutes, she felt a lot less tense.

She glanced over at Ryan. "Do you know the story of Angel's Bay?"

"There's a story?" he said, arching an eyebrow.

"Yes. I looked it up on my phone on the way down."

"Why?"

"Because I wanted to know more about the place that I was going to. And it was a long drive." Not to mention the fact that she'd wanted something to occupy her mind besides Ryan and Brandon.

"You've always been a planner."

"You may have come late to the planning party, but I know you don't just fly into the wind anymore," she said dryly. "You have flight routes and computer backup systems and contingency plans."

"True, but that's when I have passengers. If it were only me, I'd take off and see where I ended up." He gave her a small smile. "You used to enjoy that kind of impulsive freedom."

"Never as much as you. I was terrified the first time you took me up in a plane."

"I remember. But you had a good time that day—after you got over being nervous. After you let yourself trust me."

"I did. You were good at pushing me to try new things."

"And you returned the favor. I would never in my life have seen a ballet if you hadn't taken me."

"You hated that ballet. You complained about how boring it was for days."

"Yeah, but I saw it. I had the experience. That's something," he defended.

She smiled. "I thought it was boring, too."

"What?" he asked in surprise. "You did not."

"I did. But I couldn't tell you that. I never would have heard the end of it. I had talked so much about introducing culture into our lives; I couldn't say I hated every second of that ballet. But the truth is that I couldn't follow the story, and while I appreciated the work that the dancers went through, I didn't feel anything, except boredom."

"Well, well, the secrets are all coming out now. Next you're going to tell me you don't really like opera, either."

"No way. I've already told you one of my secrets. You tell me one of yours. Something you think I don't know."

"Something you don't know," Ryan echoed, thinking for a moment. "Okay, I've got it."

"Really?" she asked warily, wondering if it was a good

idea to be sharing secrets with a man she was about to divorce.

"Senior year in college, I finished your paper on the Odyssey."

She frowned. "No, you didn't."

"Yeah, I did," he said, looking her straight in the eye. "You were pulling an all- nighter, but you'd been cramming for finals for days, and that paper was the last thing you had to do. I got up at two a.m. to see if you were coming to bed, and you were fast asleep, your head on the desk. I tried to wake you up, but you were out. I read through what you had on the screen and saw you were just missing an ending. So I wrote it for you."

She stared at him in astonishment. "How would you have known what to write? You knew nothing about the Odyssey."

"You talked about your paper for days, Nicole. Don't you remember?"

"I remember, but still…"

"I knew what you were trying to say. I looked through the beginning of your paper and repeated some of your main points at the end. I was going to tell you, but then I fell asleep. When I woke up that morning you were gone. It was a little late to tell you what I'd done, and I must admit I was worried that I was going to get you flunked out of that class. But two days later, you had an A, and I felt very good about myself."

She saw his smug smile and shook her head. "I can't believe you did that, Ryan."

"What you can't believe is that I got you an A," he said pointedly. "It was your first A in that class."

"That wasn't because of you. You couldn't have written more than a few paragraphs."

"I think it was about a page."

She frowned. "It's weird, because now that you say that, I

do remember waking up feeling groggy and wondering when I'd actually finished the paper. I was so tired. But it looked done."

"You're welcome."

As she gazed into Ryan's eyes, she felt the old connection between them. "I can't believe you could finish my paper and I wouldn't know. You must have written the end in a way that sounded like me."

"Well, I knew you pretty well then, Nicole."

"Yes, you did," she said slowly, wondering if now was a good time to talk about what had happened between them. They were getting along so well, she was almost reluctant to bring it up, but something compelled her to open her mouth. "Ryan—"

"No," he said, cutting her off with a wave of his hand. "Not tonight."

"How do you know what I'm going to say?"

"I know."

"You're always the one who wants to talk, and I'm usually the one who doesn't," she reminded him. "This is your chance."

"I understand, and I'll probably regret not having this conversation, but it's been a long day, and I don't want to fight with you, Nic. We need to work together to find Brandon. And I don't think we should let ourselves get distracted by anything else."

"You're right," she said, feeling both annoyed that he was trying to control things but also relieved not to get into their emotional history.

Ryan stretched out onto his back, pillowing his head with his arms. "So tell me the story of Angel's Bay."

"Well, okay," she began, trying to remember what she'd read. "It starts around the time of the Gold Rush. Ships were going up and down the coast of California, bringing miners to the Gold Country. When they had found their fortunes or given up, they took the same ships back down the coast. Sometimes, those ships were laden with gold and filled with joyous miners. Other times, the holds were empty and people were filled with discouragement and despair."

"You are loving this," Ryan interrupted. "I can hear the excitement in your voice."

"I do love a story, and this one is pretty good, so don't interrupt."

"Fine. Go on."

"One of those ships got caught up in a terrible storm. The boat broke apart and many, many people were flung into the sea. There were legendary tales of heroic rescues but also selfish acts of survival. It was even believed that one man was murdered on the ship before it went down in the storm. But no one really knows what happened. Or, at least, I didn't see it in the articles I read." She cleared her throat and continued. "When morning came, the survivors gathered together by the bay and mourned their lost loved ones. As they waited for help to arrive, they built shelters and eventually a town was born. They called it Angel's Bay, in honor of the lost souls. Legend says that miracles still happen here, and that sometimes in the misty fog you can see the angels keeping watch over their descendants."

"That's quite a story."

"It is. Oh, and the female survivors of the wreck made a memorial quilt, a square for each person or family that was lost at sea. Sometimes they used remnants of the actual clothing the people wore. That quilt became the centerpiece of the town and still hangs in the Angel's Heart Quilt Shop in downtown Angel's Bay. I bet it's an amazing piece of history, telling a story of a generation that lived a very long time ago." She paused, knowing she'd gotten caught up in the story. She couldn't help herself. It was always amazing to her to look back into history and see how people reacted to the events of their times, and how sometimes heroes emerged in the most unlikely place. "Ryan, are you awake?"

He smiled. "Yes. I'm just thinking."

"About the quilt? I bet Brandon would like it. He's always interested in angles and squares and things that match. Although these squares probably don't match. Each one is most likely completely unique."

"Yeah," Ryan said, distraction in his voice.

Her gaze narrowed on his face. "What are you thinking about?"

"I was thinking about the way Brandon likes to match things up, rocks, blocks, leaves of grass, the petals on a flower. If there's a group of anything, he has to find two of a kind."

"He's obsessed," she said. "The day that Brandon disappeared he was doing just that, matching up pebbles along the school fence. And we had a moment, Ryan, a really small moment, but Brandon found a perfect pair, and he looked right at me, and there was a gleam in his eyes. It was triumph. He was sharing his success with me." She bit down her lips as tears came into her eyes. "I wanted to freeze that moment in time. I wanted to hang on to it for as long as I could, but it was gone so fast. He turned away and began the search again, the way he always does, because no victory is ever enough."

Ryan sat up straight. "Do you think…?"

"What?" she asked, not sure what he wanted to say.

"The need to match. This is going to sound crazy, but do you think Brandon has been looking for his twin? Has he always known deep inside that some part of him is missing?"

She shivered at his words. "I guess it's possible. He's certainly driven to find the other half of something. Maybe it's a need that he doesn't understand, but something his subconscious drives him to do."

"Did he do it before he was diagnosed?"

"I don't remember. He was so active as a toddler. When I picture him in my mind at that time in his life, I see a blur of smiles and movement. And he was so verbal. I can still hear his voice. It was so strange when he went silent. I think that's what I missed first—the sound of his voice, the tenor of his laugh." She blew out a breath, feeling another huge wave of emotion. They just kept coming, much like the waves pounding the beach in front of her. "Who would separate identical twins, Ryan? It was wrong to split the two boys apart. They're brothers."

"Maybe the family or one of the lawyers thought it would be easier to adopt them out."

"So many couples are desperate for babies. We can't have been the only ones who would have loved to have twins. I bet the Schillings would have taken two children, too. Unless they didn't want two, and suddenly there was an extra." Her nerves tightened. "Maybe that's why Brandon suddenly became available." She shook her head in frustration. "I'm tired of having questions and no answers."

"We'll get answers tomorrow. Let's go back to the inn." He got to his feet and held out his hand to her.

She hesitated and then took it, his warm fingers curling around hers as he pulled her to her feet. When he let go, she was surprised at how she missed that simple touch.

By the time they got back to their room it was after midnight. She grabbed her pajama bottoms and a T-shirt and went into the bathroom to change and brush her teeth. When she got out, Ryan took a turn. It felt both perfectly normal and incredibly awkward to be sharing a room with him.

She climbed into the bed nearest the window and left the light on between the beds. A moment later, Ryan came out of the bathroom, got into the other bed and turned off the light.

She closed her eyes and tried to sleep, but when she wasn't thinking about Brandon, her mind was on the man so close, and yet so far away.

A few minutes later, she said, "Ryan, are you asleep?"

"No."

She rolled onto her side. A small stream of moonlight lit up his face. "I don't think I can sleep."

"Try not talking," he said dryly.

She thought about that suggestion for a good minute. "Nope, that's not going to work. I feel tense."

Silence followed her words. Then he said, "Do you want a backrub?"

Have Ryan's hands on her? A new tension entered her body. "That might not be a good idea."

"No, it's a lousy idea," he agreed. "Because if I touch you, I'm not going to be able to just rub your back. And we both know you don't want anything more from me."

His words sent a jolt through her body. It had been a long time since he'd said something provocative. Or maybe it was just the first time she'd let herself hear him. Part of her wanted to refute his statement, because maybe she did want something more. Maybe she wanted to get rid of some of the tension and worry running around inside of her, and having sex with Ryan would probably accomplish that.

But it was never just sex with Ryan. She couldn't be with him without really being with him, without opening up her heart as well as her body. And that was dangerous.

She flopped onto her back and stared at the ceiling. She could hear him breathing and knew he wasn't close to being asleep, either.

"Did you ever think life was going to be this hard?" she asked.

"I should have, because I came from a childhood that was hard. But when I met you and your family, I thought all the bad stuff was behind me." He sighed. "And don't take what I just said the wrong way. Brandon isn't the "bad stuff". It's his illness. It's the frustration of knowing that the kid I love has to live with challenges that he may not be able to conquer."

"I know what you mean. It's the disappointment that overwhelms me. I'm so sorry for Brandon. When he was a tiny baby, and I used to rock him to sleep, I would whisper in his ear about all the adventures he was going to have, all the big moments that make up a life. I still want him to have those moments."

"I do, too." He sighed. "You should try to sleep. Morning will come faster."

"And then what?"

"Then we take the next step to getting our son back."

Nine

⟶➤➤◄◄◄⟵

Saturday morning Jessica Schilling walked into her kitchen and was surprised to find Charlotte Adams at the counter making coffee. "You're still here? Did you spend the night?"

"Yes. I wanted to keep an eye on you." Charlotte gave her a worried look. "I didn't think you should be alone."

"Thanks. I appreciate that. I can't believe I slept so long." She glanced at the clock. She'd collapsed after Joe had told her about Kyle's identical twin. That last shocking piece of information had done her in. She remembered Joe and Charlotte helping her into bed, and then everything else was a foggy blur. "Sorry I fell apart like that. Did I dream the part about Kyle having a twin?"

Charlotte gave her a sympathetic smile as she handed her a mug of coffee. "Sorry, but no. Kyle has a twin named Brandon. Joe is still trying to get information on the biological parents to see if they might be involved, now that we know both boys have disappeared. Apparently it's not that easy to find out who they are."

"Why not?"

"For one thing, the attorney Travis used died a few years ago."

"But aren't there birth certificates or something?"

"Joe said he'd be over this morning with an update."

Charlotte had no sooner finished speaking when the doorbell rang. "That's probably him."

As Charlotte went to answer the door, Jessica sat down at the table and glanced around the kitchen. Everything was neat and tidy, nothing on the counters save for a plastic container of cookies. She knew a few of the parents in Kyle's class had stopped by with casserole dishes and salads, but there was no sign of them now. Charlotte must have put everything away.

As Joe entered the kitchen, she got to her feet. There was a serious expression on his face, and she couldn't help but worry about what was coming next.

"Hello, Jessica."

"Joe. Do you have any news for me?"

"I've been looking into the circumstances of Kyle's adoption. I was able to track down the daughter of Travis's attorney. She lives in San Diego. She told me that all of her father's paperwork was in storage a few miles from her house. I've sent Detective Marlow down there to go through the boxes, but I'll be honest; the daughter said her father was disorganized and forgetful toward the end of his life, and she has no idea if he kept good records."

Jessica's heart sank. Feeling suddenly weak and tired again, she sat back down on the chair. "That doesn't sound very hopeful."

"We'll know more once Jason gets there." Joe shot Charlotte a quick look. "Did you tell her about the Prescotts?"

Charlotte shook her head. "I didn't have a chance."

"Who are the Prescotts?" Jessica asked.

"The parents of the other missing child," Charlotte explained. "They called here last night when you were asleep. They drove down from San Francisco yesterday and would like to speak to you. They're on their way over now. I gave them your address. I hope that's okay."

"I guess," she said halfheartedly, feeling completely

overwhelmed by everything. "But I don't know anything about the adoption. That was Travis and Sharon's deal." She'd barely finished speaking when the doorbell rang again. "Could you get the door? I need to brush my hair and pull myself together."

"Of course. I have to take off for a while, Jessica. I have a patient going into labor. I'll check in on you later."

"That's fine. Thanks for all your help, Charlotte. I couldn't have gotten through the last few days without you." As Charlotte left the kitchen, Jessica looked at Joe. "Do you know how lucky you are to have her?"

Joe smiled. "Believe me, I do."

"I better get dressed." She dashed across the hall and up the stairs. She felt a little nervous about meeting the other family. Although they were probably the only people in the world who could relate to what she was going through. Maybe teaming up was a good idea.

Nicole glanced around the block of small, charming houses set in the foothills of Angel's Bay. It looked like a family neighborhood. She could see bikes in the driveway next door, and a red rubber ball peeked out from under the bush in the Schillings' front yard. But there were no children playing outside on this Saturday morning. Perhaps the parents were keeping their kids indoors, afraid of the kidnapper who had stolen Kyle out from under them.

"Ring it again," Ryan said impatiently.

Before she could do so, the door opened, and an attractive blonde in her mid-thirties gave them a warm smile. "Mr. and Mrs. Prescott? I'm Charlotte Adams. I spoke to you on the phone. Mrs. Schilling will be down in a few minutes. Won't you come in?"

Nicole was relieved by her words. For a moment, she'd been afraid that Mrs. Schilling would not want to see them.

Charlotte ushered them into a warm, cozy living room, filled with a large couch, a matching loveseat and armchair, and a piano by the window. There was evidence of a child everywhere: books on the coffee table, toys on the floor and photographs on all the walls. Over the mantel was a large photo of a little boy about four, who looked exactly like Brandon.

She swallowed a knot in her throat. She wanted to look away, but she couldn't. She was drawn to that picture. She heard Charlotte say something, but her words didn't make sense to her. Her entire focus was on the boy in the picture.

And then Ryan's hands came down on her shoulders. She felt his hard chest against her back and was grateful for the support.

"Look at that smile," she whispered. "It's full of light and life. And he's looking right at the camera."

"Yeah," Ryan said gruffly. "Let's sit down on the couch, Nicole."

"I don't know if I can stop looking at him. He's Brandon, but he's not." She turned to Ryan and saw pain in his eyes. He might not be saying much, but he was just as affected by the picture of Kyle as she was. His hands slipped down her arms, and he gripped her fingers.

"We can't go there," he said.

She nodded, knowing exactly what he meant. Comparing the boys would only distract them from their goal. They were here to find Brandon. Learning more about his twin could come later. Her fingers tightened around Ryan's. "You're right. I'm glad you're here with me."

"I wouldn't be anywhere else," he said, his voice filled with emotion.

"Mr. and Mrs. Prescott?"

The male voice broke them apart.

A tall, brown-haired man with dark eyes entered the room. He wore a suit and tie, and there was a glint of a badge at his waist.

"I'm Joe Silveira, Chief of Police," he said, his voice crisp.

"Ryan Prescott," Ryan said. "This is my wife Nicole."

"I'm glad you're both here," the chief said. "It will be helpful to have you and Mrs. Schilling in the same place. Hopefully, we can put our heads together and come up with some new leads."

Nicole liked the chief's positive attitude. "That's what we're hoping for as well."

"What can you tell me about your adoption process?" the chief asked. "How long did you work with your attorney before you got your son?"

Nicole glanced over at Ryan. "It was about six months, wasn't it?"

He nodded. "Yes, but we'd been working with other agencies for five years before that. We always knew that Nicole couldn't have children, so we started our quest for a child soon after we got married."

"Did your attorney tell you anything about the biological mother or father?"

"No," Nicole said. "What about Mrs. Schilling? Does she know anything?"

"I wish I did," a woman said from the doorway. She gave them a tentative smile. "Hi. I'm Jessica Schilling."

The slender, leggy brunette who walked into the living room in a clingy black sweater, tight jeans and boots surprised Nicole. Jessica Schilling couldn't have been older than twenty-five or twenty-six. Her dark brown hair was pulled back into a ponytail, and there was a beauty in her face despite the dark shadows under her eyes and the reddened tip of her nose. How could such a young woman have adopted a child six years ago?

As the questions raced through her mind, she realized that Jessica was staring at her with the same curiosity. Regardless of their ages or backgrounds, they were both mothers of missing children, and that gave them an immediate bond. She introduced herself and Ryan, and then they all sat down.

She and Ryan took a seat on the couch, Joe Silveira sat in the chair across from them, and Jessica curled up on the adjacent love seat, her feet tucked under her.

"I'm sorry you've come all this way," Jessica said. "But I don't know anything about Kyle's birth. I don't know if Chief Silveira filled you in on my situation—"

"I didn't," the chief replied. "I thought I'd leave it to you."

"Oh, okay." She twisted her wedding ring around on her finger as she took a deep breath. "Well, here's the story. My husband Travis adopted Kyle with his first wife, Sharon. Sharon had cancer as a teenager, and while it had been in remission for a long time, she had difficulty getting pregnant. When Travis and Sharon reached their mid-thirties, they decided to adopt. It's my understanding that it took a few years before they got Kyle. They were happy for a while, and then things went bad. Sharon's cancer came back. She passed away when Kyle was two."

"I'm sorry," Nicole murmured. She hadn't expected such a sad story. Sharon had finally gotten the child she'd always wanted and then had died knowing she wouldn't be able to raise him. It was heartbreaking.

"Travis told me that he was grateful that he had Kyle to distract him from the pain," Jessica continued. "His little boy kept him going through the sadness. The two of them were inseparable. They loved each other so much." She bit down on her bottom lip. "This is hard."

Nicole could see that Jessica was fighting back tears, and while her heart went out to her, they needed to hear the rest.

"Take your time," Ryan said gently.

Jessica drew in a deep breath. "Travis and I met when Kyle was four. We had a whirlwind romance. I think I fell in love with both of them at the same time. In three months we were married, and I was a wife and a mother. I thought I'd won the lottery. Everything was great. But good luck never seems to stay with me long. Travis was killed in an accident a few months after our first wedding anniversary." She cleared her throat and licked her lips, pain in her eyes. "That was almost a year ago. Since then it's been Kyle and me. I really love that kid, and he loves me. We're a team now."

Nicole heard the defiant note in Jessica's voice and wondered where it came from. But all she said was, "I'm so sorry about your husband."

"Thank you."

"Did Travis tell you anything about the adoption proceedings?" Ryan asked.

Jessica shook her head. "He said that it was a blind adoption. He didn't know anything about the birth parents, and they didn't know anything about him. That's the way he and Sharon wanted it. They didn't want to confuse Kyle with two sets of parents. Kyle doesn't know that he's adopted," she added. "Travis wanted to wait until he was old enough to understand, and, to be honest, I didn't even think about it after Travis died. It's been difficult enough trying to explain the concept of death and heaven to a six-year-old."

Kyle had certainly suffered a lot of losses in his young life, Nicole thought, her heart going out to Brandon's brother. The pictures she'd seen of him hadn't told the whole story.

"I wish I could be of more help," Jessica added. "I had no idea Kyle had a twin brother, and I don't think Travis knew, either. He and Sharon had hoped to adopt more children before she got sick. I'm sorry you wasted your time coming down here."

"It wasn't a waste. We wanted to meet you," Nicole replied. "And we still want to know more about Kyle. He's our son's brother, even thought that feels weird to say out loud."

"Kyle is a great kid. He's friendly, outgoing, curious, and way too trusting. He loves people. I've told him not to talk to strangers, but he's too young to understand the danger."

Nicole's stomach twisted with every word that came out of Jessica's mouth. The other woman had no idea that her simple description of her son had caused Nicole pain. Brandon was about as far from outgoing, curious and trusting as a boy could be.

"Could you show me Kyle's room?" Nicole asked impulsively, the words coming out of her mouth before she considered what she was asking.

"Nicole, that's not a good idea," Ryan warned.

He was probably right, but it was too late to take back the request. And she wanted to see Kyle's room, almost as much as she didn't want to see it. "If it's okay with you?" she asked Jessica.

"Sure," Jessica said, getting to her feet. "It's upstairs."

Nicole glanced at Ryan. "Are you coming?"

"Not yet. I want to talk to the chief."

After Nicole and Jessica left the living room, Ryan saw speculation in the chief's thoughtful gaze.

"What?" Ryan asked shortly.

"Why wouldn't you want your wife to see Kyle's bedroom?"

The police chief obviously didn't miss a thing. Ryan

hoped that boded well for the investigation.

"Because our son, Brandon, is autistic. And seeing Brandon's identical twin so full of life is hard on Nicole, and on me."

"I understand."

"I'm not sure that you do," Ryan said. "Autism comes in like a thief in the night. Brandon was fine until he was three years old. He was talking, walking, laughing, singing, dancing around; he was a totally normal kid, and then one day he got sick. He retreated into a world that we couldn't enter. He barely talks now. He can occasionally squeeze out a word if he's desperate, but for the most part he's silent. He's hypersensitive to light, colors, noise, and he becomes extremely agitated around people he doesn't know."

Ryan realized he was telling the police chief more than he needed to know, but the words kept pouring out of him. "It's been a struggle to have him in public school. He has special aides, but Brandon doesn't like being around other kids. We're trying to keep him in the world, but it's a battle. That's why seeing Kyle, the mirror image of our child, and yet so completely different, is rough."

"I'm sure it is," the chief said with compassion in his tone.

"Nicole and I worry that the kidnappers won't be able to deal with Brandon's illness, that they'll become frustrated or angry with him."

"I'm going to do everything in my power to bring both boys home as soon as possible. How long are you planning to stay in Angel's Bay?"

"As long as it makes sense," Ryan replied. "The boys are together, and my gut tells me that we'll be able to make more progress if we join forces with Jessica, although it doesn't appear that she has any more information than we do."

"No, but she may remember more as time goes by—

things Travis may have said in passing."

"I hope so. Did you know Travis?"

The chief nodded. "I only met him once, but after his death, Jessica became friends with my fiancé, Charlotte, so I actually know Jessica better, and Kyle, too, of course. He's exactly the way Jessica described—an open, loving child. He's the light of a lot of lives, and everyone in my department is committed to bringing both children home to their parents."

"Thank you."

The chief stood up, and Ryan followed. As they walked to the door, Ryan said, "I keep wondering why the boys were split up. It sounds like Travis would have wanted two children, and Nicole and I certainly did. It doesn't make sense."

"Splitting up the boys would make finding them more difficult. The mother may have wanted to prevent the father from going after the kids. Or it could have been about money. Splitting up the twins might have been more profitable. But those are just theories. We need facts."

"Yes, we do."

"Charlotte gave me your phone number, so I'll be in touch."

As the chief left the house, Ryan thought about the theories he'd presented, wondering if either or both were true. At least Joe Silveira was considering all the options. He liked the chief's open mind and willingness to cooperate, not that Max wasn't working his ass off in San Francisco, but Max had to work through the various departments and there were more missing children in San Francisco, all of whom deserved attention and time. Here in Angel's Bay, Kyle was the focus of the department, which meant Brandon was, too.

Ryan glanced toward the stairs, wondering how Nicole was handling being in Kyle's bedroom. He'd always been impressed with Nicole's fight, her courage, but standing in the bedroom of Brandon's twin couldn't be easy. There was a part of him that wanted to join her and another part that wanted to keep Kyle in the background. He didn't want to be distracted by emotion or by wondering what their life would be like if Brandon wasn't autistic, because that wasn't going to get him anywhere.

But as the minutes passed, he found himself moving slowly toward the stairs.

Ten

⟶≫⟪⟨

Kyle's bedroom was a chaotic, colorful mess, with an unmade twin bed, toys everywhere, and clothes tossed on the floor or in the hamper by the closet. It was a totally normal room for a totally normal six-year-old, which reminded Nicole again how different Brandon was from his brother.

Brandon didn't like clutter. He got agitated when things fell on the floor, and with the exception of building blocks, he had no interest in toys of any nature.

"It's a mess," Jessica said, a guilty note in her voice, as she picked up some clothes and put them in the hamper. "I try to get Kyle to pick up, but the room is never clean for more than ten minutes. He has such a short attention span. He moves from one activity to the next. Is Brandon like that?"

Nicole swallowed hard, a knot growing in her throat. "Not really," she said, not wanting to discuss Brandon's illness. She walked over to the dresser where a plaque and a small trophy were displayed. "What are these for?"

"Soccer and swimming. Don't be too impressed. Everyone who played on the soccer team got a trophy. The plaque for swimming was when Kyle graduated out of the tadpole group by swimming one lap across the pool. Kyle is a little fish when it comes to water. Does Brandon like to swim?"

"Not really," she repeated. Realizing she wasn't giving Jessica much in return, she said, "Brandon likes to build things."

"Oh, that's interesting. Not Kyle," Jessica said with a smile. "He likes to knock things down. He's a little bulldozer. It used to make Travis crazy. Travis's company puts up buildings all over the world, and Travis was always trying to get Kyle interested in construction, but Kyle didn't have the patience. He doesn't like puzzles or putting things together. It's more about action for him."

"Brandon likes puzzles. And he can show extraordinary patience when it comes to matching things up." As the words came out of her mouth, she was reminded of her earlier conversation with Ryan. Had Brandon been subconsciously looking for his twin all these years? Was that what had driven his obsession to pair things up?

She looked at Jessica. "I wonder what the boys thought when they saw each other, when they realized they looked exactly the same."

"Kyle was probably excited. He loves to meet new people, especially other little boys." Jessica paused. "I've been trying to find comfort knowing that they're together. It was worse the first few days when we didn't know who could have possibly snatched him. Not that I'm happy your son is also missing; I didn't mean it that way."

"I didn't take it that way," she reassured Jessica. "I've also been trying to feel better about the boys being together. It's not really working that well for me."

"Okay, thank you for saying that. I was lying before. It's not working for me, either." She let out a sigh. "You and your husband are the only ones who understand what I'm going through." Jessica crossed her arms in front of her chest. "I wish Travis was alive. I could use his support right now. Although if Travis were alive, Kyle probably wouldn't be missing."

"I don't think that's true. Knowing now that the boys were targeted, it's clear that someone or several people planned their abductions for some time. It wasn't a crime of opportunity, Jessica. This was purposeful." She stopped talking as Ryan appeared in the doorway.

"How's it going up here?" he asked.

"All right," she said.

His jaw tightened as he looked around the room, and she knew he was seeing everything she'd seen. As his gaze caught on a pair of small cleats on the floor, her heart broke a little more. Ryan had had big plans for Brandon. He'd talked endlessly about not being able to wait until Brandon was old enough to play baseball, soccer and basketball, and all the other sports that Ryan had excelled at.

And it wasn't only athletics that Ryan had wanted to share with his son; it was everything else. He'd wanted to take Brandon camping and teach him how to fly. He'd wanted to be a part of his son's life. He'd wanted to be the kind of father he'd always wanted to have.

It suddenly occurred to her that when Brandon had withdrawn from the world, Ryan had taken it like a rejection, probably feeling the way he'd felt when his father rejected him. She'd never really looked at it like that before, but now it seemed so clear. That's why Ryan had had more trouble dealing with Brandon's illness. Not that it was easy for her to communicate with Brandon, either. But she'd never taken the broken connection as a personal rejection.

And she'd pushed herself into Brandon's life. She'd forced him to deal with her, even though most of the time she annoyed him. But she kept hoping that some day he would see her constant presence as love, and not just see it, but also feel it.

"What's that?" Ryan suddenly muttered. He walked

across the room and squatted down next to the laundry basket. Then he pulled out a small colorful quilt.

Her heart leapt into her throat. "Oh, my God," she said as he held up the quilt. She looked at Jessica. "Where did you get that?"

Jessica frowned. "Kyle has had it since he was a baby. Travis told me it was a gift from the local quilting guild. It's a tradition in Angel's Bay for every newborn to get a handmade quilt. Why do you ask?"

"Because Brandon has a quilt like that," Nicole replied. "Exactly like that."

"I don't understand," Jessica said slowly. "What do you think that means?"

"Brandon came to us wrapped in a quilt just like this one, so if this quilt was made in Angel's Bay, then Brandon has a connection to this town."

"Maybe the birth mother lived here," Ryan suggested, clearly on board with her train of thought.

"I don't think that's possible," Jessica said doubtfully. "I got the impression the birth mother was from somewhere else. And Angel's Bay is a tight community. If a teenager had a baby here, it would be impossible for her to give it up for adoption and have it be a secret."

Nicole could see Jessica's point, but there was a connection between the boys, the quilts and Angel's Bay. "Well, someone made our two boys matching quilts. And even if the birth mother didn't live here, maybe the quilter did or still does."

"How old was Kyle when Travis adopted him?" Ryan asked Jessica.

"I think he was a few days old; I'm not completely sure. What about Brandon?"

"Four days," Ryan replied. "And on one of those days, someone wrapped our son in a blanket that was made here in

Angel's Bay." He looked at Nicole. "This is important."

"I agree. I don't know what the link is, but I know there is one." She turned to Jessica. "What else do you know about the quilts? You said it's a town tradition?"

"Yes. I don't know if you've heard any of the town history—"

"I know some of it," Nicole said.

"Then you probably know there was a shipwreck a long time ago, and the survivors built a town here. One of the first things they did was put together a quilt in honor of their lost loved ones. The quilt still hangs in the shop, a reminder of where a lot of people came from. It's crazy how many people in this town trace their roots back to people who were on the ship, including Travis and his family."

"Who can we talk to about the newborn quilts?" Ryan asked. "We need to know who made the quilts for Brandon and Kyle and who ordered them."

"My friend Kara Lynch would be a good person to start with," Jessica replied. "Her family owns the quilt shop, and Kara knows everyone in the guild."

"Where can we find her?" Nicole asked.

"It's Saturday, so she's probably at the quilt shop."

"Let's go," Ryan said abruptly.

"You should come with us," Nicole said to Jessica. "You know Kara, so she'll be more willing to talk to you."

"All right," Jessica said. "Do you really think we're on to something?"

"I do," Nicole said. "I have a feeling those quilts are going to bring our boys home."

Fifteen minutes later they were in Ryan's car and on their way to the quilt shop. For the first time since Brandon had disappeared, Nicole felt hopeful.

"It's strange to be outside," Jessica murmured. "How can everything look so normal when my life is upside down?"

Nicole turned in her seat to meet Jessica's gaze. "I feel exactly the same way, but we're going to find our way back to normal."

Even as she said the words, Nicole realized that her version of normal would be far different from Jessica's. But she wouldn't think about that now.

Jessica gave her a tentative smile. "I'm glad you came down here. My friends have been supportive, but as the days go by, everyone goes back to their own life, and I can't ask them not to."

"I understand. I'm glad we came, too." As she finished speaking, her phone rang, and as she grabbed it out of her bag, her brother's name flashed across the screen. She'd had a few missed calls from Sean, but she hadn't had a chance to call him back.

"Sean," she said. "Sorry I never got back to you."

"No problem. I've been worried about you and Brandon. Mom filled me in on the twin brother, which I can't quite believe, but is there any more news?"

"Not yet. We're in Angel's Bay now talking to the other parent."

"That's what I heard. How long are you going to be there?"

"At least until tomorrow, maybe a few more days after that. We'll see how things go. We think we'll get further faster if we all work together."

"Sounds like a solid plan. Look, I'm about an hour from Angel's Bay," Sean said. "I thought I'd come up and meet you, see if I can help."

"Really?" she said in surprise. "I thought you were in San Diego with your band."

"I was, but when I heard you were coming down the coast, I decided to drive up and meet you. I don't have another show until next weekend. I know you have Ryan with you, but you're a little short on Callaways. I can't believe no one from the family came along."

"Everyone offered, but it's more important that they keep things going in San Francisco."

"I get it. But I'm free, so I'd like to help. I'll call you when I get in. Okay?"

"That would be great." She was touched that Sean was going out of his way to meet her. Sean was four years younger than her, and while the gap in age wasn't that much, their lives were very different, and they hadn't been close in years. She was a wife, a mother, and a teacher, and Sean was still chasing his dream of being a rock star.

"What's great?" Ryan asked, having only caught her side of the conversation.

"Oh, Sean has been performing in Southern California. He's coming here to meet us and should be in town in about an hour." She shifted in her seat to look at Jessica. "Sean is one of my five brothers, younger by four years."

"Five brothers?" Jessica asked, awe in her voice. "That's a lot."

"And I have two sisters, which makes eight siblings. Sometimes the family seems way too big, but in times of crisis, I can always count on them." It suddenly occurred to her that Jessica seemed very much on her own. "Do you have family in Angel's Bay?"

"Travis's family is in town." Jessica's lips tightened. "They don't care much for me, especially Travis's mother, Paula. She hated me from the second Travis brought me home. I didn't think it was possible for her to dislike me more, but since Kyle disappeared, she's practically foaming at the mouth."

"That's rough."

"As for my family, it's just me and my mom, and she lives in Vegas," Jessica continued. "She couldn't come out here, which is fine. She'd only add more drama, and that's the last thing I need." Jessica crossed her arms in front of her chest. "I just want to get Kyle back. He's the only person who makes sense in my life." She took a breath. "Take the next right, Ryan. "The quilt shop is about halfway down the street. Park anywhere you can find."

→⇒⇐←

The quilt shop was located in the center of the downtown area, and the streets were crowded with locals running Saturday errands and tourists strolling along the charming streets, checking out the antique stores, art galleries and cafés. Angel's Bay was a beautiful town, Nicole thought, wishing they'd come here for another reason. Then she could have enjoyed the small town atmosphere. Instead, she was tense and silently praying that Jessica's friend Kara would be able to tell them who had made the quilts.

When they entered the store, Jessica said, "Kara is probably upstairs. That's where they run a lot of the classes. Wait here, and I'll go check."

Jessica disappeared down the aisle, heading for the stairs.

As Nicole's gaze followed Jessica, it caught on a large glass display case by the stairwell. "I think that's the original quilt," she murmured.

Ryan frowned. "What?"

She smiled at his awkward stance. Ryan had never liked to shop, and she'd always been amused by how uncomfortable he got in places like lingerie departments and now apparently quilting stores. "I said I think that's the original memorial quilt from the shipwreck. I want to take a look."

"Let's just wait here."

"It's right over there," she said, ignoring him.

Despite his protest, Ryan followed her over to the glass case. There were probably more beautiful quilts than this one, but there was so much history in the quilt that Nicole saw the beauty in every stitch.

There was a placard next to the case that detailed the history of the quilt and the names of the quilters and their loved ones.

"Look," she said, pointing to a name. "Helen Schilling— she must be a relation to Travis's family. She made the quilt for her son Donald, who died in the wreck at the age of five," she added, feeling a kinship with that young mother. But Brandon wasn't dead, she reminded herself. He was coming home. She was going to be with her son again. "It's amazing to think that this quilt was made over a hundred and fifty years ago; a beautiful reminder of a terrible tragedy." She looked back at Ryan. "You aren't saying much."

"I'm not that interested in that old blanket," he said tersely.

She frowned. "What's going on with you? You're so uncomfortable in here."

"There's a lot of estrogen in this place."

"True, but is that really the reason?" she questioned. "Something else is up."

He met her gaze and let out a sigh. "I don't want this to be a dead end, Nicole. Every hour that passes, every day that goes by—"

She cut him off by putting her fingers against his mouth. "Sh-sh. I don't want to think about the time passing. It's too scary."

"Sorry," he muttered.

She dropped her hand, her fingers tingling from the warmth of his mouth. "We have to stay in the moment. It's the only way I'm going to survive."

"You're right." His gaze bored into hers. "You know why we used to be so good together? When you were weak, I was strong, and when I was weak, you were strong. We were always able to pull each other up."

"Until we both went down at the same time."

"Yeah."

All the emotions of the past few years passed between them in one long glance. And then the connection was broken by the arrival of Jessica and Kara.

Kara Lynch was an attractive and pregnant redhead with a warm, friendly smile.

"This is Nicole and Ryan Prescott," Jessica said.

"Nice to meet you but very sorry it's under these circumstances," Kara said. "Jessica tells me you're looking for the quilter who made the quilts for your sons."

"Yes, would you have a record of that?" Nicole asked.

"My grandmother should. While we've started to computerize, we've only put in the last couple of years, so the information would probably be in one of my grandmother's many journals. I'll be finishing up here in the next ten minutes, and I can stop by her house on my way home. Will that work?"

"That would be great," Nicole said. "Of course, we need everything as fast as possible."

"I completely understand. I have a child, and I know what you're going through is horrible. My husband is also a cop here in town. He's been working overtime on the case, along with all the other officers."

"We're very grateful," Nicole said.

"We'd like to know not only who made the quilts but also who ordered them," Ryan interjected. "I assume someone has to notify the guild of an upcoming birth."

"If it's not for a local child, yes," Kara replied.

"Otherwise, usually the pregnant woman knows someone in the guild. But lately we've been taking orders for newborn quilts from all over the country."

Nicole's heart sank. She didn't want the order to have come from the East Coast. She wanted to feel like they were getting closer and not farther away.

Kara gave them a thoughtful look. "You know Sharon, Travis's first wife, was a quilter. She might have ordered the quilts, although why would she order two if she only adopted Kyle? I guess that doesn't make sense." She turned to Jessica. "I'll talk to my grandmother, and then I'll give you a call."

"Thanks," Jessica said. "We really appreciate it."

"It's the least I can do. I'll fill Colin in and Joe, too, if that's all right with you," Kara added.

"Of course," Jessica said. "That will save us a call."

As Kara left, Nicole turned to Ryan. "Speaking of calls, I should phone home and get someone to take a photo of Brandon's quilt. Then we can match his blanket to Kyle's and see if there are any differences."

"Good idea," he said. "Do you want to do that now?"

"I'll wait until we get back to the house."

As they left the shop and walked down the street, Nicole glanced at Jessica. "This is a beautiful small town."

Jessica nodded. "Travis loved it here. He told me it was the kind of place where people looked out for each other and bad things didn't happen. Unfortunately, he was wrong about the bad things."

"But not about the people," Nicole said. "I feel like everyone in Angel's Bay is looking for Kyle and now for Brandon." Her phone rang as she got into the car. It was Sean again. "Where are you?"

"Just driving past the *Welcome to Angel's Bay* sign," he said. "Where can I meet you?"

"We're on our way back to Jessica's house now. That's

Kyle's mother. Why don't you meet us there?" She gave him Jessica's address and said, "We'll see you in a few minutes." As she slipped her phone back into her bag, she glanced back at Jessica. "I hope you don't mind if my brother meets us at your place."

"Of course not. And if anyone is hungry, I have plenty of food that the neighbors have dropped off."

"I could eat something," Ryan said.

Nicole nodded. She was hungry, too. They'd been in such a hurry to get to Jessica's house, they'd skipped breakfast, and it was now past one o'clock. "I don't want you to go to any trouble, though."

"I'll just be opening up containers," Jessica said. "That's actually my best skill when it comes to cooking. I thought about taking some cooking classes when Travis and I got married, but he loved to cook. So I let him. Do you cook, Nicole?"

"I used to cook more," Nicole replied, thinking how lazy she'd gotten in that department. She was always rushing back from some appointment, too tired, or too busy to do more than throw a few things together. And since Brandon would only eat a very small variety of foods, it wasn't that much fun to cook for him. It had been a lot more fun when Ryan was around, when they were first married, when they'd drink wine and chop vegetables and make dinner together.

"What about you, Ryan?" Jessica asked.

"I'm better on the grill than the stove," he said, shooting Nicole a smile. "Wouldn't you agree?"

"You can grill a mean steak. But when it comes to side dishes…"

"That's all you, babe."

Her stomach fluttered at the casual caress of his words. It had been a long time since he'd called her *babe*, and she hadn't realized until just this second how much she'd missed it. She deliberately forced herself to look away from him. She had enough to handle right now. She didn't need to get lost in the past.

Eleven

 ——⟫⟫⟪⟪⟪⟪⟪⟪—

After arriving at Jessica's house, Ryan and Jessica headed into the kitchen to find some food while Nicole sat down on the front steps to call Emma and wait for Sean to arrive.

Emma answered on the first ring. "Hey, Nic. Any news?"

"We're working on a possible lead. The little boy here in Angel's Bay has a baby quilt exactly like the one that came with Brandon when we adopted him. If we can figure out who made the quilts and gave them to the boys, we may have a better chance at locating the birth parents."

"That's amazing. Have you told Max?"

"Not yet. We haven't come up with any names yet, but we have someone in the quilting guild looking into the records for us. Can you let Max know?"

"Of course. I'll call him as soon as we're done."

"I also need a favor," Nicole continued. "Can you go over to my house and take a picture of Brandon's quilt? It's on the top shelf in Brandon's closet, wrapped in plastic. We want to compare the two, see if there are any differences."

"I'm headed to a fire scene right now, but I should be able to get to your house in about an hour. Is that soon enough, or should I call Mom? I think she's still at your place."

"An hour is fine," she said. "If I need it sooner, I'll call

Mom myself."

"How are you and Ryan getting along?"

"Surprisingly well. Ryan seems different. He's determined, optimistic, and his mind is whirring with ideas. He seems like the old Ryan."

"Does that mean you're turning into the old Nicole, the one who was madly in love with him?"

Nicole didn't know how to answer that question. "I don't want to talk about our relationship right now. It's not the time."

"Someday you're going to have to make the time."

"That day is not today. I'll let you get to work, Em. Send me the photo as soon as you can."

"Will do. Good luck, Nicole."

As she finished the call, Sean pulled up in a twenty-year-old dark green minivan that had definitely seen better days. But apparently the van still worked well enough to haul his music equipment up and down the state.

When Sean got out of the car, fast food wrappers fell onto the sidewalk, and she smiled. Sean had been on the road awhile, and whatever money he made was usually put back into the music or the band. Her brother was a free spirit, and in some ways the rebel of the family, the one who couldn't quite conform to the Callaway image put forth by their father, Jack.

But like the other Callaway men, Sean had dark hair and blue eyes, an attractive combination that made her brothers very popular with the ladies. Nicole suspected that adding a guitar into the mix made Sean even more appealing.

"Nicole," he said, greeting her with a hug. "How are you holding up?"

"I'm still standing. Thanks for coming."

"No problem. So this is the other family's house? Will they mind if I'm here?"

"No. Jessica Schilling, Kyle's mom, is very nice. She's actually a widow. Her husband died last year. And since then she's been raising his kid."

"Not hers?"

"He adopted Kyle with his first wife. It's a complicated story, but the bottom line is Jessica is Kyle's mom, and she's worried sick about him."

"Got it."

Nicole opened the front door and ushered Sean into the house. As they entered the dining room, Ryan came out of the kitchen with a salad bowl in his hands. He set it down on the table and then came forward to shake Sean's hand.

"I'm sorry," Sean said to Ryan. "This whole situation sucks."

"Yeah, it does. Thanks for coming."

"Mom said Dad was thinking of driving down here, and I figured you'd rather have me than him."

Ryan nodded. "I certainly would. I'm not Jack's favorite person these days."

Nicole knew that her father had been hard on Ryan the last year, but deep down Jack Callaway had a lot of love for Ryan. He just treated him like a son, which meant his love came with high expectations.

Jessica came out of the kitchen holding a casserole dish with two potholders. She set it down on the table and then came over to meet Sean.

"I'm so sorry about your son," Sean said to Jessica.

"Thank you. It's nice of you to come and help your sister."

"It's the least I can do. I was kind of an annoying brother when we were growing up. So I probably owe her."

Nicole liked how easily Sean could take the tension out of any situation. "No *probably* about it; you were annoying. Sean used to drive me crazy playing the same screeching chords on his guitar over and over and over again," she told Jessica.

"I was practicing," he said defensively. "I got better."

"Not fast enough for me," she teased. "Although I am now one of your biggest fans."

"Why don't we eat?" Ryan suggested. "You can share family stories over lunch."

"I wouldn't want to bore Jessica," Nicole said, as she pulled out a chair.

Ryan gave her a smile. "Your stories are never boring. Like Jack, you know how to spin a tale."

"He's right," Sean added. He looked at Jessica. "Whenever Nicole would babysit us, she would make us listen to endless stories about Gods and Goddesses. And they were actually somewhat entertaining."

"I hope my students think so. I teach Greek mythology at the local community college," she explained to Jessica. She hadn't given much thought to her job in the past few days, but she knew the college would cover her classes with subs until she got back.

"That sounds like an interesting job," Jessica said. "I never went to college. I always wanted to, but I barely made it out of high school, and there wasn't money for more, so I went to work."

"What did you do?" Sean asked as he helped himself to salad.

"I did everything. I worked at fast food restaurants, retail shops. I even did some dog walking. But I made the most money when I started dancing. My mother is a former Rockette and Vegas showgirl. When she stopped dancing, she started teaching. I was usually tagging along, so I learned how to dance before I could walk. I didn't really want to follow in her footsteps, but I didn't have any other skills. For the most part it was fun."

"And Vegas is where you met Travis?" Nicole asked.

"Yes," she said, a smile parting her lips. "He was working as a project manager for a building going up on the strip. It was a six-month job, so he'd packed up Kyle and himself and moved to Vegas. One night he came to a show, and the next night he invited me to meet him for dinner. Two days later I was introduced to Kyle. It was very fast, but Travis treated me so much better than anyone I'd ever met, and I loved seeing him with his son. My father bailed on me when I was little, so I was impressed with a man who could be family-oriented. When his job ended, he asked me to marry him and move to Angel's Bay, and I said yes." She cleared her throat. "And that's enough about me. Sorry. I didn't mean to go on like that."

"It's nice to get to know you better," Nicole said.

"So what do you do, Ryan?" Jessica asked, eager to distract attention from herself.

"I'm a pilot. I fly commercial jets."

"How fun!"

"Best job in the world," he said with a nod. "I started flying when I was in high school. Actually, it was Nicole who pushed me to take my first lesson."

"Well, you'd been talking about it for weeks," she said, meeting his gaze.

"I don't know why I was afraid to go for it," he said. "But in the end, I did, and I never looked back. Flying gave me perspective, and I needed that. My world was too small when I was growing up. Up there, in the sky, I could see all the possibilities."

As Ryan spoke, Nicole realized how small her world had gotten the past few years, and this trip, this frantic search for Brandon, was actually giving her some perspective, too.

Jessica turned to Sean. "What about you? Nicole said you're a musician. What kind of music do you play?"

"Alternative rock."

"I'm not sure I know what that means," Jessica said.

Sean grinned. "It means I take rock music and give it my own spin."

"Sean is extremely talented," Nicole told Jessica. "He writes all of his own songs."

"Amazing. Do you sing, too?"

"Yeah."

"When is your tour going to be over?" Nicole asked.

"Next month. We have three more shows and then we're going to head home and get back into the studio. I like performing, but it's nice to have a break."

"I couldn't live on the road," Jessica said. "My mother used to tour when I was little. She'd get hired on to some show as a dancer and play a few weeks in a bunch of different cities, and she'd drag me along with her. The only part I liked was playing with all her makeup when she'd go out on stage. I probably still wear way too much, at least that's what my mother-in-law says." Jessica put her hands to her face. "Although I don't think I have a speck of makeup on right now. I can't imagine what I look like."

"You look like someone who doesn't need any makeup," Sean said.

"That's a nice lie to tell a girl," she said with a smile. "I think I saw some cookies on the counter in the kitchen. I'll get them."

As Jessica left the room, Sean said, "So what can I do to help you? Tell me what you need."

"I don't really know," Nicole said. "We're waiting for callbacks on some leads we've been following, but right now we're on hold."

"Then I'll wait with you."

Jessica came back into the room with a plate of cookies. "I have an idea for something we could do while we're waiting," she said, catching the end of their conversation. "Talking about Travis got me to thinking. I know there aren't any adoption records in the house, but I just remembered that after Travis died, his firm sent over a bunch of boxes from his office. I had them put in the garage. I didn't bother to unpack them. It's doubtful there's anything about the adoption in there, but we could take a look."

"We should definitely take a look," Ryan said with a nod. "And it's better than sitting around and waiting for the phone to ring."

Nicole couldn't agree more. She grabbed a cookie off the plate and said, "Let's get to work."

—➤➤◄◄—

Ryan started out optimistic, but three hours and six boxes of paper later, his mood had soured. He'd learned a lot about Travis Schilling's business but absolutely nothing about the adoption or anything else remotely personal. He could see the same frustration on Nicole's face as she shoved the last box aside and gave him a tired look. "Is there more?"

"I don't think so."

"We have the last box here," Sean said. He and Jessica were sitting at a card table with a stack of papers in front of them.

"And it doesn't look good," Jessica said, an apologetic gleam in her eyes. "I'm sorry. I feel like I've led us on a wild goose chase."

"It's not your fault," Ryan said. "It gave us something to do, and we now know that Travis didn't keep any paperwork regarding the adoption in his office. It was a long shot, but one we had to take. And honestly, I'm not all that surprised. I was thinking about what we were given at the time of the adoption, and aside from our contract with Mr. Reynolds, the only other piece of paper we received was a revised birth certificate that all adoptive parents are given. I was hoping Travis had more, but he probably didn't." He glanced at his watch. "What does surprise me is that we haven't heard back from your friend Kara." How long could it take to look through some quilting logs? Kara had called once to tell them she and her grandmother were starting the search, but that had been hours ago.

"It must be taking her longer than she thought," Jessica said. "I know she'll call us as soon as she knows anything."

Nicole looked up from her own phone. "Emma just texted me the photo of Brandon's quilt. Let's go upstairs and compare our picture with Kyle's quilt."

"I'm coming," Jessica said, getting to her feet.

"Me, too," Sean added. "I'd like to see Kyle's room. From what you've told me about him, Jessica, he sounds like an amazing kid."

"He really is," Jessica said. "I'm sure he's a lot like your nephew."

At Jessica's casual words, Nicole paled, and Ryan tensed, knowing that they were coming close to a moment of truth.

They hadn't told Jessica about Brandon's autism. He didn't know exactly why they hadn't told her, but Nicole had seemed reluctant to say much about Brandon, and he'd followed her lead. But now that Sean was in the mix, it was going to come up, and he had a feeling it would be coming up sooner rather than later.

Twelve

——➤➤◄◄◄—

When they entered Kyle's room, Nicole immediately went for the quilt, which they'd left on the bed. Ryan walked to her side, eager to compare the two blankets.

"It's an exact match from what I can see." She held her phone next to the quilt, zooming in on each square. "Wait a second." She pointed to the center square on the blanket and the matching block on the photo. "One bird here, and two birds there." She looked at Ryan. "What does that mean?"

"Maybe Kyle was born first and Brandon was born second?" he suggested.

"That could be it. But why would that be important to note?"

"I have no idea."

"Do you see any other differences?"

"No. Although it's odd that a lot of the squares have matching items—two building blocks, two butterflies, two teddy bears. Everything is two, except the square in the center with the birds. The pairs remind me of Brandon."

She frowned. "But Brandon doesn't like the quilt anymore. Every time I brought it out, he'd kick it under the bed or stuff it in a drawer. Finally, I just put it away."

"Can I take a look?" Jessica asked.

"Sure." Nicole handed her the phone and the blanket.

Jessica studied the photo closely. "They do look exactly the same, except for what you said about the birds. I think the matching items were done because they were twins. That's why there's two of everything."

"We really need to know who ordered these quilts," Ryan said, acutely aware of every hour that was passing. It would be dark soon. And Brandon would be gone for another night. He hated that thought.

"So Kyle is a swimmer?" Sean asked, interrupting their conversation as he picked up a trophy on the dresser.

"Yes," Jessica said, handing Nicole her phone, then moving across the room to Sean's side. "Kyle can stay in the water for hours."

"Not Brandon," Sean said with a smile. He threw Nicole a pointed look. "I remember when you tried to get Brandon in the water at Aunt Margaret's house. He screamed so loud, we thought someone was attacking him."

"Your son doesn't like to swim?" Jessica asked.

"No," Nicole said shortly. She looked at Ryan, and he saw the plea in her eyes.

"Maybe we should go back downstairs," he suggested.

"One second," Sean said, completely unaware of the tension building inside of his sister. "This is a great picture." He held up a photo of Kyle, who appeared to be dancing with two teddy bears.

"That was taken at the school play," Jessica said. "I have the actual video on my phone. Do you want to see it? It's really funny. Kyle is such a goofball."

"That would be great."

Jessica pulled out her phone and punched up the video while Sean leaned over her shoulder to look at the screen. Ryan wanted to get Nicole out of the room, because he could see the emotions building inside of her. But she wasn't looking at him; she was looking at Jessica and Sean.

"What a funny kid," Sean said, looking up with a smile. "Great moves. You should see this, Nic. It's hysterical. Wait, is he singing?"

Jessica nodded, turning up the volume. "Off-key but as loud as he can."

Ryan stiffened as Kyle's voice rang through the room, a voice with all the same tones as the one Brandon had once used to speak to them, to recite nursery rhymes, and to sing silly songs, a voice that had gone quiet almost three years ago.

A wave of sadness and grief ran through him, and he could see the agony on Nicole's face. She wrapped her arms tightly around her waist as if she was in physical pain, and he thought she probably was.

"Turn if off," she said abruptly. "Turn it off right now."

Jessica and Sean stared at her in surprise.

"Nicole," Ryan said, putting a hand on her shoulder, wanting to comfort her.

She immediately stepped away from him.

"I can't do this," she said, panic in her eyes as she looked back at him. "I can't hear his voice. I can't see him." She started shaking her head as she backed toward the door. "It's too much."

"Nicole," he said, but she was already gone, flying out of the room and down the hallway.

He bolted after her, ignoring the stunned looks on Sean and Jessica's faces. He had to get to Nicole. She was heading for a big fall, and he needed to catch her.

—➤➤◄◄—

Ryan's voice rang out behind her, but Nicole didn't stop running, not even when she reached the sidewalk. She had to get away from the house, from Kyle, Jessica, and Sean. She didn't want to see anyone, and she didn't want anyone to see her. She'd been holding on to her control by a thread, and the thread was breaking. Her emotions were building up inside of her, demanding to be set free, but if she let them out, if she broke down now, she didn't know if she'd be able to pull herself together again.

So she ran.

The sun had set, and twilight surrounded her. She liked the darkness. In the shadows she could hide from herself and from reality. In the light, she couldn't pretend that things were better than they were, because everyone could see right through her.

Ryan called her name again. He was getting closer. He'd always been a faster runner than she was. Damn his long legs.

"Nicole, stop."

"Leave me alone," she said, flinging the words over her shoulder. She jumped off the curb to cross the street. A horn blared, and she realized she hadn't seen the car that was fifteen feet away.

Luckily, she made it through the intersection without getting hit. She had no idea where she was, but houses had given way to small businesses, cafés and restaurants. A few blocks away, she could see sailboats and the harbor. Sailing away seemed like a fine idea about now.

And then a hard hand came down on her shoulder. She stumbled. Ryan grabbed her arm, bringing her to an abrupt stop.

"Are you trying to get yourself killed?" he demanded. "You ran right in front of a car. Where the hell are you going?"

"I don't know," she yelled.

They stared at each other for a long moment, their breath coming fast, emotions charging the air.

"Then at least let me go with you," he said. "I know why

you ran from them, but you don't need to run from me."

"I don't want to talk to you. I don't want to talk to anyone. Go away."

"I'm not leaving you. I know how you feel, Nicole."

"No, you don't."

"You think I didn't feel pain when I heard Brandon's voice?" he asked, his voice rough and angry.

"It wasn't Brandon."

"But it sounded just like him." His gaze bored into hers. "When Kyle laughed, we heard Brandon laugh. And we haven't heard that laugh in three years. We've been praying to hear it again. And tonight we did. But it wasn't Brandon."

"No, it was Kyle. And it broke my heart." Her voice caught, her eyes blurring with tears. "Kyle is normal. He's what Brandon should be. Why isn't Brandon like his brother? What did we do wrong, Ryan?" She waved her hand in the air. "How did we break our son?"

"We didn't break him, Nicole."

"It can't be biology. His twin is fine. It has to be something else, something we did."

"It's nothing you or I did. And you know that." He paused. "You *know* that," he repeated. "Brandon's illness isn't about you. It's about him. Something went wrong in his head."

Her mouth trembled, and she bit down on her bottom lip, fighting for control, but she was losing the battle. "I'm so angry, Ryan. And I'm sad, bone-deep sad. There's a pain and an emptiness in my heart, and it doesn't go away. I'm so tired of feeling that way."

Compassion filled his eyes. "Nic," he said softly.

"And I'm tired of fighting for Brandon and fighting for you and losing everyone. All I ever do is lose." Emotions that she'd locked away for three years welled up within her. And then the dam burst. "It's not fair," she said, tears streaming down her cheeks. "Why did Brandon have to get this horrible disease? Why couldn't he be normal and happy like Kyle? Why did it have to happen to him? To us?"

He had no answers, because there weren't any.

"I feel like I've been climbing this mountain," she continued. "And every time I get close to the summit, another peak appears in front of me. There's no end. There's no moment of victory, no triumph. There are just more mountains to climb. And I can't do it anymore. I'm exhausted. I'm defeated."

Ryan hauled her into his arms, and she had no strength to resist. In fact, she welcomed his strength. Right now, he was the only reason she was still standing.

"It's okay, Nicole," Ryan whispered, holding her tight against his chest. He stroked her back with one hand. "You don't have to do anything right now except breathe."

"Even that seems too much," she said, feeling completely overwhelmed. "I wish you would leave me alone, Ryan."

"Why?"

"Because I'm about to lose it."

"Then lose it. Let it go, Nic. There's no one here but me. No one you have to be strong for; no one you need to impress. It's just me. It's just us."

His words released a tidal wave of tears that soaked her face and Ryan's shirt. Sobs choked her breath. Waves of pain ran through her, each one worse than the one before. She'd held herself together for three years, and she couldn't do it anymore. She couldn't not be sorry for herself, so she cried for Brandon and for Ryan and for herself—for the happy, healthy family they should have been, for the life they should have had.

And all the while Ryan held her, his face buried in her hair, his arms around her like tight bands of steel. He was not going to let her fall. And for the first time in a long time, she felt safe and protected.

Finally, the tears began to slow and the sobs turned to hiccups. She was a teary mess, but she felt better having released some of the pain that had been turning her inside out.

When she finally pulled back and lifted her watery gaze to Ryan's, she saw nothing but tenderness in his gaze. No condemnation. No impatience. Just the intimate love she used to see there.

"Feel better?" he asked.

"I feel stupid." She looked around, wondering if there had been any other witnesses to her breakdown, but the nearest building was closed, and there was no one else on the street. Thank goodness for that.

"You always feel stupid after you cry, which is why you never ever cry," he said, a small smile crossing his lips.

He knew her too well. She sniffed and wiped her eyes with her fingers. "I'm a mess."

"Yeah," he agreed. "But you've been holding everything in for too long."

"Definitely longer than the last three days."

He nodded, understanding in his eyes. "You don't know how many times I've wanted you to let go like that."

"Why?" she asked, bewildered by his comment.

"Because I was tired of living with a superhero."

"I wasn't that," she said defensively.

"Yes, you were. And you were amazing. But the bigger you were, the smaller I seemed to get."

His words surprised her. "I—I didn't mean to make you feel small."

"Didn't you? Didn't that make you feel better about yourself?" he challenged.

It was a harsh criticism. Unfortunately, there was a ring of truth in his statement. Had she tried to make herself feel better by being the one who knew what to do, who could save

Brandon when no one else could?

"Can't we be honest for once, Nicole? Can't we admit that this whole situation sucks big time? Can't we be human and feel unfairness and injustice? Can't we talk frankly about how hard it is to deal with a kid who can't connect, who won't look at us, who seems to feel nothing, no matter how hard we try? Do we have to be perfect every second of every day? Can we stop feeling guilty if we think about ourselves or something else for five damn minutes?"

She stared back at him, his passionate words resonating with every syllable. "If I did any of those things, what kind of mother would I be?"

"The same kind of mother you are now, only you'd be admitting that you're not a robot. You're a person who is capable of feeling every emotion, good and bad," he said, waving his hand in the air. "I know you're probably thinking right now that I just want to pull you down to my level so that I can feel better about myself. But that's not true. No matter how low you sink, you'll always be higher than me. So maybe you should stop trying to prove that all the time." He let out a breath and stepped back from her, shoving his hands into the pockets of his jeans.

It was crazy how well he could read her mind. Had she been trying to prove she was better than Ryan? Had fighting for Brandon somehow turned into a competition?

"We need to stop being angry with each other and be mad at the real enemy—autism," he added. "That's what broke us apart, and the worst irony of all is that when Brandon lost his ability to communicate, we did, too."

She was stunned by the simple truth.

"We stopped talking to each other, Nicole, and we also stopped listening. And I'm not saying this is all on you. I was probably to blame, because I had a more difficult time dealing with Brandon's rejection than you did. When he turned away from me, it reminded me of all the times my father looked away or walked away, making me feel like a piece of shit. But I was wrong to turn Brandon into my father. I was wrong about a lot of things. I just wish we could call it even, move forward from here, and stop having the same fight over and over again. That's it. That's all I have to say. Your turn."

Silence followed his words.

"I'm a little speechless," she said finally. "But in a good way."

He nodded, his jaw tight.

"I wish you would have said some of that before, but maybe before I wasn't ready to hear it," she admitted.

She knew she'd been a partner in the demise of their marriage. She just hadn't had anyone hold up such a bright mirror before. Her family had walked on eggshells around her, knowing she had so much on her plate that they couldn't put one more thing on her. They couldn't tell her that maybe she wasn't handling things as well as she could be. And they were on the outside. They didn't really know what was going on. But Ryan did, and he knew her better than anyone.

She'd thought she'd known him better than anyone, but she hadn't realized that Brandon's rejection had made Ryan feel like the loser his father had tried to turn him into. Ryan had always had more emotional baggage than her, but she sometimes forgot that, because for the most part he kept his past buried. And she had more pressing things to worry about. But maybe she shouldn't have let her husband and her marriage become such a low priority in her life.

She drew in a deep breath. "I need to clean up. But I can't face Sean and Jessica right now. I know we should, but—"

"Forget doing what you *should* do all the time. We'll get the car, go to the hotel and regroup. Okay?"

"Okay," she said, relieved by his proposal.

They walked back to Jessica's house and retrieved the car without seeing anyone. She'd apologize to Jessica and her brother later. Her emotions were too fragile right now to get into any explanations.

When they entered their hotel room, she went into the bathroom. One quick glance at her tear-streaked face and red, puffy eyes was enough to send her into the shower. She let the warm water pour over her head and across her tense shoulders as she thought about everything Ryan had said. He'd been surprisingly insightful, and some of that insight had been painful, but she'd heard him, and she'd felt closer to him than she had in a very long time.

Their conversation had stripped away all the guard walls they'd put up to protect themselves from getting hurt more than they already were, but now those walls had come down. She wasn't seeing Ryan through a haze of anger, but rather through the eyes of love, and that was more than a little scary. It was much easier to hate him than to love him, because his love had taken her not only to the highest high but also the lowest low.

Did she want to put herself through all that emotion again?

Did she really have a choice?

Ryan stepped onto the balcony and looked out at the crashing sea. The moon was moving higher in the sky, the stars coming out one by one as dusk turned into night.

His shirt was damp from Nicole's tears, and as the wind hit him, a chill ran through his body. With Brandon missing, today probably hadn't been the best time to get into it with Nicole, but the words had just come pouring out of him. He'd been as shaken by the sound of Kyle's voice as she had.

But he knew that even with all the challenges, he would never trade Brandon for Kyle, because Brandon was his son. Brandon was the one he'd rocked in his arms, read to, played ball with, and loved. And even though they were like strangers now, the love was still there, waiting for a chance to reconnect.

He hadn't given up on that hope. He'd become more realistic about the odds of that happening, but deep down inside, he could imagine it in his mind. And he wanted that image to come true, just as much as Nicole did.

Nicole...

He let out a sigh, feeling so many emotions for her. He wanted her love back, too, and in the past few days, he'd started to see flashes of the old Nicole again, the woman he'd fallen in love with, someone who was soft and vulnerable, creative and imaginative, who didn't hide her feelings behind a tough, hard exterior. Not that he didn't love the kick-ass side of her; he did. He'd just missed the other side of her, the side who loved him and needed him.

His phone rang, startling him out of his reverie, which was probably a good thing. Yearning for Nicole was only going to worsen the ache in his gut.

"Sean," he said.

"Where are you guys?"

"Oh. Sorry to bail on you. Nicole just couldn't handle seeing and hearing Kyle. She had a little breakdown, and I brought her back to the hotel."

"How is she doing now?"

"She's better. She's in the shower. I can have her call you when she gets out." He suddenly realized they'd left Sean with Jessica, someone he barely knew. "Do you want to come over here? We can get you a room. We're at the Seagull Inn."

"I'll be over later. Don't worry about me. I'm going to hang with Jessica for a while."

"You sure?"

"Yeah, she doesn't seem to have a lot of friends around to support her. But I need to ask you what you want me to tell her about Brandon's autism. She's been asking me questions about why Nicole suddenly freaked out, and I've been putting her off, not sure what you want me to say."

"You can tell her about Brandon."

"Are you sure? Will Nicole be all right with that?"

"She will be," Ryan said decisively. "In fact, I think it will be easier if you tell Jessica. You'll be able to do it in a less emotional way."

"All right."

"Has Jessica heard back on the quilts yet?"

"No. We'll call as soon as she does. Take care of my big sis."

"I will," he promised.

When he returned to the bedroom, Nicole was coming out of the bathroom in a white terry cloth robe that had been provided by the inn, her hair wrapped up in a towel. She stopped abruptly when she saw the phone in his hand. "Who were you talking to?"

"Sean. He was worried about you."

"I feel bad that I ran out on him after he came all this way to see me."

"He's fine. I told him to come here, and we'll get him a room, but he said he's going to stay with Jessica for a while. And, no, she hasn't heard anything more about the quilts." He paused. "Nicole, Sean asked what he should tell Jessica about why you were so upset. I told him he could tell her about Brandon. I hope that's all right with you."

"It is. I don't know why I didn't tell her. Although you didn't say anything, either."

"I was following your lead."

"There never seemed to be the right moment, and I didn't

want to make things more complicated."

"That makes sense."

She stared back at him, a mix of emotions playing through her pretty blue eyes, and his gut tightened as the quiet between them slowly filled with tension.

"So what do we do now?" she asked.

A half dozen answers ran through his mind, all of them tempting and dangerous. He didn't know where he and Nicole stood anymore. And he was afraid one wrong step would wreck the tenuous truce between them.

"I'm going to take a shower," he said finally, thinking that that was the safest choice. "Why don't you order room service? We can eat and then figure out what to do next."

"All right, but Ryan…"

He waited for the rest of her sentence, but she couldn't seem to come up with any words.

Then she said, "I'm sorry—for a lot of things, and I know you are, too. You said earlier that maybe we should call it even, and I'd like to do that."

"So would I."

"Good."

As he moved to walk past her, she caught his arm with her hand.

He gave her an enquiring look.

She hesitated, and then pressed onto her toes so she could kiss him.

It was soft and sweet, a tender kiss that felt like the start of something new. But it was way too short.

There was a glittering spark of desire in her eyes when she pulled away, a spark he hadn't seen in a long time. He wanted to put a match to that spark. He wanted to build a fire and have it consume them.

But Nicole was too fragile right now, and he didn't want to mess up what seemed like a new beginning.

"Go take your shower," she said, letting go of his arm.

He would. But now it was going to have to be a cold one.

Thirteen

Jessica hesitated as she came downstairs, hearing Sean on the phone with Ryan. Ever since Nicole had run out of the house, Sean had been making vague excuses for his sister's behavior, but Jessica hadn't believed any of them. There had been a stricken look in Nicole's eyes when she'd left Kyle's bedroom, almost as if she'd heard the voice of a ghost. And while Jessica understood better than anyone how on edge they all were, there had been something different about Nicole's reaction.

"Is Nicole all right?" she asked, walking into the living room as Sean got off the phone.

"She will be. They went back to their hotel. They need to regroup."

"Can you tell me now what happened? Or is it a secret?"

"It's not a secret, but I wanted to check with Nicole before I spoke to you."

"So, what's the story?" she asked.

"Brandon is autistic," he said.

His short, blunt statement took her by surprise. She didn't know what she'd been expecting, but it hadn't been that. "I—I don't understand."

"Sit down." Sean took a seat in the armchair as he waved her toward the couch.

"Was he born that way?" she asked.

"No, it came on when he was about three. Before that, he was fine. Nicole has been working hard to get him better. She's taken him to different doctors and treatment centers. She cut down her hours on her job so she could work one-on-one with him every day, but nothing has worked. It's been really difficult for Nicole and Ryan. Quite frankly, it's rocked their marriage."

"Wow," she murmured. "I don't know what to say. I'm sorry. Why didn't Nicole tell me?"

"I don't think she knew how to bring it up. But when she heard Kyle's voice on the video, it pushed her over the edge. He sounded like Brandon when Brandon was okay. I'm a dumbass for asking you to show me the video. I should have realized that Nicole would have a hard time with it."

Jessica sat back against the cushions. She hadn't been a mother very long. And in some ways she felt like an amateur, but she'd fallen hard for Kyle, and she couldn't imagine how she would react if he suddenly got sick and withdrew from her. She knew she'd miss him, because she missed him like crazy now. But he would come home, and he would be all right. When Brandon came home, he'd still be autistic, and Nicole and Ryan would still have a battle to fight.

She glanced back at Sean. "Nicole and Ryan seem like they're in perfect sync. You said they've been having problems?"

"Yes, but I definitely talk too much, so maybe don't share that with them."

"I won't."

"We all hope that they'll work things out. They've been together since they were teenagers." He frowned. "I don't want you to think that any of us wish Kyle wasn't healthy and happy. It's not about that."

"I understand. When you look at Kyle, you think of

Brandon and what he might have been like if he hadn't gotten sick."

"Exactly."

"Maybe being with Kyle will be helpful to Brandon."

"That would be something positive to come out of all this," he said.

"I wish Nicole had told me about Brandon. I feel like I've been bragging about Kyle every other second."

"You should brag. Kyle is a great kid, and he's your son. It's okay to think he's amazing."

"He is amazing. And resilient," she added. "Kyle has lost so many people in his short life—his real parents and then his adoptive parents, first Sharon, then Travis. And losing his father was a huge blow, because he was old enough to really feel that loss. He couldn't sleep alone in his bed for weeks. He kept asking me when Travis was coming back, and every time I saw the hope in his eyes, I had to kill it with the truth."

"That's rough."

"I tried to love him through the loss so he wouldn't feel like he was getting stuck with the short end of the stick—me. But in reality, that's exactly what happened."

"You're not the short end of any stick."

"You don't know me well enough to say that."

"I have good instincts about people," he said with a smile.

"And you're modest, too," she said, smiling back at him.

For some reason, she felt surprisingly at ease with Sean. He was her age, or a few years older, and he wasn't judgmental. It was nice to talk to someone who wasn't part of the Angel's Bay world and didn't fall into either camp, her friends or her enemies.

"Never said I was modest," he replied.

As his smile broadened, she had a feeling he was a killer with the women. What girl didn't like a hot guy who could also sing love songs? But he was probably a player, with a woman in every city. She knew what musicians were like. Her mother had dated enough of them.

Her thoughts were distracted by the buzz of her phone. It was Kara. Finally!

"Hi, Kara," she said. "Do you have any information for me?"

"Unfortunately, no," Kara said, regret in her voice. "My grandmother's journals from six years ago haven't been located. We've been looking all day for them. You know, she recently moved in with my mother, so a lot of her stuff was put into storage. I'm really sorry. I'm making phone calls and sending out emails to the guild members to see if someone remembers making the quilts. I didn't want to leave you hanging, so I thought I better let you know where I am in the process. I'm confident someone will come through with an answer before too long."

"I hope so," Jessica said, disappointed that they still didn't have a name.

"I'll be in touch. Do you need anything else? Do you have people with you? I don't want you to be alone. I spoke to Charlotte, and she's tied up with a complicated delivery at the hospital, so she said she probably won't be available until tomorrow."

"I'm fine, and I'm not alone," she said. "Don't worry about me. You've both done so much already. Just call me when you know anything."

She finished the call and looked up to see Sean's expectant gaze. "No news on the quilter, but Kara is continuing to work on it."

He gave her a thoughtful look. "You said you weren't alone, but you would be, if I wasn't here. Where are your friends?"

"I don't have many in town besides Kara and Charlotte. I

told you that my in-laws don't like me, and I haven't really connected with the mothers at Kyle's school. A lot of them know the Schillings, so they kind of treat me like I have the plague sometimes."

"I thought this was supposed to be a wonderful small town."

"It is. Some of the blame is on me. When Travis was alive, I spent all my time with him and Kyle. And after he died, I was too upset to worry about leaving the house and doing anything but keeping Kyle going. I wasn't worried about making friends, and as a result I don't have too many, but the ones I have are great. Charlotte and Kara have spent a lot of time with me the last few days, but they have jobs and families, too." She took a breath. "I don't know why I'm talking so much. You're a good listener."

"I grew up in the middle of a family of eight, with lots of big personalities on either side of me. It was hard to get a word in. So I didn't try that hard. I just played my guitar and let the rest of the world go on around me. Music was my escape."

"I tried to make dance my escape, but it didn't really work. I was good at it, but it wasn't my passion or my dream."

He leaned forward, his eyes intent on hers. "So what was your dream?'

"I don't know," she said.

"I think you do."

"Well, I guess it was family," she said slowly. "And I got that family with Travis and Kyle. But now..." A knot grew in her throat. "Let's talk about something else."

"Do you want me to go, Jessica?" he asked.

"Do you want to go? You can, if you want," she said, even though she didn't really like the idea of him leaving. The house felt too quiet without Kyle.

"Not really. I was thinking about trying out your piano,"

he said, getting to his feet. "Do you play?"

"No. The only one who pounds those keys is Kyle, and while he plays with enthusiasm, he's pretty bad."

Sean smiled. "Enthusiasm is where it starts."

"Can you play me one of your songs?"

"I can," he said with a nod, as he walked over to the piano and sat down on the bench.

She got up from the couch and walked across the room to stand next to the piano.

Sean ran his fingers along the keys and then began to play. It was a ballad, the melody beautiful. But it was when he started to sing that he took her breath away.

His tone was so deep, so pure, and it fit the song perfectly. The lyrics about finding courage, standing strong, being brave enough to smile resonated on so many levels. She found herself feeling surprisingly hopeful by the end of it.

When he finished, he lowered his hands to his thighs and looked at her with his piercing blue eyes. "Well?"

She had to force a breath into her tight chest. "Not bad," she said, which was a lie. She hadn't been so moved by a song in a long time.

"Not the best review I've gotten—also not the worst," he said lightly.

"It was great," she said. "How is that song not on the radio?"

"Maybe someday it will be."

She tilted her head as she studied his expression, wondering where the depth of emotion in the song had come from. "I thought you said you played rock."

"My band is rock. I do some Indie stuff that's different."

"Where did the lyrics come from?"

He shrugged. "I have no idea."

"They felt personal."

"There's something personal about all my songs."

"You're not going to tell me, are you?"

"I let my songs speak for themselves. But I will play you another one, if you want."

"I want," she replied, her curiosity piqued by his evasiveness. If his songs did the talking for him, maybe she'd find a clue in the next tune. Not that she needed another mystery to solve. But concentrating on Sean was a lot better than thinking about Kyle and what he was going through right now.

⇒⟫⟪⇐

While Ryan showered, Nicole threw on a pair of leggings and a sweater. She towel-dried her hair and ran a brush through the tangles, then she picked up the room service folder to look at the menu, but she couldn't focus on it. She kept thinking about Ryan, about their conversation, about the brief kiss they'd shared. And then her mind strayed to the fact that he was naked in the shower, and she remembered how much fun they'd had together under a hot spray before.

Shaking her head, she tried to change the images running through her mind. But she couldn't seem to concentrate. She was feeling tingly and a little nervous about the idea of Ryan coming out of the bathroom, probably dressed only in a towel, because he hadn't taken any clean clothes in with him, and she had used the only robe in the room.

It was ridiculous. She'd seen him naked a million times. She'd kissed and touched every inch of his body. She knew everything about him, so why did she suddenly feel like a teenager again? Like every casual glance, every word that he spoke, every smile that he gave her was somehow incredibly important and earth-shattering?

She hadn't been that girl in a very long time. She'd barely remembered that girl before tonight. She'd been too caught up in being superwoman, just like Ryan had said.

But she wasn't feeling much like a wife or a mother right now, the two labels that had defined her life for the past ten years; she was feeling like a woman, a restless, edgy, tense woman, whose barriers had come down with her earlier storm of tears.

She needed to get those walls back up. She needed to protect herself, because Ryan had brought her joy but also incredible pain. Wouldn't it be smarter—safer—to let him go? He was already living somewhere else. And while their problems might have been more clearly communicated, they weren't gone. Their son was still missing, still autistic. What had really changed?

She'd changed and Ryan had, too. They'd started to remember who they used to be.

Could they be those people again? Was it too late?

The questions ran around and around in her head. She had no answers, only mixed emotions, and at the heart of the chaos in her mind and her body was desire, attraction, a longing for an intimate connection…

Shaking her head, she told herself to stop fantasizing about Ryan.

Then the bathroom door opened and Ryan walked out, just the way she'd imagined.

The towel hung low on his narrow hips. Beads of water clung to his muscled abs and the fine dark hair that covered his chest. His long legs peeked out from beneath the small towel, and her mind immediately wanted to lift that towel.

He stared back at her, and judging by the way his dark eyes suddenly glittered with gold sparks, he'd read her mind.

She licked her lips, feeling like she was standing on the edge of a cliff. And she wanted to jump; she wanted to fly.

Ryan walked towards her. She told herself to move, to back up, to say something, anything to break the look between them.

She couldn't seem to speak. All she could do was look at him and feel a shivering need to get closer.

He stopped right in front of her. She could smell his aftershave. As he moved his head, a drop of water landed on her mouth. She licked her lips, feeling as if she were tasting him, but it was just water, she thought, feeling a little desperate. There were so many sensations running through her, so many reckless thoughts.

"Nicole," he said, his voice deep and husky.

How she remembered that voice, and the way he'd say her name—so many different ways, sometimes a soft caress, then an impatient demand, a cry of satisfaction, a promise of love.

She was in trouble. She needed to fight, to listen to her brain instead of her body, but her heart was getting in the middle, reminding her of how long and how much she'd loved this man.

Ryan moved closer, his chest brushing her breasts, a light, feathering, teasing touch. And then his hands were on her hips, and his head was coming closer.

She couldn't move. She needed his kiss as much as she needed air. Just one kiss, she told herself. Then she'd stop, then she'd come to her senses—

His mouth came down on hers, the pressure firm and oh so familiar. His lips were warm and seductive, yet minty and cool, a heady, dangerous combination.

And Ryan knew just the way she liked to be kissed with seductive purpose. His hands cupped her face, holding her still for an onslaught of pleasure. He nipped at her lips, then slid his tongue inside. She opened up for him as their tongues tangled together in a long, slow dance of love.

She wanted to get closer, to feel every heated inch of his body against hers. Reason was long gone. Her nerves were on fire. Her body tingled with anticipation. This was her man, her lover, the other part of herself. And she was meant to be his. She wanted everything he wanted—and more.

Desire ran through her as he devoured her mouth, as he whispered her name in a way that made shivers run down her spine. Every kiss was a taste of heaven. And any last lingering doubts slid away—along with his towel.

She gasped as he pulled her into the cradle of his hips, as she felt his erection, his need. And then he lifted his head and looked at her. The long, tense look stirred her senses even more. She could feel herself trembling.

"Nicole?" he said, a question in his voice.

"Yes." She wasn't even sure what he was asking her; she just knew the answer was yes to anything he might want.

He reached for the hem of her sweater and pulled it up and over her head, tossing it onto the bed. She pulled off her leggings, her thong coming off at the same time, and then Ryan was flicking open the clasp of her bra and pulling it off her shoulders.

Her full breasts spilled out, so pale against his tanned hands, her nipples peaking with the touch of his fingers. He walked her back toward the bed. They tumbled onto the mattress together, his body covering hers.

He moved his mouth from her lips to the side of her neck, the sensitive spot just beneath her ear, and he took his time.

Ryan could be so impatient in every other aspect of life, but when it came to making love, he was never in a hurry. In fact, she was usually the impatient one, feeling a need now to urge him on, to get his mouth on her breasts, his hand between her legs.

But he wouldn't be hurried, and deep down she loved the way he savored every inch of her body, making each nerve tingle with pleasure before moving on to the next. With his body pressing hers against the pillows, she could do little more than hold on to him and run her hands up and down the hard muscles of his back and buttocks.

Eventually, his mouth reached her breasts, and she arched up against him, sighing with delight as his tongue swirled around her nipples, laving, then nipping and tugging, until she moved her legs restlessly under his.

"Faster," she murmured.

He lifted his head to give her a knowing smile. "No way. I have you right where I want you."

"What about where I want you?"

"We'll get there." He pressed a kiss on her abdomen.

"Ryan, I need you," she said. "Now."

His gaze met hers, no humor left in his eyes, only desire. "I need you, too," he whispered, as he pulled her hips into his and slid into her.

They moved together in perfect harmony, the time apart only making their desire greater. Tension built within her with each thrust, each retreat, until she was shaking and crying out his name.

As he reached his own release, she wrapped her arms around him and held on tight. She didn't want to break the connection. She didn't want to let him go. She didn't want to think beyond this incredible, mind-blowing moment. So she closed her eyes and cherished the quiet, the stillness, wishing it would never end.

But of course it did end.

A few minutes later, Ryan rolled over onto his side, letting out a breath. He put his arm around her waist and pulled her onto her side to face him.

He stroked her cheek with his fingers, his gaze tender and loving. "You're so beautiful, Nic."

Her heart swelled. He hadn't looked at her like this in a very long time.

"I missed you," he added. "You don't know how much."

"I do know how much, because I missed you, too."

He kissed her again, a brief caress that made her feel cherished.

Ryan rested his head on the pillow, his eyes drifting shut. She looked at his face for a long minute, enjoying the way a strand of hair fell across his forehead, the strong planes of his face, and his sensuous mouth. She'd watched him sleep a hundred times, and she'd always loved having him in her bed, having his hand rest on her hip as he slept, exactly the way it did now.

But all those other times she hadn't had to worry about what was coming next, what would happen in the morning.

With her physical needs fulfilled, her brain was firing back up again, and she was plagued with uncertainty and a little guilt that she could find pleasure, be happy, while her child was missing.

Her sigh brought Ryan's eyes open. His hand tightened on her hip. "Don't do it, Nicole."

"What are you talking about?"

"Don't start having regrets already."

"I don't regret it. I just…"

"Feel guilty," he finished. He let out a sigh and rolled onto his back, his hand falling away from her hip. He stared at the ceiling, his expression hard and a bit angry.

"I'm sorry," she said.

After a moment, he said, "Yeah, I know."

But as they lay in silence, she had a feeling he didn't understand at all. She sat up, pulling the comforter off the bottom of the bed up and over her body. "Ryan." She waited for him to look at her.

"What?" he asked.

And with that one word, she felt as if they were as far apart as they'd ever been. It was her fault. She'd driven them apart with her guilt, making Ryan feel as if he'd done something wrong. And he hadn't.

"I wanted you," she said. "And I don't regret being with you."

Surprise passed through his eyes. "Okay," he said warily. "And the guilt?"

"Doesn't change what I just said." She paused. "I really have missed you, missed us. We were good together."

"I think we just proved that we still are good together." His tension eased as a smile turned up the corners of his mouth. "Give me a few minutes, and we can prove it again."

She smiled back at him and stretched out next to his body, resting her head on his chest as his arm came around her shoulders. She closed her eyes as emotion and exhaustion drove everything else out of her head. She'd worry about tomorrow later. Tonight she was going to be with Ryan.

Fourteen

Sunday morning, Ryan woke up a little after seven. Faint rays of sun were coming through the slits in the blinds, bathing Nicole in soft, morning light. Her blonde hair fell in waves across the pillow and around her shoulders. Her cheeks were pink from sleep, and her lips looked warm and inviting. He hadn't meant to sleep all night. He'd wanted to make love to her again, but the pace of the past few days had caught up with him.

They'd caught up with her, too, he thought, as he watched her sleep. She'd needed this rest, and so had he.

But he couldn't help thinking he'd missed an opportunity to have her again, because he had a feeling that the light of day was going to put them back to where they'd been, separated and distant, and that's the last thing he wanted.

Nicole began to stir. Her lids flickered, and a sigh passed through her parted lips. Then her eyes opened. She blinked a few times, giving him a sleepy smile. "Ryan," she said. "What time is it?"

"Seven."

She blinked again, awareness coming into her eyes. "It's morning already? We slept for like—"

"Eleven hours," he finished.

"My phone?" She glanced around. "Where's my phone?"

He tipped his head toward her purse. "Probably in your bag."

She scrambled out of bed, pulling the comforter around her naked body as she walked across the room to retrieve her phone. She grabbed it out of her bag and said, "No calls. No messages." She glanced up at him. "I wish that made me happier."

"Today is a new day."

He got up and pulled on some boxers and a pair of jeans as Nicole moved across the room to open the blinds.

"It's sunny," she said as he came up behind her. "And beautiful."

He put his arms around her waist. "Kind of like you."

She turned in his embrace and gave him a smile. "Charming so early in the morning?"

"I had a good night, and I'm not just talking about the sleep."

Her cheeks warmed with his comment. He liked that she could still be shy around him, but that was just Nicole—his Nicole.

"We should order breakfast," she said.

"Are you trying to change the subject?"

"I'm not trying—I am changing the subject. What do you want? Eggs, pancakes, waffles?"

"What if I said you?"

Her tongue darted out, and she licked her lips. "Ryan, we can't."

"Can't or shouldn't?"

"Both. We need to focus again. And I can't do that when you're kissing me. In fact, it would be really helpful if you'd put on a shirt."

"Me? I'm the problem? You do know that I can see your breasts through the holes in that blanket you're wearing."

"I'm getting dressed now, so let me go."

He didn't want to let her go—now or ever. "Nic," he said, his arms tightening around her. He couldn't find the right words to express what he wanted to say, so he settled for a kiss, a long, meaningful kiss that he hoped would tell her what he couldn't.

She swallowed hard as they broke apart. "Why don't you order breakfast while I get dressed," she suggested. "You know what I like."

He did know what she liked when it came to breakfast, but what she liked in him wasn't quite as clear. He knew he could make her happy in bed, and there had been a time when he could make her happy everywhere else. But that time had passed. Could they get it back?

She'd turned to him last night for comfort. He was smart enough to know that. She'd had an emotional breakdown, and he'd been happy to give her what she needed, because he'd needed her, too, but he wanted more than that going forward.

It would take some work. They'd both lost trust in each other, and they needed to rebuild that trust. He'd start by ordering her favorite breakfast.

-►►◄◄-

Nicole took a long shower, needing time to get her head together. She'd been so tempted to follow Ryan back into bed, and lose herself in his arms for another hour, but it was smarter to put the night behind them and move forward in their search for Brandon. Surely, they'd hear from Jessica's friend Kara sometime today, and hopefully the police would be successful in getting the adoption records opened. Those were the matters she needed to be thinking about.

But as she soaped her body in the hot, steamy shower, she couldn't help remembering how great it had been with Ryan. She could still feel his hands on her breasts, still taste him on her lips. He'd always known how to love her in just the right way.

But what about the other parts of their lives?

After yesterday's very honest and eye-opening conversation, she'd realized some truths about herself and the way she'd treated Ryan after Brandon got sick.

And Ryan was willing to accept blame, too. They'd both made mistakes. They'd been trying to handle a really difficult situation to the best of their abilities, but their best hadn't been very good. Instead of coming together, they'd split apart. And they'd hurt each other.

She'd never meant to hurt Ryan, and she knew that he hadn't wanted to hurt her. But that's exactly what they'd done.

They could do better. They *would* do better, she silently vowed. They just needed to bring Brandon home, so they could prove that.

With new resolve, she turned off the water and stepped out of the shower. She dried off, wrapped herself in a towel and pulled a brush through her hair. Then she used the blow drier until her hair was damp and a little curly. She didn't have time for styling, so she grabbed a band out of her make-up case and pulled her hair up into a ponytail.

When she returned to the bedroom, she realized that breakfast had already arrived. Ryan was sitting at the table, munching on a piece of bacon.

"That smells good," she said, grabbing some clothes out of her suitcase.

"I got blueberry waffles. Apparently, they're a specialty," Ryan said.

"And one of my favorites," she said, as she pulled on jeans and a sweater.

"I also got some eggs benedict and crispy bacon. I told them to cook it well and then cook it some more, the way you like it."

She buttoned her jeans and walked over to the table. "It looks perfect. The food came fast," she added, as she sat down across from him.

"Not really. You were in the shower a long time."

"I didn't realize," she said.

For several minutes they just ate. Nicole hadn't realized how hungry she was until she'd cleaned her plate. But then again, they'd skipped dinner the night before, so it shouldn't have been a surprise.

As she sat back in her seat, she wiped her mouth and said, "I wonder where Sean is. I feel a little guilty for abandoning him. I don't even know if he has enough money to rent a room."

"He's a big boy. He can handle himself."

"But he's here because of me. I should help him out."

"If he wanted your help, he'd ask for it."

"I doubt that. My brothers are very proud men."

"And you and your sisters are very stubborn women. So you should all just accept that about each other," he said with a smile. "I know it's in your nature to worry about everyone, but I think Sean is all right. He may be your younger brother, but he's twenty-eight years old, and he's been taking care of himself for a long time."

"I know he's super independent. He hates to take any help from the family."

"He wants to prove to your father that he doesn't need help."

"He and my dad have a very complicated relationship. Sean and Aiden probably have the hardest time with my father. They haven't been able to fall in line as well as everyone else. But while I could always see why Aiden and Jack clashed, Sean's relationship with Jack was different. There was almost a mystery to it. I don't know how to explain it. But I often felt like there was some underlying tension that only the two of them could explain, and they never felt inclined to do so—at least not to me or Emma. Did Sean ever tell you anything?"

"No."

"Maybe I'm just imagining something." She shot him a warning look as he started to open his mouth. "And don't tell me that it wouldn't be the first time."

He smiled. "I wasn't going to say that. You do have a good imagination, but you also have good instincts about people. What I was going to say was that it's funny how sometimes you call Jack your dad and other times you call him Jack."

She had always been a little torn when it came to calling her stepfather *Dad.* Even though her real father had basically abandoned her and Emma when he'd divorced their mother, she'd still felt a connection to him. As the years passed, it became clear that Jack was a better dad than her father ever could be or wanted to be. But she still hadn't been able to let go of wanting some kind of a relationship with her real father, and that relationship had come after she started working in a field similar to his. Now they had mutual interests. Sometimes he seemed to treat her more like a colleague than a daughter, but at least they talked occasionally, and strangely enough that meant something to her.

She frowned, wondering now about the strength and power of that biological bond. Would Brandon feel some inexplicable connection to his birth mother or his birth father? Would something down deep inside his soul recognize that they were blood?

She found that thought disturbing.

"Nicole," Ryan said, drawing her gaze back to his. "Where did you go?"

"Some place I didn't want to go. I was just thinking about biological parents and adoptive ones. I know there's a strong blood bond that runs through everyone. It's genetic."

"I don't believe that blood is more important than love. At least, it wasn't in my case." He paused. "We're Brandon's parents. He knows us. He loves us on some level, and he doesn't know these other people."

"He's been with them for a few days now. And he's with his brother." She let out a painful sigh. "God, I just realized he's with his real family."

"No, he's not with his real family," Ryan said forcefully. "He's with the people who gave him up for adoption. If that's in fact who he's with; we don't know for sure." As he finished speaking, his cell phone rang. "Hello?" he said. "Yes, my wife is with me."

Her nerves tightened at his words. "Who is it?" she asked impatiently.

He held up a hand as he listened. "I understand. We'll be right there." He put down the phone and said, "That was Chief Silveira. He wants us to come down to the station. They've found some security video that may be helpful."

"Security video? Of Brandon?"

"Apparently, it's from a fast food restaurant somewhere between here and Los Angeles. He said the images are not good, and the boys are not completely identifiable, but he wants us to take a look in case it is them. He has already called Jessica. She'll meet us at the station." His gaze turned grim. "It may not be them, Nicole. This could be a false alarm."

"Or our first big break."

→➤◄←

Ten minutes later Nicole and Ryan pulled into the police station parking lot behind Sean's green van. The four of them met up on the sidewalk, and Nicole could see the excitement and hope in Jessica's eyes that they might finally have a real clue.

As they walked toward the station, Nicole fell into step with her brother. "Sorry I bailed on you last night," she said.

He gave her a smile. "No problem. You had a lot on your mind."

"I did, but that's not really an excuse. You drove up here to help me, and—"

"And nothing," he said, cutting her off. "I don't want you to worry about me, Nicole. Brandon is your sole focus, and I am more than okay with that."

"Thanks. Did you stay with Jessica all night?" she asked, a little curious about how they were still together.

"I kept her company until she went to bed and then I slept on her couch," he said, meeting her questioning gaze. "I was going to get a hotel room, but she didn't want to be alone in the house. So I stayed."

"That was nice of you."

"I can be a nice guy," he said lightly. "And, frankly, I thought you and Ryan needed to be on your own for a while. You were upset when you ran out yesterday, and he's the person you needed to be with."

Her brother was a pretty smart guy. "You're right. But I'm better now, and I'm ready to hear some good news."

"I hope that's what's coming," Sean said, as he followed her through the front door.

After checking in at the front desk, they were ushered into a conference room and told that Chief Silveira would be with them in a moment.

Ryan and Nicole sat down on one side of the table, Jessica and Sean on the other. For a moment there was nothing but tense silence.

Then Jessica sent Nicole a hesitant smile. "Are you feeling better today? Sean told me about Brandon, and I'm really sorry. I hope I didn't make things worse by talking on and on about Kyle."

"You didn't do anything wrong; you didn't know. I should have told you. I don't know why I didn't. I guess it just felt like too big of a story to get into. We'll talk more later."

"Whatever you want, Nicole."

They all fell silent again, the only sound in the room provided by the ticktock of the big clock on the wall.

"Where the hell is Silveira?" Ryan muttered, his gaze darting to the door every other minute.

Nicole was wondering the same thing.

Finally the door opened, and Joe Silveira walked into the room dressed in his usual dark suit with white shirt and tie. With him was a uniformed officer, a blond, blue-eyed man, who was built like a linebacker.

"Hello, everyone," the chief said. "This is Officer Lynch."

Colin gave them a compassionate smile. "Hello. You met my wife Kara yesterday, and she asked me to tell you that the search goes on for who made the matching quilts. She hopes to have something for you today."

Nicole nodded, not really surprised to learn that this cop was married to Kara. There seemed to be many intersecting relationships in Angel's Bay, but it was all good. The more people who were working on the boys' behalf, the better.

Colin set a laptop computer down on the table and took a seat in front of it, while the chief stood behind him.

"All right," the chief said, pressing his fingers together. "This is what we know. Last night we got a call from a cashier at a restaurant in Carpinteria, about two hours south of here. The woman saw the boys' photos on a local news broadcast and believed that the same children had been in her restaurant yesterday, Saturday afternoon."

Nicole felt a rush of anxiety at the chief's words, and she

found herself reaching for Ryan's hand. He gave her a quick look, then squeezed her fingers reassuringly as the chief continued.

"We followed up with the manager of the restaurant," the chief continued. "He was able to send us video from their security camera. Unfortunately, the identity of the boys is not clear. That's why I asked you to come in."

Nicole bit down on her bottom lip and tried to breathe through her nerves. She wanted the chief to stop talking and play the video so she could see her son.

Joe dimmed the lights as Colin punched several keys on his computer. A minute later, a video appeared on the television screen on the wall.

Nicole squinted at the grainy images, wishing she could see more clearly. A parking lot, play structure and outside patio were visible as well as a portion of the front door leading into the restaurant. At one of the patio tables, she could see a family enjoying a meal, but there appeared to be a woman, a man and only one child. "Is that one of the kids?" she asked.

"No, watch the door," the chief replied.

Ten agonizingly slow seconds later, the front door opened. They could only see the bottom third of the doorway, but it was high enough to show two small boys walking out holding hands. They wore big gray sweatshirts that fell past their thighs, and the hoods were pulled up over their heads, hiding their hair color. Dark sunglasses covered their eyes.

Nicole's heart stopped as Colin froze the frame. "Oh, my God," she whispered. Was one of the boys Brandon?

As she studied the small figures, she was almost certain Brandon was the boy on the left. Her gaze moved down his body to the black tennis shoes and she knew. "That's him," she said. "That's Brandon on the left. He wore those shoes the day he disappeared. Oh, God. That's really him." She squeezed Ryan's hand. "That's our son."

Ryan shot her a tense, worried look. "Are you sure?"

"I'm positive," she said, meeting his gaze.

He nodded, his jaw tight. "I am, too."

Nicole looked across the table at Jessica. Her gaze was fixed on the screen.

"Kyle was wearing jeans like the boy on the right," Jessica said slowly. "But I wish I could see his face."

Nicole felt the same way. She wanted to pull down the hood and yank off the sunglasses and gaze into the eyes of her son. Even if he wouldn't make eye contact with her, even if his expression was as withdrawn and dull as it always was, she would be happy, because she would be able to see him.

But she still wouldn't have him. They had a grainy video taken at a restaurant miles away. And who knew where the boys were now? There had to be another clue, some other lead to follow.

"Play the rest," she ordered.

Colin nodded. "You got it."

As the video began again, Nicole could see a pair of jean-clad legs that appeared to belong to a man just behind the boys. But they couldn't see anything above his hips.

"What the hell kind of security camera doesn't capture the entire doorway?" Ryan demanded, anger in his voice.

"The manager said that the camera's position was altered by some high winds during a big storm two weeks ago. They hadn't fixed it yet," the chief explained.

"Did the cashier tell you who the boys were with?" Ryan asked.

"She didn't wait on them at the counter, but she noticed them when they came out of the bathroom with a male, who appeared to be in his early to mid-thirties. She was struck by the fact that he was dressed very much like the boys with the hooded sweatshirt and sunglasses. She thought at the time he was simply dressing his twins like him. But later when she saw the news, she wondered if the sunglasses and hoods were meant to be more of a disguise."

"Of course they were a disguise," Ryan said. "Anyone can see that. Someone should have called in the second they saw the boys."

As Ryan spoke, Nicole focused on the unseen male. It had been easier to think of the biological mother, or a woman having her little boy, than some guy. Who was he? The biological father? The biological mother's boyfriend?

She wanted more answers instead of more questions.

"Can you go back to the boys?" she asked, feeling a desperate need to look at Brandon again.

Colin rewound the video.

Nicole searched for any other detail that might be important.

"They look okay, don't you think?" Jessica asked, a hopeful note in her voice. "They're not crying. They don't look hurt. I guess that's something."

Nicole knew that Jessica was trying to find some peace in her fear, but she didn't know if she could believe Jessica's conclusion. Who knew what the oversized clothes and big sunglasses were hiding?

"They're holding hands," Ryan muttered. He looked back at Nicole. "I can't remember the last time Brandon willingly held someone's hand, can you?"

She stared at the two small hands clinging together. "No," she said. She'd had to force Brandon to take her hand sometimes, just to make sure he wouldn't suddenly dart into traffic if he got spooked when they were outside. But he never liked the contact. He always resisted her.

He wasn't resisting now. Her heart turned over at the sight.

"Maybe somewhere in Brandon's subconscious, he

recognizes his brother," Ryan said.

"I guess that must be it," she said slowly.

"Kyle is very protective," Jessica put in. "He always watches out for kids who are getting picked on. It's his natural instinct. And Brandon is his brother, so he'd definitely watch out for him."

Nicole didn't want to think about Brandon getting picked on, but how could she not? If the kidnappers were going to get annoyed or frustrated with one of the kids, it would probably be Brandon.

"I wonder what Kyle and Brandon thought when they saw each other," Jessica continued. "Wouldn't it be strange to suddenly see a mirror image of yourself?"

"I don't know what Brandon would think," Nicole said. She turned to the chief, who was watching them all with sharp, perceptive eyes. "What do you think the kidnapper would tell the boys so that they wouldn't run away from him? Would he threaten them?" she asked, finding it hard to get the words out, but she had to ask the question. She needed some reassurance.

"If the kidnapper is related to the boys, then I think he'd tell them they're back with their real parent," the chief said. "If this man is their father. If he has some other relationship to their mother, maybe her friend, then he would probably bring her up. He'd point out that they look alike, that they are brothers, and that they're back together the way they were supposed to be all along. He'd probably tell them that they're now with their real family."

Nicole sucked in a quick breath, his words stabbing her like a knife to the gut.

"I'm sorry," the chief said. "I was too blunt."

"No, you were honest," she said. "Do you think they'd be threatened or hit?"

"I think it's better to focus on what we've just seen, which is two kids who do not look like they've been harmed," he said. "Speculation is not going to help."

She knew he was right, but it was difficult to stop her mind from racing to every worst possible case scenario. She was a mother. Her child was in danger. And she had to save him. That was all that made sense to her.

"What's the next move?" Ryan asked.

"The detective I sent to San Diego to dig through the attorney's records has not located any information on Kyle Schilling's adoption. On his way back up the coast, he will stop in at this restaurant and talk to the cashier and manager."

She liked the sound of that. Maybe they would remember something else.

"Before you go, can I ask you to take one more look at the video?" the chief enquired. "We don't know if the boys ate at the restaurant, or if they did, whether they were inside or outside, but it appears that someone recently left the first table on the patio. You can also see some cars in the lot. Anything else look familiar?"

Nicole watched the video as Officer Lynch played it again. "I thought I saw a white car near the school when Brandon was taken, but none of the cars in that lot are white." She frowned, wishing she could find something that the police had missed.

"Hang on," Ryan said suddenly. "Can you zoom in on the first table?"

"What do you see, Ryan?" she asked.

"Crayons. And a picture."

She put a hand to her mouth, seeing what he was seeing. "Oh, my God."

"How is a kid's picture going to help us?" Jessica asked in bewilderment. "Kyle can only draw stick figures."

"Brandon has a photographic memory, and the ability to draw what he sees, what's around him, where he's been,"

Nicole explained. "It's what they call a savant skill. When he stopped talking, he started drawing."

Colin zoomed in on the table and brought the hand-drawn picture to full frame. Brandon had sketched two matching boys, himself and his brother, sitting side by side at a picnic table. He'd gotten every last detail right from the sweatshirts, to the sunglasses, to the different colors of their sneakers. Across from them on the table was a big set of keys and a pen that had some writing on the side.

"What does the pen say?" Ryan asked.

"Looks like Haywood Plumbing," Colin said. "A six-year-old drew this?" he asked in amazement.

"He's really good," Nicole said.

"I'll say."

"And there's a car in the picture," Nicole added, pointing to the far side of the picture. "The square license plate had a stripe of green and a round orange in the middle. On either side of the orange were two letters, J on the left and S on the right. "Can you find a car with only a partial plate?" she asked.

"We can search the databases and see how many cars match," the chief said. "That looks like a Florida plate, which could narrow things down."

"Florida," she echoed. "That's a long way from here." She'd preferred to think that Brandon wasn't too far away, but Florida was on the other side of the country.

"Well, he's not in Florida yet," Ryan said. "Not if they're driving. Not if they were in Carpinteria yesterday."

She appreciated the reminder. "You're right, but we have to find them soon, before they leave the state."

"Your little boy may have given us the break we need," the chief said as he turned the lights back on. "We'll check out the pen and the partial plate, and hope one of them takes us somewhere. I've shared this video with the San Francisco

Police Department. They get everything I get and vice versa. We'll be in touch as soon as we know more." He gave them an encouraging smile. "You've all been very helpful. Thank you."

"Thank you, Chief," she said. "For letting us help."

"In my experience, it's always a mistake *not* to let the parents help. You know your kids better than anyone. I saw that video another time and never picked up on the fact that that crayon drawing might hold some clues. You've got a smart kid."

Nicole nodded, thinking how rare it was that anyone gave Brandon a compliment. But he was smart and hopefully he'd just given them the clue they needed to find him and his brother.

Fifteen

—➤➤➤◄◄◄—

"What should we do now?" Nicole asked as they left the police station. "Should we go somewhere and talk, compare notes…"

"We can go to my house," Jessica suggested. "Unless it's uncomfortable for you to be there?"

"No, it's not at all uncomfortable," Nicole said, seeing concern in Jessica's eyes. "I'm fine now. I'm not going to break down again, and your house would be great." She glanced at her brother. "Are you sticking around today?"

"Yes. We'll meet you at Jessica's house."

"Great," she said, a little surprised at how quickly Sean and Jessica had become friends. But then Sean didn't judge, and he was easy to be around, two qualities that Jessica probably liked, considering she was involved in some kind of battle with her in-laws.

"Are you really okay with going back to Kyle's house?" Ryan asked as they got into his car.

"Yes. I'm moving on. What did you think about the security video?" She shifted in her seat so she could see him better. "It was weird to see Brandon in that big sweatshirt and those sunglasses. I wonder what he's thinking about it all. Is he even aware of what's going on?"

"We never know how aware he is of anything."

"That's true."

"He seems to like Kyle."

"Yeah, he does," she agreed.

"In fact, he seems to…" Ryan's voice trailed away.

"What were you going to say?" she asked curiously.

He shook his head. "It doesn't matter."

"Just say it, Ryan. We're way past keeping secrets from each other."

"You won't like it," he warned.

"Say it anyway."

"I was thinking about all our efforts to communicate with Brandon and how we just haven't been able to find a way to connect with him. But with Kyle, with his twin, maybe Brandon finally has the one and only connection that he wants—his brother."

Nicole frowned. Ryan was right. She didn't like the idea of Brandon having a connection to a kid he'd just met when she'd spent the past three years doing everything she could to build a link between her son and herself. But she couldn't deny what she'd seen on the video. Brandon had been clinging to his brother when they left the restaurant. Somewhere in his head, Brandon recognized Kyle as his brother, as blood.

Had he also recognized someone else as blood—his biological mother or father?

Her stomach clenched at that thought. It was one thing for Brandon to connect to his brother, but she really hated the idea of him connecting to his biological parents. That would be wrong and unfair and very painful.

But was a blood tie stronger than an adoptive relationship? She didn't want to believe that it was, but maybe genetics played more of a role than she knew.

"I'm sorry, Nicole." Ryan shot her a worried look. "I shouldn't have said that. I was thinking about my relationship with Brandon, not yours. He connects with you. He always has. I'm the one on the outside, not you."

He was offering her an olive branch, but she couldn't take it. "No, you were right. Brandon doesn't relate to me, not really, not in the way I want. I pretend that he feels something for me, that he sees me as his mother, because the lie keeps me going. It stops me from giving up. But the truth is this—I can't comfort Brandon when he's scared or angry. He pushes me away when I try. And he hasn't wanted to hold my hand in years. Brandon hates for anyone to touch him. But apparently there is something about Kyle that gets through to him."

"I have to say I'm a little surprised you'd admit the lie to me," Ryan said slowly. "You've always been so positive that you were making progress. I never saw any doubt in your eyes. You were so sure of even the smallest victories."

She sighed. "I couldn't let there be doubt. When you wanted to be realistic and pragmatic and have a reasonable conversation, I tuned you out. I couldn't go to that place of logic. I had to stay hopeful; I had to believe in the possibilities. I told myself that you might quit, but I never would, because I believe in miracles even if you don't."

"Who said I don't believe in miracles?"

"You did. You told me that when you were a little kid you used to pray for a miracle, an escape from your dad for both you and your mom. But no miracles came, so you stopped believing. And I understand why you felt that way. I didn't grow up the way you did. I came from a broken home, but my mother created a second family that was far better than the first. You didn't get that second chance as a kid."

"No, I didn't. No second chances, no miracles. By the time I was a teenager, I was cynical, frustrated and angry. I thought I'd gotten the short stick in life."

"You had."

"But then I met you."

He abruptly changed lanes, pulling the car over to the side of the road. Then he turned off the engine.

"Why are we stopping, Ryan?"

He looked her straight in the eye. "Because I want to say something important, and I want you to hear it. I can't do that and drive at the same time." He drew in a deep breath. "I didn't know what family was supposed to be like until I met the Callaways, and I didn't know what love was supposed to feel like until I met you. You changed my world in so many ways that you'll never know. You were smart, beautiful, passionate, determined, and you didn't just believe in miracles and dreams; you believed in me."

She caught her breath at his words, at the serious and loving look in his eyes.

"The first day we met, you couldn't stand me," he continued.

"You were so cocky, so full of yourself," she murmured. "But it wasn't that I couldn't stand you. I was afraid of how you made me feel. I had my head down, eye on the prize, good grades, getting into a great college, and I was worried you were going to distract me from that. I was right to be worried, because you did distract me."

"But I didn't stop you," he reminded her.

"No, you supported me in everything that I wanted to do," she said, tears pricking at her eyelids again.

"And you supported me. You made me believe that life could be good," he said. "That love could be real and that I could be more than the piece of shit my father thought I was. You made me look up into the sky. You're the reason I followed my dream to fly. It was all you, Nic."

"You would have become a pilot even if you'd never met me. Flying is your passion."

"I love to fly, but *you're* my passion. I don't know how the hell we ended up like this, but I do know that I never should have let you go."

He paused for a long moment, so long her heart started to beat faster in anticipation of what he was about to say next.

"I'm sorry, Nicole. I don't know if I've said that out loud before, but I've thought it a million times in my mind. I'm sorry for letting you down, for disappointing you, for not being the person you thought I was. I should have been a better husband, a better father. I have no excuses, just a lot of regret."

She sucked in a breath, shaken by the deep intensity of his words and all the emotion behind them. He had stripped himself bare in front of her, something she knew had taken a lot of courage. After all the pain he'd endured as a child, Ryan knew first-hand the danger of being vulnerable. But he was putting it all on the line for her. And she had to do the same.

"I'm sorry, too, Ryan. I could have been a better wife and a better mother."

"No, you're a fantastic mother," he cut in.

"What kind of fantastic mother drives her kid's father away?"

"You didn't do that."

"I did. And I need to apologize. Let me."

They stared at each other for a long moment, and in that moment, she felt the last lingering remnants of anger and pain slide away.

Ryan finally nodded. "I accept your apology."

"And I accept yours," she said, wiping the moisture from under her eyes.

"Okay," he said, a smile curving his lips.

"Okay," she echoed, smiling back at him.

He started the car and they finished the drive to Jessica's house in peaceful quiet.

→→←←←

When they arrived at Jessica's house, Ryan felt as if he'd dropped ten pounds of weight from his chest. His guilt and his anger were gone. He felt free. He'd said what he needed to say, and Nicole had heard him.

He'd been a little surprised by the apology he'd gotten in return. They had truly turned the corner when it came to being honest with themselves and with each other.

Sean opened the door before they had a chance to ring the bell. "What took you guys so long?"

"Uh, we took a wrong turn," Nicole said awkwardly.

"Actually, it was a right turn," Ryan corrected. "Don't you think?"

Nicole met his gaze. "Yes, I do."

Sean cleared his throat. "Great. When you two are done talking in code, why don't you come in?"

"Where's Jessica?" Nicole asked.

"She'll be down in a minute."

"I'm going to get some water," Nicole said. "Do either of you want anything?"

Sean shook his head, and Ryan said, "I'm good." Then he followed Sean into the living room.

He sat down on the couch while Sean took a seat at the piano, running his fingers lightly over the keys.

"So what was all that about?" Sean asked after a moment. "Right turn, wrong turn…"

"Nicole and I had a good conversation. Something we've needed to do for a while."

"Well, I am glad to hear that. I've been waiting for you two to stop fighting against each other and start fighting for each other—the way you used to do." Sean gave him a smile. "I remember when you first started dating. My father was not too thrilled with you, Ryan. He knew about your dad, knew you'd taken some hits, and he was afraid that you might take out your anger on Nicole."

"I know. Jack took me aside when Nic and I first started seeing each other and told me that if I ever hurt her, I'd have him to deal with. I told him I would never hurt her, but I broke that promise."

"Not in the way my father was worried about."

"No, but pain is pain. Jack was right to be concerned about the two of us together."

"No, he wasn't right, and Nicole told him so. It was the night before her high school graduation. I'd never heard her talk to my dad like that. You two wanted to take a trip that summer, and Jack was not happy about it. Nicole told him that she loved you, that you were the best man she'd ever known, and that she was going to marry you one day. She told him that he would need to change his attitude about you, because you were always going to be in her life." Sean gave him a smile. "My dad was stunned by her passion. I was impressed, too. I thought some day I'd like to have a woman stand up for me like that." He paused. "Nicole fought for you back then, Ryan. Maybe you need to fight for her now."

"I'm trying."

"Good. Because I've had a front row seat to the Ryan and Nicole show since I was thirteen years old, and I want to see a happy ending."

"So do I."

Nicole came into the living room with a bottle of water in her hand. She'd barely sat down on the couch when Jessica came flying into the room with her phone in hand, and a glitter of excitement in her eyes.

"I just heard from Kara," Jessica said. "The woman who made the quilts for the boys is Marian Kelton."

Nicole jumped to her feet. "Does she live in town? Can we talk to her?"

"We can," Jessica said. "But I haven't told you the most

interesting or horrifying part yet, depending on how you look at it."

"What's that?" Ryan asked impatiently.

"Marian Kelton told Kara that the quilts were ordered by Paula Schilling—my mother-in-law."

Ryan was shocked. "Your mother-in-law? Are you serious?"

"Yes. I couldn't believe it, either."

"If that's true, then she had to know there were twins," Nicole said. "We need to talk to her. Where can we find her?"

Jessica glanced down at her watch. "She goes to the eleven o'clock church service every Sunday. It should be getting out in a few minutes."

"Then let's go to church," Nicole said.

—➤➤◄◄—

They piled into Ryan's car and headed across town. The church was set in a beautiful oasis of green lawns and sheltering trees. Just beyond the church property, Nicole could see the blue waters of the Pacific Ocean. It was a peaceful setting, but Nicole felt anything but peaceful. Her emotions were churning. She felt excited and nervous and terrified about where this new development might lead.

"Looks like a lot of people around here go to church," Sean commented as they found a spot in the crowded parking lot.

"They do," Jessica agreed. "I used to go with Travis, but since he died and we had the funeral in there, I haven't been able to make myself go back inside."

Nicole heard pain in Jessica's voice and was reminded that Jessica had been hit hard with loss the past year, first her husband and now Kyle. It was a wonder she could get out of bed. But despite Jessica's quiet personality, it was clear there was a core of strength inside of her that kept her going through the hard times.

"You don't have to go in now," Nicole said.

"I wasn't planning on it," Jessica said. "Although I feel a little guilty about missing this particular service. Andrew told me he was going to lead a special prayer for the boys, and I probably should have forced myself to go. Andrew Schilling is the minister, and also Travis's cousin," Jessica explained. "He's been very supportive, but it's been difficult to be around Paula and the rest of Travis's family. Anyway, Paula will be one of the last ones out. She always sits in the front row with her sister, Andrew's mother, and they usually leave last."

They walked through the parking lot, pausing under a tree at the edge of the lawn as the church doors opened and the congregation began to spill out.

"There she is," Jessica said, pointing to a tall, brown-haired woman leaving the church with the minister.

Nicole led the way across the grass, Ryan, Jessica and Sean on her heels.

When they were a few feet away, Paula Schilling looked up and saw them. Her gaze settled on Jessica, and she visibly stiffened.

"What's happened?" she asked. "Has Kyle been found?"

"Not yet," Jessica replied. "We need to speak to you. These are the Prescotts—

the parents and uncle of Kyle's brother Brandon. Paula Schilling, Andrew Schilling," she added quickly, finishing off the introductions.

Paula stiffened. "What can I do to help?"

"Kyle received a quilt when he was a baby," Jessica said. "I was told that you ordered that quilt, and not just that quilt, but a second one as well. Why did you order two quilts for one baby? Did you know Kyle had a twin?"

Shock passed through Paula's eyes. "What? What are you

talking about?"

"You heard me," Jessica said forcefully. "The quilts. Explain why you ordered two."

Paula drew her head up and gave Jessica a stern look. "I ordered two quilts, because I wanted to have a replacement. When Travis was little, he had a blanket that he adored. He carried it around everywhere, but one day it was left behind at a park, and Travis was devastated. He cried for days. I didn't want the same thing to happen to Kyle, so I ordered a backup. Now what's all this about?"

"The second quilt ended up with my son," Nicole said. "If you simply ordered one as a spare, how do you explain that?"

"I have no idea. I haven't thought about those quilts in years. Why are they important now?"

"Because if you knew there were twins, then you probably knew the identity of the biological parents," Nicole said. "And the police believe the birth parents may be involved in the kidnapping."

Paula stared back at her with anger in her eyes. Was it a cover for knowledge or guilt? Nicole couldn't tell.

"I don't know anything about the biological parents," Paula said. "And I don't know how the second quilt ended up with your son. When I heard Travis and Sharon were getting a baby, I ordered the quilts because they're an Angel's Bay tradition. I don't recall what happened to them after they were delivered. I wish I could help, believe me. I adore Kyle. He's my grandson, and I want him to come home. He never should have been in a position where he could get taken by a stranger." She tossed her last statement in Jessica's direction.

Jessica stiffened but didn't try to defend herself. Instead, she said, "You were very close to Travis, Paula. Is it possible he thought he might be getting two children and that's why you ordered two quilts? Did something happen to change that? Was he concerned about adopting twins? Maybe he thought two children would be too much for Sharon?"

"No, he never suggested any of that," Paula said flatly. "I don't know where you get your ideas, Jessica. I already told you why I ordered two quilts." She pressed a hand to her temple. "This is very upsetting. I feel a little dizzy." She turned to her nephew. "Andrew, would you drive me home now?"

"Of course," Andrew said. He gave the group a compassionate smile. "We're praying for Kyle and Brandon. Please let me know if there's anything else I can do to help."

"Well, you weren't exaggerating," Sean said as the Schillings left. "Your mother-in-law is a mean old bitch. But you stood up to her."

"She pissed me off," Jessica said. "And I don't think she was telling us the whole truth."

"I agree," Nicole said. "She was cagey, choosing her words carefully."

"Exactly," Ryan said with a nod. "As if she was trying not to get caught in a lie."

"We should talk to Marian Kelton," Nicole said. "Maybe she will have a better recollection of the order. Do you have her number, Jessica?"

"I can get it from Kara."

As Jessica reached for her phone, Ryan's phone began to ring.

He stepped a few feet away to answer, and Nicole followed.

"Max," Ryan said. "What's up?" He paused. "Thank God." He reached out a hand to Nicole and she grabbed it, wondering if Max had found Brandon.

"Can you text me the address?" Ryan asked. "I know the police are on it, but that's only a few hours from here, and maybe the mother will give us more information because we're not cops." He listened for another moment, then released Nicole's hand to text himself a note. "Thanks." He ended the call and said, "They got the birth certificate and the name of the biological mother. No father was listed."

"What is the mother's name?" she asked, feeling both excited and fearful. Brandon's biological mother had always been a ghostly figure, a threat in the beginning, someone who might change her mind, and then as time went on, she'd just disappeared. Now the ghost was about to get a name.

"Andrea Holt. Before you get too excited, they haven't been able to locate her."

"Why not?"

"I don't know, but they have found Andrea's parents."

"Brandon's biological grandparents?"

Ryan's jaw tightened. "Yes. Andrea's mother, Carole, told the police that she hasn't seen her daughter in three years and has no idea where she is. She said that her daughter has had substance abuse issues for a long time and could be homeless."

"That doesn't sound good," she muttered.

"Carole and her husband live in Beverly Hills. Both police departments have spoken to her on the phone, and Inspector DeCarlo is catching a plane out this afternoon to meet with her in person.

"We're going to Beverly Hills," she said, not making it a question—because there was no question. They were only a few hours from L.A. They might even be able to beat Inspector DeCarlo to the house. But even if they didn't, it didn't matter. She had to meet Brandon's biological grandparents. She had to know what they knew.

"What's going on?" Jessica interrupted, as she and Sean joined them.

"The police got the birth certificate unsealed," Nicole said, repeating the information Ryan had given her. "Ryan and I want to drive down to L.A. and meet Carole Holt. Hopefully, she can help lead us to her daughter."

"Should I come?" Jessica asked.

"If you want to, sure."

"I just told Marian Kelton that we'd be over to her house in a few minutes. Maybe we don't need her information anymore," Jessica said. "We already know that Paula ordered the quilts."

"We should still talk to Marian," Ryan said. "She might be able to refute Paula's explanation or point us in another direction. We may have the biological grandmother, but we don't have the birth mother. Marian might have some clue that would help us. I think we should split up and follow both leads at the same time."

"That makes sense," Jessica said. "You two should meet the biological grandmother. You have a longer history with Brandon than I have with Kyle, and you were the ones who arranged the adoption, so it's logical that you should speak to her. I can talk to Marian, and my mother-in-law again, if I have to."

"I'll stay here with Jessica," Sean offered. "You two don't need me, and I don't want Jessica to have to deal with the monster-in-law on her own."

Nicole nodded, pleased to have a plan worked out so quickly. She hadn't wanted to waste time deciding who should do what, but she really did want to be the one to speak to Carole Holt.

They got back into Ryan's car and drove to Jessica's house. After Sean and Jessica left the car, Nicole looked over at Ryan. There was hope in his eyes, and she felt the same sense of optimism.

"We have the grandmother," she said.

"Yes, we do." He leaned over and gave her a quick kiss. "And soon we're going to have our son."

Sixteen

—→➤➤◄◄←—

"Thanks for staying," Jessica told Sean as they walked toward Sean's van. "I hope I made the right decision staying here instead of going with them."

"You did."

He put a hand on her arm, and she felt a tingle run down her spine. It was a weird, unexpected feeling. She'd been numb for almost a year, but suddenly she wasn't. She didn't know what to think about that. In fact, she didn't really know what to think about Sean. He was a stranger in so many ways, and yet he also felt like a friend.

"I know why you let them go on their own, Jess."

"What do you mean, you know why?"

"You didn't adopt Kyle at birth, and I think deep down you feel that because you haven't had Kyle as long, you're not as *real* a mother as Nicole is. But that isn't true, and you have to stop thinking that way."

She was shocked at how well he'd read her. She didn't know what to say.

Sean shrugged. "Or I could be wrong."

"You're not wrong," she said after a minute. "I do feel a little like an imposter sometimes."

"You have to remember that your husband chose you to be Kyle's mother. It's tragic that he died so young and left you and Kyle on your own. But if I were him, I'd be happy that the woman I loved was raising my kid. And from everything you've told me about Kyle and your lives over the past year, I think you're doing a good job."

She blinked back a tear at the kind words. "Stop, you're going to make me cry."

"I was trying to make you smile," he said dryly. "I never seem to get it right with women."

"You got it right. Thanks." Sean had reminded her of something she'd forgotten—that Travis had chosen to marry her. And he had thought she was a good mother. Sure, he'd laughed at her a few times in the beginning when she'd fumbled things, because she hadn't really been around kids before Kyle. She'd been an only child, and she'd never done much babysitting, so meeting Kyle as a four-year-old and having to learn how to deal with him had been an eye-opener.

But she and Kyle had forged a bond. And since Travis had died, they'd gotten really, really close. Kyle called her *Mommy*. And Kyle's opinion was really the only one that mattered.

"So where are we going?" Sean asked, as they got into his van.

"A few miles from here. Marian lives on the outside of town."

"Tell me where to go."

"I will. I appreciate your support, Sean. You don't judge, and I like that."

"I've been judged a lot in my life. I try not to return that favor, if I can help it."

"I guess all artists get judged."

"I wasn't talking just about my music. My family has been fairly critical of my choices the last few years. The Callaways have a longstanding tradition of serving the community. It started like five generations ago. My father, grandfather, great-grandfather and great-great-grandfather all served in the San Francisco Fire Department. My brothers Burke and Colton are firefighters. Aiden was a smokejumper up until last year."

"I take it you didn't want to be a firefighter."

"No. Nor a helicopter pilot like my brother Drew or a doctor like Shayla or a teacher like Nicole. They're all doing important things with their lives. They help people. They serve the community. I serve myself."

She had a feeling he was echoing someone else's words. "Your music isn't just for you. I'm sure you entertain people and make them feel better for a little while."

"According to my father, entertainment is not service. I should be helping people, giving back to the world, making it a better place, and not thinking only of myself."

"Maybe you should take your own advice and not let other people's opinions define your life," she said pointedly.

He grinned. "Easier to give advice than to take it. My father is not completely wrong. I do live for myself. I don't have anyone else to worry about, and I like it that way. I go where I want, when I want. No responsibilities, no commitment. What could be better?"

She was a little disappointed in his words. Now he sounded like a lot of guys she'd met, especially the ones who ran through Vegas for a weekend of parties and fun. But despite Sean's candor, she didn't believe he was as selfish as he painted himself.

"Sean?"

He turned to look at her. "What?"

"You're helping me, and I'm a total stranger. I don't think you've strayed as far away from the Callaway traditions as you think."

He shrugged. "I didn't have anything else to do this weekend. Believe me when I tell you that I am nobody's hero.

Anyone who tries to make me into one will be very disappointed. I know my limitations. And everyone else finds out eventually."

There was a dark edge to his tone. Sean might be easygoing on the surface, but he obviously had some secrets. But those secrets were none of her business. He'd be gone in a day or two. He was just a stranger passing through, and she'd had plenty of those in her life.

"You know I'm going to keep driving straight until you tell me to turn," Sean said.

"Sorry." She sat up straighter in her seat, realizing she'd lost track of what they were supposed to be doing. "Turn left at the next corner. Marian's house will be a few blocks down. Hopefully, she'll be home."

Ten minutes later, Jessica rang the bell at Marian Kelton's house. The older woman opened the door with a smile.

Marian was a short, plump woman with red hair and freckles that mixed with the lines on her aging face. She had to be in her seventies, but she had a lively sparkle in her green eyes.

"Come in. Come in. Can I get you something to eat or drink? Tea? Cookies?" Marian asked as they entered her house.

"No thanks," Jessica said. "We just have a few questions if you don't mind."

"Oh, of course not. I've been worried sick about that little boy of yours. And when Kara told me about the other child, I was flabbergasted. Who would have ever imagined that Kyle had a twin brother?" Marian motioned them toward the living room. "Let's sit down so we can chat."

As they took a seat on the red sofa, Jessica glanced around the colorfully decorated room, taking note of the beautiful wall-hanging quilt and another smaller quilt tossed over the side of an armchair. Marian obviously spent a lot of time at the sewing machine.

"So what else can I tell you?" Marian asked. "You already know that Paula was the one who ordered the quilts. I didn't realize that was a secret or important in any way until Kara called me."

"It's important because Paula ordered two quilts when Travis was only adopting one baby," Jessica said. "My mother-in-law explained that she ordered two so she would have a backup. But to be honest, I'm not sure that's true. I was wondering what she told you, if you remember?"

Marian nodded. "I remember everything. Paula did tell me she wanted a backup, but I did find it strange that she wanted one detail on the quilts to be different."

"The birds. Kyle's quilt has one and Brandon's has two."

"Exactly. I guess Paula thought that would be a subtle way to tell them apart. I didn't ask, because Paula doesn't like to explain herself. She's been that way since she was a little girl."

"You've known her that long?" Sean asked.

"Since kindergarten," Marian said with a nod. "And let me tell you, Paula was bossy when she was five. She used to rule our group of girls like she was the queen and we were her servants."

Jessica didn't think that Paula had changed much since she was five. She still liked to be in charge, and everyone had to dance to her tune. "Since you knew Paula, you must have known Travis as well," she said.

"Oh, sure, and Sharon, too." Marian's face softened. "But I won't talk about her if it's too painful for you."

"It's not painful. I know Travis loved Sharon and that she

died too young."

"She did," Marian agreed. "It was so sad. She'd just gotten everything she ever wanted—a child—and she didn't get to see him grow up. It was heartbreaking. And Travis was grief-stricken for months after her death."

Jessica frowned, Marian's words more painful than she'd expected. She turned the conversation back to the quilts. "Do you remember when Paula ordered the quilts, how long before Travis and Sharon got Kyle?"

"I think it was about a month before Kyle was born." Marian replied. "I remember worrying that something might go wrong. Travis and Sharon had had another adoption fall through at the last minute. They were on the way to the hospital when they got a call from a social worker saying the adoption was off. That was about eight or nine months before they got Kyle. Everyone had their fingers crossed that the same thing wouldn't happen again."

Travis had never told her anything about that baby, Jessica realized. He'd been open and up front about his love for Sharon and their desire to have children, but he hadn't gone into detail about their adoption struggles, and she hadn't asked. That part of his life didn't belong to her, and she hadn't really wanted to think that much about his first love.

"Was there any mention of Kyle's biological parents?" Sean interjected. "Did Paula share any details about who the mother was?"

"No, she didn't say anything about the birth parents to me. Maybe you should try talking to Paula again. I know she can be difficult, but she loves Kyle, and I can't see why she would keep any secrets that might bring Kyle home."

"I can't, either," Jessica said. "But I do think she's keeping a secret, and I need to figure out what it is."

"Well, unless she's willing to tell you, I doubt you'll figure it out," Marian said. "When Paula wants to keep a secret, she keeps it. In fact, sometimes she holds that secret over you. She used to do that to me when we were in high school. I remember one time I had a mad crush on this boy named Eric. Paula told me he liked someone else, but she wouldn't say who it was. She used to drive me crazy. Finally, she told me it was our other friend, Carole. I shouldn't have been surprised, because Carole always got a lot of attention from boys, but I was annoyed that Paula chose not to tell me." Marian stopped. "Good grief, I'm rambling on. What else can I tell you?"

Jessica frowned, the name Carole running around in her head. Wasn't that the same name as the biological grandmother that Ryan and Nicole had gone to see? "Where does Carole live now?" she asked.

"In Los Angeles. She married a very wealthy man. We always knew she'd end up living the good life."

Jessica's nerves tightened. "Did she have any children?"

"One daughter. Why do you ask?"

"We've been trying to find Kyle's biological parents. The police have the name of the birth mother, Andrea Holt. And her mother's name is Carole Holt. I'm wondering if they're the same person."

Marian's eyebrows shot up in surprise. "Carole married Raymond Holt and had a daughter named Andrea. Are you telling me that Kyle is Carole's grandson?"

Jessica's stomach began to churn. "I think so," she murmured, turning to Sean. "We need to call Nicole and Ryan."

He nodded.

She glanced back to Marian. "Can I ask a favor?"

"Of course, dear. What is it?"

"Please don't tell Paula that we were here or that we've found a possible link between her friend Carole and Kyle." She didn't know how involved Paula was in anything, but if

Carole was truly Kyle's grandmother, then Jessica couldn't believe that Paula didn't know about it.

But why hadn't Paula said something when Kyle disappeared? And if not then, why hadn't she come forward when the news about Brandon came out? They might have had Kyle home by now, unless Paula was somehow involved?

That thought made her sick. Had her mother-in-law harbored such hatred for Jessica as a mother that she'd had her own grandson kidnapped to get him away from her?

No, that was ludicrous, she told herself. Paula wouldn't go that far. Would she?

Seventeen

❯❯❮❮

It was a three-hour drive from Angel's Bay to Los Angeles, and after an hour in the car, Nicole was feeling impatient and frustrated. Judging by the speed at which Ryan was driving, he was as eager as she was to get to the end of their journey. She braced her hand on the side of the car as Ryan sped around a slow, lumbering truck.

He shot her a quick look. "Sorry, that truck was making me crazy."

"I completely understand." She was more than a little happy to have left the truck behind. "But we can't afford a speeding ticket or an accident right now."

He eased his foot off the gas pedal. "I just want to get there already, and I'm used to flying. If there had been an airport in Angel's Bay, I would have gotten us a plane."

"And I would have been happy to get on board. This drive seems endless."

He gave her an understanding smile. "We're halfway there, so it won't be too much longer."

She glanced out the window, watching the scenery fly by. So much had happened in the last few days, so many huge life changes, and probably the biggest change was her relationship with Ryan.

A week ago she'd thought that they were done, that Ryan

was out of her life forever, that their past love was a faded memory.

But there was nothing faded about Ryan now. He'd come back to her in vibrant color, reminding her not only of the man he used to be but also the woman she used to be.

They'd broken down the walls between them and realized that they'd gotten lost in the details of their life—the big picture completely forgotten. Now they could move past the blame and pull away the curtain of resentment. They could see each other again, the way they really were. And the truth was that they'd always been a good team when they worked together, when they balanced Ryan's logic with her passion, his realism with her optimism, his desire to fly and her desire to make sure they also had roots, a home, and family.

And then there was the undeniable chemistry between them.

She'd pushed Ryan away the past year, because making love with him always opened up her emotions and took her to an incredible level of need and desire. She felt vulnerable in his arms, and she couldn't feel vulnerable and deal with Brandon's illness. So Ryan had been the one to shove aside.

It hadn't been fair to either of them. She'd punished herself as much as Ryan, because she'd missed their intimacy. Tears pricked at her eyes. Ryan was truly the love of her life. She'd known it when she was seventeen, and she knew it now. What she didn't know was how they could make it work.

Right now they were alone; it was just the two of them again. But when Brandon came home, when they got their son back, all the old problems would return as well.

Brandon wasn't going to be miraculously cured. He might even be worse.

"Nicole?"

"Yes?" she asked, not looking at him, not wanting him to

see the moisture in her eyes.

"Why are you crying?"

"I'm not."

"I know the way you breathe when you're trying to keep it together. Your breath comes short and fast and a little ragged, and every now and then you draw in a bigger breath and then let out a sigh."

His words brought her head around, and she stared at him in amazement. "Seriously? You know how I breathe when I'm trying not to cry?"

His eyes were dark and tender as he said, "I know everything about you, Nic. So there's really no point in trying to hide from me. I don't even know why you feel you need to. When you're hurting, I hurt, too. And I want to fix things for you, just like you want to fix things for Brandon. We're not so different, babe."

"I guess not."

"So what's making you sad now?"

"I'm just feeling emotional. I'll be okay." She glanced down at her phone as it began to ring. "It's Jessica."

"Put it on speaker so I can hear."

She punched the button and said, "Hi, Jessica."

"Nicole, where are you?"

"We're about an hour outside of Los Angeles. I'm putting you on speaker."

"Okay. So, Sean and I just left Marian's house. You're not going to believe what we found out. The woman you're going to see, Carole Holt, grew up in Angel's Bay with Paula Schilling."

Nicole was shocked to learn that Paula Schilling and Carole Holt were friends. "That is unbelievable."

"Apparently, they were best friends when they were younger but had some falling out years ago. Marian Kelton can't imagine why Carole would give Paula one of her grandchildren, but it looks like that's exactly what she did. We still don't know why she split up the twins, though."

"Your mother-in-law has known all along that Carole is the biological grandmother?" Nicole asked. "That means she also knew about Andrea." She couldn't believe that Paula Schilling had kept such an important secret.

"Yes. She lied to our faces this morning," Jessica said angrily. "She knew we were looking for the birth parents. She could have told us days ago that Andrea was the mother of the boys."

"I wonder why she didn't. It doesn't make sense. She loves her grandson, doesn't she?"

"Sean suggested that Paula might have wanted to use Kyle's kidnapping as a way to discredit me," Jessica said. "Maybe sue for custody. It's hard to believe that she would hate me that much, but I need to confront her."

"Don't do that yet," Ryan interrupted.

"Why not?" Jessica asked.

"Yes, why not?" Nicole echoed, giving Ryan a questioning look.

"We don't want Paula to alert Carole Holt that we're on to her. As far as Paula knows, we're still in the dark about the identity of the birth mother. I think we should keep it that way for the time being," Ryan said.

"All right," Jessica said slowly. "That makes sense. I'll hold off. Call us as soon as you talk to Carole."

"We will," Nicole promised. As she disconnected the call, she glanced at Ryan. "This just gets crazier and crazier. What do you think?"

"That we may have only hit the tip of the iceberg."

"Now, I really wonder why Brandon and Kyle were separated. Wouldn't Carole and Paula have wanted the boys together?"

"It doesn't make sense, but I can't say I'm sorry that they

separated the boys. We wouldn't have gotten Brandon if they hadn't split them up. Maybe that's selfish, but that's the way I feel."

"I feel that way, too." She liked the fierce love in Ryan's voice, and she was once again reminded of the past—the first night with their son. She'd been sitting in the rocking chair, with Brandon in her arms, and Ryan had squatted down in front of them, putting his hand on Brandon's tiny head. Ryan had sworn that he would love Brandon and her every day for the rest of his life.

She didn't even bother to hide the fact that she was tearing up again. Ryan was right. They didn't need pretense between them. She wiped her eyes with her fingers and gave him a watery smile. "I was just thinking about how happy we were when we got Brandon. He was all of our dreams come true."

"And you don't have a secret wish that we'd gotten Kyle instead?"

The question stabbed her right in the heart. It was the elephant in the room that no one had wanted to mention, but now that Ryan had said the words, the answer was so obvious.

"Not for a second. Brandon is our son. I wish he didn't have to suffer the way he does. I wish that he could have all the joys his brother has, but I wouldn't trade him for a second. I mean that, Ryan." She paused. "I was shaken up when I first saw Kyle, when I heard his voice, when I realized that we'd gotten the twin with all the problems, and maybe there was a brief moment when I wondered why. But I know why. We were meant to be Brandon's parents. That's the plan for him and for us. And I'm good with it." She blew out a breath, realizing how much better she felt saying that out loud. "I'm really good with it. I don't think I knew how good until this second. Brandon is our kid, and he sure as hell doesn't belong to Carole or Andrea or anyone else, and I can't wait to tell them all that."

→→◄◄←

An hour later they exited the freeway and Nicole consulted the map on her phone for directions. "There it is— Sycamore Drive. Turn right. Her house should be a few blocks down."

As they passed by beautiful mansions set back from the street, Nicole felt as if she'd entered a different world, a world that was very quiet. Many of the properties were imprisoned behind iron gates and security cameras. "I wonder how many secrets are behind those gates," she muttered.

"Probably more than you can imagine," Ryan said.

She glanced at him. "It's weird to think that Brandon was born into money. I always assumed that his mother was some poor teenager who couldn't take care of her child."

"Maybe her parents were unwilling to help her. I think you should take the lead with Carole, Nicole. Talk to her mother-to-mother. You're better at winning people over than I am. We need Carole to be our ally, someone who can help us find her daughter and her grandchildren."

Ryan was right, but there was a part of Nicole that rebelled against the idea of Carole Holt being her son's *grandmother*. Jack and Lynda were Brandon's grandparents. They had been present for all of the big moments in Brandon's life—not this woman, this stranger.

But she had to keep her eye on the big picture, and getting Carole Holt on their side would help them get to the kids that much faster.

"There it is," she said, happy to see there were no locked gates or security cameras in front of Carole's house.

The home was a large, two-story manor with a circular drive in the front. The landscaping was lush and beautiful with a small fountain in a corner of the front yard.

As Ryan parked the car, a silver Mercedes passed them and turned into the drive, stopping near the front door.

"Is that her?" Ryan asked.

"Let's find out."

They walked quickly down the drive. The thin, blonde, middle-aged woman was too distracted with her grocery bags to see them approach.

"Carole Holt?" Nicole asked.

The woman jumped in surprise. "Who are you? What do you want?"

"I'm Nicole Prescott, and this is my husband Ryan. We're the parents of a six-year-old boy who was kidnapped a few days ago. His name is Brandon."

Carole's face paled. "I already spoke to the police."

"Then you know that your daughter Andrea is Brandon's biological mother. And I'm sure they told you about Kyle, Brandon's twin. He's also missing."

"I don't know where Andrea is. I haven't seen her in several years, but I don't believe she had anything to do with this kidnapping. My daughter is a drug addict. She can barely take care of herself, much less anyone else. The idea that she could plan some elaborate kidnapping is unbelievable." Carole shook her head. "Someone else must have done it."

"What about the biological father?" Nicole asked. "Do you know who he is?"

"No, I don't. Andrea never said." She took a breath. "I'm very sorry about the children. But I really don't think my daughter is involved. I need to go inside. My ice cream is melting."

"Let me carry that for you," Ryan said, grabbing the remaining bag off the back seat.

Carole frowned. "I can handle it myself."

"We want to talk to you about your daughter, Mrs. Holt,"

Ryan said firmly. "You may not believe she had anything to do with kidnapping our son, but the police think she's involved. Wouldn't it be better for your daughter if we found her first, instead of the cops? It doesn't sound like Andrea needs the police coming down on her. We don't care what Andrea is involved in. We just want to get our child back, and we believe your daughter either has the kids or knows who does."

Carole gave Ryan a long look and then slowly nodded. "All right. I can give you a few minutes, but that's all. My husband Philip will be home from his golf game soon, and he doesn't allow anyone to talk about Andrea in his presence."

"Is that because of her drug addiction?" Nicole asked as they followed Carole up the drive.

"Among other things."

When they entered the house, Nicole was more than a little impressed by the beauty of the home. The entry boasted marble floors, dark wood paneling and a beautiful glass chandelier. The huge living room was decorated with large white furniture, glass tables, and what looked to be expensive art on the walls. The adjacent dining room was just as grand and very formal, with a long mahogany table and twelve chairs.

This was a house for entertaining, for showing off, Nicole thought, but it didn't feel lived in or even very personal.

They entered the kitchen, and Carole set the grocery bags down on a large center island topped with beautiful sparkling granite. She pulled out a few perishable items, including a carton of ice cream, and set them in the freezer. The she motioned them towards a large table in a windowed nook overlooking a garden and a pool.

As they sat down at the table, Carole drew in a deep breath and clasped her hands together. "This is so strange. I never thought I would ever meet you. The adoption was supposed to be closed. No contact from us. No contact from you. It was going to be easier that way. Which—which boy did you say is yours?" Carole asked, then quickly put up a hand. "Actually, I don't want to know. It doesn't matter."

"Our son is Brandon," Nicole said. "When was the last time you saw the twins?"

"I suppose it was the day of their birth. They had blue eyes, just like their mother."

"Why did Andrea give up the boys for adoption?" Nicole continued.

"Her father insisted. Andrea was fifteen years old and six months pregnant when she finally came to us. It was too late for an abortion by then, but she was too young to be a mother. I considered allowing her and the baby to live here—we didn't realize there were twins at the time—but my husband was not interested in raising more children. He was so angry with Andrea. She had disappointed him, and he wanted nothing to do with her. He told Andrea she would have to give up her baby for adoption. I couldn't persuade him to change his mind. Andrea didn't think I tried hard enough, and maybe I didn't, because part of me thought he was right."

"I wanted Andrea to have her own life," Carole continued. "I thought being a mother would hold her back. There would be no opportunity for her to go away to college, no wonderful career to embark upon." She uttered a bitter laugh. "Not that giving away the boys made any of that come true."

"So Andrea didn't go to college?" Nicole asked. Now that they had Carole talking, she wanted to learn as much as possible about Brandon's birth mother.

"Andrea dropped out of high school her senior year. Giving away the babies broke her in some way. She never recovered from the loss, and her friends were terrible people.

They got her into drugs. Once she started, she couldn't stop. I tried to help her. I paid for rehab three different times. She'd stay clean for a while, then go back to the drugs. She said she needed the high so she could look herself in the mirror. She felt horribly guilty about giving up her children. We underestimated how hard it would be for her to go on without them."

Nicole frowned, not liking the idea that Andrea had been somewhat coerced into giving up her babies. She didn't want there to be any type of technical reason that might allow Andrea to get her children back.

"Those first two days after the birth were the hardest," Carole added. "Andrea cried for hours. She kept asking for the boys, begging me to bring them to her. My heart broke for her. But it was too late. The boys had already been taken from the hospital. I tried to reassure her that the children were in a good home, that they would have a good life, but she couldn't hear me. She couldn't stand that their life wouldn't be with her."

"Why didn't she try to stop the adoption?" Ryan asked, a grim note in his voice.

"She couldn't. She'd already signed the papers. Everything was done. The boys were gone, and we didn't know where they were."

"But that's not true," Nicole said. "You knew where Kyle was, because he was adopted by Travis Schilling, the son of your good friend Paula."

Carole's eyes widened. "How do you know that?"

"Marian Kelton," Nicole replied. "She told us that you and Paula were friends."

"Marian was always a big gossip," Carole said with a sigh.

"We put the rest of the story together," Nicole continued. "But what we don't understand is why the kids were separated."

"That was Philip's idea," Carole said. "Originally, the boys were going to be together. Paula had told me about the trouble that Travis and his wife had had adopting a child. I knew they would be good parents, so I told Paula that we should try to work something out. But that it had to be a secret, because Philip didn't want to know where the kids were going, and, of course, he didn't want Andrea to know. I was working with the lawyer at that point, so we kept it amongst the three of us. Unfortunately, Philip found out, and he was furious. He wanted the kids with strangers on the other side of the country. He was worried that Andrea might go looking for them. Eventually, he agreed to go along with the adoption as long as Travis only took one child and the other boy went to another family."

"How did Paula react when you told her Travis was only getting one boy?" Nicole asked.

"She was angry, but it was one or none, and she wanted Travis to have a chance to be a father."

Nicole sat back in her seat, digesting everything Carole had said. One thing was clear—it was only by the slightest chance that they'd gotten Brandon.

"Tell me something, Mrs. Holt," Ryan said. "Did you and Philip enjoy playing God?"

Carole flinched. "We didn't think of it that way."

"You didn't?" he challenged. "You split up identical twin brothers. You lied to your daughter about where her children were."

"Both boys were going to have a better life," Carole said. "And two families were going to have children. Everyone would win."

"Except for Andrea," Nicole said, feeling sorry for the fifteen-year-old girl who'd been railroaded into giving up her babies by her domineering parents.

"Yes," Carole agreed. "I truly thought Andrea would move on with her life and that she would have more children, but instead she spun out of control. I wish I could turn back time and make different decisions, but I can't. You may not believe this, but I still love my daughter very much, and I would do anything to help her feel better."

"Have you looked for her?" Nicole asked. "You have plenty of money. Why not hire a private investigator?"

Carole gave her a sad smile. "I've had investigators drag Andrea home twice, and she was barely in the house before she was out again. She wanted nothing to do with us." Carole paused. "When I first got pregnant, I dreamt about having a little girl, a sweet daughter who would wear pink dresses and let me French braid her hair. We'd go shopping together and have lunch, and we'd be best friends as well as mother and daughter. But Andrea was not that girl. She hated pink, didn't like to shop or do her hair. She was a tomboy and a rebel and we didn't understand each other at all. When she reached puberty, she became uncontrollable, breaking rules, drinking, staying out until all hours of the night, and having sex with boys she barely knew. I didn't know how to make any of it stop. And I couldn't spend all my time on Andrea. My husband needed me, too. I had to make difficult choices. I wish I'd been a better mother, but I did the best I could."

Nicole didn't think Carole's best had been that good, but then she hadn't walked in Carole's shoes, so how could she criticize? "You mentioned that Andrea had sex with different boys. You must have had some theory as to who the father of her children was."

"Andrea said she didn't know who it was, that there had been several boys. She loved telling me things like that. She knew it would hurt me." Carole cleared her throat. "There were a couple of boys that she spent time with that summer— Devon Bolles and Malcolm Segal. Neither one of them came forward when the babies were born, so I have no idea if either was involved with her in that way."

Nicole texted a note to herself to check into those two boys. They would be young men now, and maybe they would be willing to answer some questions.

"Are we about done?" Carole asked. "I want to be helpful, but I do have some things to take care of."

"I think we've got enough," Ryan said. "Would it be possible for me to use your bathroom before we leave? It's a long drive back to Angel's Bay."

"Of course. It's down the hall on the left."

He got to his feet. "Thanks, I'll be right back."

As Ryan left the room, Nicole drew Carole's attention back to her. "Where was your daughter when you saw her last?"

"In a run-down apartment in Hollywood. She called me asking for help, but when I arrived, all she wanted was money. I knew she'd spend it on drugs, so I said no." Carole shook her head, sadness in her gaze. "Andrea looked terrible, thin and fragile. I told her I'd drive her to rehab right then, but she just gave me this look of hopelessness and said, 'What's the point? Nothing can take the pain away.' I tried to tell her that things would get better, but she wouldn't hear me."

"Is it possible she's still in that apartment building? Can you give me the address?"

"I'm sure she was evicted. She had no money."

"But someone there might know where she is now."

Carole hesitated. "It was on Vermont Street. I think it was one-eleven, but it's been awhile."

Nicole jotted down the address. "What about Andrea's friends? There must be someone who keeps in touch with her."

"I don't know who her friends are anymore."

"Well, maybe the police will be able to track her down,"

Nicole said, frustrated with Carole's reticence. Or maybe the woman truly didn't know anything. She'd obviously lived a life of denial and pretense for a long time. She doubted any of Carole's friends knew anything about her daughter or the pregnancy or the twins. It would have been swept under the rug years ago.

"I gave the police the same information I just gave you," Carole said.

"What about your husband? Has he talked to the cops?"

"Not yet. An inspector said he would be by later this afternoon. I'm not looking forward to that. Philip doesn't care to acknowledge Andrea's existence any more."

"He doesn't care at all about what's happening with his daughter?" She thought Philip sounded like a cold, ruthless person.

"I think he does care, somewhere down deep," Carole said. "But he doesn't let anyone see it, not even me. We don't talk about Andrea in this house. We haven't said her name in probably five or six years. I'm sure you don't understand that. Unless you've had to deal with someone who has an addiction, it's impossible to know how difficult it is. Andrea is a different person on drugs. She's not herself."

"It doesn't sound like she got along that well with you and your husband when she was herself."

"I suppose that's true." Carole sighed. "I really wish everything had gone differently. Andrea deserved to have a better life than the one she has, and believe me when I say I know I'm not blameless. Being a mother is the hardest job I ever had."

Nicole could relate to that even if she couldn't relate to much else that Carole had said.

Ryan reentered the kitchen and said, "Ready to go?"

"I guess." She was reluctant to leave Carole, feeling like she was the closest link to Andrea, but Carole was already standing up, and it was clear she was done with their conversation.

When they reached the front door, Carole said, "I really hope the boys are all right. Perhaps you could let me know when you find them."

"Sure," Nicole said.

"Thanks," Ryan said to Carole. "We appreciate your help."

"I only wish I could help more," she said, then shut the door behind them.

Nicole frowned as she followed Ryan down to the car, wondering why Ryan had suddenly been so nice to Carole. His mood seemed to have changed between the time he'd left the kitchen and come back.

"Ryan," she began.

"Get in the car," he said, a sparkle in his eyes.

"Okay, I'm in," she said, as she got into her seat and closed the door. "What's going on?"

"I made a side trip through Carole's study on the way to the bathroom, and I found a flyer for the Serenity Healing Center on top of a pile of papers. I did a search on my phone and found out it's a drug rehab and psychiatric clinic in Santa Monica. I'm thinking maybe Andrea made one of her stops in rehab there." He turned the key in the ignition. "I think we should go there and see if anyone has any information on Andrea. It's another long shot, but it's not that far away, so we might as well check it out."

"Sounds good to me. I wasn't ready to go back to Angel's Bay yet." She looked up the Serenity Healing Center on her phone. "I've got directions. We need to get on the freeway. Turn right at the next light. Then drive about a mile, and we should see the on-ramp."

"Got it." As he pulled away from the curb, he said, "Did Carole tell you anything else while I was in the bathroom?"

"She gave me the address of where Andrea was living when she saw her a few years ago. We can check that out after we go to the rehab center." She thought about everything they'd learned in the past hour. "It's weird how we almost didn't get Brandon, isn't it? Sometimes, one random decision can change your whole life."

"And not just your life, but a lot of other people's lives. A fifteen-year-old girl has unprotected sex and becomes pregnant, and look how many people have been affected by that one, probably impulsive, moment."

"Yeah. It sounds like Andrea suffered a lot when she gave up the kids." She glanced at Ryan. "I didn't want it to be that way. I didn't want to become a mother at someone else's expense. I didn't want our joy to be the result of someone else's heartbreak."

"We didn't know, Nicole. All we knew was that we were going to give Brandon a good home, and that's what we did. You need to keep your eye on the ball."

She smiled at his sports metaphor. "Don't worry, my eye is still on the ball."

"Good, because it sounded like you were feeling a little sorry for Andrea. And it's more than likely she's the one who kidnapped our boy."

"I know. I get it. We find her, we find them."

Eighteen

—➤➤◆◆◆—

On their way to the healing center, Ryan got a call from Chief Silveira. He put it on speaker so that Nicole could hear their conversation.

"We believe we located the owner of the pen that was depicted in your son's drawing," the chief said.

Ryan shot Nicole a quick look, then said. "Who's that?"

"Jonathan Haywood. His parents own Haywood Plumbing. Jonathan is twenty-six years old, and the third of their five children. He's been in and out of trouble and rehab the past five years. He works at the company sporadically, but last month he said he was quitting for good. He had a better opportunity."

"How do you know he's the owner of the pen?" Ryan asked. "It sounds like there are a lot of Haywoods. Although Carole Holt told us that Andrea has been involved with drugs, so there's a connection."

"I've got a better one," the chief said. "I spoke to Beverly Haywood, Jonathan's mother. She told me that the Holts lived next door to them for twelve years when they lived in North Hollywood. Beverly Haywood was best friends with Carole Holt, and her daughter Kelly was good friends with Andrea.

"That's definitely a link," Ryan muttered.

"Yes. The Holts moved to Beverly Hills when Andrea

and Kelly were about fourteen, and after that the Haywoods saw little of them. Beverly said that she was hurt that Carole didn't keep in touch, but she knew that Philip controlled a lot of his wife's time, and they were moving up in the world."

"Philip sounds like a hell of a guy," Ryan said dryly, thinking about the man who had forced his daughter to give up her kids and apparently kept his wife on a tight rein as well.

"We haven't been able to speak to him yet," Chief Silveira said. "But he's on the list."

"You still haven't told us why you think Jonathan is the owner of the pen," Ryan said. "It was his sister that was friends with Andrea, right?"

"Yes, but the families were close, and Beverly said that Andrea and Jonathan used to go to concerts together. However, what really points to Jonathan is the statement I got from his roommate. He said that Jonathan called him from Santa Barbara a few days ago and said he was going to move to Florida with his girlfriend. That he was going to finally get what was due to him. That was a direct quote."

"The Florida license plates," Nicole muttered.

He met her gaze and his jaw tightened. "How long will it take for you to bring in Haywood?"

"We're working on it right now. Where are you two?"

"We just left Carole Holt's house," Ryan replied, filling the chief in on the information Carole had given them, including her relationship to Paula Schilling.

"Sounds like I need to have another chat with Paula," the chief said. "I can't believe she's been sitting on this information with her grandson's life in the balance. Keep in touch."

"We will," Ryan promised. After disconnecting the call, he looked at Nicole. "What do you think?"

Her eyes sparkled with excitement. "I know it's a leap,

but I think that Andrea and this Haywood guy kidnapped the boys."

"It's certainly looking that way," he conceded. "Maybe Haywood is the biological father."

"It's all adding up," she said. "Brandon's picture showed us the Florida license plates, the pen on the table. Santa Barbara is not very far from Angel's Bay. The Haywoods were close to the Holts. Jonathan and Andrea were friends, and they've both been involved in the drug scene. The puzzle is coming together."

He could see the excitement on her face, and he wanted to feel as optimistic as she did, but he wasn't quite sure they weren't still missing an important piece of information. "Let's see if the rehab center can give us another clue."

Ten minutes later they arrived at the Serenity Healing Center, which was a three-story building across the street from the Santa Monica beach and pier. It looked like a boutique hotel with views facing the ocean. Ryan thought it was just the kind of place a woman like Carole Holt would send her daughter for help. It was clean and upscale. One could almost pretend that they were on vacation or at a retreat instead of getting treated for a drug addiction.

"It's nice," Nicole said as they parked in a small lot behind the building. "Serene."

He smiled at the touch of sarcasm in her tone. "I was thinking the same thing. What better place for the drug addict daughter of a wealthy family to go?"

"Exactly, but I'm worried now that this kind of place probably gets celebrities and other people who are extremely private. They're not going to turn over Andrea's personal information to us. Should we call Chief Silveira or Max? Get them involved in this?" She paused. "I noticed you didn't mention our lead to Chief Silveira."

"We don't know if it is a lead yet. We can always call the

police after we check things out."

They got out of the car and walked across the lot. Ryan held the door open for Nicole, then followed her inside the building.

The lobby was beautiful. Along one wall was a gentle waterfall that ended in a swirling dark blue tiled pool of rippling water. Soft music played in the background, and the lighting was warm and muted. There were comfortable couches and chairs next to reading lamps and bookshelves. But there was no one sitting on those couches, no one reading any of the books. There was, however, a young woman sitting at a desk by the far window.

As they approached, the woman gave them a warm, welcoming look. She was probably in her mid-twenties, Ryan thought. He flashed her a smile, knowing that getting her on their side was probably the first step.

"Hello," he said.

"Hello," she replied. "Can I help you?"

"I hope so. We're trying to find a friend of ours. She disappeared a few weeks ago, and we think she might be here."

"I'm afraid I can't give out any information regarding our guests."

Ryan noted her deliberate use of the word *guest* when *patient* probably would have been a more accurate word.

"I completely understand," he said, stalling for time as he searched for the right words to say. "We wouldn't be here if we had another choice, but we have information regarding Andrea Holt's children, and she's been waiting for this news for a long time. We really need to find her. It's very important. If there's anything you can do to help us, we'd be extremely grateful."

The woman drew in a big breath, debate going on in her eyes. "Why don't I get the director for you? He can answer your questions."

"That would be great."

"Have a seat." As they moved toward the couches, she picked up the phone. "Dr. Robertson. There's someone here with information on Andrea Holt's children." She listened for a moment, then hung up the phone and turned to them. "He'll be right out."

"Nice," Nicole murmured as they sat down on the couch. "I haven't seen you use that kind of charm since you needed to talk Mrs. Mulligan into giving you a higher grade in physics so you could graduate on time."

He smiled. "I save it for when I need it."

She gave him a weak smile in return, but it was obvious her thoughts were somewhere else. He put a hand on her thigh, quieting the rapid tapping of her leg.

"You okay?" he asked.

"Just nervous, excited, worried."

"We're on to something here, Nicole. You heard the way she talked to the doctor; they know Andrea, they know about her children."

Nicole straightened. "That's true. You're right. She definitely recognized the name."

The ding of the elevator door interrupted their conversation. They both rose as a man stepped off and headed in their direction. He wore an expensive suit with a dress shirt and tie and was probably in his forties. He moved with a purpose and a confidence that suggested he was in charge.

"Hello," he said. "I'm Edward Robertson, the medical director of the center. And you are?"

"Ryan Prescott," he said, shaking the man's hand.

"And I'm Nicole Prescott," Nicole said as she also shook hands with the doctor.

"You've been asking about Andrea Holt?"

"Yes." As Ryan looked into the doctor's sharp gaze, he

knew that no amount of charm was going to sway this man. He decided to go with the truth. "I don't know how much you know about Andrea's background, but when she was a teenager she gave up two children for adoption. Nicole and I adopted one of her twin boys when he was four days old. He's six now, and his name is Brandon." A knot grew in Ryan's throat as the image of Brandon flashed through his head, reminding him how important it was that they get this doctor to help them.

"Brandon was kidnapped from a playground last Thursday afternoon," Ryan continued. "And his twin brother was taken from a party the day before that. Since then the police from two counties as well as the two adoptive families have been looking for the boys. We believe that Andrea may be able to help us find them." He didn't go as far as to say that they believed Andrea had the kids, because he didn't want the doctor to think he had to protect Andrea from them.

"I'm sorry to hear about all this," Dr. Robertson said, his expression more somber now. "Unfortunately, Andrea is not going to be able to help you."

"We just want to talk to her. If she can't help, then we'll move on," Ryan said, sensing that the doctor was about to send them out the door without any information.

"Carole told us you might be able to help," Nicole interjected. "We just came from her house."

"I was wondering how you found us," the doctor replied. "I must admit I'm a little surprised Carole talked to you about us."

"She's worried about her grandchildren," Nicole said. "Can you please help us? We need to talk to Andrea. And it would be better if we spoke to her before the police did."

"Come with me," the doctor said abruptly. He walked over to the elevator and pushed the button.

Ryan and Nicole quickly followed. "Where are we

going?" Ryan asked.

"You asked for help, and after hearing your story, I'm inclined to give it," the doctor said as they stepped into the elevator. "I'm very sorry about your children. I have a son, and I know I would be desperate if something happened to him."

"We are desperate," Nicole said. "We'll do whatever it takes to get our kids back."

They got off on the third floor and walked down a hallway filled with low-lit lamps and expensive artwork. There was no one around. Everything was very quiet, almost eerily quiet.

Ryan wondered where all the patients were.

Dr. Robertson led them to the end of the hallway. He opened a door and waved them inside.

Ryan stepped across the threshold first. He'd thought they were entering the director's office, but this was a small observation room with a computer system and phone on the counter. And beyond the glass was a woman lying in a hospital bed. She was small and still with long blonde hair that fell over her shoulders. She was lying on her back, and she was so pale for a moment he thought she was dead.

Nicole gasped and put her hand on his arm. "Is that…"

"Andrea Holt," Dr. Robertson replied.

"What's wrong with her?" Ryan asked, stunned that they were looking at Andrea Holt, at Brandon's biological mother.

"She's under sedation. She's dealing with psychological disorders and withdrawal from substance abuse. She had an intense session this morning and became quite agitated, so we sedated her. As I told you, she's in no condition to answer any questions."

"How long has she been here?" Ryan asked, staring through the glass window.

"About three weeks," the doctor replied.

Which meant Andrea could not have kidnapped Brandon or Kyle. The realization almost knocked Ryan off of his feet. He was grateful for Nicole's hand on his arm. He needed the contact, the connection to reality. It was the only thing keeping him upright.

"She looks like Brandon," Nicole murmured.

Andrea did look like Brandon. His stomach turned over seeing his son's familiar features in this young woman's thin face. This was his son's mother. But, no, that was wrong. *Nicole was Brandon's mother*. This was just the person who had given birth to Brandon and Kyle, although even that was difficult to believe. Andrea didn't look old enough now to be a mother. He couldn't imagine what she would have looked like at fifteen. It really hit home to him just how young she had been when she'd given up her boys—barely more than a child herself.

"She doesn't have the boys," Nicole said, drawing his attention. "She didn't take them, Ryan."

He saw the shocked pain in her eyes, and heard the bewilderment in her voice, and he knew exactly how she felt.

"We were wrong," Nicole continued. "Oh, my God!" She put a hand to her mouth. "We were wrong. We've been on the wrong track all along. What do we do now?"

"We keep looking," he said firmly, seeing the panic in her gaze. "We keep asking questions."

"I don't even know what to ask anymore."

He didn't, either. He'd been so sure that finding Andrea would lead them to Brandon, but they were back where they'd been when they started. He wanted to hit something, but he had to hold it together—for Nicole and also for Brandon.

He turned to the doctor, seeing a speculative look on his face.

"You thought Andrea had kidnapped your child?" Dr. Robertson asked.

"We thought it was a possibility," Ryan conceded. "Or that she might know who did. Has anyone else visited Andrea?"

"Only her mother. She came the day after Andrea was admitted, but Andrea wouldn't see her. Andrea has a lot of issues with her parents."

"Did Andrea tell you about her babies?" Nicole asked.

"Yes. It's a subject that's very much on her mind."

"Did she say who the father of her children is?" Nicole continued.

"No, she's never said anything about him. Do you think he's involved?"

"Probably," Ryan said. "Are you sure that no one else has visited Andrea?"

"Positive. However, a man dropped her off here when she first arrived. I spoke to him briefly in order to ascertain what medications Andrea had been taking."

"What can you tell us about him?" Ryan asked.

"He was young, early twenties, Andrea's age. He had blondish hair, on the longer side. I didn't really pay that much attention to him. I was more concerned with Andrea at the time." The doctor paused and then said, "I think he said his name was Devon. Or Dylan. Something like that."

"That's the name of one of the boys Carole told me about," Nicole said. "Devon Bolles."

"I didn't get a last name," Dr. Robertson said. "And he didn't wait around. I admitted Andrea, and he took off."

"What about a Jonathan Haywood?" Ryan asked. "Has he been here, either as a guest or a visitor?"

Something flickered in the doctor's eyes. "I'm sorry I can't confirm or deny that."

"So the name means something to you?"

"I really couldn't say."

"When will Andrea be awake?" Nicole asked. "When can

we talk to her?"

"I will speak to Andrea in the morning," Dr. Robertson said. "And I'll ask her if she's up to talking to you."

"Up to talking to us?" Nicole snapped. "Our kids are missing, and she may be the only one who knows who took them."

"I seriously doubt she knows anything. She's been here for almost a month, and during that time she has spoken to no one outside of this center. Your kids disappeared last week," he reminded them. "Andrea didn't orchestrate anything."

"But she could tell us who the father is and whether or not he might have taken them," Nicole said.

"As I said, I will speak to her. I have to protect Andrea's interests. She's my patient, and at this point in her recovery she's fragile. I brought you up here so that you could see that for yourselves. I do understand the urgency of your situation," he added. "And I will do everything I can to help. But Andrea is more likely to speak to me than to you. She's very guarded, and you're strangers."

"We're the parents of one of her children," Ryan said. "And if she still cares about the kids she gave up, I think she'd want to help us find them."

Dr. Robertson nodded and handed Ryan a card. "This is my direct number. Call me tomorrow around ten, and I'll let you know what I find out."

"Not until ten?" Nicole asked, frustration in her voice.

"I'm sorry," Dr. Robertson said, an apology in his eyes. "I promise to do everything I can to help you. But there's nothing more that can happen today."

Dr. Robertson opened the door and escorted them down the hall, onto the elevator, and through the lobby. At the door to the parking lot, he said goodbye and waited for them to leave the building. It was clear he had no intention of letting them wander around on their own.

When they reached the car, Nicole gave him a look that was filled with shock and hopelessness. It reminded Ryan of the way she'd looked at him the first time they'd heard that Brandon had autism. And just like before, he wanted to fix it. Unfortunately, just like before he couldn't—at least not this second.

They needed to look at everything they'd learned and figure out what to do next.

But Nicole didn't appear to be in a thinking mood. Her heart was in her eyes. She was completely devastated.

"Andrea doesn't have the kids," Nicole said again. "All this time we thought she had them, but she doesn't. We've come all this way to get nowhere."

There was nothing he could say that would make her feel better, so he did the only thing he could do—he opened his arms.

She walked into his embrace and slid her arms around his waist, her face pressed against his chest. He held on tight, needing her as much as she needed him. And they stayed there for several long minutes.

Then she lifted her head and looked up at him. "I'm lost."

"You're not lost. I'm here. And you'll always know where you are when you're with me." It might have been a cocky statement to make given their history, but it was one that came from his heart. "And I feel the same way about you. As long as you're with me, I'll always know where I am."

"What if we're both lost?" she asked with a defeated shrug.

"Then we'll find our way together."

"I really thought Andrea had Brandon."

"I did, too."

"Now, we have to start over. We're back at the beginning. I don't know how much more I can take. I'm so tired." Her lip trembled. "And I really don't want to cry again."

He gave her a soft smile and tucked her hair behind her ear. "You can cry if want to. There's no shame in it."

"But it doesn't get me anywhere. What are we going to do now?"

"We need to go over everything we learned today and figure out our next move."

"I can't imagine what that would be," she said wearily.

He didn't know, either. "Let's find a hotel and get some food. It's almost dinner time."

"You want to stay here tonight? You don't think we should go back to Angel's Bay?"

"Not yet. Let's wait until tomorrow—until after we speak to Dr. Robertson. Perhaps Andrea will be willing to talk to us."

"That sounds like a long shot," Nicole said as he stepped away from her to open the car door.

"Long shots can pay off big."

"Or leave you broke," she said gloomily.

"When did we switch places?" he asked lightly. "You used to be the optimist."

"I feel beaten," she admitted.

"You just need some time to regroup. Get your second wind. You'll bounce back; you always do."

"I don't know, Ryan. I need more than time or a second wind."

He smiled. "Then we'll get you a cheeseburger, too. I know just the place."

"A cheeseburger is not going to make me feel better," she said grumpily.

"We'll see," he said, as he got in the car and started the engine.

"Okay, I was wrong," Nicole admitted an hour later, as she popped the last bite of her World Famous Tommy's chili cheeseburger into her mouth. "That was the best cheeseburger I've ever had, and I actually do feel a little better." She had energy again, and she didn't feel nearly as beaten down as she had when they'd left the clinic.

"Told you," Ryan said with a cocky smile. "Sometimes I'm smarter than you."

"Let's not get carried away. It was my idea to bring the food here," she added, as Ryan pushed his chair back from the small table by the window.

They'd managed to pick up the burgers and find a decent motel only six blocks away from the Serenity Healing Center.

"That's true. That was a good call," he said.

"I wasn't in the mood to sit in a restaurant with a bunch of strangers."

"Neither was I. It's been a rough day."

"I felt bad telling Jessica that Andrea didn't have the kids. She was really disappointed."

"We know how she feels," he said.

"I'm glad she's not alone. Sean will help keep her spirits up."

She tossed the remnants of her meal into a paper bag and then sat back against the pillows on her bed, watching Ryan stretch out on the opposite bed. He put his arms under his head as he stared at the ceiling. Then he yawned and said, "I think I'm about to fall into a cheeseburger and French fry coma."

"We need to talk about what we're going to do next. Make a plan. Come up with a strategy."

"You got your second wind fast," he said, as he rolled onto his side to face her. "Okay, I'm awake. I'm totally with you. Let's discuss strategy."

"Good. I'll take some notes." She grabbed her cell phone

out of her bag and sat cross-legged on the bed. "Carole gave us the names of two guys that Andrea used to date—Devon Bolles and Malcolm Segal. We think Devon dropped Andrea off at the clinic. We also have Jonathan Haywood, who grew up with Andrea; their mothers are friends, and he is also a druggie." She looked up. "We can look them all up on the Internet. Maybe we'll get lucky and actually be able to find someone's phone number."

"That would be lucky," Ryan said.

"Or they may be on social media."

"Another good idea."

"We should probably talk to Carole again tomorrow. She lied about not knowing where Andrea is. Why would she do that? If Andrea has been in the hospital for three weeks, then she didn't take the kids. So why wouldn't Carole tell us that?"

Ryan shook his head. "The Holts seem big on pretense. Maybe she didn't want to admit that her daughter is seriously ill."

"She told us that Andrea was a drug addict, so she wasn't trying to keep that secret." Nicole thought for a moment. "She's protecting someone else. Maybe Jonathan Haywood. Maybe Carole has some loyalty to Jonathan's mother, Beverly. She could be trying to protect her friend's son. Or maybe she's protecting Jonathan because she knows he's the father of Andrea's kids and that he went to get the kids for Andrea."

"That's a lot of *maybe's*," Ryan said.

"True," she said with a frown. "We need to narrow things down. I have three possible candidates for biological father with Jonathan Haywood at the top."

She pulled up the Internet on her phone and typed in Malcolm Segal's name. Five minutes later she found him on Facebook. Six minutes later she knew she could eliminate him as a suspect, because Malcolm Segal was a marine who had been deployed for the past seven months.

"It's not Segal," she said.

When Ryan didn't reply, she glanced over at him and realized that he was asleep. As much as she wanted his input, she couldn't bring herself to wake him up. He was exhausted, and she couldn't blame him. He'd been the one driving them all over the state for most of the day.

So she settled more comfortably on the bed and searched next for Devon Bolles. He wasn't too difficult to find, either. Devon Bolles was a professional DJ, and he had a photo on his website, which matched the description Dr. Robertson had given them of the man who had dropped Andrea off at the center.

As she surfed Devon's website, she found a gallery of photos, many of which had been taken over the past weekend. It soon became clear that Devon had been working in a club on the other side of the country for several weeks. There was no way he could have been involved in the kidnapping.

"Damn," she muttered. That was two suspects off the list. She was left with one, Jonathan Haywood.

Her search for Haywood didn't turn up anything. There were several Jonathan Haywoods on the Internet, but none that were the right age or in the right part of the country.

She set down her phone with a sigh and gazed at the man slumbering so peacefully across from her.

When they'd asked for a room, they hadn't specified how many beds, but they'd ended up with two. Now she had to admit that she would have been happier with one. Ryan felt like he was too far away. She didn't want to sleep on this bed by herself. She wanted to curl up next to Ryan, the way she had for most of the ten years that they'd been together.

After another minute of indecision, she got up and stretched out next to Ryan. She'd barely settled her head on the pillow when he flung his arm across her waist and pulled her into the curve of his hips.

As Ryan's steady breath soothed her nerves, she found her eyes getting heavy. She told herself she'd take a little rest and then she'd continue on with the research. But soon she was drifting off on a wave of exhaustion.

And then she saw real waves pounding the beach.

She was standing on the sand, watching Brandon play at the water's edge. He was building a sand castle. Ryan was helping him. Every few minutes they would fill the bucket with seawater and then dump it onto the sand. Ryan then showed Brandon how to mold the wet sand with his hands.

Brandon watched his father with rapt attention, a sparkle in his blue eyes. Then with a mischievous smile, he grabbed the bucket and tossed the rest of the water at Ryan's face.

Ryan sputtered. Brandon squealed and went running down the beach.

Ryan chased him, and soon they were wrestling on the beach. Ryan was tickling Brandon, and Brandon was laughing and squirming in his arms.

Nicole felt her heart swell with joy as they played together.

Ryan saw her watching and gave her a smile and a wave.

She was about to join them when she heard a woman call Brandon's name.

Her little boy was pulling away from Ryan. Brandon was looking at someone else down the beach, a pretty blonde woman. She was motioning for Brandon to come to her.

And Brandon responded. He ran down the beach to the woman.

The two of them hugged. Then the woman raised her gaze. Her eyes met Nicole's.

"He's mine," she said. "He's my baby. Not yours."

Nicole screamed, "No, he's mine." But they were walking away from her.

They met up with another woman, an older woman, who looked like Carole Holt. She pulled out a bag of gummy bears and gave Brandon a treat. He popped it into his mouth, and then he put one hand in Carole's, the other in Andrea's, as they walked away.

"Brandon, come back," she yelled. "Come back. You're my son. Mine."

"Nicole," Ryan said.

She pushed him away, wanting to move, to run, but her feet were stuck in the sand. She couldn't get free.

"They're getting away," *she yelled, flailing her arms and legs, kicking out at whoever was holding her back.*

"Nicole, wake up!"

Ryan's voice was suddenly louder.

"Wake up," he said again, giving her a little shake.

She didn't want to open her eyes. She didn't want to lose sight of Brandon, but Ryan was calling her back.

"You're dreaming," he told her when her eyes finally fluttered open.

She wasn't on the beach anymore. She was in the hotel room with Ryan.

"What—what time is it?" she asked, blinking at the unexpected brightness.

"It's seven," he said.

"In the morning?" she asked in surprise.

He smiled. "Yeah. We slept all night."

"I just laid down for a minute."

"What was wrong with your bed?" he asked.

"It was a little cold. I didn't think you'd mind."

"I've always liked sleeping with you—even if we're just sleeping." He sat back against the pillows as she turned on her side. "So what were you dreaming about?"

"I saw Brandon."

Ryan nodded. "I figured that much. You were yelling his

name."

"You and Brandon were building a sand castle on the beach. It was weird, because I don't think you've ever done that together. But Brandon was laughing and smiling. He dumped water on your head."

Her words brought a painful spark to Ryan's gaze, but still he asked, "What happened next?"

"You chased him down the beach, and you were wrestling together. It was so sweet, so perfect a moment. But then Andrea came. She took Brandon's hand, and he went with her. I wanted her to bring him back to me, but she said he was her baby."

His eyes softened. "It was a dream, Nicole. Brandon is our child. Andrea gave him up."

"Not willingly. Andrea was a mixed-up girl whose parents forced her to give away her children. She didn't want to do it."

"Andrea was a fifteen-year-old who wasn't ready to be a mother," he reminded her. "And she did a wonderful thing. She gave her children to two families who could take care of them better than she could."

"But she didn't want to."

He frowned. "I told you not to feel sorry for her."

"It's hard not to feel bad for someone who has ended up the way she has. She's only twenty-one years old and look at where she is—in a mental hospital going through drug detox. Did she go crazy because she lost her kids?"

"Or because she was into drugs?" he suggested. "We don't know her whole story yet. And maybe it doesn't matter. You can't pick a moment in time and decide that that was the catalyst for everything else. Maybe she doesn't get pregnant, but she still gets involved with drugs. Obviously, her family wasn't close. Carole is certainly no treat. And when Carole talked about Philip, she reminded me of my mother, the way she used to get nervous when my father was in a bad mood. She would make me tiptoe around him, as if he were some kind of king. He was just an asshole."

"We don't know if Phillip is like your father," Nicole pointed out.

"He probably isn't like my dad. But I didn't like the way Carole talked about him, as if his wishes were more important than hers, or her daughter's."

"Carole was in my dream, too. She gave Brandon gummy bears, and she had the orange ones that he likes."

As she said the words, the image flashed through her mind again, followed by another one. She sat up. "Oh, my God!"

His gaze narrowed. "What's wrong now?"

Her heart began to race. "Gummy bears. She gave Brandon gummy bears."

"So?" he asked in confusion. "Sugar treats in dreams don't count for poor nutrition."

"That's not what I'm talking about, Ryan. There were gummy bears in the grocery bag that Carole took into her house yesterday. When she set the bag down on the counter, the gummy bears fell out. I didn't think anything of it at the time." Excitement rushed through her as she tried to make sense of her shocking new theory. "Why would a fifty-something woman who lives in Beverly Hills, with only her husband, be buying gummy bears?"

Ryan stared back at her, his lips tightening.

"And why would this same woman lie about her daughter being alive?" she continued. "Why would Carole want us to continue searching for Andrea when she knew where Andrea was all along?" She didn't wait for an answer. "I think Carole knows exactly where the boys are. In fact, I think she might be our kidnapper." She bounded out of bed, wondering why Ryan wasn't jumping to his feet. "What?" she demanded.

"You dreamt about gummy bears," he said. "Are you sure you saw them in Carole's bag? And that it wasn't part of your dream?"

"They were in my dream, but they were also in that grocery bag." She met his gaze. "I am absolutely, positively sure, Ryan. We need to talk to Carole again."

He stood up. "All right. Let's go."

Nineteen

➤➤➤◄◄◄─

It took Nicole and Ryan far longer to get across town in the Los Angeles morning commute than either one of them expected. By the time they pulled up in front of Carole's house, it was almost nine. There was no car in the driveway, although certainly Carole could have put her car in the three-car garage at the side of the property.

Nicole jumped out of the car as soon as Ryan cut the engine. He followed her up to Carole's front door. She gave the bell an impatient jab. No one answered. She tried again, this time holding her finger down on the bell.

Finally, the door swung open, but it wasn't Carole in the entry, it was an older woman dressed in black slacks and a long-sleeved black sweater. A housekeeper, Nicole thought.

"We're here to see Carole Holt," Nicole said.

"Mrs. Holt is not home."

"Do you know when she'll be back?"

"No, she didn't say."

"We really need to speak to her. Do you know where she went? It's an emergency."

The woman shook her head. "Sorry."

Nicole let out a sigh as the woman closed the door in her face. "That's great. Carole is gone, and we don't know where she went. We need to call the police, Ryan. Maybe they can find her."

"Let's talk about it in the car," he said, heading back down the drive.

As they got into the car, she pulled out her phone. "Who should I call? Max? Inspector DeCarlo or Chief Silveira? What do you think?"

"Hold that question."

He drove down the block, then pulled a three-point turn and parked behind a white van on the opposite side of the street.

"What are you doing?" she asked.

"I saw someone look out the window when we were at the door. Carole may be home and just doesn't want to talk to us again. I think we should wait here for a bit and see if anyone leaves the house."

"All right," she said, not sure that they wouldn't be waiting all day, but at the moment she didn't have a better idea. She settled more comfortably into her seat. "By the way, after you fell asleep last night, I did a search on the two male names that Carole gave us, and they're both dead ends as far as I can see, at least in terms of one of them being the kidnapper. Malcolm has been overseas with the Marines for the past several months, and while Devon might have dropped off Andrea at rehab, he's been in New York the last few weeks performing as a DJ at a nightclub."

He gave a nod of approval. "Nice work."

"I think our most likely suspect, aside from Carole, is Jonathan Haywood, but I couldn't find anything on him beyond what Chief Silveira told us yesterday. What do you think?"

"I agree that Haywood is probably involved. I can't explain the gummy bears in Carole's bag, unless they're some sort of guilty pleasure for her. I have seen adults eat gummy bears."

"Maybe, but seeing them in her bag—"

"And in your dream," he reminded her.

"I do know the difference between reality and a dream, but we'll just have to see what comes of it."

"You have good instincts, Nicole, so if you think the gummy bears are important, so do I."

"I appreciate that."

"And I'm sorry I fell asleep on you last night."

"You were exhausted." She paused. "I'm going to call Max and tell him what we know so far. It's been awhile since I checked in with him, and I want to make sure that Chief Silveira is keeping him in the loop." She punched in Max's number. "Hey, Max, it's Nicole."

"I was just going to call you," Max said. "Inspector DeCarlo told me that you spoke to Mrs. Holt yesterday. How did that go?"

"Well, she lied to us, so not that well."

"What are you talking about?"

She suddenly realized that no one else knew about Andrea. She'd been so distraught after leaving the center that she hadn't given a thought to sharing the information with the police. "We found Andrea Holt," she said.

"What?" he asked in surprise. "Where?"

"She's in the Serenity Healing Center in Santa Monica. She's undergoing psychological treatment and rehabilitation for substance abuse. She's been there for three weeks, Max. She doesn't have the kids. She's not the kidnapper. I saw her with my own eyes."

"Did you talk to her?"

"No, she was sedated."

"You should have called me, Nicole."

"I know. I really am sorry. I was shaken up when I realized she didn't have the kids, and I wasn't thinking straight, but you can follow up with the director of the center,

Dr. Robertson. He's going to speak to Andrea this morning and see if he can get any information from her about the biological father."

"So you haven't found the father yet?"

"No, but I hope Chief Silveira filled you in on Jonathan Haywood."

"Yes, I'm up to date on that part of the investigation. We're trying to find Haywood now."

"I think Carole Holt is also involved," she said. "She lied about not knowing where Andrea is. Dr. Robertson told us she visited her daughter the second day she was there. And Carole also had gummy bears in her grocery bag."

"What?"

"Gummy bears. I know it sounds far-fetched, Max, but I don't see this Beverly Hills woman having a desire to eat a sugary kids treat like gummy bears. I think she bought them for the kids."

"Where are you now?"

"Outside of Carole's house. Her housekeeper claims she's not home. We're waiting to see if that's a lie."

"Nicole, you need to get out of there. If Carole is involved in the kidnapping, she could be dangerous."

"Ryan is with me. We're okay."

"Ryan is a pilot, not a cop, and I don't think he has a gun—does he?"

"No. But we're not doing anything dangerous. We're just waiting for her to come home."

"Or to leave," Ryan interrupted, tipping his head toward the silver Mercedes backing out of the driveway.

"I've got to go," she told Max. "She's leaving. We need to catch her."

"No, you don't need to catch her. I'll call the local police and have them bring her in for questioning."

"Do what you need to do," she said to Max. "I'll call you

later."

"Nicole, do not go after her on your own."

She ended the call and then turned the ringer to mute as Ryan drove down the street, careful not to get too close to the Mercedes.

"Max is calling the local cops," she said. "They'll bring her in for questioning."

"Only if they can find her," Ryan said grimly. "I'm not letting her out of my sight until the cops pull her over, or she gets to where she's going."

Ryan followed Carole through Beverly Hills and onto the freeway. There was enough traffic for them to remain inconspicuous, but not too much that they couldn't keep Carole's car in view.

"Where is she going?" Nicole muttered fifteen minutes later, as Carole left the freeway and turned north up the Pacific Coast Highway towards Malibu.

Ryan didn't bother to answer, his focus on the Mercedes.

Nicole felt her nerves tighten with every passing mile, and she was filled with anxiety. She hoped that Carole was leading them to the boys and not on another wild goose chase. But they wouldn't know for sure until Carole stopped. One thing was clear; Carole was the only one in the car. Whatever she was doing—wherever she was going—she was on her own.

They drove past the mansions of Malibu, continuing north along the coast. The highway ended as they entered a town called Oxnard. Carole continued through the residential streets, driving past much more modest homes, as well as fruit stands and small farms.

As the traffic thinned, Ryan deliberately stayed behind a slow-moving truck for some cover. But it didn't appear that Carole knew anyone was following her since she didn't make any sudden moves or lane changes.

Nicole's phone rang twice. Max and then Emma's number flashed across her screen, but she didn't pick up either call. She knew they would try to talk her out of this chase, and she had no intention of letting Carole out of her sight. Once Carole got to wherever she was going, she would let Max know where they were.

"She's turning," Nicole said.

"I've got it," Ryan said, hugging the back of the truck until the next intersection came up.

A few turns later, they saw Carole pulling into the driveway of a small one-story house whose backyard faced the ocean.

Ryan slowed down, pulling in behind a parked car five houses away.

Nicole's heart leapt into her throat as she saw Carole get out of the car with two grocery bags and head up to the front door.

Ryan turned off the engine. "Call Max," he said. "Tell him where we are."

She dialed Max's number.

"Where the hell are you?" Max asked.

"I'm on Branson Street in Oxnard. The 400 block. Carole pulled into the driveway of a small house and went inside with grocery bags. I think she has the kids, Max. There's no way she has friends in this small, random neighborhood an hour away from her home."

"I'll send the local police," he said. "Wait where you are, Nicole."

"Okay," she said, knowing that if Carole tried to leave or if she saw any movement in the house, there was no way she'd be able to stay in the car, but there was no point in fighting with Max.

She set down the phone and looked at Ryan. "Max is sending help. He wants us to wait here."

"I figured," Ryan said grimly.

She met his gaze. "We're not going to wait, are we?"

"We don't know who's inside. They could be armed."

"And they could have our son," she said, impatient to get Brandon back now that they were so close. "I don't think Mrs. Holt will try to shoot us."

"Whoever she hired to kidnap our kids might be willing to do that," he reminded her. "Carole had to have paid someone to do the dirty work."

She understood that it might be risky to go up to the house, but she didn't want to wait anymore. "Ryan, if the cops come and arrest Carole, she'll get a lawyer. And if the kids aren't in that house, she sure as hell isn't going to tell us where they are."

"Fine. I'll go. You stay here."

"No. We're doing this together."

"Nicole, I don't know if I can protect you," he said flatly. "And I don't want to have to make a choice between saving Brandon and saving you."

"If that was the choice, you would save Brandon," she said quietly, looking him straight in the eye. "But I can take care of myself."

"I don't want to be stupid about this. We can wait for the cops."

He was thinking logically, and he was probably right about waiting, but every instinct she had was screaming at her to act.

And then the decision was made for her. The front door of the house opened, and a young woman came out. She carried two small backpacks in her hands. She walked over to Carole's car, opened the back door and put the backpacks inside.

"They're leaving," Nicole said, her heart jumping into her throat. "We can't let them get away now."

"Let's go," he said decisively. "I'll take the front. You go around the back, just in case there's another way out of the house. Be careful, Nicole. Stay out of sight as long as possible.

"I will. You be careful, too."

They got out of the car and walked down the sidewalk, then split off as they neared the house. Ryan headed toward the front door, Nicole to the side gate.

She paused in front of the gate, watching as the young woman walked out of the door again—this time right into Ryan. The woman squealed in surprise.

"Who are you?" she asked in alarm.

"I want to see Mrs. Holt," he said, not bothering to identify himself.

"I don't know who that is," the woman said, stepping in front of him as he tried to move past her. "You can't go in my house."

"Mrs. Holt walked through that door not more than five minutes ago," Ryan told the woman. "So get out of my way."

"I'll call the police," the woman said.

"Don't worry. They're already on their way." He flung the words over his shoulder as he pushed past her.

As Ryan disappeared from view, Nicole moved through the side gate and into the small, fenced-in backyard. She kept out of sight behind a tall bush, wanting to see who else might be around before she made a move.

There was a play structure in one corner of the yard with a tunnel and a slide. There were toys on the grass, colorful balls and big blocks, and on the deck were sketch pads and paints.

She heard a voice, a little boy's voice, asking what was happening. It had to be Kyle, she thought, her heart leaping with anticipation.

The boys were here!

She peered around the bush and saw the French doors open onto the deck. Her breath caught in her throat. Carole was coming through the door, dragging two little boys with her. One was Kyle, and the other was Brandon.

Nicole's heart stopped as she saw the face of her son for the first time in five long days. He wasn't happy. He was trying to pull away from Carole, and he had a look of agitation and fear on his face.

"Brandon, stop," Carole said. "We have to go now. I have presents for you in the car. You're going to love them."

"What kind of presents?" Kyle asked.

"Lots of them," Carole said as she wrestled to keep a grip on Brandon, who was trying desperately to get away from her.

Nicole slipped out from behind the shrubs just as Brandon broke free of Carole with a high-pitched scream. He ran toward the play structure, but before he could get there, a man came around the far side of the yard and grabbed Brandon, holding him in front of him like a shield as Ryan came charging out of the house.

"Stay back," the man warned.

"Don't hurt my son," Nicole said.

She heard Carole gasp at her sudden arrival, but all of Nicole's attention was on the man holding her child.

"I said stay back—both of you," the man yelled. He was a big guy with broad shoulders, long brown hair and a scruffy beard.

"It's over," Ryan said. "The police are on their way. There's nowhere to go."

"Oh, there's somewhere to go." The man looked at Carole. "Take out your wallet and throw it over here."

Carole hesitated.

"Do it," the man said.

Brandon squirmed in the man's arms, his little legs

kicking the man's big thighs.

"He's right, Jonathan," Carole said, defeat in her voice. "It's over. Let Brandon go."

"No way. I'm not getting away with nothing. Throw me your wallet now, or the kid takes a swim." He moved towards the waist high fence that was meant to prevent people from climbing on the crumbling cliff or falling into the ocean below.

Swamped with fear, Nicole took another step forward. So did Ryan.

"Don't move," Jonathan repeated, anger in his eyes. "I got nothing to lose."

"Kidnapping is not the same as murder," Ryan said. "Let Brandon go now."

"Not without cash."

"Give him the money," Nicole said to Carole. Beyond the fence, the sea swirled like an angry, impatient and hungry monster.

As Carole reached for her wallet, Jonathan cursed at Brandon, who was fighting as hard as he could.

"Knock it off, kid," Jonathan yelled.

Brandon screamed and then he planted his mouth on the man's arm, biting through his skin with a fury that came from somewhere deep inside.

"Shit!" the man swore, stumbling backwards.

Ryan rushed forward and yanked Brandon out of the man's arms. He set Brandon on the ground a few feet away and then rushed toward Haywood, swinging his right fist into Jonathan Haywood's face.

Haywood flew back against the fence from the force of Ryan's punch. When he tried to move, Ryan hit him again. Haywood sank to the ground, covering his bleeding nose with his hands as he rolled around, howling in pain.

Nicole ran to Brandon. She wanted to throw her arms

around him, but she didn't want to agitate or frighten him even more. He was huddled on the ground, his arms wrapped around his waist as he stared at his father.

Ryan gave Haywood a kick when he tried to get up. "Stay down," he ordered.

"Brandon," Nicole said. "It's Mommy. Everything is going to be okay now." She paused. "Brandon, can you look at me?"

Usually, when she asked him to do that, he ignored her or pretended not to hear her. But today, his head slowly turned.

She caught her breath, not wanting to spook him.

His gaze met hers, and there was a spark of recognition in his eyes that made her stomach clench. "Daddy and I have come to take you home," she told him.

A part of her wondered if he remembered her or Ryan or home.

She held her breath, hoping he wouldn't reject her or put up a fight, but he seemed to be all out of fight.

His gaze moved past her, and she saw Kyle coming up behind her, a tentative, worried look on his face. He looked at her and then at Brandon. Something passed between the two boys. Then Brandon got up and walked over to his brother. He held out his hand, and Kyle took it.

Then Brandon brought his brother over to her.

It was the craziest, sweetest, most heartbreaking thing she'd ever seen.

Then it got even better.

Brandon put out his other hand to her, his gaze on her face.

Her eyes blurred with tears as she covered his small fingers with hers. The warmth of his touch was shocking and wonderful, strange and familiar, all at the same time.

"Oh, Brandon," she said. "I've missed you."

He didn't answer her, but he didn't look away.

Then Kyle said, "Are you really Brandon's mommy?"

"Yes, yes, I am," she said. "And I'm going to take you home to your mommy, to Jessica. She's told me a lot about you."

"She said this is our home now," Kyle said, pointing to Carole. "She said she was taking us to our real mother."

Rage ran through Nicole. She looked at Carole and wanted to hit her the way Ryan had hit Haywood. But there was no point. Carole was done. There was defeat in her eyes, and she made no move to run.

"She was wrong," Nicole told Kyle, a firm note in her voice. "Jessica is your real mother."

"I thought she was," Kyle said with a nod. "Can we go home now?"

"Soon," she promised.

"I just wanted Andrea to see them," Carole said. She moved her sad gaze from the boys to Nicole. "My daughter was killing herself. When I saw her three weeks ago, she was close to death. She told the doctor that she hated me for not fighting for her kids, and she didn't want to live without them anymore. I had to do something. She's my daughter. I love her. I had to try to save her, and I knew there was only one thing that would make her happy."

"So you decided to kidnap her kids?" Nicole asked in amazement.

"It was the only way. I couldn't get them back legally, so I hired Jonathan and his girlfriend to help me. I knew they'd do anything for enough money. But I made sure that the boys weren't hurt. I gave them presents and toys and food. They were well taken care of," she said, as if she were making some sort of defense.

"You stole them from their homes, from their parents. And now you're trying to justify it?" Nicole asked, shaking her head in bewilderment. "Are you serious? You have no defense."

"Kyle's adoptive parents are both dead. Paula told me Travis's second wife was a terrible mother."

"She's not a terrible mother," Nicole said. "And neither am I. So don't try to tell me that you were saving the kids from us."

"No, I was saving my daughter. If Andrea could see them, she would feel better. She could get her life together."

"This isn't about your daughter; it's about these boys. It's about what they need, not what you or Andrea need."

"I thought they would be happy together. They never should have been split up."

"No, that was another mistake you made. How did you find them anyway?"

"I always knew where Kyle was, and I had a private investigator find Brandon. The investigator told me that Brandon wasn't—normal, but I didn't know exactly what he meant. What's wrong with him?"

"Nothing," she said, hating the way Carol had said *normal*. "Brandon is exactly the way he's supposed to be."

Carole stared back at her. "How did you find me? What did I do wrong?"

"You bought gummy bears. I saw them in your bag yesterday when we were at your house. I knew you didn't buy them for yourself."

Carole's eyes widened. "Kyle asked for them." She shook her head in disbelief. "Gummy bears. I'm so stupid."

"Why did you tell us yesterday that you hadn't seen Andrea in years?"

"I thought looking for her would keep you busy. You were so convinced that she was the kidnapper; I wanted to buy time. I was going to keep them safe until she got better and then set them all up in a house somewhere. She was finally going to have her family, and I was going to see my daughter happy again."

Nicole wondered if Carole really believed the fantasy she'd created in her head. "And you didn't think we'd keep looking for them?"

"I was hoping you'd give up eventually."

"I would have never given up." She heard the police pulling up in front, and a moment later officers stormed the yard.

Nicole's hand tightened around Brandon's as the officers cuffed Haywood and marched him out of the yard.

Ryan came over to join them as the cops read Carole her rights.

"Brandon is holding my hand," she whispered to Ryan, afraid that Brandon might pull away if he suddenly realized what he was doing.

"I can see that," Ryan said with a tender smile. He squatted down in front of Brandon. "Hey, buddy. I missed you."

Brandon stared at Ryan, but didn't say a word. Nicole wanted Brandon to give something to Ryan, too, the way he had to her, but he didn't, and she felt her heart break a little on Ryan's behalf.

Ryan didn't react negatively. He just kept smiling, and then he turned to Brandon's brother.

"You must be Kyle," he said.

The little boy nodded, but crept closer to Nicole. Obviously, watching Ryan fight Haywood had made Kyle a little nervous about who was the good guy and who was the bad guy.

"Why don't we go out front?" she suggested.

"Good idea," Ryan said. "I'll talk to the cops. You get the boys out of here."

She took the boys through the side yard and down the street.

When they reached the car, Kyle said, "Where's my Mom?"

"She's at your house in Angel's Bay," Nicole replied, giving him a reassuring smile. "Ryan and I are going to take you home as soon as we can."

"Is she mad? She told me not to talk to strangers, but the girl asked me to help her find her puppy. Then she made me get in her car. She said the man was going to drive me home, but he didn't."

"That must have been scary."

"They didn't have a puppy," Kyle added. "But then they said they were going to take me to see my brother. I always wanted to have a brother. My friend Mark has two brothers, and they play catch with him." He shot Brandon a quick look. "I don't think Brandon knows how to play catch."

"Maybe you can teach him," she said.

"I will," Kyle said with a vigorous nod.

Nicole felt another rush of emotion as Kyle put his arm around his brother's shoulders.

"Brandon was sad," Kyle told her. "I told him it was going to be okay."

"I'm really glad you were with him. You're a very brave little boy."

"I wasn't scared at all," Kyle declared. "Can we go home now?"

"Soon," she promised.

She opened the back door of the car, and Brandon immediately let go of her hand and scrambled inside. She was sorry to lose his touch, because she might not ever get it back again, but she was also happy to see him reach for his favorite bucket of blocks. She'd thrown them in the car so he'd have something to do when they found him. He put the bucket on the seat between him and Kyle. Soon the two boys were pulling out pieces and fitting them together.

She took a few steps away as Ryan came down the sidewalk.

"What's happening?" she asked.

"Mrs. Holt and Jonathan Haywood have been arrested. The other woman has disappeared for now, but I'm sure Carole will give her up or Haywood will. Neither one of them seems willing to take all the blame."

"What about the kids? Can we take them home? We don't have to go through any red tape, do we?"

"A little red tape. We need to go down to the local station and make an official statement, but after that we've been cleared to take Kyle back to Angel's Bay and Brandon to San Francisco. We'll have to give a statement to both of those departments as well, but everyone wants the boys returned to their homes as soon as possible."

"All right. That's good."

He put his hands on her waist and smiled into her eyes. "We've got our boy back."

Tears slid down her cheeks at his words. "Yes, we do. God, I can't believe I'm crying again."

He gave her a soft smile as he wiped away the tears with a gentle thumb. "I feel like crying, too."

"You? My hero? You were great back there, Ryan. I was afraid that Haywood was going to hurt Brandon, that we were so close and yet not close enough."

"Brandon distracted him. He's a fighter—our kid. How could he be anything else with you as his mother?"

"And you as his father," she said, not wanting to take all the credit. "I couldn't have made it through the last few days without you."

"I don't want you to have to get through any day without me," he said quietly. He lowered his head and kissed her as if he were making a promise. "Ready to go home?"

"I am. Ryan?"

"Yeah?"

"Brandon has changed."

Ryan nodded. "I know. I saw him go to you and take your hand. It was amazing. He knows you, Nicole. He loves you. You're his mother. His safe place."

She wiped her eyes as more tears fell. "He loves you, too, Ryan. I know he does; he just can't say it or show it."

"He doesn't need to say it or show it. He just needs to be who he is."

"I wanted him to take your hand, too. I wanted you to feel his touch."

He drew in a quick breath. "It will happen someday. I can wait. One step at a time, right?"

"Right."

He glanced over at the car. "Look at that."

She followed Ryan's gaze. "They're playing together," she said, as Brandon and Kyle exchanged building blocks. "Brandon is actually playing with another child."

"Not just any child, but his brother. Maybe we didn't just get one miracle," Ryan said. "Maybe we got two."

Twenty

—➤➤◄◄◄—

"Where are they?" Jessica asked impatiently, as she paced around the porch, pausing every now and then to peer down the street, wishing for a car to appear. "It's been over an hour since Nicole called and said they were finally done giving their statement to the police. They should be here by now."

Sean leaned against the porch railing and gave her a smile. "Kyle is fine, Jess."

"I know, but I have to see him for myself. Then I'll be sure."

"Maybe you should call your friends, your in-laws."

"Not yet. I know I'm being selfish, but I don't want everyone to come storming over here until I have a chance to talk to Kyle, to know that he's okay. Plus, I think Paula can sweat it out for a while longer. She could have ended all of this several days ago if she'd told the police who Kyle's biological mother was."

"She has a lot to answer for," he agreed. "And I'm glad you're not going to let her off the hook. When I first met you, she seemed to intimidate you."

"That's when I still thought she was better than me. Now I know differently. She's a scheming liar. And she's going to have to pay for what she did. Maybe she won't go to jail, but she'll have to explain to her friends and her family why she lied and kept secrets while a little boy's life was in danger. People are finally going to see her the way she really is. They've treated her like a queen for years, but she's no better than anyone."

"Certainly not you." He cocked his head to the right. "Why did you ever think she was better than you?"

"I grew up poor, no money, no father, and a mother who made more money stripping than she ever did as a real dancer. And when she wasn't taking off her clothes on stage, she was doing it in private, for high rollers, and later for anyone who'd pay. She embarrassed me, and for a long time I couldn't separate who she was and who I was. When I met Travis and he brought me here and introduced me to his perfect family, all the old insecurities came back. I wasn't sure I belonged, that I was good enough." She blew out a breath. "And that is way more than you needed to know."

"You're not your mother, Jess."

"I know."

"Do you?" he challenged.

"Most days I do," she admitted with a smile. "Thanks for staying with me, Sean. I know you came to help Nicole, but you ended up helping me." She didn't know what she would have done without him. He'd been a stranger two days ago, but now he felt like a friend, maybe even more than a friend. She pushed that foolish thought away.

Sean had made it clear that he liked to wander, to play his music wherever his band got booked, to have no commitments and no responsibilities, except maybe to the fans who came to hear him play. She was a single mother with nothing but responsibility and a lifetime commitment to her son.

"What are you thinking about?" Sean asked curiously. "You went somewhere in your head."

"I don't know. My thoughts are all over the place," she

said vaguely. "I feel like Kyle's disappearance was a turning point in my life, and I'm not really sure where I go from here. I wanted to keep everything the same for Kyle after Travis died, but I don't know that I can go back to the way things were. I don't want to deprive Kyle of his grandmother or anyone else in Travis's family, but things are going to have to change. I won't have anyone talking bad about me to my son, especially not someone in the family."

Sean nodded. "I think you're going to be more than a match for Paula."

"I used to be pretty scrappy. I knew how to survive, because I had to. But when Travis came along, he wanted me to be a stay-at-home wife and mother, and I loved that idea. He wanted to take care of me, and I wanted to let him."

"Nothing wrong with that."

"But I'm not that girl anymore, either. I feel like I'm starting my third life. I'm not the daughter of the stripper, and I'm not the beloved wife of a great guy. I have to figure out how to be me, whoever that is."

"Good luck," he said dryly. "I don't know what number life I'm on, but I haven't figured that out yet, either."

"Really? You seem very confident in your choices."

"I know what I don't want more than what I do want."

"That's an interesting statement. Are you talking about your decision not to follow in the family traditions?"

"That's definitely part of it."

"I think there's a story you haven't told me."

"Lots of stories. But none of them that interesting, believe me. I'm just a guy with a guitar. Or as my father would say—a loser."

"You're not a loser. I've met a lot of losers in my life. Vegas is full of them," she said. "Trust me, I know."

"But you don't know me, Jess."

As he stared into her eyes, her stomach did a little

nervous flop. It was a good thing Sean was leaving soon, because even though she didn't believe for a second that he was a loser, she did believe that she could fall for him. And that was the last thing she wanted.

A car came around the corner, and everything else went out of her head.

"There they are," she said, running down the steps.

Ryan had barely stopped the engine when Kyle opened the back door and ran into her arms.

She fell to her knees and hugged him as tightly as she could. "I love you, I love you, I love you," she chanted, feeling as if a part of her heart had just come home.

"Mommy, I can't breathe," he complained.

She loosened her grip with a teary smile and gazed into his blue eyes. "I missed you, honey."

"I missed you, too," he said. "But I didn't cry at all."

"You were very brave," she said, impressed with his spirit and resilience. But that was Kyle. He didn't let anything get him down.

"Can I have ice cream?" he asked.

She laughed. "As much as you want." She got to her feet and looked at Nicole and Ryan, wondering how she could ever thank them. If they hadn't come to Angel's Bay, if they hadn't been so determined to find Brandon, who knew how long it would have taken the police to find the twins?

"Thank you," she said. "You are both my heroes."

"You're more than welcome," Nicole said. "Kyle is an amazing kid."

Jessica hugged Kyle to her side as Nicole walked to the back of the car. Brandon sat inside, staring down at the two blocks in his hands. He seemed reluctant to leave the car.

Nicole peered into the car. "Brandon, honey. It's time to get out and meet Kyle's mom."

Brandon's ears perked up, but he didn't actually look up.

Kyle slipped out from under Jessica's arm and ran to the car. "Hey, Brandon, come on," he said. "I want to show you my room and my toys. I have lots of blocks, too. It's okay. My mom is really nice."

Kyle held out his hand. Brandon slowly lifted his gaze to his brother and then took his hand. Kyle pulled Brandon out of the car.

"This is my mom," Kyle said.

"Hi, Brandon," Jessica said.

"He doesn't like to talk," Kyle told her.

"That's okay. He doesn't have to talk," she said. "Why don't you take Brandon up to your room?"

"Okay," Kyle said.

Nicole moved over to Jessica's side as the boys ran up to the house. "Brandon has never been able to connect with any other child or adult, but Kyle has found a way in," Nicole said. "It's a little bit magical."

Jessica smiled. "Travis used to tell me that Angel's Bay was a good place for magic and miracles. I never really knew what he was talking about—until now. Let's go inside. We'll get the boys some food, and you can tell me what happened. I know Carole Holt was responsible, but I still don't understand why she did it."

"Don't worry. I'll tell you the whole story," Nicole said.

"Good. And I hope you're not thinking of driving back to San Francisco today."

"No. It's been a long day, and we don't want to pull the boys apart yet. They're incredibly bonded. If you don't mind, Ryan and I thought we might stay here. We can sleep on the couch, a chair, even the floor. We don't care."

"Of course you'll stay here," Jessica said. "I'd love to have you. You and Ryan can have my room. I'll sleep on the pull-out couch in the living room. The boys can share the bed in Kyle's room."

"We'll take the pull-out," Nicole said.

"You saved my kid. I can give you a bed."

"The pull-out will be fine," Nicole insisted.

Jessica glanced over at Ryan who simply shrugged. "My wife is very stubborn," he said. "I'd probably give in if I were you."

"Fine. We'll figure it out later. Shall we go inside?"

"Actually, I'm going to take off now," Sean said.

She'd known Sean was planning to leave, but she was surprised that he was leaving now. "You don't want to spend some time with Brandon?"

"I think it's good for the two families to be together."

"You're family, too," Nicole said. "You're Brandon's uncle, and my brother, and I haven't told you how grateful I am that you came here."

"I didn't do anything," he said dismissively.

"You did a lot for me," Jessica put in. "You kept me from going crazy with the waiting."

"That was my pleasure," he said, giving her a warm smile.

"I want to hear the rest of your song one day," she said. "It's going to be a hit, I'm sure."

"We'll see." He gave Nicole a hug, shook Ryan's hand, gave her a wave, then got into his van.

"My brother wrote a song?" Nicole asked as Sean drove off.

"He only has one verse, but it's beautiful. Sean is very talented. Is your father as disappointed in Sean as Sean thinks?" Jessica asked as they walked up the path to the house.

Nicole frowned. "I don't know if disappointed is the right word."

"I do, and it is," Ryan cut in. "Sorry, Nic, but you know it's true."

"My father has high expectations," Nicole agreed. "But he loves Sean very much. They're just different people, and they can't seem to understand each other. Maybe one day they will." She paused. "Anyway, I'm glad Sean was helpful to you."

"He was," Jessica said, casting one last look down the street. She felt an odd sense of loss, wondering how she could miss someone she barely knew.

→➤◄←

Ryan had barely finished sharing a pizza with Brandon, Kyle, Jessica and Nicole when the doorbell started to ring, followed by the phone. Soon, Jessica's house was filled with visitors, including Kara and Marian, who had been instrumental in deciphering the mystery of the quilts, as well as Andrew Schilling, Travis's cousin. Andrew let them know that Paula was extremely sorry for not coming forward and would be expressing her apologies for some time to come.

Ryan didn't give a damn about Paula's apologies. He hoped he would never have to see the woman again.

With Jessica tied up with her friends and neighbors and Nicole playing with the boys, Ryan spent some time filling in the local police department: Chief Silveira, Detective Jason Marlowe and Officer Colin Lynch. Then he got on the phone to talk to Max and Inspector DeCarlo from the San Francisco Police Department.

Finally, he called Dr. Robertson. The doctor had spoken to Andrea, and while she was shocked by her mother's actions, she was happy to know that her children were all right. Ryan expressed concern that Andrea might now want to see the kids, but the doctor assured him that for the time being, Andrea was focused on her own recovery. Maybe someday they could discuss some type of visitation, but, of course, that was up to them. Ryan told him that was an issue that he would have to discuss with all the parties involved, but he doubted anyone wanted to confuse the boys even more at this time.

With the last call out of the way, Ryan made his way into the kitchen where Jessica was washing dishes.

"I think we finally finished all the casseroles," she said. "But if you're hungry, I can make you a sandwich."

"I'm just thirsty," he said, grabbing a coke out of the refrigerator. "You had quite a crowd here tonight."

"Everyone is happy the boys are safe and healthy."

"Can I help you with the cleaning?"

"No, I'm done." She set the last dish to dry and wiped her hands on a towel.

There was a sparkle in Jessica's eyes now, and she looked more like the young woman that she was than the exhausted and panicked mother who'd been worried sick about her son.

"You look happy," he commented.

"I feel great—like a huge weight has been lifted off my chest. I can breathe again."

"I know the feeling," he said, taking a swig of his soda as he leaned against the counter.

"I know you do. I was a little scared when you and Nicole first showed up here. I wasn't sure what you'd be like, what you'd think about me, but you've both been great. And I feel like we're family in a strange kind of way."

"I think we are family," he said with a nod. "Tied together by our children."

"What are we going to do, Ryan?"

It was a question that had been running through his mind all day. The boys needed to stay together. But Brandon needed Kyle far more than Kyle needed Brandon.

"The kids love each other," Jessica added. "But I live here and you live in San Francisco."

"We'll figure something out, something that makes sense for all of us."

"I don't think that will be easy."

"Hey, compared to finding our kids, anything else is a walk in the park."

She smiled. "You're right. There's been enough worry the past few days. I just want to feel good about Kyle being home. I think I might actually be able to sleep tonight." She paused. "Are you sure I can't talk you and Nicole into taking the bedroom?"

He shook his head. "We're happy with the pull-out couch."

"I don't think it's very comfortable."

"I can sleep anywhere, as long as Nicole is with me."

Jessica smiled. "You two make a great team."

"Yeah, we do."

"I'm going to go upstairs and check on the boys. Last time I looked, Nicole was reading to them, and they could barely keep their eyes open. It's been a long few days for them."

"For all of us. I'll go up with you."

Nicole was sitting on the foot of Kyle's bed, but she was no longer reading. She was staring at the two boys who were tucked in next to each other in Kyle's twin bed.
Kyle was on the outside, Brandon against the wall, and they were both fast asleep.

"They're so sweet," Jessica murmured.

"Yeah," he said a little gruffly, unexpectedly choked up by the sight of his son sleeping so close to his twin brother.

Nicole slid off the bed with quiet grace and walked over to join them. "They didn't last more than a few pages," she said.

"I'm going to say goodnight," Jessica said.

"Goodnight," Ryan and Nicole echoed.

As Jessica walked down the hall, Ryan put his arm around Nicole's shoulders, and they both turned their gazes back on the boys.

"Kyle has his hand on Brandon's arm," Nicole remarked. "Even in sleep, he's protecting his brother. It's as if Kyle senses that Brandon needs his touch." She drew in a shaky breath. "I'm so happy that Brandon isn't alone in his head anymore. If we can't reach him, at least Kyle can."

"Let's go downstairs."

"I'm not sure I can leave him."

He gave her a loving smile. "They're not going to wake up until morning, and we'll be close by."

"Okay. You're right." She gave the boys one last look and then flipped off the light, closed the door, and followed him down to the living room.

Jessica had already pulled out the couch and tossed some extra blankets and pillows onto the mattress.

Nicole started to sit down, the stopped. "Darn, I forgot something."

"What?"

"I'll be right back."

While she was gone, he stripped down to his boxers and T-shirt and climbed into bed.

Nicole returned a moment later. She scrambled onto the bed and handed him a piece of paper. "Brandon drew this earlier tonight. I wanted you to see it."

He stared at the picture. There were two small boys, a monster, and a large, super-hero raising his fist to the monster. "Is this Superman?"

She gave him a soft smile. "It's you, Ryan. It's you, rescuing your son and his brother from a monster. Don't you recognize yourself?"

Looking more closely, he could see his features, but he was shocked that Brandon had drawn him as a hero. "Usually his pictures are more accurate to life," he murmured.

"This sketch *is* accurate. Brandon saw you as his hero today, and I saw you that way, too."

He caught his breath as she turned her pretty blue gaze on him. "Today, maybe, but I haven't been very heroic the past few years."

"I haven't, either. But we already agreed that we're even. Although now I have to say you're ahead by one good right hook."

He grinned. "It was a damn good punch. He fell to his knees."

"How's your hand?" She pulled up his hand to look at his knuckles. "Bruised," she said, then raised his hand to her mouth and gave his knuckles a gentle kiss. "Better?"

He knew she'd meant it to be a playful, tender gesture, but her mouth on any part of his body sent desire through him.

"Ryan?" she asked, her gaze on his, her expression more serious now. "What are you thinking?"

"I love you, Nicole. I never stopped, not for a second. There's never been anyone else in my life but you."

"Not even while we were apart?"

He shook his head. "No. It's been you since I was seventeen years old, and I want it to be you for the rest of my life."

She blinked away tears. "I don't know why I keep crying."

"I'm hoping they're happy tears now."

"They are." She drew in a deep breath and then said, "I love you, too, Ryan. And I never stopped, either. If we're being honest, I have to say I wanted to stop loving you, because it hurt so much to be without you. And I wanted the pain to go away. I thought maybe with time it would, but time only made things worse."

"I know I let you down—"

She put a hand over his mouth. "Even, remember? No more hashing out the old problems. They're done."

"Can you really forget the past?"

"Yes. We're starting over. But it won't be easy, Ryan. Brandon might be showing a little improvement, but—"

"But he's still autistic," Ryan finished.

"Yes," she said with a sigh. "And as much as I want him to get better, I don't know if he will. He might never be more than he is, but I can accept it now. I can be okay with it and not feel like I'm giving up."

He was really happy to hear that. "Good. And I'm going to stop seeing Brandon's rejection of the world as a rejection of me. His illness is not my failure or yours. It's just what it is." He paused. "I might need some help, if I sometimes forget that."

"I promise to help you."

"Even if it means giving me a kick in the ass?"

"I will be the kicker," she promised.

He laughed. "You look a little too happy about that prospect."

She grinned back at him. "You know, while you were gone, I didn't just miss being your wife, I also missed being your friend. Talking to you, laughing with you, having incredibly fantastic sex with you."

He picked up her hand and brought it to his lips. "I missed that, too—all of it, especially the last part. We can do better, Nicole."

"I'm counting on it. I think we should start now."

"I agree," he said, his heart speeding up. "So what do you want to do?"

"Well, we've talked, and we've laughed a little, so I'm thinking we move on to the incredibly fantastic sex."

"You're setting the bar high."

"I think you're up to it." She leaned over and kissed him on the mouth, her lips seductive and warm. "Love me, Ryan."

"I will—for the rest of my life," he promised.

Epilogue

Three weeks later

Nicole got to her mom's house early in the morning on Thanksgiving. It was a tradition for the Callaway women to stuff the bird and make the pies together, and after almost losing her son at Halloween, Nicole had a lot to be thankful for this year. She had Ryan and Brandon back, and her life was filled with love and joy.

As she glanced around the kitchen at some of the other females in her family, she felt even more blessed. Her mother Lynda was at the stove stirring a pan of simmering onions to go in the stuffing. Emma was at the kitchen table, mixing the pumpkin pie filling, while Sara, who was overdue to have her baby, was slicing up apples for the apple pie. Ria, Drew's girlfriend, and her adopted daughter Megan were at the opposite end of the table peeling an enormous number of potatoes, and Shayla, who had just run in after an all-night stint at the hospital as part of her fourth year of medical school, was preparing the turkey to go into the oven.

Nicole was in charge of making the pie dough, and she'd already kneaded, pounded and rolled the dough out. She now had four pie pans waiting for filling. She wiped her floury hands on a towel and joined Shayla by the kitchen sink. A glorious twenty-six pound bird was sitting in a large pan.

"Do you need any help?" Nicole asked.

Her youngest sister gave her a dry smile. "I just put thirty-two stitches into a man's hand; I think I can handle tying two turkey legs together."

"We're not stuffing the bird first?" she asked.

"Not this year," her mom said from the stove. "We just put some herbs and chopped vegetables inside."

"Mom doesn't want to poison anyone," Shayla said.

Nicole nodded. "Probably a good plan, although we've survived all these years with stuffing from the bird."

"It will cook faster, too," Lynda put in. "Where's Jessica? I thought she was going to join us this morning."

"Ryan is bringing her with the boys. She and Kyle moved into their new apartment last night, and she wanted to get a few things unpacked."

"How far away is her place from yours?" Shayla asked.

"It's around the corner. We're lucky she could find something that close. And I'm extremely grateful to Jessica for being willing to uproot her life and move to San Francisco. We wanted to keep the boys together."

"It would have been hard for you to move to Angel's Bay," Shayla said.

"Yes, it would have been a challenge. Ryan needs to be near the airport to work, and Brandon's doctors are all here. Thankfully, Jessica was ready for some distance from her in-laws, and she has enough money to live on for now. She can take her time thinking about what she wants to do next."

"What does she do?" Emma asked, joining them at the sink. "I don't think you ever said."

"She used to be a dancer in Vegas, before she was a full-time mom. Now, I think she's considering going back to school part-time."

"So what are you guys going to do? Take turns watching

the boys?" Shayla asked.

"We're working it all out," Nicole said. "Brandon definitely does better when Kyle is around, so keeping them together and happy is a top priority."

Emma and Shayla both gave her concerned and sympathetic looks.

She smiled. "Don't worry. I'm not going to get all depressed on you. This is a happy day. Brandon is doing better than he has in years."

"And you and Ryan?" Emma asked. "How's that working out?"

"Great," she said unable to keep her smile from growing bigger.

Emma laughed. "That good, huh?"

"He's moved back home. We're talking to each other again. We're having fun. We're better than we ever were."

"What about Brandon and Ryan?" Emma asked. "Any improvement there?"

"Little ones," Nicole said. "Ryan plays with both boys a lot, and Brandon actually tossed a ball to him the other day. He was so happy, I thought he was going to cry."

"Men and their ballgames," Emma said with a grin.

She smiled back. "Yes. We're all doing really well."

"I'm so happy for you," Shayla said with a smile. "I was just a little kid when you and Ryan got together, and you were always my example of the perfect relationship, the perfect couple."

"We were never perfect," Nicole said. "We both wanted to be, but it took admitting that we weren't perfect to bring us back together. Honesty is so important." She paused as the back door opened and Sean walked in.

Emma screamed with delight, and soon Sean was being enveloped in a series of female hugs.

"Okay, where are the men?" he asked, as he set a twelve-pack of beer on the counter.

"In the living room watching football," Lynda replied with a dry smile. "Where else?"

Then that's where I'm headed."

Nicole followed him into the dining room. "I'm so glad you came home, Sean. You weren't sure when we spoke last."

"I changed some plans around. Where's Brandon?"

"He'll be here soon. Ryan is bringing him, along with Jessica and Kyle." She couldn't help noticing the spark of interest that lit her brother's eyes when she mentioned Jessica. The two of them had certainly hit it off during the few days he'd spent in Angel's Bay. Although neither Sean nor Jessica had been inclined to share anything about those days with her. "Jessica moved up here a few days ago," she added. "We're going to raise the boys together. She's going to live a block away from me."

"That's great."

"It is great. Jessica is family now."

"Yeah." He cleared his throat as a cheer erupted from the living room. "Sounds like someone scored. I'll catch up to you later."

"Hey, Nic, the pies are ready to be filled. Can I go ahead and do it?" Emma asked as she came out of the kitchen. She paused. "What are you looking so thoughtful about?"

"It's nothing—probably."

Emma raised an eyebrow. "That sounds like something."

She looked around, and lowered her voice. "I think Sean might like Jessica."

"Really?" Emma asked. "That's interesting."

"No, it's not at all interesting," she said. "Because Jessica is Kyle's mother, and Kyle is Brandon's brother, and I know there aren't any blood connections, but she's practically a Callaway."

Awareness dawned in Emma's eyes. "I see where you're

going. You don't want Sean to get involved with her."

"Or hurt her. Sean doesn't do long-term relationships. He's here today, gone tomorrow. Do you think I should say something to him?"

"You mean, wave a red flag in front of his face?" Emma asked. "If you tell Sean not to do something, he's only going to want to do it more. If you're going to warn anyone, I'd start with Jessica. But maybe there's nothing to worry about. As you said, Sean is here today, gone tomorrow. He won't be around long enough to start anything."

"I think something might have started when he came to Angel's Bay."

"Well, if it did, it did. Now is not the day to be worrying about something that may never happen," Emma reminded her. "You've got your boy and your man back. That's all you should care about. Speaking of which—I think I hear Ryan."

A moment later, Ryan came into the dining room with Brandon and Kyle. The boys immediately ran upstairs, heading for the playroom in the attic. Ryan smiled at Emma, then put his arm around Nicole and gave her a loving kiss.

"Happy Thanksgiving, babe," he said.

"You, too," she said, blushing at the look in his eyes. "They'd celebrated their own private Thanksgiving much earlier in the morning.

"Oh, my God, you guys really are back," Emma said dryly. "This reminds me of high school when I used to walk into our bedroom and catch you making out on the bed when Mom thought you two were doing homework."

Ryan laughed. "Then maybe you should beat it, Em, like you used to."

"She never beat it," Nicole reminded him. "She'd stay and ask us questions just to be annoying."

Emma grinned. "Are you kidding? You think that was my idea? Dad used to pay me five dollars to go up there and bug you."

Nicole's jaw dropped. "Are you serious?"

"I got rich your senior year in high school."

"Your dad never did trust me," Ryan said.

"Well, he does now, and so do I," Nicole said firmly. She grabbed his hand and pulled him close to her, giving him a promising kiss. "And people are going to have to deal with me kissing you whenever I want to."

"I like the sound of that," he said.

Another loud cheer came from the living room, and a minute later Sean strolled into the dining room. "49ers are up by seven," he said. "I'm getting a beer. You want one, Ryan?"

"No, I'll pass. I told Brandon and Kyle I'd help them build a fort."

Nicole had been impressed with Ryan's devotion to Brandon the past few weeks. Since they'd come back from Angel's Bay, he'd made good on his promise not to take Brandon's rejections personally. Instead of shutting down when Brandon withdrew, Ryan was more patient. And if one effort to engage Brandon failed, Ryan would try again.

"Hello," Jessica said, coming through the kitchen with a tray of veggies and dip. "Your mom said I should feed the guys something more than chips." She paused when she saw Sean, and a sparkle entered her eyes. "Sean, I didn't know you were here."

"Just arrived," he said, giving her a warm smile. "I heard you moved here."

"Yes, still settling in, but I think it's going to be a good change."

"Let me take that for you," Sean said, grabbing the tray out of her hands. "Have you met everyone?"

"I'm not sure. There are so many of you."

He laughed. "That there are. Come on, I'll introduce you around."

As Sean and Jessica disappeared into the living room, Emma looked at Nicole and said, "I see what you mean."

Nicole met her sister's gaze. "Right?"

Ryan's gaze narrowed. "What are we talking about?"

Before she could answer, they heard a crash in the kitchen. And then Lynda came out, calling for Aiden.

"What's wrong?" Nicole asked, as her mother headed to the living room.

"Sara is in labor," her mom said.

A moment later, Aiden came running through the dining room. They followed him into the kitchen where Sara was sitting in the chair breathing heavily and clutching her abdomen.

Sara sent Emma an apologetic look. "I knocked over your pumpkin pie filling, sorry."

"Don't worry about that," Emma said. "You're having a baby."

Ria was already wiping up the mess while Megan watched the action with wide eyes.

"Let's get you to the hospital," Aiden told Sara.

"It's Thanksgiving. I can't have the baby today. My doctor is visiting her parents. And we're having dinner here," Sara said, rambling and distracted by the pain.

"I don't think you have a choice, honey," Aiden said gently.

"I'll drive," Shayla said. "And I'll make sure you get the best doctor available."

As Aiden and Shayla helped Sara out to the car, Nicole turned to Ryan and smiled. "Isn't this crazy? In a few hours there's going to be another Callaway."

"It wouldn't be a Callaway holiday without a little excitement."

"Brandon is going to have another cousin."

"He's lucky. So are we. Nicole..." he began. "I know I

said it before, but I want to say it again and again and again. "I love you."

She gazed into his eyes and saw her heart, her soul, and her future in him. "I love you, too, Ryan. Now—"

"And forever," he finished.

THE END

NOBODY BUT YOU

A Callaway Wedding Novella

BARBARA FREETHY

One

⟶⟫⟪⟵

"You're a beautiful bride, Emma," Nicole Callaway said, smiling at her sister in the full-length mirror.

Emma stared at herself in bemusement. This woman in the lacy white wedding dress wasn't her, was it? She was a tomboy turned firefighter turned arson investigator. She spent her days in coveralls and fire suits. She was lucky if she remembered to run a brush through her blonde hair, much less put on makeup, but today her sisters, Nicole and Shayla, had done her hair and forced her to wear eyeliner and lipstick. She barely recognized herself, but she was impressed.

"Damn, I look good," she said.

"Like a princess in a fairytale," Shayla said with a wistful sigh.

Emma turned around to give her youngest sister a smile. At twenty-four, Shayla was the baby of the Callaway family, and while on most days she was a pragmatic, logical, and rather brilliant medical student, today she was obviously caught up in bridal fantasies.

"Princess?" Emma challenged. "I look good enough to be the queen."

"Always so ambitious," Nicole teased.

"I can't help it. I like to be on top."

Nicole laughed. "And how does Max feel about that?"

"I wasn't talking about *that*," she said. "Although, now that you mention it…"

"We don't need any more information," Nicole said quickly.

"I wasn't going to give you any," she replied. "And I've had to be ambitious. I'm a woman in a man's profession. If I don't fight, I'm done."

"I know," Nicole said with an understanding nod. "And it's not just doing the job well that motivates you, it's Dad's respect."

That was true. Jack Callaway's respect had been a driving force behind many of her ambitions, which was probably true for most of her siblings. Her father had a big personality and demanded achievement from everyone around him, his coworkers and his family members. But for her, his opinion was even more important, because Jack was second in charge of the San Francisco Fire Department, which technically made him her boss.

"It's different for me than for you," she said. "I work in Dad's world, and I can't let him down. I have to continually prove I'm as good as the boys."

"You've already proven that a dozen times over," Nicole said. "And today you're not a firefighter, you're a bride. This is your night, Em. You're the star, and the only one you have to share the spotlight with is Max. I don't think he'll steal your thunder."

"I don't know about that. He's going to look hot in that black tuxedo I forced him to rent," Emma said with a grin.

"I'm sure you're right, but everyone will still be looking at you," Nicole said with a smile. "If for no other reason than this may be the only time they see you in a long dress."

She tipped her head. "Good point." Her gaze moved to the clock on the bedside table. It was half past four, and the wedding ceremony was scheduled for six at a beautiful church in the presidio, followed by a reception at the San Francisco Yacht Club. "We should get going, don't you think?"

"I'll check on the limo," Shayla said. "It's supposed to be here now." On her way out of the bedroom, she paused in the doorway. "In case I don't get a chance to say it before the wedding, I'm really happy for you, Em, and I'm even happier that you got us bridesmaid dresses that aren't hideous. Thank you for that."

Emma smiled, thinking how pretty Shayla looked in the gold cocktail dress. She'd wanted a color to fit her holiday wedding, and what could be better than dresses the color of champagne? "I'm glad you like it." After Shayla left, Emma turned back to Nicole. "This whole day feels surreal. Here we are, standing in the bedroom we shared when we were teenagers, when we used to dream about the guy we were going to marry. Remember all the talks we used to have after we turned the lights out?"

"I do," Nicole said with a soft smile. "We were so worried we wouldn't find the right guys, but we did. I have Ryan, and you have Max. Life is good."

"Almost too good. I feel a little nervous, like this kind of happiness can't possibly last. It's silly to feel that way—isn't it?"

"Yes," Nicole said firmly. "That's just nerves talking, Emma. Love can last forever. Look at our grandparents. And look at Mom and Jack."

"But Mom's first marriage with our dad didn't work out. I'm sure she thought it would. How does anyone really know?"

"You don't know. You have to trust your feelings. Sometimes marriage takes work. Ryan and I have certainly had our challenges. But I believe that real love triumphs in the end." She paused. "Ryan and I lost our way for a while, but when Brandon was kidnapped, all the stupid stuff seemed so unimportant. I never want to lose my perspective like that again."

"Well, you're back together now."

"Stronger than ever," Nicole said with a nod, then she frowned. "You're not really having doubts about marrying Max, are you?"

She quickly shook her head. "No, I'm just jittery, and I don't know why. Max is wonderful."

"And he's the perfect man for you. He's smart and strong, and he'll always protect you and love you, even when you don't want protection and you're being a little too annoying to love," she teased.

Emma made a face at her. "Thanks for that."

"Seriously, stop worrying and enjoy the moment."

"You're right. I'm just nervous because this day has taken so long to get here." She had originally planned to marry Max in August, in a double wedding with her best friend, Sara, who, at the time, was engaged to her brother, Aiden. But Sara had gotten pregnant and needed to move up her wedding day. Emma had been forced to cancel the double wedding venue, which she couldn't afford on her own, and had rescheduled her wedding for two weeks before Christmas.

Now that December had arrived, she was happy with her new date. She loved winter—cold foggy mornings, the drizzle of rain on the window, and the holiday lights that turned ordinary streets into winter wonderlands. This time of the year felt magical, and so did her love for Max.

She hadn't liked him much at first. She'd met him on the job. She'd been working on an arson case, and he'd been the detective assigned to the homicide that resulted from the arson. She'd found him cocky and annoying and very territorial. It had soon become clear, however, that the sparks between them were not just the result of anger or irritation but also attraction.

She'd fought against that attraction, because she'd just gotten out of a bad relationship and wasn't eager to start another. And Max had been wary, too. He'd lived through his parents' bitter divorce and wasn't a big believer in marriage. But in the end, the love between them had been too strong to resist.

They'd fallen hard for each other, and their relationship had become the best possible mix of passion, friendship and respect. Max accepted her for who she was. And she did the same for him. It was the most honest relationship of her life, and today they would make an official and public commitment to each other. She couldn't wait.

"It may seem like the last few months have been really long to you, Emma," Nicole said. "But I think the year has flown by. So much has happened in our family. You and Max fell in love, Aiden and Sara had a baby girl, Drew fell for Ria and is now helping her parent her seventeen-year-old niece. It's been crazy!"

"Don't forget you found Brandon's twin brother, Kyle."

"And we met Kyle's mother, Jessica, who is already starting to feel like a sister," Nicole said with a nod. "We've had a lot of blessings this year."

Emma saw the moisture in her sister's eyes and felt a little teary herself. "Stop already. You're going to make me cry, and I know you don't want to have to do my makeup again."

Nicole laughed. "Very true. Okay, let's talk about a more practical matter."

"What's that?"

"I am so touched that you and Max want to include Brandon and Kyle in your ceremony, but I'm worried about Brandon being one of the ring bearers."

"Brandon and Kyle did fine at the rehearsal last night,"

Emma reminded her, understanding the concern in Nicole's eyes. Six-year-old Brandon was autistic, but since being reunited with his twin brother, Kyle, Brandon was showing marked improvement when it came to interacting with others, and she thought he could handle the ceremony. "Kyle will be there to help him," she added. "Besides, they're not going to carry the actual rings. Even if they bolt down the aisle or drop the pillows, it will still be fine."

"I just don't want anything to mar your perfect night. I can never predict what Brandon is going to do or what might spook him. He could freeze in the middle of the aisle and start screaming. Or he could run out of the church."

"Don't worry about it, Nicole. Jessica said she'd stand at the back in case Brandon decides to take off. She'll make sure he's okay. You said she's really good with him."

Nicole nodded, but there was still a little doubt in her eyes. "Brandon does like Jessica, or at least he tolerates her. The fact that Kyle loves her seems to carry some weight with him."

"It's going to be fine. And whatever Brandon does is not going to ruin my night. I want my family around me. That's all that's important. Speaking of family, have you heard from Sean yet?"

"Not since yesterday."

Emma frowned. "I texted him an hour ago, but he didn't reply," she said, worried that her younger brother wouldn't make the ceremony. Sean was a touring musician, and he'd been on the road the past six months with his band, but he'd promised to drive down from Seattle for her wedding. Unfortunately, he'd gotten caught in a snowstorm on the California-Oregon border, so he'd had to pull off the road for a few hours. "He should be here by now."

"He'll do everything he can to make it," Nicole reassured her.

"I hope so. But we both know he's not big on family events."

"Your wedding is different. Sean will be here."

"I just hope nothing has happened to him."

Nicole shook her head. "You're not normally a worrier, Emma. Where is the icy calm you display when you run into burning buildings?"

"It seems to be on vacation," she admitted. "I keep feeling an odd chill run through my body, and I don't know where it's coming from."

"Limo is here," Shayla interrupted, returning to the room with Emma's other two bridesmaids, her best friend and sister-in-law, Sara, and Drew's girlfriend, Ria. Emma had a feeling that Ria would be the next to get engaged, but Drew and Ria were pretty close-mouthed about their plans these days.

Her bridesmaids were certainly an attractive group of women, she thought. Her sisters, Nicole and Shayla, were both pretty blondes. Ria had wavy light brown hair with gold highlights, and Sara was a gorgeous brunette.

"First a toast," Sara said, handing Emma a glass of champagne. "To a fantastic friend and an incredible sister. We wish you nothing but happiness, Emma."

"To Emma," the others echoed.

"Thanks you guys," she said, blinking away another tear as she looked around the circle of females. "You all mean so much to me."

"You mean a lot to us, too," Sara said. She set down her glass and picked up Emma's bouquet of white roses. "Shall I carry these for you?"

"If you don't mind," Emma replied.

As the other bridesmaids picked up their bouquets and bags, she took one last look at herself in the mirror.

"You're gorgeous, Emma," Ria said, coming up behind

her.

"Thanks." She gave Ria a sheepish smile. "I feel a little vain. I haven't looked at myself this much in years, if ever."

"You're entitled. You're the bride."

"I can only use that excuse for a few more hours."

"So where are you going on your honeymoon?" Ria asked as they headed toward the door.

"Max is surprising me. He wouldn't even let me pack my own suitcase. He had Nicole do it."

"Then you must know where they're going, Nicole," Ria said.

"Not really. I only know what clothes she's taking," Nicole replied. "Max was afraid Emma would use her interrogation skills to break me, so he only told me as much as I needed to know."

"I don't care where we go," Emma said. "And I'm not even worried about what's in my suitcase, because I'm not planning on wearing too many clothes, if you know what I mean."

Nicole laughed. "Let's go get you married."

"Finally," she said.

As she followed her sister out the door, she tried to ignore the anxious flutter in her stomach and the goose bumps running down her arms. Everything was going to be fine. It was her wedding day. What could go wrong?

Two

⟶ ⟫ ⟪ ⟵

"So where are you going on the honeymoon?" Spencer Harrison asked his brother, Max as they entered the bank. "You can tell me now. I won't see Emma until she meets you at the altar, so there's no way I can accidentally tell her."

Max gave him a smug smile. "I'm taking her to Paris. That's why we're here. I want to get some euros so I don't have to worry about changing money at the airport."

"Paris—nice. I'm impressed."

"Emma has never been out of the country, so we're going to do five days in Paris and five days in London. We'll be back on Christmas Eve."

"You should have stayed in Europe for Christmas."

Max shook his head. "Emma wouldn't dream of missing a Callaway family Christmas. She didn't grow up like we did, Spence. Holidays are big, joyful occasions with lots of food, family and presents. She's been shopping for cousins I've never even met. It's going to be crazy, certainly nothing like I've ever experienced."

Spencer nodded in understanding. Their parents had divorced when they were kids, and for years the holidays had been a battleground of who was supposed to go where and with which parent. His mother had usually ended up in tears at some point. Both he and Max had come to dread the season. There had been a short time in his early twenties when he'd had a different feeling about Christmas, when he'd been in love, and dreaming about a future, a family of his own, but those dreams had been crushed, too.

The last thing he was looking forward to was another holiday to remind him of how empty his life was, how much he'd lost, and how far he had to go to get any of it back. He wished he could move the calendar to January second and skip straight to the next year without having to live through holiday carols, mistletoe, and even worse, another New Year's Eve. Whoever had invented that holiday should be shot. Instead of New Year's Eve, it could have been called the night of high expectations followed by massive disappointment.

Max frowned. "You look suddenly grim. What are you thinking about?"

"Nothing." He didn't want to put his bad mood on Max, not today.

"Liar," Max said, as they got into line. "What's wrong? Is it the wedding? Are you thinking about Stephanie?"

Stephanie had been the love of his life and his fiancé, but his love for her had sent him to prison. In attempting to defend her from a stalker, he'd accidentally killed a man. In his mind, he'd acted to protect his girlfriend, but a clever and aggressive prosecutor, egged on by the wealthy family of the victim, had portrayed him as an angry, jealous boyfriend who'd been paranoid about anyone talking to Stephanie. And Stephanie hadn't been as much help as she should have been.

"Please tell me you're not still thinking about her," Max added, an irritated note in his voice. "She let you down, Spence. She's a big reason why you went to prison for seven years. I don't want to see you waste any more time thinking about her."

"I was only thinking about her because you mentioned

her name. I'm not in love with her anymore. That's over."

"Seriously?" Max challenged.

"Yes. She's moved on with her life, and so have I. I have no interest in going backwards."

"I'm glad to hear that. So what's on your mind? Is it the job? You mentioned earlier that you're thinking about a change."

"I'm thinking about something," he said vaguely, not sure he was ready to talk about his plans yet.

"What?" Max asked curiously.

"I don't want to say."

"Why are you being so mysterious?"

"Because you'll probably laugh."

"Try me."

Spencer shifted his feet and dug his hands into his pockets. "Fine. You know the deli job was just supposed to be short-term, a way to make some cash while I decided what I wanted to do for a career."

"Right, so…"

"So, Gus has been letting me help in the kitchen. We don't make much at the deli beyond sandwiches, soups and the occasional pasta special, but I've discovered that I like cooking. It's creative and doesn't involve dealing with the customers, which I don't care for as much. I've been experimenting with dishes at home and toying with the idea of becoming a chef. I know it's ridiculous," he added quickly, sure he was taking the words right out of Max's mouth.

"Why do you say that? It sounds like a great idea to me, Spencer."

"I'm probably too old."

"You're thirty-seven."

"That's old for a career change."

"No, it's not. What do you need to do? Cooking school?"

"I could definitely use some training. I saw some classes

I could take, and Gus has some connections in the city. He thought he could get me a job as a sous chef if I learn a few more things."

Max nodded, an approving light in his eyes. "You should do it."

"I'm thinking about it." He was already regretting sharing the plan with Max, because he could see the excitement in Max's gaze. His brother was itching to fix his life in some way, because that was Max. He liked to fix things, save people, make everything better. It's what made him a good cop. But Spencer had to find his own way to his future.

"What's to think about?" Max asked.

"It will take me years to make even a tenth of what I was making as a commodities trader."

"It's not about money. It's about doing something that makes you happy. And you just said you don't want to go backwards. So go forward. You have to start somewhere. It sucks, but it is what it is."

Max was always pragmatic, and in this instance, Spencer appreciated the lack of bullshit. "Yeah, it is what it is," he echoed. He shifted his feet and tugged at his tie. "At least I won't have to wear suits as a chef. It's been a long time since I wore a tie. I forgot how constricting they are."

"It wasn't my idea. Emma told me the tuxes were non-negotiable."

"Emma is going to keep you on your toes."

"Agreed. She's beautiful but stubborn."

He grinned at the love in his brother's eyes. "I knew it would take someone like Emma to break down that wall around your heart. You fell hard for her."

"I tried not to, but how could I resist? She's one of a kind. You should see her in action, Spence. She charges into burning buildings like it's nothing. She's fearless and determined and a really good investigator. And you know she's taken a lot of shit being a female firefighter, but she doesn't get down when people try to put her down. She just proves them wrong."

"She's tough."

"She always tries to be, but she has a softness about her, too. Sometimes she cares too much about her cases, about the people involved." He shrugged. "But I like that about her as well. She's just the whole package."

"You're lucky you found her."

"I am lucky." He checked his watch. "I'm also late."

"You still have a few minutes. There's only one more person in front of us. How long could it take?"

Max pulled out his phone as it began to vibrate. He looked down at the screen and muttered, "Damn."

"What's wrong?"

"A case I'm working on. I need to take this. Hold my place."

"No problem."

As Max moved a few feet away to take his call, Spencer glanced at the woman standing in front of him. Her wavy, dark red hair fell halfway down her back. She wore a black wool coat over a gray sweater, with blue jeans and black boots completing the outfit. A colorful scarf was draped around her neck. As she impatiently shifted her feet, he caught a glimpse of her profile, beautiful pale skin with a few freckles on the bridge of her nose, full pink lips, and green eyes set off by dark lashes. She was pretty. If she weren't scowling, she'd probably be even more beautiful.

His gut tightened. It was stupid as hell to feel a spark of attraction for a complete stranger. However, the fact that he could feel any spark at all was surprising. He'd been deliberately numb for a long time, because if he couldn't feel anything, then he wouldn't feel pain, and he'd had enough hurt in his life. So he'd tried to stay detached from everyone.

It had been fairly easy to do. There hadn't been anyone around he wanted to attach to.

But now he was feeling hot and cold at the same time and a little off-balance. It was crazy. He didn't even know her, but he want to know her.

He'd once been good at talking to women. In high school and college he'd had more dates than he could remember, but that had been a really long time ago. He was out of practice.

But he had to start somewhere…

Giving in to impulse, he tapped her on the shoulder.

She jumped and gave him a startled look.

"What?" she demanded, anger in her eyes.

He cleared his throat, her green eyes so dazzling he couldn't think of what he wanted to say. "I was just wondering how long you've been waiting. And if this is the only line to exchange money?"

Real smooth, he thought, feeling like a complete idiot with his inane questions.

"This is it, and I've been waiting almost twenty minutes," she replied. "I didn't think there would be a line this close to the end of the day, especially on a Saturday. I can't miss my flight."

"Are you going somewhere exciting?"

She shook her head. "Excitement is the last thing I'm looking for. I just want a wide, sandy beach, a beautiful blue sea, and a lot of rum."

"Sounds like the perfect vacation," he murmured, wondering what her story was and where the shadows in her eyes had come from. "How long will you be gone?"

"As long as it takes to forget."

"Forget what?"

A shutter came down over her eyes. "Everything."

"That's a lot."

"I just want to go where no one knows me and start over.

Ever have that feeling?"

"Many times," he said, meeting her gaze. "Unfortunately, it's not easy to outrun the past or ourselves. Believe me—I know."

She tilted her head, giving him a speculative look. "You don't look like a man who has anything to outrun. Unless, maybe it's your wedding…"

"I'm the best man. My brother, Max, is the groom. He's getting married in an hour and taking his bride to Paris later tonight."

"Very romantic. I hope their marriage is everything they want it to be."

"That's cryptic."

"Is it?" She shrugged. "I'm not very good at finding words these days."

"Why not?"

"That's way too long a story."

"Maybe not for this line," he said lightly.

Her frown deepened. "True. I think the man at the counter must be going around the world. He keeps asking questions about every kind of currency, some I've never even heard of." She paused as she glanced back toward the counter. "I think he's finally done. She's putting his money into an envelope."

Spencer felt an unexpected wave of disappointment that in a moment this beautiful woman would be gone, and this oddly random conversation would be over. "What's your name?" he said, feeling a need to know something more about her before she disappeared.

She hesitated. "Why do you want to know?"

"Because I do."

"Hallie Cooper. You?"

"Spencer Harrison. We should get a drink sometime."

"Do you always try to pick up women at the bank?"

He smiled at her comment. "I never pick up women at the bank—or anywhere else for that matter. It's been a while."

"Yeah? So why me?"

"You have a mirror, don't you?"

A sparkle flashed in her eyes. "You're direct."

"I sense that time is running out. What do you say— Hallie Cooper? When you come back from your trip, we could get coffee, or something with rum, in case you didn't get enough on your island. All I need is your phone number." He pulled out his phone.

"I don't know if I'm ever coming back."

"You can't lie on a beach forever."

"I'd sure like to try," she said with a sigh. "My turn," she said as the man at the counter walked away.

"Seven digits, that's all I need," he said, feeling a little desperate.

"You don't want to call me. Trust me."

"Why should I do that?"

She turned away, then flung a quick glance over her shoulder. "The last person I gave my number to ended up dead."

And with that unsettling comment, she stepped up to the counter.

He stared at her back, at the six feet of space separating them. He'd wait until she finished her money exchange, then he'd tell her he wasn't scared of ending up dead. In fact, there had been many times in the past seven years when he'd wished he were dead. Dying was sometimes easier than living. But he couldn't tell her any of that. He didn't want to scare her away.

Although, hadn't she already made it clear she wasn't interested?

Actually, he thought she was interested. She was just scared.

Scared of what he wondered? What had happened to make her want to run to the other end of the world and never come back?

"Looks like we're next," Max said, returning to his side.

"Yeah," he said distractedly, his gaze still on Hallie.

"What is it with you and redheads, Spence?"

He smiled. "I like the fire. She's beautiful, don't you think?"

"Did you get her number?"

"Not yet, but I haven't given up."

"Good for you. It's about time you got back in the game."

He didn't know about getting back in the game, but he did know that he felt a compelling need to not let this woman walk out of his life without another word.

As he waited for Hallie to finish her business, he glanced around the bank, noting the holiday garlands, poinsettias and the Christmas tree in the corner. Christmas was less than two weeks away, and there was a festive atmosphere in the air, which probably had as much to do with closing being minutes away as with the upcoming holidays. There was only one other customer at the main bank of teller windows, and two female loan officers were chatting by one of their desks.

He was about to look away when the front door opened, and two men walked in. They were probably in their twenties or thirties. Both wore jeans. One had a gray sweatshirt with a hoodie pulled over his head and sunglasses covering his eyes. The other had on a black jacket and a Yankee baseball cap, his eyes also hidden by dark lenses. These two did not want to be recognized. Why? He suddenly had a bad feeling.

One man lingered by the door as the other got in line, waiting for the last customer to finish at the main counter. As the older woman left the teller window and headed out of the bank, the guy in line seemed to exchange some sort of signal with the man by the door. Then he stepped up to the waiting bank teller, a young Asian woman.

Spencer frowned, looking around for a security guard, but there was no one in sight. "Shit!" he muttered.

Max gave him a surprised look. "What's wrong?"

"We've got trouble."

Spencer had barely finished speaking when the man by the door turned the dead bolt and pulled out a gun. "Don't move. Don't anybody move," he yelled.

Three

———❖❖◆◆◆———

As the limo passed by the front of the church, Emma could see her grandparents and parents standing on the steps, welcoming their guests. She hadn't wanted a huge wedding, but being part of the Callaway family had made anything small impossible. She was not only one of eight siblings; she had over twenty cousins, and a dozen aunts and uncles. Along with family, came the fire department, which was her second family, and quite a few members of the police department, who were Max's second family. So they'd given up on trying to cut down the guest list and decided to have a big crowd and a night to remember.

"Is Max ready to deal with all the Callaways?" Nicole asked.

"He's getting used to the constant crowd," she replied. "His mother is a little overwhelmed though. She seemed very nervous at the rehearsal dinner last night."

"She's been nervous every time I've seen her," Nicole commented.

Emma nodded. "Susan is high strung and emotional. She drives Max crazy with her drama. He's been taking care of her ever since his dad took off. And I guess she was even worse while Spencer was in prison. She's a sweet woman though. She just gets overwhelmed with what are usually little problems."

"What's the deal with Max's father? Is he coming today?"

"Max didn't invite him. He said his dad hasn't been part of his life, so why should he be part of his wedding? I can understand that feeling. I should have stuck with not inviting our father," she added, unable to keep the bitter note out of her voice. She'd spent weeks debating whether or not to invite her biological father to the wedding. He'd deserted her and Nicole and their mother, Lynda, when Emma was a toddler, and while there had been some sporadic contact over the years, she didn't think of him as a father. Jack Callaway was her dad. He was the one who'd been there through all the important moments of her life.

"I'm sorry," Nicole said quietly, meeting her gaze. "I know you invited him at my urging. I thought it would be a good opportunity for you to reconnect."

"He wasn't interested in reconnecting. He's never been interested in me at all."

"That's not true."

"It is, Nicole. You share his love of history and teaching, but he doesn't understand me, and I don't understand him. It's fine. I just wish I hadn't given him another chance to reject me. I shouldn't have wasted all that time worrying about whether or not to invite him. He was never going to come."

"Don't let his absence spoil the day."

"It won't. I'm actually glad he's not here. Jack is the only father I need." She paused. "It's weird that Max and I both have a history of deadbeat dads, isn't it? Although, you and I got lucky when Mom married Jack. He's always treated us like his daughters."

"I wonder why Max's mom didn't remarry."

"I don't think she ever got over Max's dad leaving her."

The limo came to a stop.

"Showtime," Shayla said. "Are you ready, Emma?"

"More than ready," she replied. The chauffeur helped her out of the car, and she moved quickly into the hallway where her wedding planner and cousin, Cynthia Callaway, waiting for them. Cynthia was a tall, willowy brunette who moved and talked at a very fast pace. She was extremely efficient and very organized. She'd taken care of every detail of the wedding and reception, and Emma didn't know what she would have done without her.

Cynthia waved them into a small room. "You can wait here until we're ready."

"Is everyone here?" Emma asked.

"The pews are filling up," Cynthia answered. "But we still have fifteen minutes."

"Any sign of Sean?"

Cynthia shook her head. "Not yet. I texted him a few minutes ago, but I got no reply. Thank goodness he's not one of the ushers. We won't have to hold up the wedding for him."

"I know he's not in the bridal party, but I still want him to see me get married."

"Then he better get here in the next fifteen minutes," Cynthia said. "There's another ceremony after yours, Emma, so we can't wait forever, but I promise we'll wait as long as we can. I'll go check again."

"Thanks." Emma had barely entered the dressing room when her bridesmaids began to disappear: Nicole to check on the ring-bearers—her son Brandon and Brandon's brother, Kyle, Sara to make sure her one-month-old baby girl didn't need a feeding, and Ria, who wanted to make sure that her niece, Megan was all set to be the flower girl and accompany the ring bearers down the aisle, which left Shayla.

"I think you should touch up your lips," Shayla said.

"Why? Max is only going to kiss it off."

Shayla laughed. "Not until the end of the ceremony.

Think of all the photos before that moment."

"Fine. I'll add some more lipstick. But that's it. I want Max to recognize me after all."

"Shoot, I left my makeup bag in the limo. I'll get it."

As Shayla left, Emma's grandmother, Eleanor Callaway walked into the room. Eleanor was an attractive older woman with platinum blonde hair and blue eyes that were sometimes sharp and sometimes lost, as she battled Alzheimer's.

"Grandma," Emma said, giving her a hug. "I'm so glad you're here."

"Me, too." Eleanor waved her hand toward her husband, Patrick, who was hovering in the doorway. "Leave us be. I want to talk to Emma for a few minutes."

"I'll be right outside," Patrick replied. "Don't be long."

"I won't be." Eleanor took Emma's hands and gave her a smile. "You look gorgeous."

"Thank you. So do you." Emma was happy to see a sharp gleam in her grandmother's eyes. "How are you feeling today?"

"Like my old self."

"I'm glad."

"I don't know how long it will last, so I want to give you this before I forget what it is or who you are," she said with a touch of painful humor. Eleanor opened her gold clutch purse and pulled out a dark blue velvet box. "My grandmother gave me this when I married your grandfather, and I thought you might want to wear it—it could be your *something old*."

Emma took the jewelry box out of her grandmother's hand and opened the lid. A beautiful gold heart with a sapphire diamond in the middle hung on a thin gold chain and sparkled in its velvet setting. "Oh, Grandma," she breathed, as she took out the necklace. "It's gorgeous."

"My grandmother told me it would bring me luck in my marriage as it brought her luck. She was married for forty-three years before she passed away. And your grandpa and I are going on sixty-two years together."

"I have a feeling it took more than a little luck for you to stay together that long," Emma murmured.

"Oh, it took work, for sure," Eleanor said with a nod. "Your grandpa isn't the easiest man to live with."

"You don't have to tell me that." She adored her grandfather, but she was not unaware of the fact that he could be angry and arrogant on occasion.

She handed her grandmother the jewelry box and put the necklace on. It was perfect for her sweetheart neckline. She had debated on what to wear around her neck for a long time, but she hadn't had the right necklace until now. "How does it look?"

Eleanor gave an approving smile. "Like it was made for you." She glanced around the empty room. "Where is everyone?"

Emma shrugged. "Who knows? But I'm happy to have a moment alone with you. Thank you so much for this, Grandma."

"You're welcome. I gave Nicole a ring from my mother when she got married, and I have something special for Shayla when it's her day." She paused. "I have to say Emma that you remind me the most of myself. I know we're not related by blood, but I feel so close to you. I always have, from the first minute your father brought Lynda to the house and introduced me to you."

"I don't remember that."

"You were just a toddler, but you were so curious and stubborn that I knew Jack would have his hands full with you. Now it's Max's turn."

She smiled. "Yes, it is. But Max has a stubborn streak, too. So I may have my hands full with him."

"He's a good man, a strong man, someone you can count

on, lean on; I like him very much."

"So do I."

"Do you want to know the secret to love and a long marriage, Emma?"

"Boy, do I," she said with a laugh.

"Don't keep score. Being right won't keep you warm at night."

"That's good advice."

"And be kind to each other," Eleanor added, her expression growing more serious. "We're all flawed, Emma. Even the best of men can sometimes make a terrible mistake."

Emma's gut tightened. "Is there something you want to tell me, Grandma?" Eleanor had been alluding to some secret in her past for the last several months, but she never stayed sharp enough to get the whole story out.

"No, dear," Eleanor said quickly.

"Are you sure? I feel like you've wanted to tell us something about Grandpa, maybe about something bad that happened in the past. You keep talking about a secret that you don't want to keep anymore."

Eleanor stared back at her, a glint in her eyes. "What else have I said about this secret?"

"Nothing specific, but whatever it is, it seems to bother you. You get agitated and upset."

"I wish I knew what you're talking about, Emma, but this condition I have—it's like I have blackouts. I'm there, and then I'm gone for a while. When I come back, sometimes it's been five minutes, and sometimes it's been five weeks."

"I'm sorry," Emma said quickly, seeing the frustration in Eleanor's eyes now. "I shouldn't have mentioned it."

"It's all right. I just hope whatever I say doesn't hurt the people I love, especially your grandfather. He's always stood by me."

"And you've stood by him."

"That's what a wife does, Emma."

"Even if a husband does something wrong?" she asked, knowing she should drop it, but how many times would she have a chance to speak this honestly with her grandmother?

"Emma, you should let it go."

"I know I should, but remember what you said about me being curious and stubborn?"

Eleanor sighed. "Everything your grandfather has done in his life has been done out of love for his family and his friends. This isn't the time to talk about the past, Emma. Tonight you begin a new life, a life with Max, and you don't need to be thinking about anything else."

"I just want to help you. I feel like you want to tell the family something, and every time you start to do that, Grandpa shuts you up. If something is troubling you, you can tell me."

"Thank you, Emma. But nothing is bothering me, at least nothing I can remember at the moment," she added with a small smile.

Before Eleanor could say more, Cynthia and Nicole returned to the dressing room. They both looked a little too serious, and Emma's pulse quickened. "What's wrong?" she asked.

"I'm sure he's just running late," Cynthia said.

Emma saw Cynthia and Nicole exchange a quick look. "Sean still isn't here yet?"

"It's not Sean we're worried about. Well, not *just* Sean," Cynthia amended. "Max isn't here yet, either. Or his brother."

Her heart skipped a beat. "What do you mean Max isn't here yet? I talked to him a little over an hour ago. He said that he and Spencer were going to leave in a few minutes."

"There's no sign of either of them," Nicole replied.

"Did anyone call Max?" she asked.

Cynthia shook her head.

"Well, give me a phone."

Cynthia handed over her phone, and Emma punched in Max's number. The phone rang six times before voice mail came on. The bad feeling she'd been fighting all day came back with a vengeance. "He's not answering."

"He's probably in the car, driving over here," Nicole put in, forced optimism in her voice. "He'll be here any second."

"Right," she said, trying to rein in her fearful thoughts. Max wouldn't be late to his wedding. Where was he? And why wasn't he answering his phone?

Four

—➤➤◄◄◄—

Hallie Cooper's heart pounded against her chest as she dropped to her knees in front of the counter, hands in the air, as instructed by the two men in the process of robbing the bank. Her pulse was going way too fast, and terror had tightened her chest. She struggled to breathe, to stay on her knees, to think through the fear, to focus on the current minute and not the one about to come. But even as her therapist's words rang through her head, her brain screamed in shock that this wasn't supposed to be happening. She wasn't supposed to be facing another gun or more evil. She was supposed to be safe now, the bad stuff behind her.

She just hoped it would all be over fast, a quick grab of cash and then they'd be gone. The man with the Yankee baseball cap stood at the counter, instructing the teller to fill a canvas bag with cash from the drawers. The second guy in the hooded sweatshirt was making his way around the bank, collecting cell phones, jewelry, and wallets from the customers and employees. He was in front of Spencer now. She watched as Spencer pulled off his watch and tossed his wallet into the bag.

As his brother pulled out his phone, it began to ring. The man hesitated.

"In the bag," the gunman ordered. "And your wallet,

too."

Spencer's brother reluctantly handed over his phone and wallet, his expression grim.

And then it was her turn.

As the man moved towards her, she could see his hand on the gun. One slight pull of the trigger, and it would be all over. She knew what a bullet could do, how it could rip apart a body, destroy a life. She'd dealt with more gunshot wounds than she could count. She'd spent the past four years as a nurse in the Army and done two tours in Afghanistan. She'd seen more horror in those years than anyone should see in a lifetime, and she was still haunted by terrifying images. The most innocent sound could set her off, a rumble of thunder, a car backfire, the snap of a branch. Post-traumatic stress syndrome was the official diagnosis, but giving her panic a name hadn't done much to stop the attacks.

She lifted her gaze from the gun to the man's face. She couldn't see his eyes, but she could see the tension in his jaw, the barely restrained energy in his stance, and the nasty looking snake tattoo on his neck. He was on edge, maybe on some kind of drug. She didn't think it would take much to make him snap.

"What are you looking at?" he grumbled.

"Nothing," she muttered, immediately realizing her mistake. She handed over her bag and looked back down at the ground, telling herself not to be stupid. If this guy thought she could recognize him or pick him out of a line-up, she would be in more danger.

Her heart beat even faster as she felt his gaze on her head, and then finally he stepped away and ordered the teller who'd been helping her to come around the counter and get on the ground next to her.

The older woman scurried around the wall and dropped to her knees a few feet away from Hallie. She looked absolutely terrified.

The hooded gunman glanced back at his partner. "Almost done?"

"Getting there. Check the door."

As the man closest to Hallie moved away, she saw Spencer give her a reassuring look. A few minutes ago she'd been thinking that it had been a long time since a handsome stranger had hit on her. And when he'd asked for her number, for one brief second she'd been tempted. If it hadn't been her turn at the counter, maybe she would have given it to him. But more likely she would have said no and walked away, because she wasn't ready to invest in anyone or anything, not even in a casual way. She needed to get over the massive hurt in her heart first. How long that would take, she didn't know.

She'd planned to start her recovery tomorrow, on a beach in the middle of nowhere, and hopefully find some much-needed peace. Her tropical island was calling to her now. Her flight was leaving in less than two hours. She was so close to escape and yet so far away.

She'd never imagined that coming to the bank to exchange her money would put her life in danger. While she'd been prepared to die every day that she'd served in the Army, she was not prepared to die now. It would be the worst kind of irony to have escaped the bombs and gunfire that had killed her fiancé only to lose her life in a bank in the middle of an upscale neighborhood in San Francisco.

It wasn't going to happen, she told herself. These guys just wanted money and then they'd be gone. A few more minutes, and this would all be over.

A phone began to ring again, the sound coming from the canvas bag where they had tossed their cell phones. Spencer's brother stiffened. She could see the frustration on his face, and she felt for him.

Was the bride waiting at the church, wondering where

her groom was?

Hopefully not. Hopefully, the wedding wasn't for a few more hours, but Hallie could see the longing in the groom's eyes. He wanted to answer that phone. She hoped he wouldn't try to get to it. She didn't want anyone to do anything to anger the gunmen. If they followed instructions, no one would get hurt.

⸻

"Don't be a hero," Spencer muttered to Max, seeing the tension in his brother's eyes. "Better we get there late than not at all."

"That's Emma calling. I know it is. She's wondering where the hell I am. I wish I had my gun."

"Well, you don't, so don't do anything stupid."

"I'm usually the one telling you that."

That was true. Max had always had more control than Spencer, but today his brother had a lot on the line.

Looking away from Max, he turned his gaze to the hooded man, who was now digging through the bag to turn off the offending cell phone. He was pissed off and agitated by the persistent ringing. Every movement he made was jerky, nervous. It was clear he was high on something. Spencer wasn't surprised. Drugs and desperation fueled a lot of robberies. He'd spent seven years of his life locked up with guys like this—exactly like this, he realized, as the man lifted his arm to wipe some sweat off his forehead. The gesture revealed a tattoo on his wrist.

The tattoo consisted of five dots, which comprised the five points of a star. It was a common prison tattoo, the outer dots representing the walls of the jail, the inside dot the prisoner. He had a similar tattoo on his wrist. It had hurt like a son of a bitch, but getting it done had made his life a little easier on the inside. He'd become one of them. It was not a group he had ever imagined joining.

He'd grown up in the suburbs, graduated from UC Berkeley, worked on Wall Street. He'd had money and clothes and a damn good life until the bottom had fallen out of it. But he'd had to bury that side of himself when he went to prison. He'd had to change in order to survive the culture. Now he was going to have to change again, find out who he was, somewhere between where he used to be and where he was now. But first he had to get out of this bank.

He glanced at Max again. He could see the wheels turning in his brother's head. Max was assessing the situation, weighing the pros and cons of two armed gunmen versus four bank employees and three customers. He was thinking like a cop, debating whether or not he could personally take down both guys without losing anyone in the process.

Spencer didn't think that was possible. The best scenario was to stay quiet and hope the robbers took off as quickly as they'd come. But not doing anything went against Max's nature.

Max had wanted to be a cop for as long as Spencer could remember. His younger brother had always had some innate need for justice. A shrink would probably say his brother's need to put away the bad guys was somehow related to their father's abandonment, but that seemed too simplistic for Spencer's taste. The truth was more than that.

Maybe Max did feel good when he took a criminal off the street, but he also liked the chase, the puzzle, and the adrenaline rush. And he was good at what he did.

Spencer respected Max's achievements. It had taken him awhile to get past the anger he'd felt toward Max for not being able to save him from prison, but in retrospect he knew that Max had done all he could. And his anger with his brother had just been a part of his overwhelming sense of injustice. But that anger was gone now. He was happy to have his brother back in his life, and he'd been honored when Max had asked him to be his best man. He wanted nothing more than to stand beside Max when he and Emma exchanged vows.

His thoughts turned to the wedding. Emma had to be worried about Max, and his mom was probably already crying hysterical tears. Susan Harrison had always been a drama queen. He couldn't imagine what they thought was going on. But they'd explain everything when they got to the church and one day this would just be a crazy story to tell.

"Damn," Max said, his jaw tightening

He followed Max's gaze to the female loan officer who was surreptitiously moving closer to her desk. There was a focus in her gaze. She was trying to get to something—an alarm maybe. He wanted to yell at her to stop, that losing the bank's money wasn't worth losing her life. In five minutes, these guys would be gone. They just had to wait it out.

He wanted to find a way to get her attention, but she was zoned in completely on her goal, so deep in concentration that she didn't see the hooded gunman turn and look right at her.

"Stop," the gunman yelled, raising his gun.

The woman froze for a second. Then she reached for her computer keyboard and pushed a key.

Shit!

Spencer started to his feet, but he was a split second behind Max, who tackled the woman to the ground just as the gun went off.

Screams lit up the air as Max fell to the ground, clutching his side, blood staining the front of his white shirt.

Spencer rushed toward his brother, and a bullet whizzed past his ear. He knelt down beside Max. His brother looked up at him with anguish in his eyes. "Emma," he murmured. "Tell Emma I love her. Tell her I'm sorry I screwed things up."

"No, you're going to tell her yourself." He glanced at the gunman, seeing the wild light in the man's eyes. The adrenaline rush had lit him up like the Christmas tree in the corner of the bank. It was surprising he hadn't shot all of them. "He needs help."

"I don't give a shit what he needs," the man replied. "And I didn't tell you that you could move."

"He's my brother."

"What did you do?" the second gunman interrupted, anger on his face. "Why did you shoot him?"

"He got in the way. She was going for the alarm. I had to stop her." He aimed his gun at the woman now cowering and crying by the side of her desk. "Bitch."

"I'm sorry," she whispered, tears streaming down her face, as she put her hands in a silent plea for mercy.

"Leave her alone. Let's get out of here," the other gunman said. He'd barely finished speaking when sirens lit up the air.

Spencer could see the panic flash across their faces. Their escape route had just been cut off. The hooded man walked over to the windows. "Cops everywhere." He started pulling the blinds closed. The man in the Yankee cap moved over to the door to see what was happening out front.

While the men were preoccupied with the cops, Spencer took off his coat and covered Max's legs. His brother was going into shock and blood was gushing from his wound. He put his hands over the injury, applying as much pressure as he could.

His brother groaned from the painful pressure.

"Sorry, but I need to slow this bleeding down," Spencer said.

"It's not going to work. You have to take care of Emma. Tell her how happy she made me. Promise me."

"Don't die on me," Spencer said forcefully, fear running through his body as Max's eyes closed. "Hang in there, Max. Emma needs you. I need you, too."

His words went unheard. Max was unconscious.

A loud speaker suddenly crackled. The voice of a police officer ordered the men to come out with their hands up.

"What are we going to do?" the hooded man asked, meeting his partner in the middle of the bank.

"Bargain," the man said. "We've got hostages to trade for an escape."

"They're not going to deal."

"They'll have to if they don't want everyone in here to die."

The phone on one of the desks began to ring. The men didn't budge.

"If you want to negotiate, you should answer that," Spencer said.

"Did I say you could talk?" the hooded man demanded.

He ignored that comment, determined to find a way to get Max some help. "Yu have to offer them something, a sign of good faith. Let me get my brother out of here. You don't want him to die."

"I don't give a shit if he dies."

"Yes, you do. Bank robbery beats a murder rap. I know what I'm talking about." He pulled back his sleeve and lifted his arm, showing his tattoo. "You can still get out of here. You can negotiate an escape car, but if this guy dies, you're done. Let me carry him out of here."

The guy in the Yankee cap looked like he was considering the suggestion, but the hooded man shook his head. "No way. We need everyone for insurance." He looked back at his partner. "You agree, right?"

The other man slowly nodded, and Spencer's heart sank.

"Everyone against the wall, over there," the man in the Yankee cap said.

The employees and customers quickly moved toward the nearby wall, but Spencer wasn't about to take his hands off of Max.

"You, too," the hooded man said, waving his weapon at Spencer.

"I'm not leaving my brother. At least let me try to keep him alive."

"He's not important," Yankee cap said. "Let him be."

The hooded man frowned but followed his partner's lead. They moved further away to discuss their options.

Spencer pressed his hands down harder on Max's wound. "Hang in there, Max," he whispered. "Emma needs you. And so do I."

Five

The man on the floor was going to die, Hallie thought, seeing the blood pooling under Max's body. He was going to bleed out right here on the floor of the bank. Her head spun with the realization, with the horror to come. Spencer was going to lose his brother. The groom was never going to get to his bride. It was tragic. And it had all happened so incredibly fast.

She wanted to help. The nurse inside of her *needed* to help, but what could she do? She'd been ordered to stay put. And even if she hadn't, she'd given up on medicine months ago. She'd told herself that never again would she be faced with a life and death situation—never again would someone's entire existence be in her hands, because she wasn't up to the task. She'd let down her profession, her father, and herself. And she just wanted to put it all behind her.

But there was a man in front of her who was dying. And Spencer didn't know exactly what to do. He was trying, but he wasn't getting it done.

She licked her lips, fighting the panic still running around in her head. She could do this. She could try to help, she told herself.

And then the hooded gunman suddenly pulled out his gun and started shooting.

She instinctively hit the ground, heart pounding, waiting for the explosion of pain. But all she heard was a shower of glass. She slowly lifted her gaze, realizing that the man had simply shot out the security cameras.

She tried to breathe, but it seemed almost impossible to take in air. The people next to her were crying. One of the women was praying. She felt like doing both, but in the past neither crying nor praying had gotten her anywhere.

Max was whispering to his brother, encouraging him to fight. Maybe she needed to fight, too. She cleared her throat, but her voice still came out scratchy and rough. "You need to make a compress," she said to Spencer.

Spencer looked at her, and she could see the fear in his eyes, but also the determination, and it gave her courage. "Can I help him?" she said more loudly, drawing the Yankee-capped gunman's gaze to her. "I'm a nurse."

He gave her a long look, then shrugged. "Fine."

Hallie got up and moved quickly to Spencer's side. She pulled the scarf off of her neck and bundled it up. Spencer lifted his fingers, and she shoved the material under his hands. "More pressure," she said. "Use the heels of your hands." As Spencer did as instructed, she took off her coat and threw it over Max's upper torso, wanting to keep him as warm as possible.

The phone on the desk rang again. The two men still didn't answer it.

She looked at Spencer. "They don't know what to do," she whispered, realizing that the robbers' indecision and inexperience might make this situation even worse.

"No," he agreed. "We have to find a way to make them work with the cops. My brother can't die, Hallie. He's getting married today."

"Then we need to do something fast," she said, meeting his gaze.

"It's bad, isn't it?"

She couldn't count how many times someone had asked her that question, how many times she'd had to crush a dream. She'd told herself she was done with all that, but here she was again. And her only answer was the truth. "Yes, it's bad."

—➤➤◄◄—

Emma stood by the small window in the dressing room at the church. She had her arms wrapped around her waist, but she was still cold—icy cold. Fear and worry knotted her stomach, bringing nausea along with the chill. Something was terribly wrong. It was now thirty minutes past when the ceremony was supposed to start, but there was no sign of Max. He wasn't answering his phone. In fact, it appeared that he had turned it off, because now it went straight to voice mail. If he had turned it off, then he'd seen her number on the screen, and he'd chosen not to talk to her. But that didn't make sense.

Max wanted to marry her. He'd told her just last night that he'd never been this happy in his entire life. And he'd kissed her like he was never going to let her go. But he had let her go, because they'd decided to spend the night before their wedding apart. She'd gone home to her parents' house while he'd stayed in the apartment they shared. Now, she wished those hours back. Had something happened during the night? Had he been suddenly filled with doubts? Had he changed his mind about wanting to get married?

No, she told herself firmly. She'd spoken to him a few hours ago, and he'd joked that she probably wouldn't recognize him in his tux, because he was more a jeans and jacket kind of guy. There hadn't been a hint of anything wrong in his voice.

She drew in a shaky breath and let it out as she watched

the parking lot. It was full. No vehicles were moving. Everything had come to a standstill. The guests were still packed in the church—waiting...

And she was alone. She'd ordered everyone out of the dressing room, because she couldn't stand the pitying looks or the endless reassurances. She loved her family, but at this moment the only person she needed was Max.

The door behind her opened. It wasn't Max who entered the room, but Nicole. At her silent question, Nicole shook her head. "He's still not here, Emma. But there are a lot of people looking for him."

"He didn't stand me up, Nic."

"I don't think he did."

"Which means something happened to him."

Nicole gave a helpless, frustrated shake of her head. "I don't know." She paused, hesitation in her eyes.

"What?" Emma demanded, knowing there was something else on Nicole's mind.

"There's another ceremony scheduled for seven-thirty tonight."

"What does that mean?"

"The priest said we can hold the church until seven. That's another forty minutes. I'm sure Max will arrive by then."

She wanted Nicole's words to make her feel better, but they didn't. The reminder of time passing only made the fear worse. "I'm scared," she whispered. "Max is never late. I'm the one who runs behind schedule. He's always waiting for me."

"Try to stay positive. I know that's not going to be easy."

"It's impossible."

"Max loves you, Emma. He's going to find a way to get to you, no matter what has happened."

The door opened again, and Emma could see her family

hovering in the hallway, but it was her father, Jack Callaway, and Max's mother, Susan Harrison, who made their way into the room. Susan was crying. At the look on her future mother-in-law's face, Emma felt another wave of terror, and she reached for Nicole's hand for support. "What's happened?" she asked.

"Max's car was located in the lot behind the bank three blocks from here," Jack said.

"He's at the bank?" she asked. "Isn't it closed by now?"

"Yes." Jack stepped forward and put his hands on her shoulders. "The bank was robbed just before closing, Emma, and it's turned into a hostage situation. Max and Spencer are inside."

"Oh, my God!" She put a hand to her heart. "But he's all right, isn't he?"

"I assume so. They haven't let any of the hostages go yet. The negotiations are just beginning."

"Let's go to the bank," she said immediately.

"Emma—"

She shook her head at her father, not letting him finish. "I am not going to stay here and wait. I want to be there when Max comes out. I need to be there. Please don't argue with me."

"I'll take you there," he said.

"Thank you."

Her mom took off her coat and handed it to her. "At least wear this, Emma. It's cold outside."

Emma pulled the coat on over her wedding dress and followed her father to the door, telling herself with every step that Max was going to be fine. He was a cop. He knew how to handle himself. At the same time, she worried that because he was a cop, he could be in more danger. At least Spencer was with him. They might have had their differences in the past, but she knew Spencer would do everything he could to protect his brother.

—➤➤◄◄◄—

"They're on something," Hallie murmured, watching the gunmen pace around the bank, their movements nervous and agitated.

"Which makes them more dangerous," Spencer said, his expression grim. "They're not thinking rationally."

"Why aren't they talking to the cops?" The phone had rung three times in the past five minutes. A hostage negotiator had gotten on a loudspeaker telling them that the bank was surrounded and to pick up the phone. But so far the gunmen had done nothing more than argue with each other.

"They don't know what to ask for."

"Does it matter what they ask for? The cops aren't going to give it to them, are they?"

"Maybe they will, if they want to keep the rest of us alive."

She swallowed hard at the thought of more gunshots, more blood, more death. She was barely keeping it together, but she couldn't lose it now. Later—later, she'd break down, let go. Hopefully by then she'd be on her beautiful island in the middle of the ocean, letting the sun soak away her troubles, and the rum flow through her veins bringing peace and forgetfulness.

But her island image was hard to cling to when she looked down at the man on the floor. Max's face was ashen, and while the blood flow had slowed down, it was still seeping through the scarf and Spencer's fingers.

"Press down a little harder," she said.

Spencer frowned. "I'm hurting him."

"No, you're saving him, trust me."

"You've worked on gunshot wounds?"

"More than I can count. I was an Army nurse."

"Was?"

"I got tired of watching people die." The stark words came out of her mouth before she could stop them.

Spencer stared back at her. "My brother can't die, Hallie. Max is the good one. I'm the screw-up. It should be me on the floor, but Max had to be the hero. He had to try to save that woman."

"I think he did save her, if that's any consolation."

"I should have jumped up first. I saw her going for the alarm. I just didn't want to draw attention to her. But if I'd moved—"

"You can't change what happened. I've been down the endless road of 'what ifs'. It doesn't get you anywhere."

"You're probably right." He looked away from her to the gunmen. The men weren't paying them any attention, too wrapped up in their own discussion of what to do next. Turning back to her, he said, "What happened, Hallie?"

She didn't know how to answer that question. "A million things."

"Give me one."

"Well, the worst thing was watching my boyfriend die and knowing that he wouldn't have been where he was if I hadn't wanted to talk to him. He would have been far away from the bomb blast if it weren't for me. And I've gone over that night so many times in my mind, thinking how one different decision would have changed it all. But like I said, playing that game doesn't make anything better."

"I'm sorry."

She shrugged, because nothing he could say would take the pain away. It was her constant companion.

"Wrong place, wrong time, doesn't make you to blame, Hallie."

"Maybe. But that wasn't the only thing I did wrong that

night." She paused. "I'm not the good one, either."

He met her gaze. "Hard to believe."

That's because he didn't know her, didn't know the depth to which she'd sunk. Her own father could barely look at her now. All her life she'd tried to live up to his very high bar, but she'd fallen short. It was another reason why she wanted to escape. The last place she wanted to be at the holidays was with her family.

She shook her father's disapproving image out of her mind and focused on Max. She wished she could do more for him, but he needed surgery. They just had to keep him alive until they could get him to the hospital.

"The bleeding is slowing down," Spencer said.

She didn't know if that were true or just Spencer's wishful thinking. But she did know if this didn't end soon, Max wasn't going to make it to his wedding or to his bride.

Six

➤➤◄◄◄

Emma spent her days racing to fire scenes. She was no stranger to sirens, crime scene tape, or strobe lights, but the beams bouncing off the dark buildings in the commercial area surrounding the bank got her heart pounding even faster. She was not going to a job; she was going to Max, and that changed everything.

The police had closed off the street, so her father double parked about a block away, and they jumped out of the car. As her feet hit the pavement, she was assailed by a wave of terror that almost knocked her down. But she forced herself to keep moving. She had to find out what was happening.

As they neared the command post, she saw the SWAT van, and the enormous police presence outside the bank, and the knot in her throat grew bigger. She wasn't surprised at the show of force. Max was a cop. The department would work as hard as they could to bring him out safely.

A tall, dark-haired man wearing body armor approached them as they ducked under the police tape. She recognized him immediately. It was Brady O'Neal, who played basketball with both Max and her brother, Burke. Brady was a hostage negotiator, and she didn't like the somber expression in his eyes. "Brady, what's happening? Is Max in there?"

"We believe so," Brady said, his mouth drawn in a tight

line. "His car is in the lot. We haven't been able to make contact with the gunmen yet."

"How many are inside?" her father cut in.

"We're not sure. The security cameras went out when we arrived, but the techs are working on getting the video up until that point. We should have it soon."

"How do you know they have guns?" she asked.

His lips tightened. "Several passerby reported shots fired."

Her stomach turned over. "God," she breathed.

"Don't go to the worst scenario," he said quickly. "We don't know anything yet."

"Max wouldn't stand by and do nothing if someone was shooting."

"He also wouldn't do something stupid," Brady said. "He's an experienced cop." He gave her a long, commiserating look. "I'm sorry, Emma."

"We were supposed to be married by now, having our first dance, making our first toast," she said. "I had this feeling earlier that it was all too good to be true. I was right."

"You weren't right," her father said. "You're going to marry Max, and you're going to be happy." He let his words sink in, then added. "I'm going to talk to Henry, see what he knows." Henry was another cop and one of her father's closest friends. While the cops and firefighters had a friendly rivalry in the city, when it came to taking care of each other, they were all brothers.

A man stuck his head out of the SWAT van. "Brady, we've got a feed."

"Stay here," Brady said, then ran toward the back of the van.

She hesitated for one second, then followed him up the steps. The cops inside were too busy looking at the monitor to notice her presence.

On the video, two men with guns could be seen walking back and forth in the middle of the bank. A teller was collecting cash. And in the corner of the shot, she could see Max and Spencer on their knees, hands in the air. She felt a wave of relief. They were okay.

Then everything changed. Someone moved, a flash of red in the corner of the screen. Max jumped to his feet. A gun went off. He stumbled and fell to the ground, blood spattering across his dress shirt as Spencer rushed to his side.

"Oh, my God," she whispered in horror.

Brady turned around and hustled her out of the van.

"That was Max. He's hurt," she said. "They shot him, Brady."

"I know," he said, giving her a little shake. "You need to stay here, let us do our job, Emma."

"I want to help."

"Then don't get in the way."

"You have to save him, Brady. You have to. Promise me."

"I'm going to do everything I can," he said grimly.

It wasn't a promise, but it was all she was going to get.

Spencer stared down at Max's face. It appeared that his brother's skin was taking on the faint hue of blue, or was that just the strobe lights flashing through the upper portion of the uncovered windows? He looked over at Hallie, needing her reassurance.

Her face was tense, her jaw tight, her eyes filled with determination but also fear. She was checking Max's pulse and after a moment she nodded. "He's hanging in there."

A part of him wondered if she was telling him a comforting lie, but he chose instead to believe her words, because any other scenario was too terrifying to contemplate. He shifted his body as his legs began to cramp from the tight position. He was careful to keep the pressure on Max's wound. Thankfully, the bleeding had slowed down.

He glanced across the bank where the men were in yet another discussion about whether or not they should answer the phone. He was desperate for them to get the negotiations started, to take some sort of action. It was Max's only chance. But these idiots didn't know what to do. "We had to get the stupidest bank robbers on the planet," he muttered angrily.

"I wouldn't tell them that," Hallie replied.

"Maybe I should. They need some advice."

"They're not going to take it from you. Unless..." She paused. "You showed them a tattoo before. What does it mean?"

"It's a prison tattoo, the same one the hooded guy has on his arm."

"You were in prison?" she asked, surprise in her eyes.

"For seven years. Manslaughter. I killed the man who was stalking my fiancé," he added, making short work of a long story.

"Sounds justified. How did you end up in jail?"

He could hear the doubt in her voice, and he wasn't surprised. Everyone had questioned his side of the story. "It's a long story."

"Tell me at least part of it."

"I can't. I have to think of a way out of this."

"There's no way out, Spencer, not unless they pick up the phone and start talking to the cops."

"How can I make them do that?"

"You already tried. Let's just do what we're doing." She drew in a shaky breath. "I feel sick."

"Hang in there," he said, seeing the distress in her eyes.

"I'm trying. I could really use a distraction from all the

blood."

He hesitated, taking another quick look across the bank. Their captors weren't paying them any attention. They were confident they had this group under control, and they did. Spencer was the only one who could probably do something, and he couldn't take his hands off of Max's abdomen.

"Spencer," Hallie said. "Please talk to me."

"Okay. I'll tell you what happened to me. There was a guy who was harassing my fiancé, one of her coworkers. He would follow her, take pictures of her walking down the street and send them to her. One night I saw him outside of our apartment. Stephanie wasn't home. He was waiting in the shadows for her, but he got me instead. I confronted him. He gave me a smug smile and said something to the effect of having my fiancé. I hit him. One punch, and he went down. He hit his head on the sidewalk and died in the hospital an hour later."

Hallie stared back at him with wide eyes, but so far there was no hint of disgust, so he went on. "The prosecutor twisted what happened between us, and he persuaded the jury that I was paranoid, jealous and angry enough to kill an innocent man who was interested in my girlfriend. The man wasn't innocent, but he was clever, smarter than me. He'd covered his tracks."

"But your fiancé must have defended you?"

"She tried, but she fell apart on the stand. Her words were taken out of context. She got confused. It was bad. In the end, I went to jail."

"It sounds so unfair."

"It felt that way to me."

She considered his words, and he was happy she hadn't rushed to judgment, although he couldn't imagine why she hadn't. Everyone else had been eager to form an immediate opinion.

"Did you mean to kill him?" she asked.

He shook his head. "I just wanted him to leave her alone. But I acted stupidly. It was a bad decision to confront him, one I've had plenty of time to think about."

"When did you get out?"

"Seven months ago. I've been trying to start over, but my old life is gone, and I haven't quite figured out where my new life is going."

"You have time."

"I guess." He fell silent as the phone on the desk rang again. This time—finally—the man in the Yankee cap strode forward to answer the call. "Looks like they're ready to deal," he murmured.

"Let's hope the cops are, too."

"Yeah?" the gunman said. After listening for a moment, he added, "You don't need to know my name." He paused again, his gaze moving toward Max. "He's fine, barely injured."

Spencer's lips tightened. Obviously, the police knew Max was hurt. They must have been able to regain some of the security video before the cameras were destroyed.

"No one is going anywhere," the gunman said. "We want a car at the door and two hundred thousand dollars in unmarked bills in a bag on the front seat." He listened again. "No one comes out until the car is here. I don't have to give you anything in return. You have fifteen minutes before we start killing hostages." He slammed the phone down without waiting for an answer.

"My brother doesn't have fifteen minutes," Spencer said to Hallie. He directed his next words to the gunmen. "You need to send out a hostage, show you're cooperating."

"We don't need your advice," the hooded man said.

"Look, you can let my brother go. I can carry him to the front door and put him outside. The paramedics can take him from there. He's no good to you. You can't use him as a shield. You can do that with me."

"Or me," Hallie put in. "I'll go with you."

"Hallie, no," Spencer said, but he could see the fighting light in her eyes.

"It doesn't matter if I die. I should be dead."

"Shut up—both of you," the hooded man replied. Then he and his partner moved away to talk again.

"They're not going for it," Spencer said. He looked into Hallie's gaze. "Thanks for the offer. That was brave."

She shrugged. "I just want to do something good for a change."

"You're doing that now. You're helping me save my brother's life."

"I hope so," she said. "If your hands are getting tired, we can switch."

"No, I'm good," he said, keeping the pressure on Max's abdomen. "Maybe the police will act quickly knowing that Max is hurt. Hopefully, it's five minutes instead of fifteen."

⟶≫⟪⟵

Emma couldn't stand the waiting. Every minute seemed like an eternity. After getting kicked out of the SWAT van, she'd been sidelined behind the police tape. Her father must have called her mother and siblings at some point, because her entire family and bridal party now surrounded her.

As she glanced over her shoulder at the group, it seemed a surreal site, a bridal party in gold gowns and black tuxedos gathered outside of a bank on a cold winter night. They were supposed to be at the reception now, drinking champagne and making toasts.

They were not supposed to be waiting out a hostage situation with Max's life in jeopardy. She could still see his body on the ground, blood spreading across his white shirt, Spencer rushing to his side and then some other woman coming over to help. Had they stopped the bleeding? Was the wound bad? She had a million questions and no answers.

She wrapped her arms around her waist and prayed for Max to make it through.

Burke came over to her side. "I just talked to Brady. They're making a deal. There should be some action soon."

"What kind of action?" she asked.

"I don't know."

"You do know, Burke, tell me." As a firefighter and arson investigator, she'd worked hostage situations before. She knew how delicate and dangerous the negotiation could be.

"They're going to get them a car and some cash," he said, compassion in his eyes.

Out of all of her family members, Burke probably came the closest to understanding her feelings right now. He'd lost his fiancé in a car crash just a few weeks before they were supposed to get married.

"Are they really going to let them walk out and drive away?" She didn't believe that for a second. "They're going to at least try to take a hostage with them."

"That won't be a man who's injured. Max won't be their shield."

"You're right. I just want this to be over."

"I'll see if I can find anything else out."

As Burke walked away, she returned her gaze to the bank. She'd gone to this branch a million times. She knew some of the tellers by sight. And nothing bad had ever happened. Why today?

"Em?"

She turned her head at the tentative voice and for some reason the sight of her brother Sean's face put tears in her eyes. He'd made it. And maybe because he'd made it, Max would, too. It was a completely irrational and illogical thought, but she grabbed on to it anyway.

He opened his arms, and she gave him a hug. "I'm so glad you're here."

"Sorry I'm late. I should have left a day earlier, given myself more time. I don't know why I didn't."

She knew why he'd put off the trip, because Sean was uncomfortable at family events. He was the lone ranger, the one Callaway who didn't fit in, the black sheep, at least in his mind, and probably her father's, too. Sean and her father had been at odds for as long as she could remember. In fact, sometimes she thought there was something more between them, something so deep and so private that only the two of them knew what it was. But whatever it was that stood between them, she hoped someday it would disappear, because she missed Sean being in her life.

"I'm just glad you're here now," she said. "Max was shot. I don't know how bad it is, but I don't think it's good."

"He's tough. Max will fight his way back to you, Em."

"I know he's trying."

"What can I do for you, Em? You need anything?"

"Just Max."

Sean nodded. "Do you want me to go? Nicole said you didn't want to talk to anyone."

"I don't want to talk, but I wouldn't mind the company," she said, knowing that Sean could stand quietly by her side and not say a word.

"You've got it."

They stood in silence for a few minutes and then Emma found a need to break the silence. "I'm going crazy. Tell me something to distract me. Tell me about your band."

"It's good. We just finished a three week tour through the Pacific Northwest."

"Where are you going next?" she asked.

"Nowhere. I'm going to be in San Francisco for a while. We're spending the next few weeks in the studio."

"That's great."

"Maybe," he said, doubt in his voice.

"What? You don't want to be home?" As she looked at him, she saw his gaze dart across the crowd to the woman standing close to Nicole. It was Jessica Schilling, the mother of Brandon's twin brother, Kyle. Nicole had told her that she thought there were sparks between Sean and Jessica, but Nicole had not wanted to encourage that connection. Jessica was practically one of the family now, and Sean didn't have a track record for long-term relationships. Nicole didn't want Sean to break Jessica's heart and cause a rift between Jessica and the Callaways, which, in turn, could hurt Brandon and Kyle's relationship.

As Sean didn't answer, she prodded, "Sean?"

He finally looked back at her. "What was the question?"

"Why don't you want to be home?"

"It's complicated."

"Is it Dad who complicates things? Or someone else?"

He smiled. "You're always so curious, Em."

Before she could press for more information, the police moved some cones to allow a car to drive past the barriers. The sedan stopped just a few feet from the front door. "Something's happening," she murmured, her heart jumping into overdrive.

Sean put his arm around her shoulder. She appreciated the warmth, because she was shaking with nervous chills.

She prayed to God that Max would be the first one out.

Seven

Max groaned, his eyelids fluttering.

"He's waking up," Spencer murmured, excitement in his voice.

While Hallie appreciated the fact that Max was regaining consciousness, she didn't want him moving. She put her hand around Max's cold fingers and said, "Stay still. Everything is okay. Don't move." Max seemed to settle a bit at her words. She looked back at Spencer. "We need to keep him quiet—for a lot of reasons."

Understanding flashed in Spencer's eyes. He knew as well as she did that besides the medical implications of Max awakening, jostling his wound and restarting the bleeding, it was better for all of them if Max remained still and didn't factor into any actions the robbers were considering. They were probably lucky that the gunmen had never looked at their I.D.'s, never realized Max was a cop. If they had, they'd probably be even more panicked than they already were.

She looked across the bank, watching the men pace and argue and then take a quick break to check the window. It was clear that they weren't in agreement about their next step or who was in charge. The hooded man seemed to be the most unpredictable. He was the one who'd shot Max without a second thought. The guy in the Yankee cap seemed more reasonable, but he was also getting worried. And why wouldn't he be? She couldn't imagine that the cops were going to let them walk out of the bank and drive away.

Max stirred again, his fingers twitching under her hand. He stretched one of his legs and then grimaced in pain. She put her other hand on Max's shoulder and leaned down next to his ear. "Don't move, Max. We need to get you back to..." She paused, looking at Spencer. "What's her name? The bride?"

"Emma."

She leaned back down. "We need to get you back to Emma, Max, but you have to stay still, so you don't start bleeding again."

His lips parted. "Emma," he breathed. "Love—love you."

Hallie's heart tore a little at his words. He thought she was Emma.

"Don't forget," he murmured.

"He thinks you're Emma," Spencer said.

"Then I'll be her." She squeezed Max's hand and said, "You have to fight, Max." She took a deep breath, not sure she could say the words she needed to say for Max, for Emma, because she hadn't said those words since her fiancé had died. In fact, her greatest regret was that she hadn't had a chance to say those words to Doug before he passed away. That night they'd been bickering a little, nothing serious, just the things couples do. What a waste of conversation and time that had been. How she wished she could have those moments back.

She couldn't change the past for herself or for Doug, but maybe the words could mean something now, to another man who really needed to hear them. She put her face right next to Max's. He was so weak, she could barely hear his breath. She needed to give him some strength.

"I love you," she whispered. "And I need you to come

back to me. You have to stay still and rest, so the bleeding doesn't start again. You can do this, Max. Don't quit on me. We're not over yet. We're getting married, and we're having a future."

She sat back on her heels, hoping he'd heard her, hoping that he could hang on for the woman he loved. While she'd seen a lot of people die, she'd also seen a few miracles, and she wanted one for this man.

"Thanks," Spencer said.

"I hope it helped. I don't know what Emma would have said."

"Exactly what you did. He's calmer now."

"I hope he stays that way." She tucked a strand of her hair behind one ear as she looked out across the bank. "I wish these guys would calm down. The longer this goes on, the more nervous they get, and that makes them more dangerous. I thought this would be over by now." She could feel the tension rising in her own body. She needed to calm down, too.

"Tell me about the island you're going to," Spencer said.

"I don't know."

"You do know. Concentrate on that, Hallie."

She tried to focus on the dreamy image of paradise that had been getting her through the last few weeks.

"Are there palm trees?" he asked.

She nodded.

"Wide beaches?"

"With sand so hot it burns your toes," she said slowly.

"Good. What else?"

"The sea is blue-green, and the fish are so colorful, snorkeling is like looking through a kaleidoscope."

"Let's not forget about the rum," he said with a small smile.

"They put those little umbrellas in the drinks. And they

have hammocks strung up between the trees where you can nap." She paused. "I think I might be able to sleep there. It will be quiet, no noises to wake me up and make me want to dive for cover. The only sound will be the waves crashing on the beach. But I've already missed my flight."

"You'll catch another one."

She nodded, realizing her pulse had slowed back down. "Thanks. I was getting wound up."

"You're doing great, Hallie. And when we get out of here, I'm going to buy you a rum drink with one of those umbrellas. I know a place right here in the city that makes them. It won't be your island bar, but it will tide you over until you can get there. What do you say?"

"That this is a first."

He sent her an enquiring look. "What do you mean?"

"It's the first time I've been asked out while I was trying to save someone's life and my own."

"I wasn't asking; I was telling," he said, a cocky note in his voice. "We're getting out of this, Hallie. And I'm going to buy you that drink. You can bet on that."

She liked his confidence. "You're on."

As she finished speaking, the phone rang again and the Yankee-capped man strode to the desk to answer it. He listened, then hung up and turned to his partner. "The car is here and the money. We're good to go."

"That's it? It seems too easy."

"I was just thinking that." Yankee set down his gun on the desk and walked to the window. "There are a million cops out there, probably snipers on the roof."

"I don't like it," the hooded man said. "They're setting us up."

"What do you want to do then? We can't stay in here all night."

Hallie sighed as their debate began again. At this point,

any action was preferable to no action, especially where Max was concerned. His momentary calm had passed, and he was starting to move his legs now. He was also trying to pull his hand out of hers. She tightened her grip, thcn looked at Spencer.

"We have to do something," he said grimly.

She nodded. "The bleeding is starting up again, and he can't lose any more blood." She licked her lips, unable to believe what she was about to suggest. "I think we have to make a move."

He stared back at her. "I agree."

"You do?"

"Yes. We can wait it out, but Max can't. You're going to have to take over here, so I can try to get a jump on one of them."

"I can help. I'm a soldier. I know how to fight, Spencer."

"Not like this."

"Close enough," she said, remembering all the hand-to-hand combat training she'd undergone. It had been a long time, but she could do it. "You take one; I take the other. I think we can do it." She actually had no idea if they could do it or if they were about to commit suicide, but she didn't want to see Max die right in front of her without trying everything she could to save him.

His lips tightened. "We're only going to have one chance, one moment of surprise."

"The guy in the baseball cap put his gun on the desk," she said, meeting his gaze. "Now is the time."

"All right," he said decisively. "Start screaming. Pretend Max is dying, and you're terrified. Get hysterical on them. It will draw them over."

"Then what?"

"I'll jump the closest guy."

"Or I will."

"They could shoot you, Hallie."

She knew that was a real possibility but she was tired of being a victim. "I'll take the risk."

"All right. Ready?"

"More than ready." She drew in a breath and then started screaming. "Oh, my God, oh my God!" She put her hands on Max's chest as if she were searching for a heartbeat. "He's not breathing anymore. He's dying. Help! Help!" She jumped to her feet.

"What's going on?" the hooded gunman demanded, running over to them.

"We have to get him out of here," she yelled, waving her hand at Max. "Look, he's not breathing anymore. I have to get help. I can't let him die." She jerked to the right, and the gunman instinctively reached for her left arm. It was exactly what she wanted. She brought her other fist down hard on the back of his hand, the hand that was holding the gun.

He swore and dropped his weapon. It skidded across the floor. As he made a move to retrieve it, she kicked in the groin. He doubled over in pain.

Spencer leapt up and grabbed the gun off the floor. He was ready when the second man raced towards them, and he wasted no time pulling the trigger.

A split second later, a blast echoed through the bank.

Hallie saw the second gunman falter, but she didn't have time to see what happened next as the hooded man punched her in the nose. She fell backwards, clipping the side of a desk with her head as she fell toward the ground. She put up her hands to defend herself from the next attack, but it didn't come.

Spencer pulled the man off of her and hit him once, twice, a third time. The man retaliated, landing a blow on Spencer's jaw. They pummeled each other with desperate fury, a fight to the death.

Hallie tried to get up. She needed to help, but she was having trouble standing up. Stars were still exploding in front of her eyes. She forced herself to focus. She couldn't get to her feet, but she could crawl. She might not be able to help Spencer, but she could help Max. She got back to his side and put her hands on his bleeding wound.

And then the front door of the bank blasted open, the glass shattering into a million pieces, as the SWAT team rushed into the building. From there it was a flurry of action, the cops pulling Spencer and the gunman apart, the other hostages crying out with relief that it was finally over.

The paramedics rushed to her side, and she lifted her bloody hands off of Max as they went to work on him. Spencer came over as they hooked Max up to an IV and put him on a gurney.

"Where are you taking him?" Spencer asked.

"St. Mary's."

As the paramedics took Max out of the bank, Spencer turned to her. "We did it."

"Yeah," she said, wiping her hands on her jeans.

"Your nose is bleeding, Hallie."

"Is it?" She had so much blood on her hands and clothes, she didn't know where it was coming from. Spencer grabbed some tissue off a nearby desk and handed it to her. She pressed a wad of Kleenex to her nose. It hurt. She had a feeling it might be broken. But if that were the worst of it, she'd be happy. "Is the other guy dead?" she asked, looking at a second set of paramedics, who were working on the gunman Spencer had shot.

"No. I hit him in the leg."

"Nice shooting."

"It was instinct. You did the hard part, Hallie. You were amazing. So fearless."

"I wasn't fearless; I was terrified. But I knew that it was

going to be him or us, so I did what I had to do."

"Yes, you did. You're stronger than you think."

"Maybe I am," she murmured.

"You need to go to the hospital, Hallie. Your nose could be broken, and your forehead is swelling up. You must be in pain."

"I'm not feeling anything right now."

"You will." Spencer called one of the cops over and told him she needed transportation to the hospital. She would have argued, because an emergency room was the last place she wanted to go, but she was feeling a little dizzy, and it probably wouldn't hurt to get checked out.

Before she left, she gave Spencer one last look. "You told me earlier that your brother was the good one. You're not so bad yourself."

"Right back at you," he said with a smile.

"Goodbye, Spencer."

"Not goodbye. I'll see you later. I still owe you that drink."

"Max," Emma screamed, as the paramedics exited the bank with Max strapped on to a stretcher.

She'd been holding her breath since the shots had gone off and the police had swarmed the bank. Her father and Sean had had to hold her back from rushing the scene. Now she broke free of their grip and sprinted across the street. She met up with Max at the door to the ambulance. His shirt was soaked in blood, and his face was terribly white. She put her hand on his. His skin was ice cold. He was so still, she couldn't even tell if he was breathing, if his heart was beating.

"I want to go with him," she told the paramedic.

"No. Sorry. Meet us at St. Mary's."

"Wait." She leaned over and gave him a quick kiss on the lips. "Fight, Max," she said.

And then the paramedics loaded him into the ambulance and closed the doors. As the vehicle raced away, she wished she'd had another second to tell Max how much she loved him, because she was very afraid she was not going to get another chance.

A fear like no other ran through her. She couldn't lose him now, before they'd even really started. She wanted years with him, marriage, children, and grandchildren.

She started to sway, and her father's arm came around her shoulders. She turned into his embrace, pressing her face against his chest. He patted her on the back. "It's going to be all right, Emma. Have faith."

She lifted her head to face him, needing the Jack Callaway power of conviction. When her father wanted something to happen, it happened.

"Max is a strong man," he told her. "And he needs you to believe in him."

"I do believe in him. But he's really hurt. I can't believe this is happening. This was supposed to be the happiest day of my life."

"The day is not over yet. You are not a quitter, Emma. Lord knows you've proven that to me on a lot of occasions. Don't you give up on me now."

She drew in a deep breath. "I won't. You're right. Max is going to be fine, and one day this is just going to be a crazy story we tell our kids."

"That's my girl."

"Will you take me to the hospital?"

Her father nodded, but as they turned to leave, she stopped, looking back at the bank. "Where is Spencer? I should find him, make sure he's okay."

"Spencer is talking to Brady. You'll see him at the

hospital. He's all right."

"Was he hurt?"

"No, from what I understand Max was the only one shot. Spencer actually took down the bank robbers and saved Max's life. He's a hero."

"Well, good for him," she said. "Max will be proud. He has tried to tell Spencer so many times that he is much more than just an ex-con. But Spencer hasn't been able to see that. Maybe he will now.

Eight

Ten minutes later, Emma and the rest of the Callaway clan, as well as Max's mother, Susan Harrison, gathered in the waiting room of the Emergency Department at St. Mary's Hospital. Information was not long in coming, but the news wasn't good.

"Mr. Harrison is being prepped for surgery," the attending physician told Emma. "He took a gunshot wound to the abdomen and suffered heavy blood loss. We won't know the extent of the internal damage until we operate."

"Oh, God!" Susan Harrison said, tears gathering in her eyes.

Emma took Max's mother's hand in hers. Then she turned back to the doctor and asked what they all wanted to know. "Is he going to be all right?"

"We're doing everything we can. The nurse will take you up to the third floor and show you where you can wait." He tipped his head to the woman in blue scrubs standing nearby. "Mr. Harrison will be in surgery for several hours. The surgeon will be Dr. Blake Holland. He will speak to you as soon as it's done."

As the E.R. physician left, Emma looked at the nurse. "He didn't really answer my question."

The nurse gave her a compassionate smile. "Let me show

you to the waiting room."

"You're not going to answer my question, either, are you?"

"I'm afraid I don't know the answer, but I can tell you that Dr. Holland is the best surgeon we have. Mr. Harrison is in good hands." She turned and headed toward the elevator.

"The doctor is one of the best," Emma told Susan, as they followed the nurse down the hall. Her words didn't seem to register. Max's mother was terrified, which only made Emma more worried. A part of her wanted to get away from the older woman's negativity, but she knew that Max would want her to make sure that his mother was all right.

"I can't lose Max," Susan said. "He's always taken care of me, even though I drive him crazy half the time."

"We're not going to lose him. I have big plans for your son." As they neared the elevator, Susan hesitated. "Maybe I should wait here for Spencer."

"They'll tell him where to find us," Emma replied.

"I can't believe my boys got caught up in a bank robbery. I blame myself for that."

"Why?" she asked in surprise.

"Because I suggested Max change his money before going to the airport."

"You had no way of knowing what would happen."

"I didn't. But I really wish I hadn't said that." She paused. "Max was so happy this afternoon. When he came by to get Spencer, he had the biggest smile on his face. It was blinding. I hadn't seen him like that in such a long time. It reminded me of the way he was as a little boy, so eager, curious, and optimistic. That all changed when his father left us. Max lost his joy. But he got it back when he met you." She gave Emma a sad smile. "You changed his life."

"He changed mine, too," Emma said, as they stepped onto the elevator. "And I'm not giving up. You shouldn't, either. Max would want us to be strong."

"He would," Susan agreed. "And I'm rarely as strong as my son would like me to be. But you are. You're going to get him through this."

"We both are."

Stepping off the elevator, they entered a nearby waiting room. Emma took a seat in a chair against the wall, happy when her mother made a point of asking Susan to sit with her, so Emma could have some time to herself. The rest of her family and bridal party spread out, smaller groups forming here and there. The cops and firefighters had stayed downstairs, so as not to crowd the family, but Emma knew there was a lot of support a few floors down.

Nicole sat down next to her. "Can I get you anything, Em? Coffee? Water? Food? It sounds like we're going to be here for awhile."

"I don't want anything."

As she shifted in her seat, her gaze caught on a splash of red on the waist of her wedding dress. Her heart skipped a beat. She must have gotten the blood on her dress when she'd leaned over to kiss Max. She put her fingers against the red stain and then her mouth started to tremble. She had to bite down on her bottom lip to stop the cry of pain from slipping past her lips.

"Emma?" Nicole asked, her brows knitting together with concern.

"This is Max's blood. He lost so much."

"If he needs blood, he'll get it. We'll line up the family, the firefighters and the police officers, and there will be plenty of blood flowing his way. And don't be thinking it's too late, because it's not. Callaways don't quit, and we don't give up."

"You sound like Dad," she said with a sniff.

"I was channeling him just now," Nicole admitted. "But

the important thing is that he's right."

"I know."

"I need to check in with Jessica, see how Brandon is doing, but I'll be right back."

"That's fine." As Nicole left, Emma settled back in her chair and rested her head against the wall. Closing her eyes, she said a silent prayer for Max's recovery. He had to get better, because he was truly the love of her lifetime. She forced the image of him lying so still, covered in blood, out of her mind and tried to bring up the happy memories.

They'd had a lot of good moments in the past year, but probably the best was the day they'd moved into their apartment.

She smiled to herself as she drifted to a happier place…

It was after midnight.

They'd spent the night unpacking boxes and arguing about where to put the ugly recliner Max thought was perfect for watching ballgames, and she thought was perfect for the dumpster.

Max had ended up winning the argument with a kiss that had turned into much, much more. After making love, they'd been lying on the floor of their barely furnished apartment when Max rolled over on to his side and gave her a serious look.

"What?" she asked. "If you thought making love to me was going to make me change my mind about the recliner, you do not know me at all. I am not that easy." She smiled, then started to worry when his expression only grew more serious. "Okay, I am that easy. If you really want the recliner—"

"Emma, I don't give a damn about the recliner."

"Then why do you look so concerned? What are you worrying about?"

"Whether or not you'll say yes, or if you'll think it's soon,

too fast."

Her heart started to beat in triple time. "Yes to what, Max?"

He gave her a long look. "Will you marry me, Em?"

The question took her breath away. She hadn't been expecting him to propose so soon after moving in together. She'd thought they were easing their way towards a more permanent commitment.

"Okay, now I'm thinking it is too soon," he said when she didn't answer. "Sorry, forget I asked."

She immediately shook her head. "No, it's the perfect time—for the question and for the answer. Which is yes. I love you, Max. I want to marry you. I want to have a life with you."

Relief flooded his eyes. "I love you, too, Emma. You are the most stubbornly annoying, beautiful, generous, smart woman, I know."

"Hey, you could leave out a few of those adjectives," she protested. "And I'm not the only one who's stubborn. You have a very hard head."

He smiled. "I know. We're a perfect match. I want to live with you and love you and fight with you every day of our lives."

"Maybe we can keep the fights to only every now and then," she teased. "Or maybe never if you agree to put that chair in the dumpster."

"Fine, the chair goes in the dumpster."

"I was just kidding. If you can't live without it, then it stays. And I'll be very happy to curl up on your lap while you're sitting in it."

"The only thing I can't live without is you."

"You don't have to. I'm not going anywhere."

"Good."

"So when did you decide you wanted to marry me?" she

asked.

"After our first fight."

"We fought the first day we met," she reminded him. "We were working on a case and you didn't want to share your information with me."

"And you didn't want to share your info with me, either. But I thought you were gorgeous with your silky blond hair and spitfire blue eyes."

"I thought you were annoying, but also kind of hot," she admitted.

"I liked that you didn't back down."

"No, you didn't," she teased.

"Okay, maybe I didn't like it that much. But I know that life with you is going to be one hell of a ride."

"Never boring. So when do you want to get married?"

"Whenever you want. But for now..." He got up and walked across the room, pulling a jewelry box out of his coat pocket. Then he came back to her. "I was going to give this to you tomorrow, on your birthday." He glanced at the clock. "Actually it's after midnight, so it is your birthday." He opened the lid. "What do you think?"

She gasped at the sight of beautiful square-cut diamond ring. "It's gorgeous. And it's so me. You did good."

"I had a little help from your sister, Nicole. Do you like it?"

"I love it."

He slipped it on to her finger. "It fits."

"It does," she said, tears blurring her eyes as she looked from the ring to him. "You just have to make me one promise, Max."

"Anything."

"Don't ever leave me."

"I promise," he said, then kissed away her tears. "You and I are going to be together for a very long time."

The memory of Max's words echoed through Emma's head as the dream faded away. She opened her eyes and looked around the waiting room, wishing she could go back to the happy place. But reality was right in front of her.

There were a lot of concerned faces turned in her direction, but everyone was giving her space. Her family knew her well. She was a strong person, and she knew how to fight, but sometimes she needed to be in her head for a few minutes so she could get past the fear and get onto the battle ahead.

She straightened in her chair as Spencer entered the room. His tuxedo jacket was missing. His white shirt and gold tie were covered in blood. His face looked battered, a golf-ball sized swelling around his right eye that was turning a dark shade of purple. His mother ran to him, giving him a long, tight hug.

"I'm okay, Mom," he said.

"You're hurt?"

"It's not a big deal," he said, gently extricating himself from her embrace. He walked over to Emma. "I'm so sorry."

"It's not your fault," she said, getting up to give him a hug. "And from what I hear, you were quite the hero."

"When will we know anything?"

"The doctor said it could be a few hours. Can you tell me what happened, Spencer?"

"Sure," he said, waving her back into her chair. Then he sat down next to her. "What do you want to know?"

"Everything. Your mom said Max went to the bank to change some money?"

"For your honeymoon. It was supposed to be a quick, ten-minute stop." Spencer shook his head, his lips tightening. "And then it all went to hell."

"How did Max get shot?"

"One of the bank employees went to hit the silent alarm

on her computer. The gunman saw her and just as he pulled the trigger, Max dived in front of her. He was acting the hero—as usual. I told him not to, but does he ever listen to me?" he said gruffly.

She heard the pain in Spencer's voice. He was covering up his fear with anger. "What happened next?"

"I tried to stop the bleeding, but I didn't know what I was doing. Fortunately, there was a nurse in the bank, Hallie Cooper. She told me what to do."

"Thank God. Was Max in a lot of pain? Was he talking?"

Spencer hesitated.

"What did he say?" she pressed.

"He wanted me to tell you that he loved you, Emma."

She put a hand to her mouth, tears welling up again. "He didn't think he was going to make it, did he?"

"You were on his mind. You're always on his mind. My brother is crazy about you." He paused. "After that, he passed out. It was better that way. His body was resting. But then, towards the end, he started to get restless. I had trouble keeping pressure on the wound. Hallie and I realized that we were running out of time. The gunmen didn't know what to do. They were afraid they were going to get shot walking out the door."

"So what did you do?" she asked, a shiver running down her spine as his words took her right into the bank, into the terrifying ordeal.

"One of the men had left his gun on the desk by the phone when he went to look out the window. It was our chance to make a move. Hallie started screaming, telling the other guy that Max was dying. When he came close, she knocked the gun out of his hand. I picked up his gun and shot the other guy. It all happened really fast. Looking back, I wish we'd acted sooner. But we kept thinking it was going to be over in a minute."

"You took the only opportunity you had, Spencer. And Hallie sounds incredibly brave."

"She was amazing," he said, admiration in his tone. "She's downstairs getting checked out. That guy might have broken her nose. I need to go check on her."

"I'll go with you."

"Really? You don't want to wait here?"

"I could use a walk, and I want to meet her—thank her."

"You can do that later."

"The surgery is going to take hours, and I've never been good at waiting." She got to her feet and turned to her mother. "Spencer and I are going to check on the woman who helped saved Max. I'll just be a few minutes, but you'll come find me if there's any news?"

"I will," Lynda promised.

As they walked out of the waiting room, Emma said, "Did Max tell you where he was taking me on our honeymoon?"

Spencer hesitated. "He did, but I can't tell you, Emma."

"Why not?"

"Because Max wants it to be a surprise."

She met his gaze and appreciated what he wasn't saying. "You're right. I'll let him tell me himself. Or better yet—show me."

Nine

—➤➤➤❰❰❰—

Hallie winced as the E.R. doctor finished his examination of her bruised nose.

"I don't think it's broken," he said. "The swelling should go down within twenty-four hours. You're going to have some nice shiners though."

"Great. Raccoon eyes. I can't wait."

"As for your head, the CT scan was normal, but you should take it easy for the next day or two. I'll give you a prescription for some painkillers, and you can be on your way."

She was relieved to hear that. Being back in a hospital felt both awkward and strangely comfortable. For the past ten years, her life had revolved around medicine. Hospitals had been her second home. All of her friends had been doctors and nurses, lab techs and orderlies. And when she'd gone into the Army, the uniforms had changed but not the medicine.

She'd always been good at her job. It was the one place where she'd felt smart, proud and in control—until her life and her love had blown up right in front of her. She forced the image out of her mind, but she knew the memories would always be there lurking in the background, bringing stress and anxiety to every day of her life.

"You should continue to ice. It will help the bruising,"

the doctor added.

"I'm a nurse. I know what to do."

"Sometimes nurses make the worse patients."

"I think they say that about doctors."

He smiled. "Probably true. Call me if you have any unexpected pain or severe bleeding."

"I will."

As the doctor left the room, Spencer walked in, followed by a blond woman wearing an overcoat over a wedding gown. Hallie knew immediately who she was. This was Max's bride—

Emma.

"Hallie, how are you?" Spencer asked, concern in his eyes. "Is your nose broken?"

"No, just bruised. How did you know where I was?"

"Emma got it out of the nurse. She was quite persistent." He smiled at the bride. "Emma, this is Hallie Cooper—Emma Callaway."

Emma walked over to the examining table, her blue eyes showing strain and gratitude.

"I want to thank you, Hallie. Spencer told me what you did for Max. I'm sorry you were caught up in such a bad situation, but I'm also really glad you were there." She frowned. "That sounds bad—"

"I know what you mean," Hallie said, cutting her off. "And I was happy to help. Max said your name a few times and told us he loved you."

Emma's eyes began to water. "I didn't think he was conscious."

"He drifted in and out," Hallie said. "But it was clear he was thinking about you." She hoped her words were making Emma feel better, but as a tear slid out of the corner of her eye, she thought maybe not.

Emma wiped the tear away. "I'm not going to cry," she

said. "Max will be all right. He's tough."

"Max is in surgery now," Spencer put in.

"That's good." She paused. "I appreciate you coming to check on me, but you should go back to your families."

"I think I will do that," Emma said.

"I'll be up in a minute," Spencer said.

"Okay." Emma smiled at Hallie. "I hope you feel better. I know Max is going to want to meet you when he wakes up."

"I would love to see him back on his feet."

As Emma left the room, Hallie swallowed a little nervously. She was suddenly aware of Spencer in a very different way. They'd been caught up in a life and death situation, no time to think, only to act, and they'd bonded, connected on a level that only an extremely dangerous moment could bring on. But that moment was over. Now what?

Now—nothing, she told herself. She'd made a plan for her life, a plan to lie on a beach for a few months and regroup. She might have missed her flight, but there would be another one tomorrow. She should be on it.

"What a day, huh?" Spencer asked, folding his arms in front of his chest. "It feels surreal. Like a dream."

"More like a nightmare. Did you talk to the police?"

"Yeah, that's why it took me so long to get here."

"What happened to the gunmen?"

"The one I shot was taken to another hospital. The other one is being booked into jail. They're going to go away for a long time."

"I hope so."

"Have you talked to police?" Spencer asked.

"I spoke to someone when I first got here. He brought me my phone, my wallet, and my now worthless plane ticket. He said he'd call me tomorrow if he had any other questions, but I'm sure all of us will tell the same story." She slid off the table, feeling a little steadier now. The dizzying adrenaline had finally worn off.

"Are you sure you're okay?" Spencer asked.

"I am sure. And I'd like to get out of here."

"How are you getting home?"

"Good question. My car is still at the bank. I guess I'll take a cab and get it tomorrow. Although, it will be weird to go back there."

"Take someone with you."

"I can handle it."

"I'm sure you can," he said with a smile. "Why don't you call a family member now to take you home?"

It was a simple question, but she didn't have a simple answer. "I don't have anyone to call."

His gaze narrowed speculatively. "No family?"

"I don't have anyone to call," she repeated, hoping he'd let it end there.

Of course he didn't. "Why not? Where are they?" he asked.

She sighed. "You don't let things go, do you?"

"I'm curious."

"Fine. My father lives in the East Bay, but we haven't spoken to each other in a few months."

"Why not?"

"He didn't like something I did," she replied.

"What about your mother?"

"She died when I was ten. And my only brother is overseas, if that's your next question. He's an Air Force pilot."

"Did your father serve in the military as well?"

"For many years," she said. "Are you done?"

He gave her a small smile. "I'm just getting started. If you're not in a rush to get home, can I buy you a cup of coffee in the cafeteria?"

She should say no. She should end this relationship—or

whatever it was—now, before anything else happened. She was broken, and her life was a mess, and the last thing she needed to do was involve anyone else in it. But there was something about Spencer that called out to her. So instead of turning him down, she said. "All right. I don't need any caffeine though. Maybe some herbal tea." As they walked out of the exam room, she added. "Are you sure you don't want to get back to your family?"

"My mother is being soothed by Mrs. Callaway, and I could use a moment to catch my breath. There are going to be a lot of questions, and I'm not ready to answer them all yet."

She could understand that. "Then let's get some tea."

—⇒≫≪⇐—

The hospital cafeteria was located in the basement and it was relatively empty, which wasn't surprising for nine o'clock on a Saturday night. Hallie couldn't believe that so much had happened in just a few hours. While Spencer went for decaf coffee, Hallie poured a cup of hot tea, and they sat down at a table in the corner.

As Spencer sipped his coffee, she let herself really look at him. When he'd first flirted with her in line, she'd been so focused on getting out of town and running away from her life, that she hadn't wanted to acknowledge how handsome he was, or the little flutter of attraction that had run through her when their eyes had met. In fact, she'd try to tell herself that flutter was indigestion, because there was no way she could feel anything for a man ever again. She was numb inside. Her soul had died.

But she was wrong about not being able to feel something. In fact, the nervous flutter was back, and it had nothing to do with indigestion, and everything to do with the tall, handsome, dark-haired man in front of her.

"You're staring," Spencer said.

She started as he lifted his gaze to meet hers. "Sorry. I was looking at your bruises. Nurse's habit," she lied. She didn't want him to think she was interested in him, because nothing was going to happen. How crazy would she be to get involved with a man she barely knew? And what she did know was a little alarming. He'd killed a man. He'd gone to prison. It sounded like a raw deal, but she'd only heard one side of the story.

On the other hand, actions spoke louder than words, and she'd seen Spencer in action. He'd been thoughtful and smart, staying calm when she'd been extremely anxious. And he'd fought for his brother and for her. He had demonstrated great courage, and she would always be grateful to him. But they were sitting here having tea and coffee because of gratitude. They both knew that.

"You said you weren't a nurse anymore," Spencer reminded her. "So my bruises shouldn't concern you."

"Some habits don't go away. You should put some ice on your face."

"I could say the same to you."

At his remark, she found herself smiling. "We must make a great looking couple."

He smiled back at her. "It's probably good we don't have a mirror."

"I wondered why the cashier gave us such a wary look. She probably thought we beat each other up."

"How's your tea?"

"Warm and soothing. I feel better."

"Good. You've probably spent a lot of time in hospital cafeterias."

"More time than in my own kitchen."

He rested his forearms on the table as he leaned forward, giving her an interested look. "Tell me your story, Hallie."

"I already told you when we were in the bank," she prevaricated.

"You said your fiancé was killed, but not why you quit nursing."

She shook her head. "I don't want to do this."

"Do what?"

"Exchange life stories. Pretend we're friends."

"How could we not be friends after everything we went through together?"

"But we're never going to see each other again after tonight."

"Of course we are. I still owe you a rum drink. You promised to let me buy you one."

"Then we won't see each other again after that."

"Hallie. Just talk to me. That's all I'm asking."

She slid her finger around the rim of her teacup. "That's asking a lot. A lot of bad things happened."

"And you're keeping them all inside."

"Why torture anyone else?" she asked.

"When it's so much easier to just torture yourself," he finished.

"Maybe I deserve it."

"I won't know until you talk to me." He paused. "When I went to prison, I was filled with rage at the injustice of what had happened to me. I couldn't talk to anyone about it, because I was so angry. I blamed the people around me for not doing enough. Max was a big target. I refused to see him after the first few visits. And after that, he stopped trying to see me. Most everyone else did, too. I had no one to talk to, because that's the way I wanted it, and I was as trapped in my head as I was trapped in that cell. Everything just festered inside of me. It was so bad I gave myself an ulcer. And I finally, finally realized that I wasn't punishing anyone else with my attitude, only myself. The anger was killing me more than the prison term."

"And you just let it go? Just like that?"

"God, no! Not just like that. It's still not completely gone, but I've done some talking the past few months. I've stopped making my world all about me about that one terrible event in my life. I'm starting to look out, instead of in." He paused. "I don't want to see you waste as much time as I did."

"Talking won't change anything."

"Maybe it will. Maybe you need to say something out loud and really hear the words. I'm not going to judge you, Hallie. I'm the last person who could judge anyone."

She stared back at him indecisively. She'd only told the whole story to one other person, her father, and he had judged her.

She tapped her fingers nervously on the tabletop, torn between a sudden desire to unload and a self-protective instinct to stay quiet. How could she trust Spencer, when the man who'd raised her, the man she adored and admired, had looked at her with disgust and disappointment? She was just setting herself up for another fall.

Spencer covered her nervous fingers with his warm hand, and his gaze met hers. "I promise, Hallie. You talk, I listen. No opinion."

She debated another minute and then said. "I'll start. I'm not sure how far I'll get."

"One step at a time."

She licked her lips. "We were in the middle East. My fiancé was a soldier. We'd been going out for almost a year and we'd gotten engaged just before Christmas, last year. Another reason why I really hate this season."

He nodded. "Go on."

"I asked Doug to meet me one night. I wanted to talk about our wedding plans. It was late, and he was tired. He'd been out all day that day, but I pushed him to meet me." She shook her head at the memory. "It was so stupid. My friend had sent me a bridal magazine, and I wanted to show him the dress I liked. As if it mattered to him what I wore. He didn't care at all about dresses or flowers or anything. He just wanted to marry me. I was getting too worked up about silly little things."

"What happened?"

She opened her mouth to answer, but instead of seeing Spencer's face in front of her, she saw blinding headlights. She heard the shouts to stop, and felt the terrifying fear of death run through her.

"Hallie."

Spencer's voice brought her back to the present.

"A truck came crashing through the gate," she said. "Not far from where we were standing. Doug instinctively moved towards the danger. That's the kind of man he was. A guy leaned out of the truck with an automatic weapon in his hand. He fired three times. Doug fell face down on the ground. I screamed. I started to go to him, and then the whole world exploded. I was thrown back ten feet."

Spencer squeezed her hand, his gaze filling with compassion. "You don't have to go on, Hallie. I'm sorry. I shouldn't have asked you to relive something that horrific."

"It's okay," she said, taking a moment to breathe. "I have to finish, because that's not where the story ends."

He stared back at her. "Where does it end?"

"On the operating table."

"You couldn't save Doug," he said flatly.

She shook her head. "I didn't have a chance to save Doug. After the explosion, he wasn't on the ground anymore. His body…Well, he never made it to the O.R." She couldn't go into any more detail than that.

His lips tightened. "So what happened on the table?"

"After the blast, there were a lot of injuries. I wanted to

scream and cry and mourn for Doug, but there were other soldiers to save, and some of them were my friends. I went to work, and I put everything else out of my mind, the way I was trained to do." She paused, her mind going back in time again. "I was moving so fast. It was a blur of faces, bodies, blood—so much blood. And then I saw someone I recognized. It wasn't a soldier. It was the man in the truck, the one who'd shot Doug."

Spencer blew out a breath. "What did you do?"

"The doctor was giving me orders, but I couldn't hear him. I couldn't move. I looked at that man on the table, and I saw a murderer. All I could think was that this man was supposed to die. He wanted to die. He was a suicide bomber. Why should I save him?" She met Spencer's gaze head on. "You can probably guess what happened."

"He died," Spencer said.

She nodded. "It was my fault."

"Was it? Or were his injuries so severe that he couldn't be saved?" Spencer challenged.

"Some of my friends made that excuse for me," she conceded. "But it didn't change what I'd done or didn't do. Medicine isn't supposed to be about right and wrong, good people and bad people. You're supposed to try to save the patient in front of you. That's all that matters, and I didn't do that. I didn't just freeze. I deliberately chose not to act. I went against everything I believed in, everything I was about." She took a breath. "I haven't been back in the operating room since that night. They sent me to counseling, and I told the psychiatrist I couldn't go back, and he eventually recommended discharge. Since I got out, I've been trying to decide what the hell I'm going to do with my life now. All I ever wanted to be was a nurse. I don't know how to do anything else."

"You were a nurse tonight. You saved Max's life."

"I hope I helped, but you did the hard part, Spencer."

"You told me what to do. And you talked to Max. You kept him quiet. You made him believe in Emma and their love."

"Instinct took over." She sipped her tea, feeling surprisingly better and a little lighter having told the whole story. Maybe she had needed to say it out loud. And Spencer hadn't judged her. There had been no disgust in his eyes, only kindness. "Thank you, Spencer. For doing what you said, offering no opinion about what I did, or didn't do. My father had a lot to say. And it was not good."

"Is that why you haven't spoken to him?"

"He's extremely disappointed in me, so yes."

"How could he not understand why you acted the way you did?"

"Because he's a brilliant doctor, and he would never walk away from a patient, no matter what they'd done."

"Maybe he's never been tested the way you were."

"I think he has. He's just stronger than me. He's really an incredible person. I've always loved him and admired him and wanted to be just like him. But I couldn't live up to his example. I fell really short."

"So you told him, and he said…"

"Nothing. He just stared at me. It was the longest silence of my life. Then I left. That was it. I don't blame him. I know what I did was wrong."

Spencer frowned. "You're being extremely hard on yourself, Hallie. You'd just seen your fiancé die. It's surprising you could do anything at all at that point."

"Don't let me off the hook."

"I couldn't do that if I tried. You're the only one who can do that. I don't know if what you did in that operating room was as horrible as you think it was. But I do know what you did today, and it was amazing. Just coming to my aid put you in danger, but you did it anyway. And then you take on a man with a gun twice your size? You were brave and selfless, and you should be proud of yourself."

Her eyes filled with tears, the intensity of his words breaking down the walls of guilt and shame she'd built up in her head. "You're being really nice, Spencer."

"You have to stop defining yourself by one moment in your past."

"Isn't that what you've been doing?"

"I'm trying to change. So should you. Because when I thought we might die in that bank, I realized how much I want to live."

"I had the same thought," she admitted. "I wanted to die for a long time. I kept asking why Doug, why not me? But when I saw death staring me in the face, I knew I didn't want that at all."

"And Doug wouldn't want it for you. He'd want you to make the most of your life."

"He would," she said, tearing up again. "You're right." He squeezed her fingers again, and she realized they were still holding hands, and she didn't want to let go. "We are quite a pair, aren't we?" she asked. "And I'm not talking about the bruises anymore."

"We've both been to hell. But we're not there anymore."

"What have you been doing since you got out of prison?" she asked, curious about who he was now.

"Working in a deli. It's a quite change from my old job as a commodities trader, but I couldn't do that anymore. And with a record, I couldn't be too choosey. Anyway, since being at the deli, I've been toying with the idea of becoming a chef.

"Really?" she asked in surprise.

"It's probably a crazy dream."

"But it's a great dream."

"I like to cook. I need to get better."

"So you'll get better. I hate to cook, but I really like to eat."

"Maybe you'll let me practice on you."

"Maybe." She paused as the staff began to close down the cafeteria. "I think it's time to go."

"Yeah." He let go of her hand. "I need to get upstairs anyway."

She nodded, feeling a little chill now that there was distance between them.

"Would you come with me?" he asked as they headed out the door.

She hesitated. "Oh, I don't know. You have your family and friends."

"But I want you."

His simple words sent a shiver down her spine.

And once again, when she should have said *no*, she found herself saying *yes*.

Ten

As they walked out of the cafeteria, Spencer stayed close to Hallie's side. It was strange and rather amazing the connection he felt to her. He'd felt closed off and numb for so long, but now his skin was tingling, and his black and white world was filling with color. He just needed Max to recover in order to really enjoy the new feelings of hope and optimism for the future.

They took the elevator to the third floor and walked down the hall to the waiting room. There were at least twenty people inside, most of them Callaways, and many of whom he'd met the night before at the rehearsal dinner. That seemed like a lifetime ago.

"I should go," Hallie murmured, holding back when they reached the doorway. "I don't belong here."

"I don't, either," he said.

"You're his brother."

"And these are mostly his in-laws. I could use a friend."

"Fine, but stop telling everyone I saved Max's life. You're giving me too much credit."

He smiled. "And you're being way too modest. You don't have to meet everyone, but I do want to introduce you to my mother."

"Really?" she asked, doubt in her voice. "Your mom?"

"It won't hurt a bit," he said lightly.

"You know when nurses say that, they're lying," she told him.

He smiled and led her across the room to where his mother was sitting next to Emma's mom, Lynda. They both got up to hug him. And when they were done, he found himself the recipient of many more Callaway hugs. By the time he got through the family, he could see Hallie caught up in the same warm receiving line, as Emma told her family that this was the woman who saved Max's life. At least, Hallie couldn't blame him for the attention.

When they'd gone through the line, they took a seat against the far wall.

"Well," Hallie murmured. "That was crazy. Are these people always so welcoming?"

He nodded. "Yeah, pretty much. They already consider Max a friend, a son, a brother, and a brother-in-law."

"I hope you're not worried about losing him to the Callaways, because I think they're officially adopting you and your mother, too."

"They've been great," he agreed. "I'm happy for Max." As he settled into his seat, he saw her take out her phone and check the messages. "Anything important come in?"

"No, just an alert that I missed my flight."

"There's probably one tomorrow. You should check."

"I'll do it later," she said.

He was happy to see her put away her phone, because the last thing he wanted her to do was get on a plane. "What do you usually do for Christmas, when you're not heading for the tropics?"

"I actually missed Christmas last year. I couldn't get home. But before that I always celebrated with my dad, and sometimes with my brother, if he could make it back. My Aunt Debbie, and her husband and kids, would come over on Christmas Eve. She was like a second mom to me after my mother died. We'd have a big dinner and exchange presents. Then on Christmas Day we always went to church in the morning and then had a big lunch after that. Sometimes we'd invite the neighbors in or some of my father's friends. It was different every year."

"It sounds nice," he said, hearing the wistful note in her voice. "Aren't you going to miss that?"

"I'd just put a damper on things."

"No one else besides your dad knows about…"

"They know about Doug, but nothing else, unless my father told Aunt Debbie, but I doubt he would do that."

"You've had no communication with him since the day you told him?"

She hesitated. "He's texted a few times."

"Really?" he asked, shifting in his seat. "You didn't mention that before. Did you text him back?"

"No."

"Hallie, what are you doing?"

"Hey, you said you weren't going to judge."

"I'm not judging, I'm asking you a question. Why haven't you responded to his texts?"

"I don't know."

"Yes, you do."

"Look, I had a plan to get out of town and take my problems with me. It was a good plan, until it all went to hell when I decided to stop at the bank."

"Maybe something good will come of today."

"Like what?"

"A chance to make things right. We both know life is short. You love your dad. You should talk to him again. Give it one more try. He deserves that, and so do you."

"Maybe. I'll think about it." She crossed her legs and folded her arms in front of her chest, as if she were settling in for the long haul, and they probably were.

He was glad Hallie had stayed for so many reasons, but one of the biggest was that he'd rather spend the waiting time getting to know her than thinking about how badly Max was hurt. He couldn't get the sight of all that blood out of his head, especially when his clothes were still covered in it. He just hoped the bullet had missed the vital organs and that they hadn't waited too long to act.

"Spencer?"

He met Hallie's gaze.

"Don't go back there," she said.

"Are you reading my mind now?"

"Max is in good hands. There's nothing to do but wait," she said.

"You're right."

"So what do you like to cook?" she asked.

"A lot of things."

"Like?"

"Well, I just made a really good curry dish with lamb."

"Sounds delicious. I love curry. Tell me more."

He gave her a doubtful look. "You really want to talk about food?"

"It seems like a good topic to me, and one that isn't going to upset either one of us."

"I might bore you to sleep."

She smiled. "I'll take that risk."

"You are the daredevil."

"Don't you know it," she said lightly.

He smiled back at her. "Okay, then let me tell you about this stew I'm working on…"

—⟫⟪—

Emma glanced at the clock on the wall, feeling as if the minutes were passing with agonizing slowness. Max had been in surgery for almost four hours, and she was tired of waiting. Her siblings and parents had been great at trying to keep her distracted, but they'd eventually run out of things to say, and she'd drunk enough coffee to sink a ship, which probably hadn't been a good idea. The caffeine had only made her more jumpy and anxious.

Nicole came into the room after having gone to check with the nurse's station. She immediately shook her head at Emma's silent question. "No news yet, but they think it will be soon."

"They said that an hour ago."

"I know," Nicole said. "But let's go with no news is good news."

She saw the weariness in her sister's face. "If you need to go home, Nicole, I can call you—"

"Don't be silly. I'm not going anywhere. Jessica is keeping Brandon overnight, so I'm all yours."

Shayla came over to join them. "I talked to a friend of mine who's an intern here. He said he thinks the surgery is almost done. He also reiterated that Dr. Holland is brilliant."

Emma was happy to hear both of those statements.

"I never think about the people waiting," Shayla said, as she took a seat. "In medical school, we're so focused on the physical body, on diagnosis, treatment, pharmaceuticals, but we don't spent a lot of time thinking about the people in the waiting room. I'm going to remember this feeling when I'm a surgeon."

"You're going to make a really good one," Emma said. Shayla had always been an academic overachiever, but it was nice to see her taking in the whole picture.

She'd no sooner finished speaking than the door opened, and a doctor walked in. He was dressed in scrubs and booties and looked like he'd come straight from the O.R.

Emma jumped to her feet and rushed across the room.

Susan was just as fast. They grabbed each other's hand as they faced the doctor together.

"I'm Dr. Holland," he said. "Mr. Harrison is doing well. He made it through the surgery without complications, and we're anticipating a full recovery."

It took a minute for his words to register through the fear. "Oh, my God," Emma said, putting her other hand to her heart. "Can you say that again?"

The doctor smiled. "He's going to be fine, but he'll need some recovery time."

She blew out a breath, feeling an enormous weight lift off her chest. "That is the best news. Thank you so much."

"Mr. Harrison did the hard work," the doctor said. "He's a fighter."

"I know," she replied, never doubting that Max would fight to come back to her. "When can I see him?"

"He'll be asleep for a few hours."

"I want to sit with him. Can I do that? Please."

He nodded. "Of course, but only one of you. We'll save the other visits for tomorrow afternoon."

Emma nodded her agreement.

"The nurse will come and get you when Mr. Harrison is back in his room."

As the doctor left, she looked around at her friends and family, the people who had stood by her on the worst day of her life. "He's going to be okay," she said again, happiness racing through her veins.

Her words were met with a chorus of cheers and smiles, all except for Max's mother, who was quietly weeping into her tissue.

"Susan," Emma said, squeezing her hand.

"Don't mind me," Susan said. "These are happy tears now." She gave Emma a watery smile. "My boy is going to be all right."

"He is." Emma hesitated. The last thing she wanted to do was give up her seat at Max's bedside, but she knew his mother was very worried about him, too. "Do you want to go in and see him first?"

"Oh, no, dear," she said, shaking her head. "Max will want you there, Emma. Just tell him we're all thinking about him."

"Spencer?" she asked, offering him the same courtesy.

He smiled. "Are you kidding? I'm not the pretty face my brother wants to see when he wakes up. But tell him next time he wants to go to the bank, I'm going to pass."

"Online banking from here on," she agreed. She looked back at her sister, Nicole. "We should make some calls, let people know."

"I'm on it," Nicole said. "I'll start with the guys downstairs."

"And I'll call the family," Lynda said.

"I'll go through the wedding list with Cynthia and make sure all the guests get an update," Shayla said. "Don't worry about anything, Emma. Just go see your man."

"I will. You've all been amazing to me. I couldn't have gotten through this without any you. I'm so lucky to have this wonderful, incredible family."

"You never have to get through anything without us," her father said, giving her a hug. "We're Callaways. All for one. One for all."

"Always, Dad." She ran to the door to meet the nurse who was coming to get her. She couldn't wait to see Max. She wouldn't feel completely better until he opened his eyes and smiled at her. Then her world would be right side up again.

—➤➤◄◄—

As Emma left the room, Spencer ran a weary hand

through his hair and looked at Hallie. "I guess that's it."

She gave him a warm smile. "I'm so glad you got good news."

"Thanks for staying with me."

"No problem. I learned a lot. I think I might even try my own hand at a stew."

He grinned at her teasing smile. "I told you I would bore you."

"You didn't. But I think I will find myself a cab and go home."

"Why don't I drive you?"

"You should stay with your mom."

He knew she was right, but he really didn't want to say goodbye to Hallie yet. He was just getting to know her, and he was afraid if he let her walk away now, he'd never see her again. The day's events had brought down her guard walls, but would they be back up in the morning? Would she get on a plane and fly off to her dream island and never come home again? "I'll walk you to the elevator then."

"Great."

The walk was far too short.

As she reached for the elevator button, he stepped in front of her. "Hallie…"

"What?"

"We need to get that drink."

"We will," she said.

"When you get back from the island?"

She shook her head. "I'm not going to the island."

"But the beach is calling, isn't it?"

"It was, until I spent half the night talking to you. You're very persuasive Spencer." She paused. "I'm going to give my dad a call in the morning and maybe go see him."

"Really?"

"You said some things that made sense."

"I'm glad. So if I'm that good, can I persuade you to give me your phone number now?"

She smiled. "I already did."

He gave her a questioning look. "What do you mean?"

"I put it in your phone when you went to the restroom earlier."

He grinned. "Sneaky."

"You really don't know anything about me."

"I'm looking forward to finding out more."

"I kind of feel the same way about you." She reached around him and pushed the button. "Before we say goodbye, I just need to know one thing."

"What's that?" he asked.

She stepped forward, put her hands on his head and pulled him into one hot and amazingly good kiss. Her lips were warm and inviting, and the spark that had been burning since he'd first laid eyes on her leapt into a full-blown flame. He felt a passion brewing that he hadn't felt in a very long time. He put his hands on her waist and held on, wanting to keep the kiss going for as long as possible.

Then the elevator dinged, and she broke away with a breathless smile. "Just as I thought," she said. "That mouth of yours is good for a lot more than talking."

He grinned. "Yours, too. That was hot. I'm going to call you tomorrow. You better answer."

Hallie stepped into the elevator. "I will," she said.

The elevator doors closed, and he walked back down the hall, feeling light on his feet and happier than he'd been in a decade.

The rest of his life was about to begin. He was closing the book on his past for good, and he was looking forward to a future—a future that was going to include one beautiful, gutsy redhead.

--->->-<-<--

Emma sat by Max's side until dawn. The sun was just creeping through the slit in the curtains when Max began to stir. She got to her feet as his eyelids flickered and then slowly opened. She put her hand on his arm as he tried to focus. His skin was warm now, and it was so much better than the icy cold she'd felt the night before.

His gaze finally met hers.

"Max," she whispered.

His lips parted, but his voice was hoarse and rough when he said, "Emma."

"Don't try to talk," she said quickly. Seeing the confusion in his eyes, she added, "You're in the hospital. You were shot, but you're going to be all right." She gave him a smile, wanting to reassure him, wanting to take the sudden flash of fear out of his eyes. She suddenly realized where it was coming from. "Spencer is all right, too."

Relief moved across his face. He took several deeper breaths and then said, "I'm sorry."

Her heart tore at his words. "You don't have anything to be sorry for."

"The wedding—"

"Will happen another day. Don't worry about it."

"All the money your parents spent—"

"Stop. It's going to be fine," she said firmly. "The only thing that matters is you. You're going to be all right. That's all I care about."

"You look so pretty."

She gave him a teary smile. "That's the drugs talking. I'm a mess."

"You have blood on your dress." He frowned. "How did you get blood on your clothes?"

"I hugged you," she said. "Right before they put you in the ambulance."

"How did I get out of the bank?"

"It's a long story. Spencer will tell you everything."

"Did anyone else get hurt?"

"You're the only one. Luckily there was a nurse in the bank. She helped Spencer take care of you."

"Did she have red hair?"

"She did."

"Spencer was hitting on her in line."

"I think he's still doing that," she said with a smile. "She spent half the night in the waiting room with him."

"Good for him."

"You should rest now." Her hand slid down his arm and she put her fingers around his.

He looked into her eyes. "Are you still going to marry me, Emma?"

"Try and stop me," she said. "Third time will be the charm. And I really don't care about any more wedding planning, Max. We can get married wherever. It's the marriage part I want, the having children and growing old together that's important. I want what my grandparents' have—the next sixty years with you."

"Only sixty?"

"Make that a hundred. Try to rest now."

"Kiss me first," he said.

She lowered her head and kissed him on the lips, infusing every bit of her love and passion for him in that one long kiss. "Sleep now."

"Now? After that?" he said. "I want another kiss."

"Tomorrow," she said with a laugh.

Despite his protest, his eyes were already drifting closed. She sat back down in the chair and then leaned back and closed her eyes, letting exhaustion sweep her into a happy dream of many more tomorrows with the man she loved.

Eleven

Two weeks later – Christmas Eve

"I thought you were taking me out to dinner," Hallie said as Spencer ushered her up the steps of the San Francisco Courthouse.

He smiled. "You'll get dinner—eventually."

"That sounds ominous. What's going on?"

"It's a surprise."

Spencer had been surprising her a lot lately. In fact, they'd spent much of the last two weeks together. As promised, their first date had been to the Beachside Bar where he'd introduced her to San Francisco's finest rum drinks. They'd talked for hours over those drinks, and found they had more in common than just dark pasts.

She couldn't remember feeling so comfortable with a man so quickly, but going through a life and death situation with Spencer had vaulted them over the initial first date awkwardness, and their relationship was moving quickly past friendship into passion and maybe even love.

They'd both been through their own version of hell, but they were coming out of the darkness. Spencer had enrolled in a cooking class and was working on the weekends as a sous chef, and she'd just spoken to one of her former bosses at San Francisco General Hospital about working in the maternity ward. She thought bringing babies into the world would be a nice change of pace. She'd missed nursing, and it was time to stop running away from what she loved. Her punishment was over.

She'd never imagined a trip to the bank could turn her entire life upside down. And it wasn't just the robbery that had shaken her out of her stupor; it was Spencer.

After telling him her story, she'd been able to go back to her dad. Her father had apologized for not reacting the way she'd wanted. And she'd said she was sorry for not giving him a chance to react any way he wanted to. They'd made up and she'd found her dad to be far more understanding of what she'd gone through than she'd thought.

Speaking of her father…

"Don't forget, we have to get to my dad's house by eight," she said. "I promised I'd bring you by after dinner. He wants to meet the man who encouraged me to talk to him again."

"And I want to meet him. We'll be there in plenty of time." Spencer paused by the front door. "Before we go inside, I want to say something."

"What's that?" she asked, feeling a little nervous. It was a familiar feeling. In fact, she was starting to get used to the fluttery dance her stomach did every time Spencer was around. She was wildly attracted to the man; she just didn't know exactly what to do about it. After their fast start, they'd been taking things slow, but she'd been finding the pace a little slower than she wanted. In fact, she'd been taking a lot of cold showers lately.

Spencer gave her a serious look. "I want you, Hallie."

She swallowed hard, not sure what to say. "Okay."

He frowned. "Not exactly the reaction I was looking for."

"We're standing outside a courthouse."

"I know it's not the most romantic spot I could have picked, but I didn't want to go another minute without telling you how I feel. We've both been hurt by love. But I'm ready to take another chance—with you. If you're not ready yet, I'll wait. I know you loved Doug, and I want to respect that."

"How long will you wait?"

"As long as it takes for you to want me, too. I know I'm not the ideal man. I've got a prison record—"

"Hush," she said, putting her finger against his lips. "We've been all through that. I know what kind of man you are. I'm not afraid of your record or your past."

"Are you sure?"

"Positive. I already want you, Spencer. I'm scared of how much I want you. And after what we went through together, I don't want to waste any more time being afraid. I'd like to see where this relationship goes. So I'm in, all the way in." As she finished speaking, all her lingering doubts faded away. She was in love again. She'd never imagined she could be, but here she was.

"Thank God," Spencer said with heartfelt sincerity. "I feel the same way." He pulled her into his arms and kissed her.

"I'm glad you feel the same," she said breathlessly, but I hope you didn't bring me here to spring a surprise wedding on me."

"Well, someone is getting married, but it's not us. It's Emma and Max."

"Really? Here?"

"Emma didn't want to wait to put together another wedding. She wants to marry Max tonight."

"Isn't this family only?"

"You saved Max's life. Trust me, in Emma's eyes, you're already part of the family."

—➤➤◄◄—

Emma glanced in the mirror of the ladies' restroom in the San Francisco Courthouse. Her sister, Nicole, met her gaze, and Emma smiled at their reflection, thinking back to the last time she'd gotten dressed for her wedding, her sister at her side. Then she'd worn a concoction of lace and silk. Now she had on a simple long-sleeve white dress with a sweetheart neckline perfect for showing off her grandmother's necklace.

"You look good," Nicole said.

"I think she could use a touch more eye-shadow," Shayla put in, as she came up behind them.

"Stop it. I look fine," Emma said with a smile, turning around to face them.

"Are you sure this is what you want?" Shayla asked, doubt in her eyes. "Maybe this is the wrong time to ask the question, but I know this isn't your dream wedding."

"My dream wedding is with the man I love, and he's waiting for me down the hall. I know he's here this time, because Sara checked for me. Nothing is going to go wrong today," she added with a little smile. "So let's get this show on the road."

"After you," Nicole said, waving her out of the bathroom.

Max and Spencer along with the Callaway men were waiting outside the judge's chambers. Max wore a dark gray suit and Emma's breath caught in her chest at the sight of him. He looked so handsome. But more importantly, he looked healthy and alive. He'd recovered quickly from his surgery, and neither one of them had wanted to wait another second to tie the knot.

"Ready to become Mrs. Max Harrison?" he asked, taking her hand.

She gave him a loving smile. "More than ready."

"Good. Let's do this so we can get to the honeymoon."

"We have the reception at my mom's house first."

"Don't remind me. I can't wait to get you alone, Emma

Callaway."

"Soon to be Emma Callaway Harrison. I love you, Max. It's going to be me and you forever."

"Forever," he agreed, kissing her on the mouth.

"Hey, you two," Spencer said. "Save something for the ceremony."

She glanced over at Spencer, pleased to see the beautiful Hallie at his side. She had a feeling Spencer was going to get his happily-ever-after, too.

Max led her into the judge's chambers. And as they stood in front of the judge, promising to love each other forever, they were surrounded by their family and friends. There was love in every breath of air that she took, and Emma drank it all in. Their vows were more poignant now, knowing how close they'd come to losing each other and the dream of their lifetime.

"You may kiss the bride," the judge finally said.

Max gave her a look of love and said. "It's about damn time." And then his mouth covered hers.

THE END

Don't miss the next book in the Callaway series

ALL A HEART NEEDS
(Coming August 2015!)

Sean Callaway is the black sheep of the Callaway clan, the sibling who refused to follow in the family tradition of firefighting. Instead, he lives his life in music. On the outside, he's a free-spirited rock star, but on the inside, Sean is haunted by the death of a childhood friend, a tragedy no one knows he witnessed. He's kept the secret for twenty years. But nothing stays hidden forever...

Jessica Schilling, a young widow, moved to San Francisco to reunite her six-year-old stepson with his long-lost identical twin brother, Brandon. She rents a house just around the corner from the Callaways, and while cleaning out the garage for the previous owner Jessica stumbles upon a very old secret—one that someone might just be willing to kill to keep.

Suddenly, Sean is thrust back into the past. He's never thought of himself as a hero, but now he's forced to face his most disturbing memories, not only to solve the riddle of the tragedy that ripped his life apart, but also to save the woman he loves...

About The Author

Barbara Freethy is a #1 New York Times Bestselling Author of 42 novels ranging from contemporary romance to romantic suspense and women's fiction. Traditionally published for many years, Barbara opened her own publishing company in 2011 and has since sold over 5 million books! Nineteen of her titles have appeared on the New York Times and USA Today Bestseller Lists.

Known for her emotional and compelling stories of love, family, mystery and romance, Barbara enjoys writing about ordinary people caught up in extraordinary adventures. Barbara's books have won numerous awards. She is a six-time finalist for the RITA for best contemporary romance from Romance Writers of America and a two-time winner for DANIEL'S GIFT and THE WAY BACK HOME.

Barbara has lived all over the state of California and currently resides in Northern California where she draws much of her inspiration from the beautiful bay area.

For a complete listing of books, as well as excerpts and contests, and to connect with Barbara:

Visit Barbara's Website:
www.barbarafreethy.com

Join Barbara on Facebook:
www.facebook.com/barbarafreethybooks

Follow Barbara on Twitter:
www.twitter.com/barbarafreethy